MW01105384

First Edition

Cover Art Contribution By MarkoTheSketchGuy Al.

Printed in the United States of America

Visit www.Outcastbooks.com

CONTENT

I would like to dedicate this book to my children. You have, and always will be my greatest achievement, and source of inspiration. I love you very much.

Dad (R.J. Simmons)

I would also like to thank my wife Cindy for her loving support and to my editor, Susan Myers for her diligent work on this book. Without their keen eye, and insight this book would not have made it to print.

PROLOGUE

****

Our world rests on the edge of peace after so many years of bloodshed. As I sit here thinking back on the events that led to this day, I cannot help but mourn the loss of the countless lives; heroes, villains, loved ones, old ones, and, yes, even children; all forfeited for the sake of a few miles of earth.

I regret that the first king, King Hakon, partook of a blood bond with a dragon, granting to himself the ability to control the elements of this world. This was the beginning of our downfall, but this alone would not have set Telekkar on a path of destruction. It was his decision to pass on his power to his four sons; each restricted to one of the elements that ultimately sealed our fate. Now, many thousands of years later, our world stands separated into two classes. The Gehage, the descendants of King Hakon who rule through their ability to control the elements, and the Ukrin who are forced to survive under their leadership.

If only separated into two classes we may have lived on in relative peace, but we are separated on a greater scale than Gehage and Ukrin. Through many years of war our world has split into the four nations. Rarely have we known a time of peace. The Fire Kingdom has warred with each of the other nations throughout our history, but none more than the Stone Kingdom. It was their assault on the Stone Kingdom's eastern gate that started this war, this Great War, so many years ago. Although the kingship of the Stone Kingdom was weak, the people of its lands proved that they would stand against any invader. As unmovable as the rocks they control, these people defied the Fire king, as well as their own, to keep the land left to them by their fore-fathers.

How I wish that war could be fought solely on the battle-field, but it is inevitable that the innocent are dragged into our folly. If only the Gehage were never formed, this world would have seen happier days. But it is useless to regret the days gone by. That has been a long and hard lesson to learn. King Hakon did make his bond with the dragon and created through his bloodline the Gehage. After countless battles I sit in this library writing down the accounts of this Great War; this war that will unite the kingdoms again. You see, I would like to tell you that the road to peace was a short and easy journey. But what little peace we feel today came at great sacrifice for others. This journey did not happen over days or months but over years; many, many years. I cannot tell you that one hero, one man of extreme power, brought this about. It took many heroes, many villains, and even more beings who I would say were shaded a bit gray to bring this world to this moment in history.

If we were to trace back to the very person who spawned the change of this tide in history, we would find not a king, but a common man, only a boy when this began. Although he became great in time, he began as ordinary as any other. His defining virtue; the one strength that led this world to the edge of peace was his inability to put himself before those around him. Some men learn to be honorable; others are born with it; and the truly great inspire those around them to do the same. These men change the world, these men make a difference, and, sadly, these men endure the hardest and most bitter trials. To say that he changed our world would be a sad misrepresentation of history. But it can be argued that through his actions, through his failures, and through his sacrifices he created the heroes who did.

2

ONE

****

THE DEADLANDS

Kale awoke from a short sleep sweating and aggravated. As his eyes opened, the film that had dried on his eyelids cracked and blurred his vision. Suffocating and sweating under the canvas covers, he could just see the light coming in through the small holes meshed in the blanket. The itch of a single bead of sweat formed on his forehead as the droplet ran down his skin to find its way to the fur pad that laid below; separating him from the clay slab that had looked so inviting the night before.

Now the slab made itself known by the aching twinge running down his lower back and proceeding up to his shoulder blade. Slowly Kale's senses became more attuned to his surroundings. In the distance the sound of shuffling feet disturbed the staleness of the air. The smell of breakfast fought its way through the heat and dust, giving his body a reason to stir.

Kale tossed the covers off and sat up nursing his sore legs and back. He had just the day before made a fifteen mile run back from a nearby trading post with the town's monthly mail.

"Uh, another day, another run, will it never end?" Kale wondered.

A gruff voice broke the silence of his room from beyond the door. "Kale, get out of bed. You're already running late."

"I'm up Dad. I'll be out in a minute," he replied.

"You'd better be. Even you can't make it to Perm in less than three hours. Now get a move on it," demanded his father.

Kale slid on his leather pants and strapped on his boots.

With a sigh, the pain in his muscles from the previous day's run emerged from hiding. Messages between the villages had increased a lot lately with the kingdoms starting their yearly draft. Kale slowly walked to the door, leaning a bit to one side to get rid of a cramped muscle. Opening the door produced a fresh smell of cooked buzzard eggs from the kitchen. With the smell of hot food, Kale's stomach finally awoke, letting off a growl.

Kale's mother, a petite women with long black hair, set the table for breakfast.

"Good morning, dear," she said as she emptied the remaining eggs onto a plate.

"Morning, breakfast smells great. I'm starving."

"You've been doing a lot of runs the last few weeks; I want to make sure you get a good meal before you take off again," she told him.

Kale straddled a stool at the table and settled in for a good meal. He took a big mouthful of eggs and began eyeing a piece of desert rodent being prepared over the fire. To most rodent would be considered a peasant's dish, but when you live in the Telekkar Desert, food is a luxury. Kale had long ago given up on being pickey of what he ate. Any meat was a welcomed change, and the eggs today were pretty good by normal standards. This time you could almost taste the eggs through all the sand that floated in the pan while it cooked. Kale was used to the grit on his teeth. A cup of water and a few licks with his tongue, and they almost felt clean again.

A few loud bumps against the door and wall brought Kale's attention to his father, Zeak, stepping out from the pantry holding his usual flask of ale. Like many other men, Kale's father used to serve in one of the kingdom's armies. He refused to talk freely about it. Either due to the horrific sights he had beheld or out of shear inability to adjust to a commoner's life, he had resorted to drink to dull the harshness of everyday living. He would sit and stare at his old sword collecting dust over the entrance way and tell tales of grandeur from the life before he had settled down.

In some of his drunken exploits Zeak would claim to have been a high ranking officer who had taken part in many battles, but the details from each story varied based on how much drink he had consumed.

He was missing his left leg, and it was replaced by a wooden peg. Even with the missing limb, if he hadn't had too much to drink, he could keep a straight course while walking. If a heroic soldier ever did exist in him it had vanished. Now, only a broken, haggard man remained. His pot belly and slender arms only added to his disfigurement.

Zeak leaned heavily on his crutch while taking a drink. "Sorry, boy, but you don't have time for breakfast. That extra hour of sleep you snuck in has cost you time. You have to have that list delivered to Perm before noon or Mr. Kecklin will have my head. He needs those supplies ordered on time!"

"Ok, I'm going." Kale took a quick gulp of water, grabbed his pack, and headed out the door. Just as he was leaving he could see his father plop down at the table and scrape the rest of Kale's breakfast onto his plate.

Kale paused to take a look at the day. As usual there were no clouds in the sky, no chance of rain. It appeared to be an expectant hot and dry day. Knowing that those leather straps could rub him raw quickly if he let them move around, Kale pushed the strap of his bag up over his head and onto his shoulder. Giving

5

it a good tug to make sure it wasn't loose, he started his warm up jog over to the message office.

Consisting of a little over a thousand residents, Yukan was a small town located in the hot sandy wasteland called the Deadlands. The terrain, harsh with little to no water, was covered with patches of sand grass that devoured what moisture there was. The only real commodity besides water were the farming of lega and snake hunting. Lega, a simple plant that could grow anywhere with an abundance of sun and when ground up could be used to make bread, provided the town with a steady income and served as the chief source of nutritious food. Yukan owned a large farm near its gates to manufacture the flour from this plant.

As for the rest of the workers in Yukan, they were generally employed as snake farmers whose occupation consisted of going into the grassy areas to capture the most poisonous snakes. The extracts of the venoms were sold to any of the armies for medicine, antidotes, and, primarily, to tip their arrows.

The streets of Yukan were nothing more than compacted sand from the walking of its inhabitants. With only twelve hours of daylight it was so hot that most people could not leave the shade during mid day for fear of overheating.

The town's key feature, a well, was located in the center of town. People came from miles around to get water. Being one of the few tradable commodities any town has in this desolate place, the town saw many visitors.

Surrounded by a thirty foot clay wall the town was well protected from the various bandits who would raid the small towns. Most of the houses doubled as shops, and Kale's family had made its trade by acting as the messenger service to the towns near Yukan.

The town received news and visitors at the message office which consisted of a small shed with a window which doubled as a receiving station at the northern gate of town. Standing both as sentry and greeter stood the old scrawny town's official, Devlin. Devlin, a nice enough fellow, had always treated Kale with kindness. Approaching the office Kale could see Devlin sorting out some letters and placing some into a bundle.

Kale took his normal position, folding his arms and leaning on the small one board counter on the edge of the window. "Hey, Devlin, how's it going this morning?"

Devlin finished his sorting and then looked up with a broad smile. "Not bad, Kale. I hear you're running up to Perm today."

"Sure am, just wondered if you had any letters that needed to go that way."

"You read my mind; I've received five letters this month that are destined for Perm. Normal price I assume, an ounce a letter?" As the primary commodity, money was gauged in weight of water in the Deadlands. Even as he was speaking, Devlin began to weigh each letter.

"Yep, sure is." Kale leaned back and unfastened a pouch on the side of his bag.

Devlin leaned toward Kale with a smile. "Ok, here ya go boy, and don't worry. I won't tell your father you picked up any extra coin for this run."

"You're a true friend. Try to stay out of the sun today. I hear it's going to be a scorcher."

"I should say the same to you, but there's not much to hide under out there," Devlin replied.

"So true, anyway, what's the news lately? I've been out for about a week at Nieha. Are there any traders in town?" Kale inquired.

"Not at the moment, but be careful on your run today. I hear there's a pack of dessert cats prowling about to the north. I doubt they will go near Perm, but with the lack of food these days, they may risk the danger," warned Devlin.

"I'll keep my eyes out. Thanks for the warning. I'll talk to you in a few days. Good day, Devlin," Kale said. Tucking the letters into his bag, Kale closed it and checked that all the pouches and pockets were secured. Starting on his way to Perm, Kale left the receiving station.

* * *

Perm was a small trading outpost about thirty miles from Yukan. It was a run that Kale had made countless times before and had long established himself as the fastest messenger in the Deadlands. Beasts of burden with any hint of real speed were unheard of in this barren landscape because it was nearly impossible to care for them; runners by foot were the fastest means of communication.

Although the run to Perm was uneventful, a few times Kale thought he saw sand cats traipsing among the edges of the sand dunes, but they faded as quickly as they came. In the sands on a hot day your mind plays all kinds of tricks on you. You can imagine almost anything on those blurred blistering horizons.

Perm, like any town with something of value, was surrounded by the typical clay wall. Perm made its way by being a trading post for the Leaf Nation villages and those of the Stone Kingdom. It was also a place where the Sand tribes came to barter for necessities. Perm had a variety of people, inhabited by refugees from towns destroyed in war, people who wanted to escape the tyranny of the Fire Kingdom, and, sadly, for the most part criminals hiding from the authorities of any one of the four kingdoms.

The main trading post was located near the southern entrance. As Kale approached, he saw men, mostly just a few scrawny slaves and one very large young man, unloading some goods from a wagon. The large man's back was turned, but he stood a hand over seven feet tall and his shoulders were as wide as any two men. He had dark skin and a bald head. He lifted two fifty gallon barrels of water onto his shoulders and stepped off the wagon. The creaking of the wagon, thanking the man for the release of its burden, was so high pitched it made Kale cringe. After placing them on the loading dock he turned around. With the exception of a large scar across his right cheek, his face was young and innocent, a flaw that betrayed his manly body and gave away the secret of his youth.

Kale shouted from the edge of the street, "Reagan, is that you?"

Reagan returned the greeting with a large smile. "Kale, you dog, when did you get to Perm?"

"Just making another run. I see you picked up a few slaves while in the Stone country. How long are they going to be with you?" Kale asked.

Reagan answered, "Like normal, as soon as they work off what we paid for them, they are free to go."

"I wouldn't say that too loud. The slave traders don't take kindly to freeing slaves. Bad for business, you know," warned Kale.

Reagan gave another big grin and leaned in closer to Kale.

"And when has my family ever feared the slave traders?"

"You're as bold as you are big. What do you say we settle in for a drink at Murah's Inn after we get done here at the post? I'd like to visit with you a bit before I head back to Yukan. It's been empty out there since your family moved to Perm."

"Sure, that sounds like fun, but I have good news. I hear my father accepted a delivery to Mr. Kecklin. The post is just waiting for his supply list, and then they'll start filling the cart," Reagan said.

Kale laughed, "Well, then I guess I'd better get in there if all they're waiting on is me."

"I should have known you would be running late. Kale, tell me how the fastest guy in all the sand is always late."

"Just bad luck, I guess. Or, it's because I like making a dramatic entrance," joked Kale.

Reagan slapped Kale's shoulder. "I think it's because you like ticking your ol' man off."

A half smile cracked Kale's lips, "Well, there is that, too. Reagan, I need to get this list in. I'll settle up and then head over to Murah's. I assume you will have an hour or so while they're loading the cart. And I might as well tag along with you on the ride back. I'm in no hurry to get home."

***

Murah's inn smelled of sweat and dust, but it did the trick of keeping the sun out, and the inn had working fans, to boot. The post had enough business it could afford to waste wood on furnishings, and for Kale, sitting down at a table not made of clay was a rare treat. A haggard bar lady came walking by balancing six mugs on a platter and carrying two more in her other hand. Kale leaned into the aisle to get her attention. "Hey, miss, do

10

you think I could get a drink when you get a second?"

The woman pursed her lips and gave an exasperated sigh. "I'll be with you in a second; right now I've got a table of Stone Troopers waiting for drinks in the back. I have no intention of frustrating them. Murah already told me if they break anything because of bad service, it's coming out of my pay."

"Stone Troopers, they're already starting their recruitment run?" Kale asked.

Repositioning herself to both stabilize her load and free up the walkway, the waitress stepped closer to the table to be heard more clearly. "Yeah, they've already picked four boys for service. You look like a strapping young lad; unless you want to spend a lifetime in their army, I'd suggest staying out of their way."

"Well, they normally don't recruit anyone who doesn't live in the village they are scouting. Do you have any idea where they're heading next?" Kale asked the bar maid.

"They didn't say where, but they came from the north so I assume they're heading south." The sound of men wrestling in the back began to increase and breaking glass could be heard hitting the floor.

"I'd better get these back there. With any luck they'll pass out and won't be any more trouble," she said, heading quickly toward the back.

Looking back Kale could see the eight Stone Troopers around a table. All but one seemed to be having a good time. It was obvious who the captain was by his vast difference in appearance. By the look of the others, they were just Ukrin. But the captain was different. His size and the sternness of his presence made it pretty obvious he was of noble blood. A key feature of the Stone Gehage was their hulking strength and immense size. Many Ukrin could be that large and some even that strong, but a Gehage carried so much strength and such superiority that they were hard to miss. It's kind of like watching an ant carrying a large piece of cactus fruit. It's unbelievable when you think about it, but it's just one of those things of nature you come to accept.

Kale had thought for years that Reagan may have been part Stone Gehage due to his size, but after seeing him receive the scar that defined his facial features, he had given up on that notion. Some Ukrin are just naturally gifted. They don't need the ancient bloodline to stand out.

Kale was awakened from his trance of concentration by the sudden jerk of the table. As he glanced back he saw Reagan sitting down. He used the table for support and was almost smashing Kale's stomach in the process.

Kale let out an exasperated breath. "Hey, man, you want to lighten up on the table. I'm not as durable as you are, my friend."

"Oh, sorry, Kale, hurt my ankle on the way over here. One of the new slaves wasn't watching his rope, and a barrel fell off the cart onto it," Reagan explained.

Leaning under the table to get a good look Kale exhaled with a whistle. "Wow, man, is it broken? Those barrels weigh a few hundred pounds."

Reagan gave his ankle a good rub down, wincing a bit when touching the tenderness of the bruise. "No, just a bit sore. It'll be okay."

"So, Reagan, what are you having?" asked Kale.

"Oh, probably a mug or two of ale. I can't drink too much.

We need to get to Yukan by mid-day two days from now; you?"
Reagan answered.

"Same as always, Keckleberry Juice," replied Kale.

"You're still not a drinking, ey'?" chuckled Reagan.

"Well, the way I figure it, my ol' man drinks enough for the both of us. One of us has to stay sober," Kale explained.

"Yeah, I guess he does," agreed Reagan.

The sounds of the inn intensified as workers started breaking for the day and travelers settled in for dinner before they took to their rooms for the night.

"Oh yeah, Reagan, before I forget, you may want to keep a low profile tonight. We've got some Stone Troopers from a recruitment group in town," advised Kale.

"Really, I may have to pay them a visit before I leave," Reagan growled.

"Have you been in the sun too much today or something? As big as you are you'd probably get drafted before you finished a sentence. In fact, I'm thinking about ducking out of here before they see me," Kale said.

"To be honest, I've been thinking about volunteering. I have no intention of hauling a cart around all my life. Some people make a good living in the Earth Kingdom's army. You just have to watch what outfit you get into, and normally, if you volunteer, they let you pick what section they base you," Reagan said.

"Yeah, but come on Reagan, unless you're a Gehage, you can't make officer. You'd be a grunt for the rest of your life," argued Kale.

"And I'm not now! But hey, man, no worries. I haven't decided yet," replied Reagan.

The sounds of the bar grew to a deafening intensity as more

people piled in and made their way to retrieve a drink.

Kale attempted to increase his volume to accommodate the change. "Well, that's good; that means I still have time to talk you out of it."

"What's that, Kale? I can't hear you. Talk up a bit. It's loud in here," shouted Reagan.

Kale cupped his hands around his mouth and leaned over the table to shorten the distance. "I said I still have time to talk you out of it."

Reagan leaned back on his chair. Even in the deafening loudness you could hear his chair give off a groan.

"We'll see. I don't see the waitress getting back to us anytime soon; I'm going to go get our drinks from the bar myself," Reagan decided.

"Ok, I'll just stay here and save our seats," Kale said.

Reagan got up from the table and started his hobble over to the bar. Reagan moved slowly, carefully moving his enormous girth through the crowd while trying not to bump his ankle.

With every passing moment the air got more musty and filled with pipe smoke. The sweet grass smell permeated everything it touched. With so many conversations going on, it was almost impossible to concentrate on any one sound. Kale thought back to when he was a boy and used to sneak into this bar in hopes of finding a partly finished glass to swipe. As a smile cracked his face from the thought of the time his mother caught him, he received a tap on the shoulder. Looking up he saw one of the Stone Kingdom guards standing above him.

"You need to clear out. My men have been doing real work all day, and we need this table," he ordered.

"I'm sorry officer; my friend and I are having a drink. You

can have it when we are finished," Kale answered.

The soldier put his hand on the table and leaned closer. "Maybe you didn't hear me, you little sand flee. I said leave!"

A shadow fell over the soldier's body. Looking up he saw Reagan standing over him, blocking the light from the lantern hanging against the wall.

In a deeper than normal voice Reagan put his hand on the table and leaned over the soldier in the same posture that the soldier was leaning over Kale. "I wouldn't be calling someone a flea if I was as small as you mister. Is there a problem?"

The soldier sprung to his feet and drew his sword. "What the..oh, you think I'm afraid of you. I'm a Stone..."

Before the soldier could get out the rest of his sentence, a large fist flew through the air smashing his jaw and sending him sprawling across the floor, knocking people against each other and others to the floor. In a crowded room in a border town all it takes is one swing to set the whole place off in a tumble. Within a few seconds, chairs, glasses, and fists were flying.

Looking at Reagan, Kale pointed towards the door to signify it was time to make a hasty exit. Reagan pushed and occasionally belted a few people to work his way out of the door. Kale wasn't so fortunate; in the twelve feet to the exit he was punched in both eyes, received a bloody nose, and had the unfortunate luck to catch a glass bottle between his legs. This caused him to tumble to the floor in a daze of colors and pain. If not for Reagan grabbing his ankle and dragging him out the door, he would have been trampled on by the crowd.

Reagan laughed as he carried Kale's groaning limp body away from the bar and to his father's cart to reclaim his dignity. "Kale, it looks like you managed to get yourself into another mess. We'd better get on the road before those troopers come looking for us. I'm in no mood to get a bad name with them. With my luck, if I sign up, I'd end up in their company."

Kale slowly composed himself and after taking a few breaths began to speak. "You're probably right. Looks like the cart is loaded. Let's get on the road. I think I'll just lie down for a bit on these sacks of flour. Walking isn't really an option right now."

Even the slaves could not repress their laughter at the sight of Kale lying on the flour sacks with his hands between his legs rolling back and forth.

* * *

By the time the cart stopped to make camp for the night, Kale had regained his composure and was getting around pretty well. The slaves made a big fire to keep the animals away and to prepare a meal.

"So, Reagan, how's that ankle hold'n up?" Kale asked.

"It's still pretty sore, but after a week or so I should at least be able to get around without a limp," Reagan answered.

"And what about your...ankle?" said Reagan, repressing a smile.

Kale picked up a stick from the nearby wood pile and sent it flying. It landed squarely on Reagan's forearm and bounced harmlessly to the ground.

"Oh, I'm sure in a week or so I'll be getting around just fine too, funny man." Kale shifted to one side. "But, seriously, I think that's only the second time I've ever seen you hurt."

"Ah, I get a few good ones now and then. Still nothing as bad as when you gave me this cut on my face," Reagan continued.

"ME! Now wait. That wasn't my fault. I can't help it if that beam broke; it was your weight that caused it," argued Kale.

"Yeah, it was my weight, but who was doing summersaults on it?" Reagan pointed to the side of his face. "I call this my Kale scar."

"Hey, how was I to know you'd fall on a sickle. I still can't believe that you didn't get your head cut off," Kale exclaimed.

Reagan ran his fingers along his scar. "Well, we all get lucky sometimes." Reagan held up his finger as if to request a pause in their reminiscing. "Kale, something's wrong. It's too quite; I don't hear any of the crickets."

"They probably got scared off by all our movement and talking," Kale replied.

"No, they were chirping not ten minutes ago, and we were much louder then. Something's wrong." Reagan turned his head toward the cart and addressed one of the slaves.

A young man was talking with two of the other slaves giving them directions for setting up camp. He stood six feet tall with short curly black hair and a short beard. He looked older than he really was. His face was stern and lines of wisdom had already started to set in. He carried a long spear on his back with a large feather hanging from the end of it near the blade. The frame of his body was thin and bony, but it was covered in layers of muscles that defied its weakness.

"Latus, take one of the new hands and circle the camp. There's a lot of meat on that wagon, and I don't want to loose any of it to hungry animals," Reagan ordered.

"Yes, Master Reagan, right away." The slave replied and immediately set to complete the task.

Now that the current concerns were addressed Reagan

turned his attention back to Kale. "I almost wish it is an animal. I just hope those Stone Troopers didn't find out who we were and come out after us."

"Reagan, you're just being paranoid. There are a million reasons the crickets aren't chirping. I think you've just had too much excitement today." Kale continued, "So, I see Latus is still with you. I'm surprised he hasn't worked off his debt yet."

"He's been with us for two years now. My father about broke us buying him from a slaver. He's a skilled hunter, tracker, guide and smart, too. Been a real help. He cost us more than what ten slaves would. I'm afraid he won't work off his debt for some time. At first I didn't see why father was willing to pay so much for him, but he always did have a good eye when judging folks."

A few minutes later Latus returned with one of the new hands. "Master Reagan, we've circled the parameter, and we don't see anything. Would you like us to sit up and keep watch?"

"Yeah, that's a good idea, Latus. Choose a few of the new hands and have them take shifts. Make sure they keep the fire going, as well. Kale's probably right, though. I've just had a busy day, but it's never a bad idea to be cautious."

Slowly the camp calmed down. One by one the slaves found a place near the cart to sleep. Reagan climbed inside his knapsack near the fire while Kale laid down his fur mat and canvas cover and used his bag as a pillow. With all the day's excitement, it didn't take Kale's body long to find its way to sleep.

* * *

Kale's eyes opened slowly, but the area was very dark. The smell of smoldering coals filled the air. A rustling over by the cart could be heard, but through the darkness nothing could be seen. The fire had dwindled to a few small flames, and occasionally they flared up when a puff of wind blew by.

Kale sat up and immediately the sound of the rustling ceased. "Looks like the new hands aren't doing a good job keeping the fire going," he murmured.

Kale grabbed an armful of twigs and desert grass and tossed it onto the low burning flames. The grass caught quickly and flared up, and the light illuminated the area, displaying a gory sight.

Three of the slaves were ripped to pieces and strewn about like bits of garbage; the cart looked to have been ransacked by something quite large. From around the back of the cart a low growl broke the silence. Slowly stepping into the light walked a large sand cat. With bloody fangs the cat stood four foot high at its back and had long fangs that hung down out of its mouth. Its short mane was mangled and its thin, prominent ribs pushed against its skin.

Kale looked over at where Reagan was sleeping, only to see that both he and his sleeping nap sack were missing. A lump began to from in his throat as he reached down to grab a smoldering stick from the fire.

The sand cat leapt in the air, clearing the fire and coming down on top of Kale, forcing his body to press into the sand under the weight. With short snaps it tried to tear out Kale's throat, but using the stick to hold the jaws at bay, Kale minimized the damage to a bite on the shoulder blade and a claw mark across the face. The more immediate danger was the loss of breath from the weight of the cat pressing down on his chest.

As Kale's strength began to fail he heard a crack, and then

the weight of the cat increased as it slumped over on his body. Slowly the cat's body rolled to one side as a bloody Reagan was exposed standing over him holding a log from the fire.

"Kale! Are you ok?" Reagan demanded.

"I'll live, thanks to you. What happened?" Kale exclaimed.

"I'm not sure myself; I woke up being drug feet first in my nap sack away from camp by one of these beasts. I slipped out in time to make it back here. I assume the other one will be back soon so you'd better get that scrawny hide of yours up quickly."

No sooner had Reagan finished his sentence than another cat leapt over the cart and landed in the camp. Shifting its weight to its front paws, it began to sniff the ground searching for hints of its prey.

Whispering, Reagan slowly backed into the darkness out of the range of the fire's light. "Kale, stay behind me. Maybe all he wants is the meat in the wagon. Let's try to back out of camp."

Backing up over the hill near the camp the two eased out of sight. Kale paid so much attention to not being followed by the cat that he didn't notice the clump of sand grass behind him and tripped over it. In an attempt to catch himself he ended up face down in the sand.

Kale froze in fear, knowing any more sound would attract the feline from over the hill. The pounding of his heart increased with every second, and just when he thought he had reached the pinnacle of possible fear, it was expanded to new heights by a new sound. Directly above him he heard a very close growling and felt the slimy drips of saliva running down his face.

As he looked up, a third cat's eyes were glinting in the

moonlight, staring hungrily down at Kale.

A lump fromed in his throat as he choked out a plea, "Oh, you've got to be kidding me...REAGAN!"

From a distance the sound of shuffling and grunting could be heard. "I've got my own problems, Kale! You'll have to deal with that one yourself."

Kale sprang to his feet just in time to grab the bottom of the cat's jaws as it leapt for his throat. The beast's claws ripped away at the flesh exposed from Kale's vest cutting deep wounds into his arms.

The weight of the cat was tremendous; if the cat had been healthy, Kale's strength would have done little to defend him from such monstrous dexterity and natural strength. Just as Kale's arms could take no more assault and the last thread of strength had left him, Kale heard a wisp of air as if something were in mid flight. The cat flexed as if hit and then rolled off Kale writhing in pain. A spear protruding from its abdomen.

Looking around Kale saw Reagan's lead worker, Latus, kneeling on the ground. His left arm hung lightly at his side and even in the darkness Kale could see blood trailing down his body. Moments later he collapsed in exhaustion.

Reagan's loud plea caught Kale's attention. "Kale! A little... little help here."

Reagan had one cat's head pinned between his knees preventing its mouth from opening. It was clawing and jerking to gain its freedom. The other cat had positioned itself on top of Reagan in the same fashion that the previous cat had pinned Kale. Grabbing the spear out of the now dead sand cat, Kale rushed to assist Reagan.

Kale stuck the spear into the side of the cat attacking Reagan's

21

throat. Between Kale's sloppy precision and his weak arms, he did little more than get the cat's attention. It darted at him. Kale waved the spear back and forth to keep the beast at bay. Finally Kale centered the spear's weight and prepared to make an aimed throw at the cat's body. With all the remaining strength he had, he sent the spear flying.

The spear sailed finely at its target and for a brief second the throw looked promising. But, at the last moment, the cat sprang to its right and grabbed the spear in mid-flight. With a vengeful growl it clamped down, breaking the head of the spear off.

"This isn't good. How you doing over there, Reagan? Anytime you want to rush in and save the day is fine by me!" shouted Kale.

Reagan was in the process of detaching his opponent's jaws from the inside of his thigh. "Still working on it. Keep him busy for a minute!"

Kale returned his attention to his cat as it began to prowl to one side, attempting to get a good angle to spring in for the kill. Kale countered the cat's movements until he was close enough to pick up the shaft from the spear. Leaning down he got a hold of it, the cat took this as its opportunity and leapt into the air towards Kale's throat. Dropping to the ground, Kale put the shaft into the cat's mouth and then put his feet into its stomach, launching it over his head like he was wrestling with another boy from town. The cat landed on its back with a loud crack and then disappeared beneath the sand.

Turning, Kale saw Reagan dispatching the other animal by beating in its skull with his massive fists.

Kale slowly approached what appeared to be a large hole. Peering over the edge Kale could see a thirty foot pit trap with large spikes sticking out from the bottom. Unfortunately, the cat had missed them and was trying to find a way out of the hole.

Reagan approached and looked into the pit. "Wow, we could have easily fallen into that ourselves. That wouldn't have been fun."

The cat began to claw at the walls and started its assent up the slope of the pit. As its head got level with the top of the hole, Reagan gave it a good kick sending it back into the pit. This time the cat wasn't so fortunate and landed on one of the spikes, suspending it in mid-air.

TWO

****

LIVE FREE

Finally able to take an inventory of the losses, they found that over half of the meat had been ruined, and all of the slaves but Latus were dead. This posed a terrible loss to Reagan's family as they were responsible for any losses that accrued during transport.

Reagan began to clean his wounds, bandaging the larger slashes and allowing the smaller ones to crust over. Sitting against one of the cart wheels, Reagan covered his face with his hands in frustration. "Kale, I don't know what we're going to do now. The slaves alone will be enough to put us out of business, not to mention the lost supplies."

Placing his hand on Reagan's shoulder, Kale began to give comfort. "I'm sorry, my friend. We'll find a way to solve this."

Latus came from around the cart holding two large desert cat furs. "Master Reagan, it's not as bad as it seems. We've got over a thousand pounds of meat between the cats and four pelts, as well. The teeth and claws alone will pay for one of the lost slaves."

Reagan lifted his head and allowed a slight smile to creep out. "Latus, you always look towards the bright side of things. Don't you? But, you're right. We can recoup some of our losses. You've proven to be most valuable my friend." Reagan stood and approached Latus examining his arm. "Latus, your arm is cut to the bone. You need to rest. Let Kale and me take care of the other cats. It wouldn't do us any good to lose you, too."

"As you wish, Master Reagan." Turning, Latus stretched the furs out on the ground with his good arm and then took Reagan's old position leaning against the wheel.

Reagan retrieved two skinning knives from the supply box on the side of the cart and approached Kale. "So, you think you're up to skinning one of these cats. We'll need to cut the best meats off of them as well and dry them on the trip back to Yukan." Reagan pulled Kale a little closer to the light of the fire and examined his arms. "My goodness, man! Your arms look like you put them through a shreader. On second thought, I'll skin the rest of the cats. You go sit down next to Latus."

Reaching out, Kale put his hand on Reagan's shoulder to prevent him from leaving to tackle the task alone. "No, Reagan, it's not as bad as it looks. Mostly they're shallow cuts. You're hurt as well. We'll split the work. I'll take the one in the pit. You're too big to get down there without getting impaled."

"If you're sure, then okay. I'll get the one over the hill. Just toss the meat onto the sand. We'll clean it off when you're done," Reagan said as he turned to complete his task.

Kale gathered some rope, a torch, some tent stakes, and a blanket to lay on the ground to catch the meat as he threw it up. Staking down one end of the rope, Kale repelled over the side, and with no great ease, he maneuved himself down far enough to wedge himself between two of the long spears protruding from the bottom of the pit and began butchering the sand cat. The chore proved very difficult. Besides Kale's inexperience, the cat hung suspended in mid air with a large spike sticking through it. The pelt was hardly worth keeping by the time it was removed, but most of the valuable meat was intact.

What Kale thought to be a sand cricket chirping progress-

25

ively got louder the longer he worked. By the time Kale finished, the noise had annoyed him long enough that he had made up his mind to seek out the little vermin and put it out of its misery. After tossing the rest of the meat and the remaining bits of fur over the edge of the pit, Kale followed the sound of the chirping until he came to a slight indention in the wall. It appeared to be a small hole no bigger than Kale's thumb caused by one of the claws from the cat puncturing the side of the pit.

"Ah, so you're hiding in there are you? Well, I've had to put up with you for over two hours now. It's time you were quieted. Taking the skinning knife in one hand and a stick in the other, Kale began to dig out the hole to force the critter to expose itself for its execution. As Kale chiseled away, both the hole and the volume of the chirping increased. The chirping became clearer, and soon it became obvious the chirping wasn't coming from a small insect, but a bird."

With a final strike of the chisel, Kale exposed one side of a small air pocket. It looked to be about one foot high and roughly two feet long. The torch, resting at the top of the pit, only allowed light to reach the first few inches. The chirping stopped for a second, and Kale could hear something small moving inside. A bird's foot darted out into the light, and then, just as quickly, retreated to safety.

Taking the stick, Kale gently guided it along one edge of the wall and then gave it a slow sweeping motion to force the creature out of hiding. As it was pushed into the light, all of its features were exposed. It appeared to be a baby Mako hawk. Often the birds in the sand regions would lay eggs in large holes or the sides of earth mounds. As protection, they would dig into the earth creating a pocket and then seal the entrance to hide their eggs.

The bird was the size of Kale's fist with dark feathers. The creature must have been near the edge of its hole when the sand cat had climbed up as the right side of the animal's face had a slash down it. The eye was completely destroyed and the top part of the shoulder blade had caught the tail end of the slash which produced a deep gash.

"It's no wonder you were chirping, little guy. Come on, let me take you out of here." Kale reached down and scooped up the bird in his hands. Immediately the creature struck out by clamping onto Kale's thumb with its beak. Fortunately, just being a young bird, it didn't have the strength to pierce Kale's gloves.

"Hey now, you better be nice, or I'll finish what I had intended to do to you." Kale climbed out of the hole and, wrapped the edges of the blanket around the meat. He tossed the bag over his shoulders and brought everything back to camp.

Approaching camp Kale could smell the bodies of the dead burning a short distance from camp. The outline of Latus could be seen by the fire tossing remains into the flames, and occasionally you could see him wiping his eyes with his good hand.

"Hey, Reagan, come take a look at this." Kale unloaded the spoils of the sand cat and went over to Reagan who had already finished hanging the meat from his kill on the side of the cart. "Look what I found."

Reagan examined the bird. "I'll be. You find this thing in the pit?"

Kale gently stroked the head of the bird that had now become more trustful of his new master. "Yeah, I guess there was a Mako nest in there."

"That's fortunate; these birds can go for a decent amount. Let's go back and get the rest of them."

"He's it, Reagan; there was only one," Kale explained.

Reagan's brow crumpled in puzzlement. "Only one? Mako's normally have twelve to sixteen eggs at a time. I've never heard of anyone finding a nest of only one."

"Well, there was only one; I don't know what to tell you. And, to boot, he's been injured." Kale turned slightly so that the full light of the campfire would hit the bird's face.

"Oh, I see. Well, that bird isn't worth much with one eye. The market for them is as hunting birds." Reagan leaned in close enough that the bird could have pecked him in the eye. "Wait a second. I don't know what this is, but it's not a Mako."

They both moved towards the fire and crouched down to better examine the bird. "Look, Kale, it has five talons, not four, and the claws are much larger than normal. The chest, just look at the size of it, not to mention its beak, is much wider than a Mako. Its feathers are dark, but they aren't black. They look almost gray. Yeah, I'm sure of it. This isn't a Mako. At least that explains you only finding one," Reagan explained.

After they had both filled their curiosity by examining the bird for all its unique properties, Reagan stood up to finish preparing the wagon for departure. "Well, I guess regardless of what it is, it won't last more than a day or two with only one eye. I'd suggest you club it, and let's get a move on."

"Oh, now, Reagan, don't be so cruel. I mean, at least you two have something in common." Kale lifted the bird up next to Reagan's face to emphasize he meant a facial scar.

"Ha.ha.. now who's the funny man? Well, if you want to keep it, that's up to you. But, you'll need two hands free to help me pull this cart," he said.

Kale picked up his satchel and made room for the bird to rest on top of his canvas blanket, and then tossed the rest of his gear on the back of the wagon. He addressed the bird as he placed him in the hollowed spot in his bag. "You're a small guy. You'll ride comfortably in my satchel."

* * *

It became obvious that Latus would be of little help pulling the cart. When day broke, the gashes in his arm became even more hideous. But, even though he had to have been in terrible pain, he endured it like a soldier, walking steadily by the cart in silence.

By mid afternoon Latus's strength began to waver. Reagan called a break, and the three sat on the ground using the cart for shade. Taking a few small samples of the drying meat and a flask of water, they settled in to recover their strength.

Kale sat reminiscing the events of the night before. His thoughts turned to Latus, and he realized how thoughtless he had been towards the fellow. Latus could have just as easily taken off during the fight and gained his freedom, but, instead he had chosen to come to Kale's aid. Even with one good arm he had carried more than his share of the work, tending to the sand cats and had volunteered to burn the bodies of his comrades. All this he did without one word of complaint or even the slightest tone of resentment. Even being in the lowliest position in society, he carried out his duty with a sense of honor.

Kale extended his hand towards Latus. "I never thanked you, my friend."

Latus sat in puzzlement in this break of policy, offering a hand of thanks to a slave. "Master Kale, I was just doing my

29

part. There is no need to thank me. I am a slave, and it is my job to protect my Master and his belongings."

Kale extended his arm a little straighter and a little further towards him. "Even still, you saved my life when you could have just as easily left us both to die. I owe you my thanks, and you have earned a friend."

Seeing that Kale wasn't going to desist with his effort for thanks, Latus turned his attention to Reagan to seek his approval.

Reagan sat up and lines of anger filled his face. "Kale, now wait just a second. You know I can't allow a slave that kind of honor. Even my father would disapprove."

The slave's head dropped slightly showing his disappointment. As anyone could imagine, for however short a time and for however small an act, anything that makes a person feel like a free man once again is a much coveted experience.

Reagan's tone returned to normal. "Well, Latus, shake the man's hand."

Latus' head darted up, and he stared deep into Reagan's eyes. "Please, do not tease me Master," he began.

Reagan reached into his pocket and put on his family's ring. Then he stood and placed his hand on Latus's head. Pausing for a second to remember the words, he began. "As Kale as my witness, I, Reagan, son of Ghen, leader of the Blackwater family, forgive Latus Diem of any and all debts, and with it, grant him deed to his life to live as he sees honorable. Rise and depart in peace."

Reagan took off his family ring and sat back down. "The depart in peace was just part of the ceremony. I would appreciate it if you could assist us until we get to Yukan, but that is up to you. Now, shake the man's hand, my friend."

In just a few hours Latus had shown to be one of the toughest men Kale had ever encountered, and it touched him to the soul when the man shook his hand and then sobbed with a joy that only a free man can experience. A few moments passed, and he wiped his eyes.

Then he extended his good hand towards Reagan. Reagan gripped it proudly, and Latus spoke. "Reagan, I give you my word that I will be by your side until the day you die. Not as your slave, but as your friend. You will not regret this kindness you have given me."

* * *

The group of men started the last part of their journey, and although Latus was still in pain, his spirit carried him on with a joyous energy. Every now and then Kale would slice off a piece of flesh from the hanging meat and toss it into the bag with his bird who he affectionately called Makko due to it's resemblance to the Makko hawk. The bird devoured each morsel with a ferocity that exceeded a bird of its size.

The trip back to Yukan felt long and draining, but by the end of the day, they made their way through the northern gate and to the trade office. Devlin came out to meet the cart in his normal fashion, brandishing his log book and smile. As he got close enough to see the three covered in bloody clothes and limping forward, the smile faded from his face and was replaced by serious concern. "I see you've made it back, Kale, but by the looks of it, the lot of you are more worse for wear. What happened?"

Kale released the poles on the cart and rotated his arms to loosen them up. "We had a run-in with those sand cat's you warned me about. If not for Latus and Reagan, I wouldn't have made it back at all."

"My goodness, lad, well, Reagan, I have to say I'm glad to see you again. It's unfortunate it couldn't be on a better condition. Let's get the three of you to Kale's house. I'll send for Mr. Kecklin. He's pretty good with a needle and thread. Oh, and before I forget, we've got Fire Kingdom troops at the trading post. They got in this morning, and they've announced they're drafting four young men from every village by order of their King. Hopefully they'll see how banged up you two are and decide it's not worth their while. But let's not test them and instead take the alley."

By the time they reached Kale's house darkness had come. Kale's father had already passed out in his bed, but his mother greeted them at the door. Their wraps were soaked with blood and had dried to their skin. Kale's mother slowly pealed them off but couldn't help reopening the wounds. The wounds of Kale and Reagan were deep but manageable. However, Latus was another case. His wound had already started to become infected, and the cat's claws had cut the major muscles in half.

About an hour after Devlin sent for Mr. Kecklin, the door swung open, and Kecklin appeared with two servants and some medical supplies. It was hard to peg his age since Kecklin was a small man, only five feet high on a tall day. He did not appear ancient, but with abundant wrinkles and a snarled grin, anyone would guess he had far passed his glory years.

Kecklin made his living importing goods to the town and then selling them to the villagers at a hefty mark-up. No one blamed him though. In every town in the Deadlands it was the same way, always someone making a little extra coin than they should. If it wasn't Kecklin, someone else would have taken the role. Kecklin had a typical shop keeper's attitude. He was always polite and helpful, but it was easy to see through the façade to his ultimate goal of getting something from you. "Oh, boys, I'm sorry this happened to you," Kecklin blurted as he haphazardly dumped his supplies onto the table, "especially when you were carrying goods to me. I assume most of the goods made the trip, or are those ruined, as well?"

Reagan replied from the chair in the corner, "Most of the supplies are fine. We lost a good deal of the meat, but we replenished it on the trip. We also have a couple of fine sand cat furs if you wish to buy them."

Kecklin paused for a moment to calculate the profits, fidgeting his fingers in the air and mumbling to himself.

Kale's mother picked up the sewing kit and tossed it lightly into Kecklin's chest to awaken him from his thoughts. "Maybe we can talk about business after the boys have stopped bleeding. I've taken care of Kale and Reagan, but their friend, Latus, isn't looking too good. He has spiked a fever, and I'm concerned about his arm. It's starting to go black."

"Oh dear, oh dear! That's not good." Kecklin walked over to where Latus was lying down and examined the wounds. Noticing the man's clothes, Kecklin instantly assumed he was a slave. "Well, slave, which one of these two is your master? I must discuss payment for your surgery."

Latus' eyes flashed with anger. "I am my own master, sir. I've recently gained my freedom."

"Well, young man," Kecklin replied with a stare of disapproval, "your arm must be removed. It will take several hours of my time and many of my supplies to accomplish this. How do you intend on paying for my services?"

The realization of his status became all too prevalent to

Latus. Even though he was no longer a slave, he was still one in other people's eyes. Just a piece of property to be weighed and measured like corn. "I do not have the means to pay you now, but I will pay you."

Peering down at Latus with a malicious grin, Kecklin replied, "Well, I guess if you work for me for the next year..well wait, with only one arm you'll get half the work done so it would be two years. We can call it even."

The pain of going back into slavery hit Latus with as much strength as the wound itself. "It is better to die a free man than live a slave." Turning his head to the wall Latus mumbled, "Leave the arm, and let me be."

The moment was heartbreaking but fleeting. Reagan instantly started his way over to the bed when he realized what Kecklin was doing. With his limp from the bite in his thigh and the damaged ankle from the barrel injury, it took him the length of the conversation to reach the bedside. Kecklin's manner changed entirely when he felt the large hand grasp his throat, and the ground from below his feet disappear.

Reagan's face was full of rage. Even through his dark skin you could see the blood rushing to his cheeks and proceeding to his ears. "How dare you make a man die over some supplies! How dare you think that this man is so worthless you would require two years of service to help him! I ought to squeeze your neck until your head flees from your shoulders and rolls on the floor, you little worm."

Kecklin's face began to turn bright red, and his pathetic attempt at gasping and gurgling for air did little to help his situation. Sprinting to the tussle, Kale grabbed Reagan's arm with both hands. To force a man of Reagan's size to do anything was foolish. Only reason could spare this old schemer from a horrific death. "No, my friend. Please don't! This will not help Latus and will only get you thrown into prison. Let him go. There is a solution to this besides murder."

Reagan slowly lowered Kecklin's body, still squeezing his throat. "Murder, it would hardly be called that, not for this animal. Murder is reserved for creatures with a heart." Pausing for a second to allow it to sink in, Reagan flicked his wrist and tossed Kecklin against the wall, allowing him to tumble to the floor like a pile of old rags.

Kecklin coughed for a few seconds and then stood. Disdain filled his haggard eyes, but he knew better than to give this brute an excuse to claim self-defense. "Hate me if you will, but I do nothing for free. I'm a businessman, plain and simple."

Reagan sat down on his chair near the door, staring at Latus. Mr. Kecklin started to collect his things and headed towards the door. As Kecklin was about to leave, Reagan placed his hand on the door to prevent him from walking out. "What do you want? What do you want to perform the surgery?"

Kecklin stood for a second and then leaned in, "I want two."

The look on Reagan's face showed his confusion so Kecklin spoke up and clarified his meaning. "Two pelts, I want two of those sand cat pelts," and then hastily added, "...and the teeth!"

Reagan's jaw tightened and his fist clamped. "I'll deliver them with your goods in the morning. But, if he dies during surgery, you get nothing!"

Kecklin gave a triumphant smile and signaled for his assistants to prepare the table as a surgery stand. "Oh, Mr. Reagan, I'm very confident in my abilities. This isn't the first amputation

I've done."

Regardless of what hatred everyone felt towards Kecklin, that night no one could deny his skill in medicine. He handled his patient with the utmost care and precision, using herbs to dull the pain and a steady hand for the gruesome task. By the next morning the surgery was complete, and Latus was resting in Kale's room.

* * *

Later the next morning Reagan and Kale brought the cart load of goods over to Kecklin's trading post. Kecklin met them at the door. "So, boy's, let's take a look at those pelts." Reagan reached into the box hanging onto the side of the cart and pulled out the bag of teeth and tossed them to Kecklin.

Catching and opening the bag he remarked, "Oh, these will do nicely. I've got a few local tribesman who will pay handsomely for these trophies."

One of the attendances who unloaded the cart walked by Kecklin with a large box of candles, and Kecklin plopped the bag on top of it, "Put that on my desk, and if you so much as break one candle in that box, I'll have you whipped." Returning his attention to Reagan, he rubbed his hands together in excitement. "Now, where are my skins?"

Reagan reached into the back of the cart and grabbed two of the skins and tossed them on the ground spreading them out. It took all that Kale could muster to hold in his laughter. The two pelts that Reagan gave to Kecklin were the ones that Reagan and Kale had skinned. Kale hadn't seen his handiwork with the skinning in the daylight and had forgotten to examine it when they got home, but, even in the darkness, he could tell the skin was almost worthless. What Kale didn't expect is that Reagan had done just as poorly a job on his skinning. Both skins looked like a netted mess of leather strips.

Kecklin threw his arms up, "What are you trying to do? This isn't what we agreed to. I asked for two hides, not a bushel of scraps!"

Reagan had no intention of hiding his laughter and delight. "Well, Kecklin, the next time you buy something with your services, you might want to take a look at the quality. As a matter of fact, you didn't even think to ask about the quality of the goods. You were too busy using my friend as leverage to gain a profit. These are two hides, and anyone can tell they are sand cat hides." Reagan paused to appreciate a good laugh, "Enjoy!"

Peering in the back of the cart Kecklin could see the two hides that Latus had skinned. They were perfect, even the skin from the head were intact. Kecklin started to reach into the back of the cart to grab them, but Kale had seen his intention and side-stepped to block his way. "Now, Mr. Kecklin, you should know the punishment for stealing. I wouldn't suggest you touch those."

Kecklin's anger raged, and he began to fume, "I will not be cheated! Those pelts belong to me. Anyone would argue that I deserve the two best pelts out of Reagan's stock. I'll take this to the elders. They'll agree with me!"

Kale thought for a second, "I don't think you'll get far with that. You see, Reagan didn't skin those pelts. Latus did, which means they belong to him. And I specifically remember Latus telling you he wasn't going to pay for your services. So, go ahead. Take it to the elders. There is a room full of witnesses to testify that what I say is truth."

Kecklin's face turned bright red, and it was his turn to grit his teeth and clasp his fists. "Just get out of here! You've delivered my goods. Now leave, go away!"

Kale looked over at the cart and saw it was still over half full as Kecklin's attendants had stopped working to watch the performance. Reagan walked to the front of the wagon and exclaimed, "Just to clarify, we've fulfilled our obligations to deliver your goods, Mr. Kecklin?"

Kecklin's tempered flared, "Yes, now get away from my shop before I have a guard drag you away!"

Reagan gave a large smile allowing his white teeth to gleam in the sunlight for a second and then put one hand on each pole of his cart. "In that case, your stuff is loitering on my cart. Let me help you unload it." Bending his knees and then giving a push that showed the whole town how massive his strength really was, Reagan tipped the cart causing the remaining supplies to roll off onto the ground. The meat tumbled from the rack and scattered across the sand covering it with dust and grit. The boxes rolled across the ground scattering their contents.

"Good day to you, Mr. Kecklin. It was nice doing business with you." Reagan and Kale began to pull the cart away with a true feeling of justice. From behind they could hear Kecklin fuming and screaming at them, "I'll get you back for this, the both of you!"

* * *

While pulling, Kale grinned as he turned to Reagan. "So, Reagan, what do you say before we head home we take Makko here out for some fun? We'll see if he can fly and maybe teach him to hunt some insects or something. You'll need to rest a few days, and Latus will need at least a week before he'll be doing anything at all so we might as well have some entertainment."

Limping along Reagan replied, "Sure, that sounds like fun. There's a bit of grass next to the mill. I'm sure there'll be some crickets there." The two left the cart at the southern gate of town and continued on foot the next half a mile to the old mill. The grass there grew taller than in most places around Yukan and made for good scavenging. Reaching down into his bag Kale pulled out Makko. "Hey, little guy, sorry for the delay. It's been an exciting night." The bird began to peck at Kale's glove searching for meat. "Oh, you want something to eat. I guess it's been awhile. Reagan, see if you can catch a cricket. We've got to teach Makko how to hunt for himself."

Reagan returned with a handful of crickets. Plucking the wings from one they placed it in a barren section of the field and sat Makko down next to it. Lesson one didn't take too long. Within a few seconds Makko attacked the cricket, gulping it up in one bite. Reagan exclaimed, "Wow! Well, I guess nature is the best training. If you're hungry, eat whatever is smaller than you. Let's see if he will chase one. Reagan, leave the wings on the next one."

"Okay, Kale, here you go, Makko. Get'em." Reagan tossed a cricket within a few feet of where Makko perched. The cricket landed on its back. Quickly flipping itself over, it leaped into the air to escape. Makko started to run towards it but seeing that on two legs he wasn't going to overtake the critter, Makko sprung into a short flight landing every ten feet. After a few more crickets, Makko was able to gauge distance and flight time to snatch each cricket from the air.

"Well, at least he can get his own food Reagan, that's good. I know he's not a mako bird, but he'll probably get as big as one. Maybe some day I can teach him to be a hunting bird."

Reagan tossed Makko the remaining crickets. "Maybe he's worth keeping around. Vicious eater but I don't think he'll be flying anytime soon. Did you notice he can only stay in the air a minute or so before he has to ground? I'm sure that shoulder of his is hurting too much. I just hope that isn't permanent."

Makko landed on Kale's extended hand, and then searched it for more insects. Finding it empty he sat perched looking around into the grass. Kale stroked his head. "I've always wanted a hunting bird. They're just too expensive to buy. He'll make a good pet. I'm sure of it." Kale's arm jerked with the sudden movement of the bird taking off into flight. He circled around them and then flew to the top of the mill and perched on one of the circulating panels the mill used to catch the wind.

"Makko, get down here," Kale called as the bird walked along the edge of the panel looking down on them. Minutes passed and the bird stayed staring. "Makko, I'm not climbing up there, and if you don't come down now, we'll leave you here for the animals to kill you. Now, come on. We need to be heading back."

Makko cocked his head to one side and stayed still for a moment. As Kale went to take a step forward, the bird let out a shriek and dove down from the top of the mill missing Kale by inches, causing him to fall backwards onto the ground. Kale sat up, "You crazy bird. What's wrong with you?" Makko circled and came swooping down again, but this time he flew over Kale's head and dove into the grass in front of him, swooping out of the grass, carrying something, and flying eighty feet into the air before letting it drop. The object hit the ground a few feet away from Reagan. Kale stood up to go look at the object and while walking over to where Reagan stood, Makko flew in and perched on Reagan's shoulders.

Reagan gave a whistle through his teeth, "Well, will you look at that?"

Writhing in its death pains, a sand viper, measuring three feet with tan skin and faded red diamonds running down its back, lay in the sandy terrain. Kale turned his head to see Makko. "I guess you are a hunting bird after all."

Reagan, stroking ever so lightly the top of Makko's head with his bulky hand, exclaimed, "Not only that, Kale, but he saved you one nasty bite. A few more steps and you would have gone right on top of that thing."

"You're right, Reagan. This bird was protecting me." Kale grabbed Makko off his shoulder and perched him on his wrist. "Well, I guess that settles it. You're staying with me."

* * *

Kale and Reagan headed back into town. As they were approaching the house, Devlin came out of the door. "Oh, thank goodness, I found you two boys. The Fire Troopers have asked me for a census of the town so that they can decide what four young men they will be drafting. I had no choice Kale. They've chosen you as one of the new recruits. They will be sending guards to retrieve each of the boys and have them ready for pickup first thing in the morning when the main caravan makes its rounds. Kale, I just informed your father so you had better get in there. He's really upset about this."

Reagan exhaled, "Oh man, that is not good Kale. The Fire Kingdom is the worst to get drafted into. I'll give you a few minutes to talk with your parents and go retrieve the cart."

Zeak sat by the window with his sword strapped to his side staring into the street. Kale's mother sat at the table with her head buried in her hands. Her shoulders were heaving and it became obvious she was trying to conceal her sorrow.

"Mother, are you ok?" whispered Kale.

Lifting her head with tears still in her eyes she replied, "Oh Kale, you've been chosen. They're going to take you away."

"I know, mother. I just heard." Kale turned to his father, "What should I do?"

Unmoving, Zeak continued staring out the window, seemingly oblivious that a question had been posed to him.

"Mother, is he okay?" Kale asked.

"I don't know, sweetie. He's been like that all day, even before we found out about you. As soon as Devlin told him the Fire Troopers were in town, he has been sitting there. No drink, no food, just occasionally stroking the handle of his sword and mumbling."

As if awaked from a sleep, Kale's father stood up with a jerk, "They're here!"

A loud knock penetrated the room. Kale started walking toward the door but was pushed aside by his father. Opening the door hastily and walking out before the troopers at the door could speak, Zeak forced them away from the entrance way and into the street near the house.

With a sternness and breadth that Kale had rarely seen in his father, he announced, "I know why you are here, and you're going to have to take another boy. You're not taking my son!"

Amidst four lower ranking soldiers a young lieutenant stood; his armor slightly different than the normal soldier. He carried twelve daggers along his belt and on his back he brandished two short swords made of red medal. This trait signified his rank as someone from the royal family, as only a Fire

Gehage of the royal line were permitted to carry them.

Although all Gehage came from the royal bloodline of the first king, within the Fire Kingdom a select family was set aside as heirs to the throne. This passed to the first born of each family and extended out to the cousins of the current king. Most were instantly promoted to leadership, and the further away from the probability of the crown, the further away from the Fire Kingdom capital city you were posted.

Being sent beyond the borders of the Fire Kingdom for recruitment would place this officer well beyond the likelihood of royalty, but still the family's bloodline must run through his veins, making him someone to take seriously.

The young lieutenant stepped forward. "Peasant, it matters not what you wish. Your son has been chosen to serve in the Fire Kingdom's army. His choices are simple. Join willingly or be taken prisoner to serve his duty as a slave building our fortresses."

Kale's father stepped forward and tossing his long jacket aside displayed his sword and his wooden leg. "Do not talk to me of duty, pup. My family has both bled and spilled our share of blood for the Fire Kingdom. Again, choose another boy. You cannot have mine." With this he rested his hand on the hilt of his sword, making his resolution clear.

At the first sign of hostility three guards drew their swords and a fourth raised his crossbow preparing to attack. The three soldiers armed with blades rushed in to overtake Zeak. Pivoting on his wooden leg he maneuvered with such poise that the three soldiers looked like no more than children waving sticks at a lion. With each swing Zeak parried, and using the attacker's weight against them, threw them to the ground. Occasionally a good kick or well placed bash with the hilt of his sword made its mark. His blade never scratched their skin, but with play-like grace he only used it to ward off their blows.

With each display of his mastery of the blade, Kale stood in awe. His father was instantly promoted in his mind. No longer was he the exaggerating, storytelling drunk. He truly had been a soldier of old, a veteran of the Great War.

Holding his hand up gently to communicate he wished them to steady their weapons, the young lieutenant smiled as he said, "I see you've had your share of skirmishes, old man. But something tells me your wife has not. Move one more muscle, and my archer will put an arrow through her heart."

At this declaration, the archer turned slightly and aimed his bow at Kale's mother. Zeak stopped his attack instantly. Two of the guards stepped up and held Kale's arms to restrain him. Kale's heart raced at the thought of his mother's danger. "No, I will go with you freely. Leave them be. Please, leave them alone. I'll go."

The officer pulled a dagger from his belt and stepping up to Kale placed the tip under his chin. "Now hear this, you little rodent, I am Fike, second cousin of the king, and I will not be defied." Turning slowly to his archer, he tilted his head slightly. At the same instant he twirled with cat-like speed and threw the dagger.

The next few moments played out in slow motion in Kale's eyes. At the instant Fike twirled, Zeak had expected his intent. Forming in the palm of Zeak's hand gleamed a ball of fire. As Fike tossed his dagger toward Zeak's chest, Zeak had already hurled the ball of flame. The dagger passed through the fiery ball gaining a glowing glint from the heat and plunged into Zeak's chest. But the last blow was dealt by Zeak as Fike took the ball of flame directly in the face sending him sprawling on the ground.

During those same few seconds Kale heard the twang of the crossbow releasing its arrow and the blur passing by his eyes. Faintly the thump echoed, hitting its target. Out of the corner of his eye he could see his mother falling to the ground as his father hit his knees and then found his resting place face down in the sandy terrain.

Kale's heart beat so intensely he could feel it in every inch of his body. The chill of wind came rushing down around him engulfing him in his sorrows. His vision blurred as if he had entered some dream-like sleep. From a distance, a cry of grief echoed through the deepness of his consciousness in which he had retreated. And then the anger rushed in, clouding thought and vision. The faces of the guards flashed across the screen playing before his eyes. Their faces were painted with terror as their death played out in the darkness. The screams in the distance increased, but now mixed with the screams of grief were the screams of horror, the screams of the slaughtered. With each beat of his heart, the grief and anger grew until nothing but tainted colors filled his vision. Then, as if gripping at sanity, a familiar voice pierced the onslaught of emotions; Reagan's voice, "Kale, settle down..Kale...it's me...Kale...Kale.." Then all went black.

* * *

The colors started to come back into focus. Hovering above him stood Reagan staring down at him holding a club. Above him the clear blue sky promenaded the background. "Are you okay, Kale? Can you hear me?"

For an instant the hope that the memories from only mo-

45

With this hope, Kale sat up and searched his surroundings. The hope faded as quickly as it came, and Kale's heart sank deep in his chest. His mother and father still lay on the ground. Strewn around them were the bodies of the four guards riddled with wounds far beyond what would be necessary to kill them.

Realizing the weight of his arms, Kale looked down, and in both hands he held the blades of the two guards who had been holding him. Kale tossed them aside as he put his hand up in the air towards Reagan.

Reagan grabbed his hand and pulled Kale to his feet. "Kale, I'm so sorry about your parents. I heard the screams from down the street and came as fast as I could. I just didn't get here in time."

Tears streaming down his face, Kale stumbled over to his mother. Dropping to his knees he mourned for several minutes before taking the arrow out of her chest and covering her face with his father's long jacket which lay on the ground close to her.

Focusing his attention to his father, he turned him over and removed the dagger. The heat from his fathers flame had heated the blade to an almost red hot state before it plunged into his chest. As the metal cooled, Zeak's blood had merged with the blade. The edges and handle were now distorted and jagged. The blade showed a twirling glint of red.

Tossing the blade to the ground, Kale straightened Zeak's body out. "I despised you until the day you died. I'm sorry I could never see what you really were. I'm sorry I'll never know the kind of person you had lived as before this place. Rest in peace, father. You died a hero."

Taking Zeak's blade, Kale strapped it around his waist and wiped the tears with the sleeve of his shirt. Reagan stood next to his cart with Devlin a few steps behind him. In all the excitement, Kale had overlooked the scrawny official. Devlin stood very still, his face white and his eyes wide open. Kale approached him slowly. "Devlin, are you okay?" As Kale got close, Devlin backed up and tripped over the block restraining the cart wheel. "Devlin, it's me, Kale."

As Kale stepped forward again, Devlin crawled backwards quickly. "Stay away from me...don't come any closer, Kale. I mean it, stay back."

Reagan lifted his hand and put it on Kale's chest. "He's afraid Kale. I'm afraid. What in the world happened to you? I've never seen someone move so fast. And you had wind wrapping around your body. I've seen Gehage do some wild stuff, but I've never even heard of someone doing that."

Kale stopped his advancement towards Devlin and turned his head toward Reagan. "I don't know what happened; I can't remember anything but bits and pieces. I saw my parents fall, and I lost it. Everything just phased out."

Reagan lowered his hand. "My friend, all I know is with all my strength, I couldn't restrain you. You threw me twice before I finally grabbed this club and knocked you out. I don't know what that was, but I know I don't want to have to deal with it again."

Kale turned towards Devlin. "Devlin, we've been friends for a long time. I'm not going to hurt you. I don't know what happened to me. Please, I need your help. The other troops will be returning soon. What are we going to tell them about what happened?"

Devlin took a second to compose himself and stood to his feet. "Kale, I don't know what that was but I know I can't have that happen in my town again. The Fire Troopers are going to tear this town apart if I don't turn you over." Pausing for a second, Devlin's posture relaxed, and then he took a deep breath and exhaled loudly as if he had come to a conclusion. "I'll tell them your father killed these men before he was taken down. But they'll still be coming after you. You'll need to run Kale. You and Reagan. Too many people saw you two together today causing a ruckus, and that Kecklin will make sure you're all wrapped up in this mess together."

Exhaling as he put his hand out to Devlin, Kale replied, "Thank you, Devlin. Please make sure my parents are buried properly."

Again Devlin backed away. "I'll make sure your mother is buried honorably. I can't make any promises for your father. But Kale, don't come back here, ever. We don't need that kind of trouble. As much as it pains me to say, you're not welcome here anymore. I can't risk it."

Even through the pain of losing his parents, the sting of what Devlin said found its way to the surface. He was alone now, outcast from his life long home.

Looking around at the matted bodies, Kale knew his exile to be warranted. "I understand Devlin. I'll gather my things, and we'll head for the Therein Gate."

Reagan went inside and carried out Latus placing him on some blankets in the back of the cart. "Latus won't be safe here either, Kale. We'll need to haul him on the cart." Reagan turned to Devlin. "Tell them we headed towards the Ereki Forest. That should buy us a few days to make it to the Gate."

Devlin folded his hands under his sleeves. "I'll do as you ask, but that's all I can do. Be on your way and I hope you make it there safely."

After loading the cart with all the supplies they could find in the house and placing Makko in the carrying case on the side of the cart, Kale paid his last respects to his parents and then departed.

The Therein Gate acted as the main entrance into the Stone Kingdom and resided to the northwest of Yukan. All of the Badlands were neutral territory, but the Stone Country claimed everything within arrow shot of their wall. No soldier from another kingdom could approach without first sending an emissary to state his business. If anyone but peasants approached, they would be shot without warning.

The next few days were slow as the cart would jostle from the dips in the road making Latus moan in pain. In spite of being forced to be mobile, his fever had decreased, and it appeared he would pull through. Camping only during the darkest parts of night, Reagan and Kale made their way towards the Gate.

Sitting at camp one night Kale and Reagan began to discuss their plans. Reagan sat calmly at the edge of the fire next to the cart. "Kale, it looks like we are both going to have to start new lives when we reach Therein. What do you think we should do? I'm sure they need runners there as well. I could start my own delivery service."

Kale leaned back, "Oh, Reagan, I'm not sure what will become of us. Right now everything is so confusing. I feel so alone. I know I have you and Latus with me, but it's different. I feel so different since my parents died. It's like I still have them with me. I feel their presence, and when I turn to look, nothing is there. I can still smell my home in my jacket. I don't want to take it off for fear the smell will go away. I just feel so lost."

Taking a stick, Kale played with the embers to give himself a reason to cut the conversation short.

Reagan, sensing his friend's pain, chimed in, knowing now to be the time to help Kale through this difficult hour in his life. "Kale, I know how it is to loose a loved one. When my mother died I felt the same way. It's hard, but it will pass. Their memories will always be with you, but the pain will lessen and eventually it will just lay dormant, only awaking when something triggers it. But, then it will fade away again."

"I hope so, Reagan. I really do. I feel so guilty for their deaths. If only I would have been brave enough to volunteer with another army, this would have never happened."

"Kale, you should know your father would have stopped any other army from taking you, too," comforted Reagan.

"Yeah, he would have, I guess. I just never believed all those wild stories he used to tell. I mean, you should have seen the way he moved. It was unlike anything I have ever seen. It resembled the Fire Kingdom stance, but it was different, such smoothness."

Reagan tossed another stick on the fire. "That comes from years of battle. I've seen my uncle fight. He's been doing it for so long it's as easy as breathing air. But it's no easy feat to accomplish; it takes years of diligent training to bring yourself to the level your father demonstrated." Reagan rose to his feet and brushed off the back of his pants. "You know, Kale, the Stone Country is actively warring against the Fire Troopers on their eastern borders. We could join up and help prevent what happened to your parents from happening to anyone else."

Kale stood up and walked over to the cart, opening the bag Makko rested in. Reaching into the bag and pulling out Makko, he placed the bird on his arm and fed him a few slivers of meat. "What do you say, boy? You want to fight some Fire Troopers."

As if answering the call to battle, Makko stretched out his wings and gave a wild squawk. And with his good eye peered into Kale's with more intelligence than any animal Kale had ever encountered.

From the back of the cart Latus sat up holding the stub hanging off his side. "That's one fine bird you have there, Kale." He then looked around. "So, where are we?"

Reagan turned quickly at the sound of Latus's voice, "Latus, you're awake. This is a good sign. You might just make it." Within a few moments the two had updated Latus on the recent events.

Latus dropped his head slightly, "Kale, I'm so sorry." And then with a furrowed brow looked to Reagan. "My friend, why did you take me with you? Surely that story of going to Ereki will only divert them a day or two, three at most. You should have left me."

Reagan placed his hand on Latus' chest and gently laid him back down. "Now, what kind of friends would we be to leave you there to be hung like a run-away slave? And don't try and deny it. That's exactly what Kecklin would do if given the chance."

Turning to Kale, Reagan leaned on the cart, "He's right, though. This cart isn't that hard to track, and by now they would have realized our deceit and headed this way. We're only a day away from the gate. We should get a move on. They can't be far behind."

Kale placed Makko on the forward post of the cart. "In case things don't go so well, it's best if you're in the open. Your eyes

51

are better than ours, and if you need to escape, my little warrior, you're going to need to be free to take flight."

The two packed up camp and began to pull the cart through the flat sandy terrain. As they neared the plateau that led to the wall, daylight began to break. The highlights of red and pink filled the sky. Slowly colors of green appeared, and within a few moments the blue tint of the sky reared its chest. By the time the sun hung mid-way through the morning sky, the group had reached the halfway point of the plateau. A mere mile separated them from the wall. In the distance its enormous towers and large entrance way heralded their safety."

Stopping to draw a last breath of rest before making the final steps of their journey, they gulped down the last of the water left in their casks. Reagan took a healthy swig, "We're almost there, almost to safety. Those Fire Troopers won't follow us into that gate."

Makko shifted suddenly and then let out a shriek as he took flight. Turning back Kale could see seven figures approaching from the edge of the plateau. "It's them. It's got to be, and they are coming fast. By the size of them, I'd say they're on horseback."

Reagan dropped the container in his hand. "We'll never out run them with this cart."

Latus again sat up and then started to pull himself off the cart. Kale gently restrained him. "No, Latus, I won't let you do that. Not while there is still hope of escape. Hear me out. If they can take one of us with little risk of nearing the archers, they will do so. I cannot pull the cart by myself, but, Reagan, you can."

Reagan retrieved the spear from the back of the cart. "No, I cannot let you do that. We will make our stand here. Together."

"Reagan, it's our only chance, and you know it. I am a swift runner. I'll divert them to the west, and when you are out of danger, I'll sprint to catch up."

Taking his father's sword off his belt, he handed it to Latus. "Hold onto this until I get back. The weight will slow me down."

Gripping the sword to his chest, Latus looked at Kale. "If only for a moment, to be entrusted with your father's blade will be a great honor. Be careful, my friend."

Placing the second harness strap into Reagan's palm, Kale said, "No matter what happens, don't turn back. It's me they want anyway."

Reagan reluctantly gripped the strap. "I haven't seen an animal yet who could outrun you, Kale. Run swiftly and take no chances."

Shaking Reagan's hand, they each exchanged a worried glance and then Kale took off to the west at a slow jog. As he started, he looked over his shoulder, "Now, run Reagan! Get Latus to the gate!"

As Kale neared the spot he had selected to take position, he looked back and saw Reagan frantically pulling the cart. A cloud of dust arose and with every second he got closer to the wall. The Fire Troopers increased their speed at first, but seeing their target stationary was enough to get them to switch directions and proceed to what they assumed to be a surrendering prey. As they got closer, their pace slackened as they assumed Kale did not intend to run.

Looking again, Kale judged that Reagan would make it to the gate even if the horses were in pursuit at full gallop. The troops had neared to within a hundred and fifty yards from his position. It was time to make his sprint for freedom.

He shifted his weight and bolted with all the speed he could muster. Immediately the troops kicked the sides of their mounts sending them into a gallop. Kale was just fast enough to stay paced with the horses. His legs started to tighten and his breath began to shorten. The pursuit lasted only minutes as they closed in on the wall. Kale slowly lost speed which allowed the troops to gain enough ground to attempt the use of their crossbows. A well placed aim sent an arrow zinging by Kale's head, shaving a cut into his cheek.

Kale passed a distance a little over two hundred yards from the gate. An archer from above sent a warning shot displaying the range of their fire toward the pursuing troops. Kale watched the arrow land a hundred yards in front of him. The sound of the flaring nostrils and beating hooves of the horses trailing so closely behind him it urged Kale to dig deeper for a reserve of energy. Passing the arrow stuck in the sand, Kale's heart started to lighten as he heard the horses come to a halt.

Then a sharp pain pierced his thigh. The sudden alteration to his rhythm sent him tumbling to the ground. Looking down, he saw a crossbow arrow had pierced through his leg. Attached to the end hung a rope that led to the saddle of a hooded soldier. The soldier turned his horse and began to trot away, dragging Kale out of the safety of the Stone archer's shots.

Reagan stood at the wall screaming while being held back by three of the gate guards. "No! Kale! Let me go! I've got to save him."

A guard planted himself in front of Reagan, "If you go out there, they'll hang you, too, and we can't interfere with them when they are in the Deadlands. I'm sorry, but your friend is gone. I saw what he did for you. You must be very fortunate to have a friend like that."

* * *

The horses drug Kale past the edge of the plateau. His ribs ached from being pounded against the clumps of sand grass and the occasional rock. His lips were dry and his lungs felt like they were filled more with sand than air. All this did not compare to the pain in his thigh from the arrow that had peirced it. While being pulled by the horse, the hole had expanded but fortunately had clotted with sand. As soon as the horses stopped, Kale reached down and broke the arrow head off and pulled the shaft out of his thigh.

The hooded soldier approached slowly as if weak from the journey. Kale sensed something familiar about his posture and fought to place it. It didn't take long for the mystery soldier to make his identity known. Stepping on Kale's wounded thigh and twisting his boot to increase the pain, the soldier spoke with a gurgled sound making his act all the more terrible. "As I said before, no one defies me!" Then removing his hood the remnants of what used to be Fike's face were disclosed. His nose and ears were seared off. Most of his lower lip and right cheek were missing, displaying a gruesome opening to his teeth while one eye was swollen shut and seared over. All the hair leading to the back of his head had been burned off and replaced by a mutilated charred scalp.

The smell alone made Kale's stomach churn. It took all Kale's restraint not to tackle Fike to the ground, but knowing the other guards where standing close by made it impossible to do so and live to enjoy his revenge.

Following behind Fike paced a messenger; another sand

55

runner that Kale had passed often in his runs throughout the eastern towns. "Sir, a message from the general. You are ordered back to the Capital immediately. He is in need of your men for an assault."

Fike seemed to ignore the messenger as his anger flared. He then reached into his belt and retrieved the dagger used to kill Kale's father, Zeak. "I should cut your heart out with this blade. How fitting you should die by the same blade that killed your father. But I think a better fate for the son of a traitor would be to spend the rest of your miserable life starving in our prison where the taskmaster can beat you daily. Where your blood can slowly stain the ground and your sweat can be mortar to my kingdom's greatness. Yes, you will suffer and when old age has gripped you, I will come and see that you die a slow agonizing death."

Fike took one final twist of his foot into the wound now pulsating in Kale's leg and then walked away expressing a satisfied sadistical laugh. As he approached the other soldiers, he sheathed his blade. "Take that rat to Durian Keep. Tell them to make sure he lives. In due time I want to be the one to kill him."

The messenger stepped forward, "But, sir, you and your men have been ordered to return immediately."

Fike spun on his heal and with both hands sent a massive wave of flames toward the messenger. The man fell to the ground engulfed in fire, his screams filling the air and echoing in the emptiness. Fike stood over his body as it stopped moving and screamed at the lifeless burning corpse. "I heard my orders, you little maggot!"

Kale's stomach began to sour at the smell of the burning flesh. The man's screams still replaying in his mind.

Fike then turned to the soldiers he had just addressed. They both hastily bowed and grabbed a few ropes off of their horses. After Kale's hands were tied, they mounted him on a pack horse; attaching the end of the rope to the saddle. All the soldiers mounted and began to depart.

Kale took a last moment to give Fike a hate-filled stare. Fike had recovered his head with the hood of his cloak but had left his face exposed as he slowly trotted his horse over to Kale. "I told you to make sure he lived. I said nothing about making him comfortable," and then planted a kick in Kale's chest sending him sailing to the ground. His body began to roll but the rope that secured him to the saddle checked his momentum with a sudden jerk.

Fike took off towards the south east, in all probability to meet up with his company to return to the Capital as ordered.

***

The first day of the week and a half journey toward Durian tried Kale's limbs to their breaking point. The terrain slowly changed to a more solid visage with dry creek beds and gravel pits littering the path. Only being able to hobble on one leg made keeping up with the mounted troops impossible and in many cases Kale resorted to just allowing the horse to drag him.

They were forced to stop countless times to tend to the major slashes on his body from being raked across the rocks. Finally, midway through the second day, they stopped to make camp, and Kale overheard the guards say it would be impossible to deliver him alive as commanded if he wasn't allowed to ride on a mount. They finally decided that they would ride Kale on a mount until they came near the keep and then make him walk into the gates. With great relief, the guards hoisted Kale's limp body up on the mount and tied him in place to keep him from falling over from the exhaustion. In truth, Kale was more disoriented from the loss of blood than the lack of energy. Any other time being so confined would have been unbearable, but being securely fastened became an all too welcome change.

With each passing day Kale scanned the horizon for hope of a rescue, and with every evening the disappointment settled in that no salvation was to come. It would be useless to bargain with the guards. Kale had nothing they needed, and anyone could tell the guards feared Fike. The risk of his retribution would be too great to betray him.

There were many hours of reflection as their course continued deeper into Fire Kingdom territory. After the seventh day Kale had accepted the hard truth that no rescue would come. If Kale had been in Reagan's position he would have thought Kale had already been hung as a traitor or more likely beheaded on the spot. Deep in his heart he knew he would rather die than have Reagan risk his life to save him. During the last few days of the trip, large groups of soldiers passed by on the main road. Hundreds of troops at a time marched toward the Stone Kingdom's eastern border. War was fast approaching.

The last day finally came with Kale's arms and legs worn raw from the constant rubbings of the ropes. The soldiers dismounted Kale and dragged him along for the last mile. It seemed like the final hour lasted longer than the previous nine days. Even the breeze hitting his open wounds stung like salt in a fresh cut. Still hobbling, the cuts that had recently crusted over from being allowed to heal the last nine and a half days broke open. What felt to be the last of Kale's blood spilt out onto already shredded and filthy clothes.

ONE

****

DURIAN PRISON

The Durian Keep, in fact, looked nothing like a keep but a small city in the making. The Fire Kingdom had first built the four stories and a quarter-of-a-mile-long prison to house the slaves who would build the remaining buildings. There were three main streets already constructed with rough shops in the works. The northern wall had been completed, but the towers were only half finished. In the right quadrant of town a barracks sat near completion. In the middle of the city stood the tallest building Kale had ever seen. Kale counted twenty five windows straight up. Its breadth stretched as wide as the entire town of Yukan. Towering above the main floors another ten stories high stood a tubular tower about a sixth of the size of the building. Resting on its corners were four large archer towers armed with catapults and tar cauldrons. The gates leading into the building were three times as tall as Kale and over thirty feet wide.

Scattering along its walls were statues of dragons and Fire kings of old battling various beasts. Highlighted as a centerpiece in front of the building stood a forty foot high statue of the legendary story of King Haken defeating Kannov; the king of the Wolfkin.

Haken stood gloriously over the dead body of Kannov with his sword buried in the beast's chest and his shield lifted high in triumph. The statue had been magnificently molded. Kale took special notice of the King's blade. It curved ever so slightly as a scimitar and featured the head of a dragon biting the blade. This head narrowed to provide a hilt and then widened again into a dragon's talon. Kale could make out a mountain rage, a tidal wave, a great oak, and a volcano etched in intricate detail on the blade; signifying the four elements within his control.

If not for the dread of a lifetime of slavery, it would have been an awesome thing to see. The awe-inspiring moment quickly dimmed as they rounded a street corner and proceeded to the back of the city. Resting against the mountain side stood a rock quarry where the slaves would spend their days in merciless toil.

As the small band approached the quarry, a dusty taskmaster approached. "Well, ain't tis just da sorriest fella ya ever laid yer peepers on. So, I guess dis here be a new unwillin recruit?"

The guard untied the end of the rope and tossed it to the shirtless pot-bellied man covered in dust and black tar. "Yeah, something like that. Though this is a special case. By order of Lieutenant Fike, this prisoner is to be kept alive. Indefinitely! Or until he can come and partake of the pleasure of killing him."

The man put one hand to his chin. "Now, look here fella. I can't go have me guards keep an eye on one fella out of four thousand. Dat's dern impossible. And I sure ain't gonna go through all dat dere trouble for some snot nosed lieutenant. And ya can tell'em I said so."

The guards returned a casual laugh as if they were partaking in some secret folly. Then, turning back to the taskmaster said, "Maybe I should make myself a little clearer. Lieutenant Fike, son of Qame, general of the twelve legions has ordered you to do so."

Kale could see the color drain from the taskmaster's face as he lowered his hand from his chin. "Well, um dat would be a different matter, now wouldn't it. I'll make sure dis young pup is kept on the brink of death, but no further." As he pronounced this, he smiled deeply, exposing his rotting teeth and black gums and slapped Kale on the back as if they were best friends.

Turning to the taskmaster, Kale spoke for the first time in over a week. His only words seeped through cracked lips and a hoarse throat. With obvious sarcasm Kale replied, "Gee, thanks mister, that makes me feel so much better."

As soon as the last syllable left his lips, Kale regretted he had spoken such instigating words. Without missing a beat, the Taskmaster punched Kale square in the chin and then proceeded to beat him with the whip he held in his hand. "Silence, you nectic worm! Silence!"

Laughing, the guards departed. As they left, he could hear the guards chatting, "Yeah, they're going to get along just great. Let's get back before the company moves out. I don't want to miss this battle."

After a few moments of venting his rage on Kale's already frail body, the taskmaster grabbed the rope and led Kale down to the quarry. As they descended the ramp, Kale could see a stack of twenty bodies being piled up to be burned. Noticing Kale's horror, the taskmaster started to speak, giving a jolly-filled guided tour. It was as if he were a guide in the majestic halls of the Ereki Palaces.

"Ah, I see you got to noticin dim bodies over yonder. Dose be the body count for today, well so fer anyway. You be countin' yourself lucky as I won't be lettin you end up dere or it'd be me hide. So if'n you like it or no you gonna live a long time in dis place. And trust me, after a short time you'd be wishin ya be dead."

Walking along, he began to stretch out his whip, pointing to various parts. "Dim dere's were we make da morder. Yah see dat poor fool who done collapsed in da pit? He'll just be a permanent part of dis here keep as some mortar for dim stones we be cuttin out of the mountain over yonder."

This twisted tour came to an end when they reached the bottom of the ramp where resided a small shack that appeared to be a blacksmith. "And dis here'd be what we call the brand'n iron." Raising his hand to a man standing behind a fire pit. "So, Waji, what be the next number in dis here line?"

"Mighty fine morning, master, sir. We're going on twenty four six forty two. We got a new one starting so late in the day, I see."

"That we do. Let's get'em fixed up right quick so we can settle em in."

The blacksmith scratched his beard as he replied, "You got it, master, sir."

Turning with a smile and a wink, the jolly taskmaster pulled Kale forward and then grabbed his arms to restrain him. "Dis here is gonna sting just a might bit."

The blacksmith had ten irons heated in the fire. At the end of each were the numbers zero through nine. Then he pressed them into Kale's shoulder. Each iron caused the skin to smoke, producing a searing sound that almost surpassed the screams coming out of Kale's mouth. Kale's legs began to wobble after the third number, but the taskmaster would have none of that. Still holding onto Kale's arms, he forced Kale to one side and then dunked him head first into the cooling trough.

The cool water felt refreshing at first, but after a few seconds of the taskmaster holding his head under water, the coolness mattered little as the struggle for air commenced. Finally Kale's head was removed from the water. Gasping for air, Kale attempted to spit out what water he had inhaled.

The taskmaster leaned in, "Now, ye try dat fainting stuff with me again, and I'll hold you in dere til you plum drown, I will."

The last two numbers were just as painful, but with each sting, Kale made it a point to keep himself steady to prevent any further insult to his injuries. After the barbaric act of numbering Kale, the taskmaster brought him down to a cart to be delivered to a guard.

Kale determined this must be a high ranking guard as his undershirt appeared to be red while all the other guards' undershirts looked to be mud brown. "Now, Celic, I want ye to put dis here prisoner with da other special case we got last year. Make sure everyone knows dis'n gotta live, too."

Celic was an enormous man, standing seven foot four and weighing nearly three hundred and fifty pounds. His biceps were larger than Kale's head, and his face was set in a permanent state of grim from the years of service in the quarry.

"I'll make sure they know, master, sir." Taking the rope, Celic led Kale away, placing him on the back of the cart and then wheeling him over to a tunnel that led under the city. If only Kale had realized that this would be one of the very few times he would see the open sky for some time, he would have appreciated its beauty. The tunnel was well lit and big enough for the cart to ride down with ease. In the cart were large stone blocks that matched the size of the ones used to form the walls of the tunnel. When they reached the end of the tunnel, a group of workers were diligently working to extend the length of the

63

supporting wall as another group, a short distance further, were lengthening the tunnel. Celic stepped off of the cart. "Okay, six-four-two welcome to your new home." Taking Kale's hands, he cut the rope and tossed them both to the ground "You won't be needing that. There is no escape from this city so don't even try. But just to make it less appealing, I want you to take a look around. This is your work group."

Peering around, Kale saw the worried faces of twelve poor souls lost to a life of torment. "If you even attempt to run, we will kill all of them." Looking over at a young man in tattered clothes with a red sash tied around his waist, Celic continued, "Well, all but this one, six-four-two meet one-eight-three. This will be your new partner. You will live together, eat together, and die together." At this Celic took two shackles connected by an eight foot chain and attached one to the other at the ankle.

He then ripped off one of his sleeves and tied it around Kale's waist. "Don't lose the sash, it means that you're under my protection. The guards won't harm you as much, but the other inmates will despise you for it. They all know better than to take it. The last one who tried to was pulled apart by horses at my command." With this, Celic gave a self-indulged grunt as if remembering the scene vividly. "Never thought he'd hang on that long; screamed clear till he separated. Well, anyway, one-eight-three will show you the ropes." With this he turned and got back on the now unloaded cart and it pulled away out of the tunnel.

* * *

Reaching out his hand in an attempt to make a casual greeting under such harsh circumstances, Kale turned to his new cellmate. "By the way, I'm Kale." While his hand was outstretched, the sting of a whip hit his back as the guard screamed, "Silence, Dog! Get back to work."

The young man looked up quickly, "Quiet, you fool, I'll talk to you tonight. Just do as I do."

The crack of the whip once again echoed through the tunnel. "I said silence!"

The rest of the day was tiring but not as painful as the previous few weeks. The job proved to be very simple; a cart would come laden with cut stones and mortar. Kale placed the stones on the wall being dug out by the other prisoners and applied mortar for the next layer. The other slaves would get cycled out for more tedious jobs, but Kale and the other 'special case' remained in the cool of the tunnel working at a steady but reasonable pace.

After the day was over Kale and the young man he was attached to were lead through the tunnels and up into the bottom floor of the prison. As Kale walked through the dark musty filth he could not help but gag at the smell of death and decay that penetrated the cells. At each door Kale would hear moaning or the occasional cries for mercy from the new inmates. Slowly they made their way up a spiral staircase to the top floor where they were placed in one of the cells located in the middle of the building.

The cell measured twelve feet by twelve feet with twelve foot walls. Because it resided in the middle of the prison, there were no windows, but, instead, in the ceiling a cylinder opening of about two feet in diameter and about four feet long with a steel grate on both ends allowed air to flow into the room. Directly below the ceiling vent on the floor rested another cylinder tube leading to the cell below. This repeated for every floor until the last, providing an air current throughout the building.

After the cell had been locked, Kale attempted another greeting. "Now that we aren't being watched so closely, my name is Kale."

The young man brushed off his hand and then outstretched it, "Hello, Kale, my name is Riggs. I've been here for over a year now, and that says a lot for this place."

Riggs, a small framed young man of no more than twenty was slightly shorter than the average man but was well proportioned and muscular. His dark hair was pulled back and tied into a knot at the back. The clothes he wore would have at one time been considered very luxurious but from a year of working in the mud and the constant beatings, they were nothing more than finely woven rags.

Kale reached out and shook Riggs' hand. Riggs stepped back and sat on a blanket laying on the floor. Reaching under the blanket he pulled out a small bone from what appeared to be a rodent. After a few seconds of fidgeting with the shackle lock it gave a click and fell to the floor. "Well, Kale, we'll need to remember to put these on before they come for us tonight."

Kale sat down next to Riggs and allowed him to repeat the process for removing his shackle. "Tonight, why would they come get us tonight? We've just been put in our cells. Don't we get any time to rest before they slave us tomorrow?"

"This isn't for work. It's fight night. Once a week the guards have this little hobby of watching us prisoners beat each other near death. It's kind of like a chicken fight, except, normally, we don't have to kill each other to win."

"Why would we be willing to do that? Wouldn't we want to preserve our energy?"

Riggs stood up and started to stretch, "Yeah, we need our energy. But there are a few luxuries I wouldn't mind getting. You see, the guards will provide a prize for the winners. On the outside you'd throw them away and not think twice about it, you know, like an old cup or book. Every once in a while they even give things like a chair or a shelf. It's not much but here, where you have nothing! You'd be surprised what people are willing to get banged up for. Desperation and neglect will drive a person to extremes they rarely find themselves capable of."

"Really, that just sounds horrible to me, Riggs."

Riggs started to shadow box. "After a few months of starvation and sleeping on a rock, you'll lose a lot of those naive sentiments. Where do you think that blanket you're sitting on came from?"

After a few minutes of warm-ups Riggs slowed his pace and began to relax. "Sorry, you'll have to forgive me. I've been here for awhile now. I wasn't always this brash, but you learn to do what you have to if you want to survive. I used to be very sophisticated. Before here I was a stelvant to a young noble named Kain." Kale looked lost in this description. "You know, a stelvant, a personal servant to a court official's family. Attached to a member of the family since the time I could walk."

"Sorry, Riggs, I'm not from the Fire Kingdom. I'm not familiar with your customs."

Riggs took a deep breath and sat down next to Kale. Looking down he began to reminisce, "From as long as I can remember we did everything together. We were best friends. But then one day we were riding horses through a field near our home and his mount got spooked. The thing bucked him off and he hit his head pretty hard. He's been in a sleep ever since. I picked out the horse he rode on so his father blamed me. If not for me and his son being so close, I would have been executed but I think the thought of disappointing his son if he awoke weighed too heavily on his mind. He put me in prison stating that if his son died, I would suffer a horrible death, but if his son awoke, I would be granted my freedom. Of course, his father had the animal mercilessly butchered. So, here I stay awaiting my fate."

Riggs refocused his attention on Kale. "So, what's your story?"

Kale started, "Well, I..." At that moment the lock of a cell down the hall echoed through the corridor.

Riggs quickly reached down and clamped his shackle on and tossed the other to Kale. "Sorry, friend, no time now. Here they come."

Kale just had time enough to clamp on his shackle before the door swung open and Celic walked in accompanied by two guards. "So, how's my new warrior doing? I assume you're going to compete tonight six-four-two." Laughing, he signaled to the two guards following him to escort the prisoners. "Well, you're going to compete, or you'll just get your face pounded in. Either way, it'll be entertaining."

Meeting up with five other prisoners from the top floor, they were led down the flights. Before stepping out into the cool night air the guards put cloth sacks over their faces. They walked along a torch-lit walkway that led behind the prison to a large pit surrounded by benches that were already starting to fill with an incoming audience. Kale's hood was removed and he saw at the highest point stood the taskmaster, adorned in a scrubby robe and surrounded like a king by guards acting as his servants. His appearance disgusted Kale as he gorged on a bowl of grapes and fanned himself with a wooden paddle.

Setting in a pile near the ramp leading down to the pit were the prizes for the evening; a pile of junk. At first glance not even a beggar would be willing to accept such 'luxuries'. The pile contained old torn blankets, rusted and broken containers, and a bowl of rotting fruit.

Kale leaned over to Riggs and quietly started talking, "Why would someone fight for a bowl of rotted fruit?"

Laughingly Riggs replied, "You're only seeing what something is, not how it can be used. That bowl alone is worth the fight, but with that bowl and the fruit, you can make some fermented drink. Now, that is a true prize for those cold nights."

"I'm afraid that would do me no good, Riggs. I don't drink."

"Well, then you'd better hope when you fight that the prize is something you can use. But, for me, I'm hoping it's the fruit."

After a few minutes the crowd settled in. Then Celic walked over to the first two people in line and sent them into the middle of the pit. He randomly grabbed something from the pile. Holding up a cup with a broken handle he set it on a small stone pedestal next to the taskmaster. Standing, the taskmaster lifted his arms as if he were a great king of old. "Let dis here fight'n begin!"

In the center of the ring the two fighters took their stances. One man looked to be fairly healthy. He looked more muscular than the average worker and had flame tattoos starting at his waist and proceeding up to his chest. His bald head was adorned with piercings and tattoos. The second man looked to be fairly scrawny but with wiry strength.

The crowd began to cheer as they rounded each other awaiting the first blows. Riggs took this opportunity to speak freely as the sound of the crowd masked his disobedience. "You see the guy with those tattoos. That's Atus. He's been here longer than me. Supposedly he's an informant to the guards and receives extra rations. I've seen him fight several times but have been lucky enough not to draw his name."

The cheers of the crowd heightened. Looking down into the ring, Kale saw the smaller man throwing a few punches, landing several directly onto Atus' face and body. Atus received the blows with little defense and rebutted with just a smile. Widening his eyes in a crazed stare after licking the blood from his lip he began. With a swift kick to the other's knee cap, he brought the man to his knees. Following this attack he brought his elbow down on the man's head, sending him to the dirt. After a few seconds of assurance that the man wasn't going to get back up, Celic walked out into the pit and handed Atus the cup. Lifting his hand as a semblance of victory, the crowd gave out another cheer.

Celic walked over to Riggs. "Well, one-eight-three, it looks like you're up." A guard leaned down to unlock the shackle off of Riggs' ankle. "Wait!" Celic commanded. "I have a great idea. A duel battle, two against two. Leave them chained."

Riggs and Kale were led down into the pit as Celic retrieved a rusted pot and the bowl of rotting fruit for the prizes. The taskmaster stood again, "Now, we'll get us some real entertainin', two on two battles." The crowd let off a loud cheer.

Two more prisoners were led down into the pit. Riggs exhaled, "Oh great, stone cutters, I hate fighting stone cutters."

The two men were massive compared to Riggs and Kale. It became obvious they were new to the quarry as they had few lash marks and had not been whittled down from malnutrition and abuse.

Kale backed up a bit, "Um, Riggs, I guess now wouldn't be the best time to tell you I don't know how to fight."

Riggs looked over his shoulder "Oh, fate hates me. Well, you'd better learn real quick, or it's both our hides."

The two stone cutters began to circle Riggs and Kale. Being the only two chained together prevented them from countering the two stone cutters, allowing them to get position on the battle. The second charged in to attack Riggs, and at that moment the first picked up some sand and tossed it into Kale's face. Kale put his hand up to prevent the sand from hitting his eyes and felt the concussion of a fist sinking into his stomach.

Falling to the ground he rolled just in time to dodge a knee being sunk into the sand where he had lain. Glancing over he saw Riggs maneuvering, dodging the second cutter's blows. Landing several quick punches, he leaped into the air and started to do a spin. This move was stopped short by the length of the chain tightening, causing him to fall to the ground. The second cutter began to kick him while he was down.

All this occurred within a few seconds as the first continued his assault on Kale. Remembering Atus' move of striking the knee cap, Kale gave a kick while lying on the ground, causing the cutter's leg to push to one side. Next Kale lifted his foot straight up in the air catching the man's chin sending him over backwards onto the sand. Slowly the cutter stood holding his chin and shaking off the blow.

Kale took this opportunity to assist Riggs who was being pummeled by the second cutter. Rolling over until he was close enough to reach the cutter, he kicked the back of the man's legs

71

causing him to drop to his knees. This brief break allowed Riggs to regain his feet. Seizing this opportunity, Riggs jumped over the man's shoulder on the opposite side of Kale and flipped his legs so that the chain between them strangled the man's throat. Following Riggs lead, Kale put his foot on the man's back and they both pushed, causing the man to loose his breath.

This advantage came to a quick end as the first cutter who Kale had lost track off sailed in cramming his knee into Kale's chest causing his breath to exit and his head to go dizzy. Within a few seconds the man had pounded on Kale's face enough to cause large black spots to cloud Kale's vision. After the few short jabs the man raised his hand high to provide the finishing blow. From behind, Riggs wrapped his hand under the man's arm and around his neck and began to choke him.

The first man had regained his breath and came up attempting to pull Riggs off of his partner. Seeing Riggs was locked tight, he began to punch Riggs in the back and head to loosen his grip.

The battle was coming to an end with Kale near unconsciousness and Riggs taking on both cutters. Kale then remembered the pain he had felt that day in the bar when he had caught a bottle in a not so pleasant place. "No time to play fair," Kale said as he kicked with all his strength between the cutters legs causing him to hunch over in pain.

Riggs, realizing the man was useless now, turned and began parrying the man's blows. This gave Kale the chance to stand up. Then with a kick of his shackled leg, Riggs forced Kale to stumble forward close enough to provide slack on the chain. Riggs then jumped in the air as before wrapping his legs around the man's neck and twisting on the way down, causing the man to do a flip. With a crackle that penetrated the sound of the crowd, the man's neck snapped.

Kale and Riggs stood in the middle of the ring dripping with blood and panting for air as Celic approached. Handing the bowl of fruit to Kale and the pot to Riggs they received their victory cheer and were led out of the pit.

* * *

After the fight two guards escorted them back to their cells. Upon entering the cell, both collapsed onto the floor and began to nurse their wounds. Kale took the bowl of fruit and slid it over to Riggs, "Trade you."

Riggs tossed the pot over, "Gladly, thank you."

After a few short minutes Riggs stood up. "We're going to have to work on your fighting, Kale. There is no way I'm going to get stuck co-oping with you when you act like that in the ring."

Kale stood up as well, "Sorry about that. I've just never had the need to do much real battle; mostly just wrestling with the guys in town or a few brawls in the bar. Nothing that serious."

"Well, here if you can't fight, you're as good as dead so you'd better be a fast study."

Kale set his pot down in a corner. "I'll do my best if you're willing to teach me. But, I thought you were this sophisticated royal. Where in the world did you learn to fight like that? That was amazing."

"Just because I come from a noble setting doesn't mean I don't know how to handle myself. I told you, Kain and I used to do everything together, even combat training."

Kale began to feel the swollen parts of his face, "Wow, this hurts. It bothers me almost as much as my growling stomach.

73

I've had next to nothing the last few weeks. Do they feed you here?"

Riggs pointed to a bowl setting on a ledge next to the door. Behind the ledge rested a small sliding door about one foot high and one foot long. "Normally they come by during the evening and put some food in that. They probably came while we were gone." Approaching the bowl, Kale saw about a cup and a half of some watery substance with yellow gunk floating in it. There were a few pieces of some yellow root and rotting fruit among the yellow slime, as well as an occasional maggot.

Kale's stomach began to turn. "I'm far from a picky eater, but that's just disgusting. And to think I use to get upset when I had sand in my food. Luckily, there is only enough for one. I'll pass."

Riggs reached under his blanket and pulled out a wooden spoon, lifting it slightly before dropping it into the bowl. "Another prize of the ring. In point of fact, Kale, this is twice what they normally give you. Luckily, I won another bowl so we can split it if you want."

Kale held his stomach and put his hand to his mouth, "That's okay. It's all yours, Riggs."

Riggs laughed slightly and then shoveled a bite into his mouth. "I wish I could tell you it tastes better than it looks, but I'd be lying. And, trust me, if you knew what it contained, you would probably get sick. Seeing as they rarely serve anything but this, I'll save you the horror and allow you to eat in your ignorance."

Kale's curiosity had been triggered, and he sat down with Riggs, examining the gunk even closer. "Okay, now you've got me curious. I know I'm going to regret this, but what is it?"

Riggs stood back up and motioned for Kale to follow him over to the door. Sliding the small door open to allow in more torchlight, he tilted the bowl to give Kale a better look.

The sight of the soup in full light didn't help the queasiness of Kale's stomach. "It looks like raw egg yokes."

Riggs smiled and used his spoon to move things around in the bowl. "Oh, I wish it were egg yokes. Now, are you sure you really want to know this? If I could go back, I would have never asked the guard."

"Just tell me, Riggs." Kale said as he examined a piece of root in the bowl.

"Okay, but don't say I didn't warn you. Do they have tobacco where you come from?"

"Yeah, my dad smoked a pipe now and again. We had a grass, though, very similar to tobacco."

"Okay, well, then you know the concept. Did anyone in your town ever chew the grass?"

"Yeah and I don't like where this is going, Riggs."

"Well, here in the Fire Country, we have this root. It's yellow but has the same properties as a potent tobacco plant."

"Okay, I don't want to know. Stop there."

"Hey, buddy, you asked. The guards chew on this plant during the day and spit it in a bucket."

"Okay, you can stop now. I think I'm going to get sick."

"Then they add water, the leftovers after feeding the dogs, plus whatever they can find laying around, and that is dinner."

Kale rushed over to the air hole in the floor. "Oh, I don't feel so well." Then, with a few violent heaves, he released his uneasiness. "I sure hope the guy below us doesn't mind."

"He used to Kale, but he got used to it. That's also our toilet.

I feel worse for the guy on the bottom floor. They haven't built his drain yet."

"How can they expect people to live like this? I've seen mistreated dogs live better."

"That's just it, Kale. They don't expect people to live. Only the few of us who fight get the nourishment we need. Normally from stuff like that fruit. They don't care about us. We're all just a number who can easily be replaced. The Fire Kingdom alone has more than enough criminals and what they call traitors to fill this place a thousand times over."

Stepping over to the bowl of rotting fruit, Riggs started to examine them. Taking up a half eaten apple he tossed it over to Kale. "Here, try this. It's not been sitting too long. It just got tossed in because it had been gnawed on by a rat."

For the most part the apple looked edible. "Thanks, Riggs." Then Kale began to work around the spots with teeth marks already in it.

By the time they were done with their meal, the sun had just broached the skyline. From down the hall the sound of locks clicking echoed throughout the empty space. One by one the prisoners were escorted into the hall to be brought down to the quarry. Kale and Riggs would perform their usual duties in the tunnel and then return at night. Unwilling to partake of the chew stew, as Riggs effectively began calling it, Kale began loosing his strength. With the exception of a few pieces of fruit, Kale hadn't eaten anything in almost a week now. Even in his degenerating state, Riggs insisted that they practice his hand-to-hand skills to prevent them from being soundly beaten in the next match.

After the day's exercise, Kale's body ached and his stomach

growled in complaint of its abuse. Curling up on the stone slab to get some rest, Kale fell asleep with memories of his home to distract him from his hunger. The very thing he had once longed to get away from was now what he longed for with all his heart. Falling into a sleepless dream, he began to see his mother cooking at her stove and his father hobbling around the house bumping into things. Memories of those spirit-filled days of delivery runs now seemed so inviting. What joy it would be to be so free! Then, as if unwillingly, the memories flashed by until he came to that horrifying day.

The images of Fike approaching his family in his haughtiness and demonizing presence invaded his dream, along with the feeling of the cold blade plucking at the bottom of his chin. Knowing that he was in a dream, Kale tried to force his consciousness to awaken before being forced to relive that tragic moment. But, it was for naught. His mind raced forward. Kale saw his mother jerk with the hit of the arrow and Fike's heated blade plunge into his father's heart.

But, unlike when the event unfolded, Kale's memory didn't stop there. The feelings of anger and grief poured in, and he saw himself from a distance screaming. With speed beyond anything he had encountered, he saw himself push the guards off and grab their blades. As if screaming at himself, Kale echoed, "Stop! Don't!" as this visage of himself mercilessly slaughtering the soldiers played out, slashing and stabbing continually even after the soldiers had fallen.

Then, within the memory, Reagan came running up the street, reaching out to restrain Kale from this wild onslaught. Kale heaved back with one arm sending Reagan flying through the air, slamming into the cart. Rushing again now with Devlin's help, Reagan grabbed ahold of Kale's arm as Devlin grabbed the other. This time a screaming gust of wind wrapped around Kale's body, throwing both Reagen and Devlin to the ground like straw. Kale continued his stabbing of the bodies on the ground. Reagan grabbed a board broken off of the cart by his first landing and, approaching from behind, swung with sternness, striking Kale on the back of his head.

Awakening in the darkness of the cell, Kale's eyes adjusted to the light of the stars above creeping in from the grated hole. Looking around the cell, Kale saw Riggs sitting up on his blanket staring. Coarsely he spoke from across the cell. "So, you're a Gehage?".

Kale sat up, "Why do you say that?"

"I heard you screaming, and when I sat up, you were floating with flames circling your body. Why didn't you use some of that power when we were getting pummeled to death just days ago?"

"This just keeps getting weirder. You don't understand, Riggs. I don't know what I am. Sometimes, now, I don't know who I am."

Kale moved next to Riggs on his blanket and began to tell his tale, starting with the recruits showing up in Yukan to his capture at the Gate.

Riggs sat for a second in silence "Wow, all that time and your father never told you he was a Gehage. That's wild."

"I know, Riggs. I can only assume he had a good reason for hiding it. I never stopped to think that I could be a Gehage, too. I always thought of it as something he hid from me, not something I could do myself."

Riggs sat up. "I could help you; I could help you develop

your Fire powers. Then, maybe we would be able to get out of this place."

Looking puzzled, Kale retorted "What, are you a Fire Gehage, too?"

"No, if I were a Fire Gehage, I would have broken out of here a long time ago. But, like I said before, we did everything together, Kain and I, that is. He was a Gehage, and I was allowed to sit in as his masters taught him the arts. All I can do is repeat what they told him. Maybe that would help you to focus your power."

"I've got nothing better to do. How do we start?" Kale asked.

Riggs stood up. "What do you know about the use of elemental powers?" he began.

"Not much, I have to admit. I know there is Fire, Stone, Water, and Plant, sometimes referred to as earth; each have their own basic properties. That's about it. I've seen a few Stone and Fire benders at a show in Yukan once. They did some pretty amazing feats."

"Well, you can forget the monkey stuff. We'll need to get you to do the basics first. Each element is triggered by an emotion. Water is triggered by compassion, Stone by fear, Earth by joy, and Fire by anger. To control your Fire ability, you need to control your anger."

Kale stood as well. "That won't be a problem. I rarely get angry. I've always regarded myself as a calm person."

Riggs laughed slightly "No, you're not getting it. You have to be able to control your anger. Turning it off is only half the battle. You need to be able to turn it on as well. By the story you tell, your powers were released when your anger reached a climax. This is often how Fire Gehage unblock the current in their bodies that channel the energy to control Fire."

Kale listened intently "Okay, Riggs, what do I do?"

"The first thing you need to do is get angry," Riggs instructed.

Kale laughed, "How exactly am I going to do that?"

Riggs stepped forward a few paces so they were close enough to reach out and touch each others' shoulders. "I know a way that will work, but you're not going to like it."

"Is this another soup story because that didn't make me angry. That made me sick," Kale retorted.

"No, it's not that." Quickly Riggs backhanded Kale, knocking him to the ground.

"What did you do that for?" Kale demanded.

Riggs jumped onto Kale's body pinning him to the ground and began smacking him in the face repeatedly. "Stop that, Riggs! Cut it out! I said STOP!" Kale screamed.

But, with each blow, Riggs hit harder and faster. "I said STOP!" The blood in Kale's body began to rise into his face until each part felt like it was being pricked with small needles. The feeling extended down his arm and into his hands. "STOP!" Freeing one arm, Kale struck Riggs in the chest causing his body to fly through the air until his chain reached it's limit, stopping him in mid-flight. His body jerked, and as he fell to the ground, he hit the wall and slid to a stop.

Kale stood, his hands shaking from the excitement.

Riggs sat, still holding his chest.

"Are you okay, Riggs? Are you hurt?"

Head bowed as if in serious pain, Riggs began to laugh. The sound echoed throughout the small cell.

"What are you laughing about? That wasn't funny, Riggs."

"Really? Maybe you should look at your hands," Riggs replied.

Kale looked down and saw his hands glowing with a feint, fiery tint. The awe of performing such an amazing act halted all feelings of anger as he stared in amazement. As the anger fled, his hands became hotter until they stung with the pain of the burning fire. "It's burning, Riggs! What do I do? My hands are burning!"

Quickly, Riggs grabbed his blanket and wrapped Kale's hands, extinguishing the flame. "Sorry about that. I guess I should have told you to put out the flame before you lost your focus."

Removing his hands from the blanket, Kale turned them back and forth to examine the extent of the damage. With the exemption of a red burned tint, his hands were perfectly fine. "I don't understand. I felt them burning."

"You are okay. Your flame isn't very hot yet, and you were still focusing when I put out the flame. A Gehage of the flame isn't naturally resistant. He has to concentrate to keep the flames from harming him. As you saw with this Fike fellow, if caught unaware, even the strongest Gehage can get burned. Getting burned is the single greatest act of disgrace a Fire Gehage can endure. I have no doubt that this Fike character would have searched you out to the ends of the earth to seek vengeance for what your father did to him."

Kale shook his head in acknowledgement and then, rubbing his hands, began to concentrate again, "Okay, Riggs, let's try it again. But this time, let's try it without the slapping."

"Sounds good to me, Kale. I doubt my chest could take another hit like that," said Riggs. "Okay, do you remember the feeling right before you punched me?"

"Yeah, I remember. My hands started to tingle," explained Kale.

"That's the spot, but you have to be able to do that even when unprovoked. Think of something that angers you. Focus on it, and when you feel the sensation of anger spreading throughout your body, push it to your hands. Your hands are the easiest place to bend fire," Riggs instructed.

Kale forced himself to think of Fike, concentrating on his one greatest point of hatred. The tingle started to form, and then, pushing it down his arms, he felt his hands begin to fill with energy. Slowly, a feint yellow aura leaked from his skin foming a barrier around his hands.

Riggs stepped back a few steps, "There it is. You've mastered the first class already. But, now you have to build it up. Practice holding it as long as you can. But, be careful." As Kale held the flame, his body started to become weaker, and Riggs became only a voice in the background of Kale's concentration. "When you control an element, you are forcing your living essence to flow through a different path in your body. This converts your living energy to an energy capable of manipulating your environment. Every Gehage is born with two different energy streams. All benders of any element must be in top physical condition. By doing this, your living stream becomes larger, allowing for a greater quantity of energy to be available to direct throughout your elemental stream. If your body isn't healthy enough to provide energy for both streams, you will slowly weaken."

As the thoughts of Fike and his actions played out in Kale's consciousness, the flames increased and then decreased, depending on the vision.

Riggs lifted his hands in a motion for Kale to pace himself. "Steady, friend. You eventually will want to start pushing your limits to increase your abilities, but, for now, I would suggest you stay at the basics until we can find some nourishment. Like a muscle, your elemental stream starts off very small and must be built up to be of any use. When your powers are unblocked, it is caused by a severe quantity of the emotion that fuels your elemental energy stream. For a Fire Gehage, that emotion is anger."

Kale's flame flickered and then went out. "I don't understand I was still concentrating. What happened?"

Riggs stepped closer once again. "Your body shut it off. Just like passing out from pain, your body has an automatic shut-off when your bending is taking too much of the living essence. This is good as it keeps you alive, but if you do not know your limits, it can be a shocking surprise. When in battle, you grow dependent on your bending abilities. If you stretch yourself, you will be left without the ability to bend and deplete yourself of energy at the same time. You can imagine how fatal that can be on the battlefield."

"At this rate, Riggs, I doubt I'll live long enough to do much on any battlefield. I just hope this week they have food as a prize when we fight," Kale said.

Riggs began to laugh, "I guess it didn't take you as long as I thought to get over your sentiments. But, being willing to fight isn't enough. Without some nourishment, neither of us will stand a chance. I'm afraid you're going to have to eat some of the soup."

"I know I said I would rather die than eat that stuff, but."

Kale walked over to the bowl sitting on the shelf. Picking it up, he walked to the center of the room under the air grate to get a better look at the soup. Sitting down on the ground, he tilted the bowl to one side to allow himself to choose from the less disgusting portions of the slop. Selecting a piece of brown carrot, he lifted it slowly towards his mouth.

With eyes closed Kale reluctantly brought the spoon to his mouth. After a practice swallow with his spit, he prepared his throat to allow the substance to flow to his stomach as quickly as possible. "Well, here it goes." Tilting his elbow, he brought the spoon the remaining inch towards his mouth and opened his eyes.

Suddenly, a black object came flying through his vision. Starting above his head, it fell down hitting the edge of his spoon and then landing in his bowl. The impact splashed the soup into Kale's face and knocked the bowl to the floor.

Using his arm, Kale wiped his eyes free of the sludge and looked down at the object on the floor. On the ground, writhing in its death spasms, a large sewer rat lay. Examining it closely, Kale could see the talon markings of some large bird.

The moment the rat fell through the grate, Riggs stepped forward to investigate. As he approached, he could see the rat lying in front of Kale "Fortune has smiled upon you, Kale. Some bird lost its grip, and this tender morsel of meat found its way through our grate."

After a few seconds, the rat's breathing stopped. Kale picked it up and, with a twist, ensured it was finished off. Riggs looked up, examining something in the grate "Kale, take a look at this."

Looking up, outlined against the moonlight, perched a large

bird. Taking a few breaths, Kale repeated the exercise from moments before. Holding his hand up towards the tube leading to the grate, his hand cast a dim glow. As the light hit the bird, Kale could see patches of golden brown feathers.

The bird leaned down and began to clean its talon, and, as its head entered the light, Kale could distinguish a slash across the bird's face hiding the solid white eye.

Riggs leaned down and picked up a small stone that had wedged into a crack in the floor. "There is a mako perched on our grate. I wonder if we can throw something at it and knock it through the hole."

Reaching out with his unlit hand, Kale quickly grabbed Rigg's wrist. "Don't you dare, Riggs. That's no mako. That's Makko."

Riggs eyebrows furled together as he shifted to give Kale a quizzing glance. "You're not making any sense. You just said it's not a mako. It's a mako? Did that rat hit your head on the way through?"

"No, that's my pet, and I might venture to say after tonight, my friend. I named him Makko because he resembled one so closely. I can't believe he found me! More importantly, I can't believe he hunted for me!" Kale turned his attention to the bird staring down through the grate. "Makko, my little hunter, although you could have chosen a better place to throw him, I will never forget this. I'm glad to see you."

Makko gave a shriek of acknowledgment and, after a few flaps of his wings, took to the sky. Kale kept the light going a few seconds longer hoping to catch a glimpse of his bird, if only for a few more seconds. After a few moments, Kale released his flame.

"Well, Kale, I have to say I like your bird," Riggs decided.

"Yeah, me too. For a second, it was like I had a piece of home here with me. I sure hope he comes back," Kale replied.

"Well, not that I didn't like the change in scenery, but I'd prefer he comes back with more food. At least for tonight, we will get some real nourishment. I can't think of the last time I had meat. And, just think, you'll have another chance to practice with your flame." Riggs took a second to retrieve a thin rock that had been chipped into a make-shift knife. "I'll skin. You cook."

The heat from Kale's flame was barely hot enough to slowly cook the rat. Riggs was forced to cut small slivers of meat off and cook them individually as the flame from Kale's hands only provided enough heat to warm the flesh. But, after numerous attempts, the meat was prepared. Both men, sitting down to dine, thoroughly devoured the small animal. Afterward, they made a fine mixture for the folowing morning's breakfast by coupling the rodent's leftover bones with some heated water in the pot they had polished with a bit of sand and a section of blanket cloth.

The next night, Kale sat watching the sky through the air shaft hoping Makko would return. Although a meal would be most welcome, the feeling of something normal, something free, was a desire that exceeded the growling of his stomach. Hours passed and the clouds began to move in, covering the moon. A drop came though the grate and hit Kale's cheek, running down like a tear. Then the thunder boomed in the distance, and a flash of light brightened the sky.

Riggs quit his repose of shadow boxing "There'll be no fight tonight. Blast that rain. We were running low on fruit, and I had hopes of winning another blanket."

Kale grabbed his pot and placed it under the grate. The downpour began and drops flooded down the shaft, filling the pot. The sounds of people in the cells below grabbing containers and whispering the word 'rain' echoed up the shafts from below. "Well, at least we'll have some water."

When the pot was about halfway full, the booming of thunder intensified as the storm increased in severity. Kale watched the drops hit the water and send ripples throughout the container. Its rhythm was soothing, and it distracted him from the walls he hated so. Then, during a particularly intense burst of thunder, the drops coming from the grate diminished to a small trickle. Kale could hear the storm outside crashing down louder than before. Peering through the shaft, Kale could see a small figure blocking the passageway.

The next burst of lighting confirmed Kale's hopes. Perched on the grate sat Makko, his wings outstretched to cover the hole as he settled in. As he folded his wings, the rain continued its descent into the pot. Makko gave a short shiver as he furled his feathers in an attempt to rid himself of the dampness. In his claws, he held a dead viper. In an attempt to drop it down the grate, Makko released it, but its length prevented it from easily sliding through. As if aggravated, Makko nudged the viper with his beak until the head made its way through one of the holes. Then, raking his right talons across the body, he forced it to slide between the grate's bars.

The viper sounded like a heap of rope being thrown to the floor. "Makko, my good fellow, I sure hope this is going to become a habit of yours," Kale said.

After a few seconds of sitting and staring at Kale, Makko shifted his head slightly. Then he turned and flew away.

***

And so the days went. During the day work would commence in the quarry, and the nights were filled with training of both the elements and the body. Makko brought food nearly every night, but, even with the morsels he provided, there was only strength enough to survive. Kale was forced to limit the use of his bending to preserve strength to get through the day and to compete in the weekly tournaments. After a few months, Kale mastered a rudimentary style of fighting and could sustain a sufficient flame.

Kale's skills and body were not the only things to grow over the next ten years. The city did, as well. New settlers continually arrived at the city setting up shops and homes. Some were enthusiasts from inside the Fire Kingdom looking for the next good opportunity to make a few coin. But, many were ordinary people migrating to find a better life.

FOUR

****

SURVIVAL OF THE FITTEST

The door of the cell creaked opened, and Celic entered in his normal fashion. "Okay, you two, it's time." That night the stars were in full bloom and the moon shone fully. Approaching the arena, the cheers of the crowd, coaxing on the warriors in the ring, echoed throughout the night. The lights shined brightly from the torches lining the walkways and positioned throughout the arena. It could be called that now, an arena. No longer was it a pit in the ground with a select few people to attend. Over the last few years, the popularity of the event had increased drastically as new drifters started settling in to the newly developing city. With each new wave of immigrants, the stands would fill until the whole of the available seating had been taken. Even the grated dome that covered the arena had been filled with brave youth willing to risk the fall.

As the crowd increased, so did the prizes for each match, as well as the complexity of the game. Instead of being an all out brawl, it had been modified to be a contest in which the contestants had to work their way through several rounds of battles until they could fight to be champions. With each victory, a small prize would be granted, but, if you reached the top, you received something truly useful. Lately the prize had been a full meal, including meat, fruit, and a vegetable, all in decent order.

Pushing through the slaves, the taskmaster grumbled and snapped at each warrior, hitting them with the handle of his whip or pushing them against the wall. Then, turning, he walked up the stairs but, instead of taking his normal seat of honor, he sat just to the left of it. In his normal place sat a tall, slender man dressed in military garb. His breastplate was comprised of the classic black metal and gleamed in the moonlight. His arms were covered with a dark chain mail, and on his side hung a long red blade indicating his rank among the people. His face looked bold but aged, and standing behind him stood a servant dressed in black cloth pants and vest with a hood hanging low over his face in a monk-like stance.

The man walked up the small ramp leading to a speaking platfrom and approached the railing. Raising his hands for silence, he pronounced over the crowd, "It is a great pleasure that I, Hakot, announce that the city of Durian has decided to officiate the arena. It will now be treated as any other licensed entertainment facility and reap the benefits of our great government."

As the crowd cheered, the taskmaster spoke from the side of his mouth to Celic, "Yeah and dem taxes an dem dere regulations an da politic'n an most specially dem dere dressed up fancy pant solder'n brats dat comes whit it."

Celic gave a half-grunt laugh and turned his attention back to the speaker. "And, my fine people, we have appointed a new master of arms to run this fine sport."

Apparently the taskmaster had been unaware of this change as at this note, he jumped clear out of his seat. As he landed, his belly gave a jiggle, his jaw dropped, and both hands sailed in the air. Screaming, he barged up the platfrom. "Now, just wait one durn minute. Ain't no body commin into me arena boot'n me outta me place."

Hakot's attendant stepped in his way and, with arms folded,

blocked his path. "You best get outta me way, or I'll break ya in two. I will." The attendant stood in his statue-like pose, staring blankly at the taskmaster.

"I said move outta me way, you little buggard." Reaching out, the taskmaster grabbed both arms of the attendant, and, with ease, lifted him into the air. As he shifted his weight to toss the attendant to one side, the attendant's eyes started to glow.

Hakot turned and lifted his hand gently, "I'd suggest you put him down before he incinerates that grotesques thing you call a head planted on your shoulders."

The taskmaster released the attendant and backed away slowly, "What in buggard bimply is goin on here? You an ya walkin candle stick better clear out. This is my arena."

Turning back to the crowd, Hakot began to speak again. "Now, I introduce the new Master of Arms for the arena of Durian. With great pleasure, I present to you, Celic."

Celic stood and began his walk up the platform, pausing just long enough to give the taskmaster a sideways glance of triumph. Standing at the top of the platform, Celic lifted his hand toward the crowd. "This is a great honor, and I will serve this city well." Awaiting for the crowd to give their cheer, he then continued, "Let the games begin!"

As Celic finished his speech, two slaves rushed down to the pit and began combat. Kale stood far enough down the line to be positioned near the platfrom. Celic and Havok turned and walked back to the seats. Only this time, Celic took the seat of honor, and Havok took the taskmaster's seat, leaving only the third seat available. The attendant stood in front of it to prevent anyone from sitting there.

The taskmaster stared into the arena in disbelief for a few

moments. Then he turned and approached Celic. "Why, you ca-nivin snake. Ya not gonna get away whit dis. I tellin' yah, I'll have yeh head before dis is through." Turning to Hakot, he continued, "And you, I don't care what rank or prestige ya carry. If it's da last thing I do, ya'll get yers."

The taskmaster turned and stomped down the platform, screaming and pushing at everyone he came close to. With each battle, the line moved up and the winners were set aside for the next round. Kale fortunately drew a fairly old sailor who, although was tough as nails, didn't have the dexterity to keep up. During the second round, Kale faced a small man with little to no skill, allowing for an easy victory. Like normal, Riggs finished off his opponents with the utmost finesse. The crowd had come to know him and his trademark move of flipping his opponents with his feet while sailing in the air. Kale had practiced it with him many times but had yet to perfect the technique of snapping the neck before release.

Kale had been so distracted by the scene of the taskmaster that he hadn't noticed Riggs staring at Hakot, his face red with rage. Finally noticing, Kale grabbed Riggs' shoulder. "What's wrong, Riggs?"

"That's him. That's the father of Kain. He put me in this hole. If only you were not tied to me, I'd stain the stones with his blood," Riggs fumed.

"But, didn't he say he would release you if his son got better?" asked Kale.

"He did. But, he also said he would kill me if he didn't. Is this the day he comes to take his revenge? If his son were awake, he surely would already have set me free. I know it," Riggs said.

"Maybe it really is just business, Riggs. You never know," said Kale.

Riggs turned his head away and focused on the moonlit sky through the bamboo grating. "Maybe, maybe," he muttered.

Those going into the third round were two stone cutters, one giant of a man , Atlas, Riggs, a recently captured priate and Kale. A scraggly pit worker in a blue bandana had also made it to the final rounds but lay still on the bench with his eyes closed. All of the excitement had been too much for his malnutritioned body. He had died with his fist still clinched and his jaw set. A guard drug him away and tossed his body into a mud pit to decompose with the other compost.

In the years Kale had been in this place, he had seen this done countless times. But, it had yet to dull itself in his heart; the cruelty still unthinkable, but the will to survive surpassed even the highest feelings of sympathy.

The third round now began, and Celic approached the platform, "Now, to present the grand prize for this evening." Celic motioned to a guard who held up a straw mattress.

All of the finalists but one gawked and pointed. Riggs leaned over to speak closely to Kale so that he might be heard over the crowd, "I'm sorry, friend, but if it comes down to you and me, I'm going to have to put it to you."

"Don't worry, Riggs. I've lucked out so far. I won't make it past this round," predicted Kale.

Two stone cutters faced off first in the third round. It was a close match, but the burly-looking fellow prevailed only to be carried away moments later due to his injuries. Next, a very tall, very large man standing close to eight feet tall and weighing near four hundred fifty pounds in his girth made his way into

93

the arena. Kale had seen him around the quarry the last few days and had pointed him out several times to Riggs. He was fighting a man taken prisoner from one of the Water Kingdom's ships. The man's shirt looked fairly new, but he had a ragged blue bandana and worn breaches. His earring and water dragon tattoos made it easy to identify his profession as a pirate. The giant of a man clapped his hands together and proceeded to rub them with delight. Smiling, the giant exposed his rotting teeth and discolored tongue. "Another victim for Tor'lam. You look like a tasty morsel."

The pirate took his stance. "We'll see, you overgrown lard sack. It'll take more than an appetite to take out ol' Captain Stonegrave."

Stonegrave took off toward the giant, leaping into the air and kicking the beast in the stomach. The giant stood unmovable, laughing at this small insect that dared to attack him. "Let's play, little man. I like to play before I eat." Grinning largely, Tor'lam swept his hand through the air smashing into the captain, sending him flying ten feet before he hit the ground tumbling.

Tor'lam grabbed his stomach and chuckled with delight, "What's the matter, little man? Do you not want to play anymore?" The captain sprang up quickly and brushed himself off. "Well, aren't you the strong bugger. Let's see what else yah got hiding in that blubber of yers."

Kale and Riggs sat studying the moves of both possible challengers. "I don't know about you, Riggs, but I sure hope that guy can find a way to take down that thing. I sure don't want to face off against him."

"I think I'm with you on that one, Kale. But this Stonegrave, I've heard his name before but not as a pirate. It could be someone else, but I know that the Stonegrave families were mighty men of war for the Water Country. Most are masters of their own ships, some even fleets. This could get interesting."

Stonegrave dodged back and forth, maneuvering around the giant's slow but mighty swings. "Hold still, little morsel. I'm trying to smash you."

"Yeah, I'll work on that." Diving through the giant's legs and coming up on his back, the captain leaped into the air and planted himself on the beast's shoulders. Tor'lam reached up to grab him, but Stonegrave stayed just out of his reach for his arms could barely lift above his mid-chest due to the large quantities of fat blocking their passage. "Just as I thought, you're so used to reaching down to attack, you don't know how to fight someone from above. I guess it's my turn to laugh now."

Stonegrave began to strike the giant in the back of the head repeatedly. Tor'lam spun in circles to try and shake off his assailant, but it did little good. Slowly the giant started to wobble; in part because of the aching in his head, and in part because he had spun himself into a daze. With a final sway, the giant fell forward, creating a large puff of dust. Stonegrave rolled off of his body and stood to see if the fight was over. With a cheer, he walked up the steps and onto the holding platform.

Kale leaned over to Riggs once again, "Let's hope you pull him."

Riggs replied, "I wouldn't speak so soon. Remember Atus is still in this."

"I nearly forgot. Maybe I should just hope you and I face off. At least I know you won't kill me," Kale replied.

Riggs began to laugh as he leaned forward to get a better view of the upcoming battle, and then he turned and smiled,

"Who says I won't?" After a short pause he continued, "And if I killed you, who would cook those delectable rodents your bird keeps bringing?"

The guard approached Atus and signaled him to the center. Next he approached Kale and Riggs. Kale's heart rose in his body. All these months he had lucked out and hadn't faced off against Atus. Most assuredly, today would be the day that monster beat his brains in. "Okay, one-eight-three, you're up."

Riggs shook Kale's hand, "I have to say, Kale, I wish he would have chosen you. Wish me luck."

"No worries. I was hoping the same for you. Good luck. You're gonna need it!"

As soon as the crowd saw the two most talented fighters take the field, they went crazy hooting and hollering. Some cheered for Atus and others for Riggs, neither by their name but by their number.

Both squared off and then took their stances for battle. Atus, in his normal form, stood half lax, as if tussling with a child. Riggs, knowing Atus's abilities, kept on guard and sprang toward him. Both attempted to strike blows but had been parried by the other. Several more attempts followed with the same result. For a short time, it seemed Riggs could hold his own, but suddenly Atus turned with a smile, shifting his weight and changing his stance.

He disclosed something new. He was not a right-handed fighter, but a lefty. The mood of the discourse changed as Atus threw quick jabs, throwing Riggs head back with each blow. Riggs landed two hits to the jaw, but it did little to hold off the onslaught of quick punches.

Riggs moved his head slightly to the left and then ducked

down under the next blow. Taking this opportunity, he threw both legs up in the air, balancing on one hand and kicked Atus in the stomach, sending him stepping backwards a few paces before tipping over onto his rear. The crowd cheered, and many of them laughed.

Standing with a glare, Atus spoke in a foreign tongue and continued his blows with increased fury. Riggs managed to dodge many of the wild punches and waited for his opportunity to strike. Then it happened. Atus swung too high, allowing Riggs to duck under the swing. With this opening, Riggs jumped into the air to perform his signature finishing move. Wrapping his legs around Atus' head, he started to come down.

As Riggs began his downward spin, Atus opened his mouth wide and heaved as if throwing up. Proceeding out of his mouth came a billowing fireball. Riggs could do little to get out of the way but release his grip. He twisted backwards to dodge the attack, and the ball just skimmed his body as it plowed into the sand. Looking down, Riggs could see flames coming off his shirt and trousers. The pain shot through his body as he rolled in the dirt to put them out.

The crowd exploded in a joyous uproar at the unexpected twist. Riggs sprang to his feet just in time to dive out of the way of another fire ball sailing through the air. With each flame, Riggs strength began to weaken from the constant darting. Atus too began loosing strength from the use of his life force in the creation of the fire.

Seeing that he could not catch Riggs by surprise again with his flames, Atus came rushing in to finish Riggs off in hand-to-hand combat. The blows were near even now as Atus had tired himself out at a faster Rate than Riggs. The battle was reaching a climax, and Riggs saw an opening to plant his foot in Atus' face, but, at the last moment, Atus ducked under and, with a sweeping motion of his foot, kicked Riggs kneecap, forcing him to the ground. Within the same effort he brought his elbow down on Riggs' head, sending him sprawling into the sand. Riggs attempted to rise, but his strength failed him. With an exhale, he dropped to the sand in exhaustion.

Atus returned to the finalist area as a guard carted Riggs out of the arena and back to the prison.

Kale followed the cart as far as he could see to catch a glimpse of Riggs moving, but no sign showed itself. His mind was so focused on Riggs that he didn't notice the guard walk up behind him. His body clenched in fright as the guard grabbed his shoulder. "You're up."

Walking down into the pit Kale faced off with Captain Stonegrave. The seaman took an overdramatic stance by waving his arms in a martial style and then coming to a stand with his foot positioned at his front. With a smile and a wink, he spoke, "Either way this goes, young chap, no hard feelings. Just trying to do right by me is all."

Kale took his stance which now looked very similar to Riggs starting positioning. "I understand, Mr.Stonegrave. Good luck."

As soon as the word 'begin' left Celic's mouth, Stonegrave charged at Kale swinging. At first, the blows were too fast, and Kale received a well-aimed blow to the chin and ribs. But, after a few seconds, Stonegrave slowed his swings down to match Kale's.

With every second, Stonegrave telegraphed his next move, making it seem as if Kale and he were on even keel. What could this man be thinking? The crowd cheered eagerly at these two fighters to see which would meet their fate at the hands of Atus in the final round.

Blow by blow, the fight continued, and then Kale's attacks began to land. It seemed as if Stonegrave was allowing them to pass by his defenses by just the slightest amount appearing to have been a near block or dodge. With a mid-strength blow, Kale swung for the Captain's mid-section. Spreading his arms just enough to allow the blow to connect, the Captain fell to his knees in a dramatic groan and then toppled over into the sand.

"What are you doing, you crazy fool? You just lost the match, and I barely touched you."

With his eyes closed, out of the corner of his mouth, the captain replied in a slur, "I'm the fool? Who has to fight that maniac? Good luck, kid."

Kale's anger burned within. He had been duped. Not only was it clear he was no match for this Captain Stonegrave in combat, but the man had outsmarted him, as well.

The long-dreaded time had come. By mere statistics, Kale knew that eventually he would have to face off against Atus. It had been obvious that Kale had been spared facing him before due to the order the taskmaster had been given to keep him alive, but that saving grace no longer existed. The short break between the two rounds seemed only a second. In the distance, Kale could hear Celic speaking, but the words blurred together. He could hear the crowd cheering as Atus finished off the remaining stone cutter. Distorted by his fear of the impending battle, Kale sunk deep within himself, his only safe refuge, time flying by unnoticed. The guard wasted no time leading Kale down to the ring.

Celic stood on the platfrom holding the prize high in the air. "And now, our two finalists will battle for the grand prize. Let the fight begin!"

Atus stood lax, letting his fists waver in the air as if this fight was nothing but a nuisance. Leading with his left foot, Atus came out swinging short jabs to get the crowd started.

Kale noticed immediately that Atus again fought right-handed. This would be his only chance; Kale must finish Atus quickly before he decided to switch to his dominant stance.

Kale rushed in, more out of fear than any hope of success. The blows came quickly. Some hit Atus, but most glanced off his shoulder or missed completely. Remembering Atus' old trick, Kale ducked under a blow and then swept his foot out to catch Atus' knees. Atus lifted his leg as if Kale had pointed to his knee before beginning the move. Atus took a step back and waved his finger in the air, and then spoke something in a foreign language. It wasn't hard for Kale to interpret, "With my own move, you should be ashamed to think I would fall for that."

Atus rushed in, and with a few short blows he knocked Kale back a couple of feet in a stumble. Then, as if to demonstrate how the move was meant to be performed, swept with all haste and ease across the sand kicking up dust into Kale's eyes and smashing his knee to one side. The bone cracked, and Kale hit his knees in pain.

The pain distorted thinking long enough to allow Atus to bring his elbow down against Kale's head, sending him face down in the dirt.

The darkness overwhelmed him for a second, but Atus must have missed his mark as Kale's mind quickly regained focus. The fear masked his pain, and the pain brought on anger.

Inner thoughts struggled with each other. "Why am I not staying down? This prize means nothing to me. Why am I getting up? Why am I so angry? This guy isn't that tough. I can take him. Come on Atus. Let's see what you have."

Quickly Kale snapped up from the sand. The crowd, already cheering their winner, stopped to admire Kale's persistence. Atus turned around, and with an angered scowl at this nuisance, he switched stances and came in to punish Kale for his insolence.

This time Atus' attacks came in swiftly, unhindered by the awkwardness of his stance. Each blow moved in rapid motion. The crowd sat in amazement as Kale ducked and turned, avoiding each blow. The rage fueled him giving him speed. Each of Atus' blows came faster, but Kale's perception had been intensified by the flood of emotion, the flood of pain and anger.

Atus heaved back and gave a mighty swing, but he overshot, allowing Kale to duck down for a mid-section blow. Gathering all of his emotions, Kale focused on his hand, heating it up, and drove it as hard as he could into Atus. The bones in Atus' mid-section cracked, and his body flung backward several feet before he slid to a stop on his knees. His arms folded over his stomach. He heaved a mouthful of blood. A slight amount of smoke seeped through his fingers covering the spot Kale had struck.

Kale's heart leapt with joy at the prospect of defeating Atus. This happiness dulled the anger, replacing it with hope. Atus took a second to compose himself and slowly lifted his head. His eyes were gleaming with fire as he slowly stood.

Kale's mind raced with thoughts once more. "How can I stop this thing? How is it possible he is still standing? What have I done? Why did I get back up?"

His thoughts were interrupted as Atus darted back towards him. Kale attempted to block the punches, but each one came in too fast and too hard to prevent. Each one that landed mangling Kale's body. Atus fueled his punches with his Fire bending, making each one sting with heat and causing even more damage. The onslaught lasted only a few seconds, but Kale could hardly stand up as Atus paused and reached out with his hand, gripping Kale's throat. Lifting Kale with one hand off of the ground, Atus pointed to him and in a slurred distant language said, "Kale, Riggs." Then, with his finger, he slid it across his throat to communicate his threat to kill them both.

It no longer mattered about himself. Kale's mind filled with the dread of loosing the only friend he had in this place. The fear of being alone, and the dread of life in a stone box with no one to talk to caused Kale's mind to race. In those short, few seconds, as Atus opened his mouth and began to collect fire in his throat, Kale's anger flared. "How dare this man impose upon our right to live! How dare he threaten me! Riggs, if I loose he will surely kill you. I can't let that happen. I won't let it happen!"

Overhead clouds began to drift in. Quickly the sky darkened, but the crowd noticed little for now they were on the edge of their seats, some even standing at the rail to see the final blow.

Kale scarcely realized his eyelids were closed. Opening them, he saw the wild look on Atus' face as his shoulders heaved forward to discharge the flame. Then... nothing, the flame squelched in his throat. Atus had committed the fatal mistake that Riggs had spoken about; he had over-used his bending and drained his life force. He was weakened.

Kale felt fueled with energy as a few drops of rain started to fall from the sky. Releasing a howl of rage, he kicked Atus in the chest forcing Atus to release him. Then, after dropping to his feet, he sprang back in the air focusing all of his energy into one punch fueled with all the energy he could muster. This mighty blow caught Atus square under the chin, sending him sprawling into the dirt.

A few groans escaped Atus as he struggled to his feet and began to take his stance once more. Clearly he was reeling from the after-effects of such a powerful attack. Atus was too week to stand without wavering back and forth.

The clouds in the sky unleashed their heavy load as torrents of rain came flooding down into the arena. The crowd that had been so attentive before rushed for their homes, shops, and carts to escape the rain.

Celic came down into the arena holding the mattress and took his position between Atus and Kale. "There is no need on letting one of you die today, not when there isn't a crowd watching." Then he grabbed the mattress at both ends and with a jerk ripped it in half. "It's a tie. Here you go." Celic tossed a half to each and then walked away laughing, satisfied in his superiority.

Clinching the once coveted mattress, Atus looked through the falling rain, and, with a fiery clench, torched the straw while raking his finger across his throat towards Kale.

Kale attempted to walk, but his knee had been crushed. The guards had to drag him back to the prison.

* * *

The cell was dark and quiet, only a small slither of moonlight pierced through the grate above. Riggs lay on the floor

103

with his eyes closed and his clothing singed; motionless as small drops of rain dripped from the hole above onto his body.

"Hey, Riggs, you okay?"

The echo of the shackles clamping shut around Kale's leg and then the second one around Riggs' motionless body was piercing. The guard turned and walked out, clanging the door shut.

Kale approached Riggs slowly. The sorrow building up in the bottom of his chest was awaiting release. "Riggs, com'on. Wake up."

Kale jumped back as suddenly one of Riggs' eyes opened up. "Are they gone?"

"Oh, I'm going to kill you; you scared the life out of me," Kale growled.

Riggs propped himself up on one elbow. "Well, I'm not too far off from death, to be sure. I'm not going to be able to stand for awhile, and I highly doubt I'll be entering the arena any time soon. How about you? You look like horse dung. Figured he'd beat you, but man, did you even put up a fight?"

Kale hobbled over and slid the half mat under Riggs' head. "Tied him actually, and I couldn't describe how sorry I am I didn't throw the match like that Captain. Now Atus has it in for me. You can count on me to nurse this leg for as long as possible."

"The captain threw the fight? Wish I would have thought of that." Kale gave a dissatisfied look. "Oh, don't look at me like that. I would have never done that to you," Riggs promised.

"Yeah, I'm sure you wouldn't have," Kale said.

The lock on the cell door gave a shriek and then clicked. Slowly the door swung open and Hakot walked in, ducking slightly to miss the top of the cell door frame. A few steps behind him his assistant trailed in, silently standing by the wall.

Riggs lowered his head, "I knew there could only be one reason you've come here. Make it quick. I've suffered enough."

Hakot reached for his blade and then paused, allowing the anger to leave his complexion. "I should kill you for speaking to me that way, you little rodent. But, no, I haven't come to kill you, not yet at least."

Hakot began to slowly circle the cell as he spoke; a subconscious habit formed from frequent talks to senators. "I have asked to be assigned to this town for the sole purpose that the physician here is said to have a possible cure for the hideous wound your stupidity inflicted on my son. I am here only to ensure you live in the event my son is cured. I am told it could be many years before he completes his research and will have the opportunity to stabilize my son. For a prisoner, he is a very intelligent man."

A look of hurtful joy filled Riggs' face. "So, he's here. He's alive."

"Yes, Riggs, he is alive. If you call lying in a bed soiling himself, unable to speak or even move, living. Then, yes, he is alive!"

Hakot folded his hands. "Now, one thing I can't allow my son to awake to is the fact that the person he cherishes as a brother has died in some arena fight. So, you can forget about competing in this little exercise of yours. I told that maggot of a taskmaster to keep you safe until this matter with my son was resolved. But, we won't have to worry about his incompetence anymore. He has been relieved of his duties and sent to taskmaster a slimy flee infested ship in Harborton. I dare say he blames you for his current misfortune. Although absurd, it was very entertaining to watch him rant."

The length of chain seemed miles long as Kale faded into the background of the situation, as unnoticed as a piece of furniture and just as silent and immobile as the stone walls surrounding them.

Riggs' face flushed red with anger. "You are a coward, Hakot. You should kill me now. We both know that you serve me an injustice. You once thought of me as a son until you found out my origins, and now just because my father wasn't native to your country, you suspect me of treachery. The only reason you haven't killed me yet is that you know your son might forgive you for my imprisonment, but he would never forgive you for my death. So, I say you are a coward. Draw your sword and put an end to my torment. I die with a clear conscience, and if I live on, I give you my word it will only be to seek justice for what you have done to me."

Hakot eyes opened widely in disbelief. "Why, you little maggot!" Drawing his sword quickly, he raised it into the air to retrieve retribution for Riggs' insolence.

Also sitting unmovable in the background had been Hakot's hooded assistant. For the first time, this figure flinched and said with a feminine tone, "Master, I beg your pardon. I just wanted to remind you that you are overdue at Captain Fike's promotion ceremony."

This slight pause in the situation was enough to check Hakot's anger. Pausing slightly, he shifted his head in thought. Then, bringing the butt of his sword handle down with swift action, he planted it against Riggs' face, forcing him to swing back prostrate on the floor.

Walking to the door, he stopped next to his assistant. "You have five minutes, Alora. I'll be in Celic's office. Do not take long."

Hakot walked out the door and closed it behind him.

Throughout the entire encounter, Kale had noticed something not in its place about this hooded soldier. It all made sense now. The slim figure, the light walk, the shadowed face, and the silent grace; it was a woman; a young woman.

Alora removed her hood and stepped forward. She was younger than Kale had expected but much stronger in presence. She walked with complete confidence, and her face was strained with experience and wisdom. Her hair was short but as red as the edges of the sun. This was a rare trait among any of the nations but most prized in the Fire Kingdom. It was a semblance of inner strength. Most were known for their tempers, and in a kingdom that defined itself on that one emotion, the women who were fortunate enough to be born with red hair were highly prized.

Taking a piece of cloth from her pocket, she knelt next to Riggs. "Riggs, are you all right? It's me, Alora. Wake up, Riggs."

"I'm awake, Alora and I know it is you. I knew it was you at the arena," he assured her.

Slapping his shoulder half in frustration and half in play, Alora sat with her feet tucked under her body. "I thought my disguise had been conceived very well. Even that fat fleabag didn't realize I was a woman, and we were almost nose to nose," she said.

"Oh, it's not your disguise that gave it away. You forget I've seen those eyes before. Do you remember the first time I snuck a kiss out of you? Those eyes of yours flared, and I swear my chest hurt for a month with that punch you gave me," Riggs teased.

"You always bring that up, but you deserved it and you know it. I was engaged then, and he was watching us," Alora explained.

"I know he was. Why do you think I did it? How else would I have gotten him to reject you?" Briggs countered.

"Oh Riggs, why did you taunt him so? You know his hatred of you. You practically begged him to finish you, knowing that I was only feet away. How could you? I could not bear to watch that," she cried.

"I'm sorry, but it was because you were there that I knew he didn't have the courage to do it. I shouldn't have used that to my advantage. I am sorry. To get just a little vengeance was too hard to let pass by," he explained.

Alora shifted her weight forward. "What's done is done, I guess. Riggs, I have come to warn you that I don't believe my father intends to let you live even if my brother awakens. He has come up with some ghastly plans of having you killed in any number of accidents. You have to escape. You have to get out of here before my brother awakens," Alora implored.

Riggs sat up. "What are you doing here, Alora? How did you get your father to agree to let you come?"

Alora lowered her head "I've agreed to marry. My only condition was to be able to tell you goodbye myself and to officially break off our engagement."

"It would have been better to let your father strike me down. How could you agree to such a thing? I know you feel for me the same way I do for you. If my father would have been of the

Fire Kingdom, we would have been married already. What cruel trick is this? Why does fate abuse me so?" Riggs raged.

Tears filled Alora's eyes, "Oh, don't say such things. I would never marry anyone else. I just had to warn you. This is the only way I could warn you."

Riggs' constitution returned "I've done it again, Alora. I'm sorry. It's just every day away from you is worse than an eternity in this prison. I cannot bear the thought of loosing you to another."

"Nor I you, Riggs. You must escape here. You must. And when you do, I want you to go somewhere. There is a little island in the Water Kingdom just outside of the Fire Kingdom's southern borders. Alchemete, remember that name. Alchemete. It's off the shipping lanes; a fisherman was stranded there for over five year before making a craft to escape."

"What foolishness are you speaking of, Alora?" Riggs demanded.

Alora looked over at Kale for the first time, "Oh, dear me, what have I done? Can this man be trusted? He's already heard so much. I am such a fool, Riggs."

Riggs sat up and gestured with his hand, "My apologies, Alora. This is my very good friend, Kale. I trust him with my life and, more importantly, with yours. He can be trusted, and, I dare say, counted on. For his part, he is a capable man."

Alora removed her hand from her blade handle. "That is very good to hear. It is an honor to meet you, Kale."

"The honor is mine. As for my sake, on my life, whatever I can do to assist Riggs to escape, I will do. His fate intertwines with mine so closely maybe we will find means for both of us to make our leave of this place." Kale lifted the chain to signify the physical bond the prison had bestowed upon the two.

Alora stood, "I will be escaping to that island in two months. I have told my father I must go down to Harborton for some shopping and dress fittings, and that time correlates with the monsoon season. This will give me the chance I need to escape. He is sending a few assistants with me, but they will not be difficult to rid myself of."

Leaning down, Alora gave Riggs a long passionate kiss and then stood and walked toward the door. "How ever many years I must wait, Riggs, I will do so even if that means dying an old maid."

The door opened, then closed, and Riggs stared blankly ahead.

"Are you okay, Riggs?" Kale asked.

Twitching slightly, Riggs came out of his daze, "I have never felt so alive, so angry, so miserable, and so happy all at one time." Riggs lay back down. "We must escape, Kale. We must find a way."

"I'm all for that. I would much rather risk my life escaping than rotting in this place." Kale approached and sat next to Riggs on the floor. "You must tell me something, though. What is all this about your father not being of the Fire Kingdom?"

"My mother was of the Fire Kingdom, for sure. She traveled with Hakot as a servant as he traversed the other nations. One year Hakot spent many months in the Water Kingdom negotiating a shipping lane treaty. My father was an inspiring young captain. My mother fell in love and had a secret relationship with him. When Hakot left, he thought nothing of his assistant bearing a child. My mother served as his assistant, but they were also secret lovers." Riggs eyebrows rose slightly, "No need to say it. I know she was a whore. I can't do anything about that. Well, anyway, Hakot always had a fancy for me growing up. Thought of me as his own son. Not just in the 'he's a great kid' way. I mean he really thought I was his son. My mother never tried to correct this thought, nor did she press him over acknowledging that he thought I was his. She knew whose son I was but was not going to mention it. I had a good life because of her deceit. But, eventually, I fell in love with Alora. She being his stepdaughter, it would have been perfectly acceptable in his mind that we marry. But, he found out the truth. I don't want to go into the details but, without any doubt, he knew that I was not his son, and he despised me for it."

"So, did you ever find out who your father was?" Kale asked.

"Yes, my mother told me when I consulted her about proposing to Alora. She felt I should know. My father is now General Wheyton Stonegrave of the first brigade. He knows nothing of me, of course; being such a short engagement between my mother and him. Anyway, I am very tired. We should get some rest. We'll still have to pull our weight in the quarry tomorrow."

FIVE

****

THE GREAT ESCAPE

The tunnels had spread to nearly every part of the city providing a sewage system and underground access to several buildings. Today's addition was a hole into the bottom of the prison. The guard passed back and forth, giving orders, and occasionally reviewing the plans with the architect pacing near by. "No, no, you idiot. I told you to have those prisoners dig to the left three feet to allow for a proper spill when we open this thing up."

The guard turned and spouted a few orders but were interrupted by the architect for nearly the tenth time. "No, I said three feet to the left, left you idiot. My left not yours. Do I have to do this myself?" Setting his plans down carelessly on the wagon loading up to leave with the load of dirt, he went down into the mix of workers and began to direct them himself. "Here, dig here, you imbeciles." With excessive emotion, the architect grabbed a shovel and began to pelt the workers.

The guard's whip was going in repetitive motion as the laborers dragged a four foot metal tube with thick crossbars. The pipe resembled the grates separating the floors of the prison with the exception that it was triple grated on both ends.

The cart was now loaded and began its retreat out of the tunnels. Riggs stood quickly and, glancing at the distracted guards, snatched the plans off of the back of the cart and hid them in his sash.

Within a few minutes the last few feet of earth and stone were removed. A gust of wind came from the hole as the new air current was established. A familiar stench filled the air. It was even more potent, but Kale associated it with home after all these years.

The architect gave up his ranting. "Well, it looks like you can do something right after all. Now, get that grate in place before the whole prison runs out. All we have to do is get the exit drain to the city complete, and we can direct the water from the mountain through here. A working underground sewer system. It will be the climax of my great career. Soon they will be calling for me in all the major cities."

As the grate was being set in place, the architect looked around for his plans and then started a brisk walk out of the tunnel waving his shovel. "That cart has run off with my plans. I'll have them whipped for their incompetence."

Kale looked up briefly at Riggs, "What are you doing? You're gonna risk your life for plans of these tunnels. We can walk this thing blindfolded and backwards and not hit a wall," Kale continued.

"Shhh, Kale, I'll explain tonight," Riggs said.

* * *

That night, Kale and Riggs sat around a recently killed chicken that Makko had been kind enough to leave for them and reviewed their plan.

"Okay, Kale, now that we're back, let me explain. Yeah, I know we can both walk that place with our eyes closed. But look," he pointed.

Riggs spread the plans out on the floor. "See, this shows where the outer edges of the walls are. And see here, this is where the exit drain is going to be. We should have it almost dug within a few weeks, and that, my friend, is our escape. Before the last day when we would break through, we'll make our move. We have to get down there and dig a hole out. That's the only way. When they put that drain grate in, we'll have no chance. It's the only one they are putting in; a single exit for the waste of the city."

Kale examined the map. "Yeah, it's a plan. But, how are we going to get down there? It would have to be at night. We aren't competing in those fights anymore so that limits our options. And we're here on the top floor the rest of the time."

"You forget, Kale. We just put in the drain for the prison today. We have a straight shot down to the sewer. All we have to do is get through these grates."

"That and four cells of noisy inmates Plus, how do you suppose we get through these bars? We would have to do it in advance, and there's no way we could do it without involving the prisoners below us."

"That's the key, though. We'll need their help. We need to find out who is below us. Surprisingly, the sound isn't all that clear. We can hear them vaguely, and they can hear us somewhat. We'll have to get through these bars and see who's below us," Riggs explained.

"Again, how are we going to do that?" asked Kale.

With a smile, Riggs looked into Kale's face, "I could smack you again if it would help."

"Oh, com'on, Riggs. I can't produce a flame that hot," protested Kale.

"You'd be surprised. By what you've told me, Atus is a Fire Gehage, and if you sent him sprawling, you can get through these bars. The trick is focusing it in a way that you don't melt them completely. We'll need to time it right, but we have to figure out our options with the cells below us. No telling what we'll have to deal with." Riggs folded up the map. "No time like the present. Keep your hand close and exhale when you get your Fire energy in your hand. It will help to expel it."

"Okay, Riggs, I'll give it a shot," said Kale.

Placing one hand on his wrist and holding the other a few inches away from the edge of the grate, Kale began to focus his energy into a flame. A faint glow filled the room and progressively got brighter.

Riggs jumped up and closed the food tray door to hide the light. Slowly the light got brighter. The metal began to heat up and then started to glow a dark red.

"Hold that flame there for a second. I have an idea." Grabbing a sharp stone from off of the cell floor, Riggs began to saw away at the hot metal slowly grinding until there was a wide indentation in the grate. "I think this will work, Kale. Keep it up."

The light went out and the room filled with darkness while Kale collapsed panting. "Sorry, Riggs, that's all I can do. Sustaining that hot of a flame drains me pretty fast."

"It's okay. We got nearly a quarter of the way through it. If we can make this progress every night, we might be able to get through the grates in time, supposing we have no issues with the prisoners below. But I doubt any of them will pass up the chance of freedom," Riggs said.

The next few days went by with tiresome repetition. But, by the end of the week, the first grate had almost been removed.

A dull gray light from the cell below displayed the only indication of the bottom of the pipe. At the bottom, a second end grate barred their descent. Kale could see the waste smeared on its surface from years of use. "Okay, Riggs, this was your idea. You go first."

Riggs sat down on the blanket. "Sorry, friend, but I can't burn off the other grate. And, um, I'm afraid you're going to have to go down head first. I don't think there will be room to bend down when you reach the bottom."

* * *

Kale removed his shirt and peered into the dark hole. Riggs sat on the edge prepared to hold his legs, barely able to restrain his smirk. Slowly, Kale crawled into the hole. Its stench was stifling. The sludge on the outer walls only purpose was to eliminate a useful hand hold by making the surface too slick to grip. As Kale reached the bottom, he supported himself on the bottom grate with one hand. From below he could hear a familiar voice. It was the man he had fought in the ring, Captain Stonegrave.

"Jenkins, my boy, surely you cannot expect me to give up my coat. It is the mark of honor for a captain, and plus, you've already won my britches." he complained.

Another voice entered the conversation. "Stoney, ol' boy, if ya didn't want to loose it, ya shouldn't bet it. Now, what right is right. I won her square. Now hand me my coat."

"Oh, you're impossible, Jenkins. Well, I'm keeping the epaulettes, and we'll play again. I swear those dice are loaded," accused Stonegrave.

Kale couldn't stand the stench much longer and decided this would be an opportune time to make himself known. "Excuse me."

"Jumpin', Josephine! what was that? Stoney, I think we have a ghost in this here cell," exclaimed Jenkins.

Kale couldn't help but laugh. "No, man, look up. I'm in the

116

grate."

Stonegrave walked over just below the grate and looked up. "Goodness, man, what are you doing in the sewage drain?"

"We're escaping, and we have to go through your cell to do it. We have a plan that I have no intention of going over while my face is so close to this muck, but if you're interested, I'm going to start burning off this grate. We can talk when I get inside. What do you say?"

Stonegrave smiled, "Well, man, if it can get us out of this place, we are in. Hurry up, man, and get to cutting."

Kale wasted no time and began the tedious process of cutting the bars. From below he heard both men in unison, "He's a Fire Gehage?"

"Yes, I'm a Fire Gehage . We'll talk more later," Kale told the men.

After an hour, Kale had Riggs pull him up. His body had been covered in muck. Before he related anything of what had transpired, he rushed to the bucket of rain water and began to sponge himself off. "That is more disgusting than anything that I have ever imagined."

Riggs could not wait any longer. "So, what did they say? Are they in or not?"

"Yeah, they are in. It's that Stonegrave fellow and a cell-mate. One of the sailor-looking men we've seen in the tunnels lately."

Kale could sense that Riggs was pleasantly surprised at this news. "That is very interesting. Maybe he can tell me more about my father, being a relative and all."

Another week passed, and Kale was able to cut through the bars on the grate below. Kale and Riggs both descended into the room with the help of a makeshift rope made from their blankets. As Riggs hit the floor, he took on an air of diplomatic seniority. Placing one hand behind his back and the other hanging lightly in the air at his waste, he made his way over to the two men. They appeared an odd couple with Jenkins in a captain's coat and pants while Captain Stonegrave wore a ratted coat over a silk shirt and ripped pants hanging over expensive shoes.

"Captain Stonegrave, pleasure to meet you. I am Riggs formally attached to Kain, son of Hakot. Pleased to make your acquaintance." It was strange to Kale to see him shift attitudes so quickly. He seemed pompous and arrogant. Barely had he noticed Jenkins to the Captain's left. The Captain, in turn, shifted his weight and began to take on his role in this play. "Many thanks, Riggs, sir. I see you are of noble breeding. As you know, I am Captain Stonegrave, formally of the Uklan family. I married a Stonegrave daughter, and as is tradition when marrying into a higher class, I took on her namesake. This is my good man Jenkins. We've seen many battles together."

Riggs tilted his head slightly and gave a nod of acknowledgment. "Good day, sir."

Stonegrave looked to Jenkins, "Jenkins, my man, would you be so kind as to help Kale with the grate while Riggs and I discuss our plans?"

Even Jenkins realized that he was now no longer a prisoner, but, once again under the command of Captain Stonegrave. "Yes, sir, right away."

Jenkins walked over to Kale, "Guess it's just you and me now, chap. Where do we start?"

"Well, first off we can introduce ourselves properly. My name is Kale." As Kale introduced himself, he wiped his hand on his pants and then extended it in greeting. Jenkins shook his and said with a nod, "And I'm Jenkins. Pleasure to meet you."

The next week went by quickly. Kale was glad to be able to talk to someone new, and apparently Riggs felt the same way. He and Stonegrave sat in a corner and chatted for hours while Kale and Jenkins worked on the grating. Finally the grate was removed, and the four of them stood around the hole.

Stonegrave looked down into the tube. "Well, Kale, I feel bad for you having to go down and talk with that brute."

"What brute? What are you talking about?"

Stonegrave turned to Riggs, "You didn't tell him? Oh, dear, my apologies. Well, you see, I know who is in the cell below us. It's that monster you had to fight in the ring, Atus."

Kale turned to Riggs. "You knew, and you didn't tell me. Well, my friend, you have a surprise coming. I'm not going down there to negotiate with him."

Riggs lifted his hands. "Sorry, Kale, I didn't know it mattered. I can't cut the grate. It has to be you."

Kale turned to Jenkins and smiled and then returned his gaze to Riggs. "That is true, Riggs, but you are the only one in this cell who speaks his language."

Riggs started to stammer a reply, but he couldn't find anything that would counter Kale's remark. Finally he lifted his hands in resignation, "Okay, okay, I'll go."

Kale and Jenkins lowered Riggs down into the hole. The tube distorted the words so that neither could understand the conversation even if they could have understood the language. After a few minutes Riggs requested to be pulled up. Wiping his hands off on his pants, he looked at the group. "He's in. He will start on his grate while Kale works on the one at the bottom of this tube. This may have turned out to our advantage as now we can progress twice as fast."

* * *

The grate was removed within a week. The work was done in silence as Kale looked down on his past enemy. Finally, with a loud crack, the last bar severed. The four men began their descent into Atus' cell. Kale placed his feet on the floor and then backed up a few feet to allow room for Riggs, Captain Stonegrave, and, lastly, the withered body of Jenkins.

This man had become a good repast for Kale the last few weeks, always kind in his sailor-like manner. Whenever the four were together, Riggs took on an air of superiority in status that more matched Stonegrave's than the others. Stonegrave and Riggs would talk for hours while Jenkins was left to assist Kale. The two talked as they worked, and Kale learned a lot about him. He had been with Stonegrave before his name changed. Jenkins had sailed under Stonegrave's colors for years now, and before that, Jenkins served on a few ships with him in boyhood as Stonegrave made his way up the ranks. Kale could truly say he liked Jenkins, mostly because of his good nature; always a smile, a pathetic, toothless smile, but a smile nonetheless.

Jenkins' body moved back and forth through the bars. First his striped breeches went through the bars. Then one arm covered in the jacket he had won from the captain passed through. When he tried to remove his second arm, one of his jacket braids caught a protruding remnant of one of the cut bars. To unravel himself, he had to loosen his grip. A few twists proved more than enough, but, with the last jerk, his hold had totally loosened and he sailed toward the floor. With a loud crack his leg hit the stone, and he toppled into a moaning heap of bone and

120

skin. "Dear, bugger me, I broke it. Curse it all. I broke it."

The group, minus Atus, huddled around their friend. Touching his leg gently, Stonegrave leaned over Jenkins, "A clean break, my friend. Dear me, this will be troublesome."

With a crinkled face and animal-like sarcasm, Jenkins grabbed Stonegrave by the shirt. "My apologies, Stoney. Next time I'll try to fall more gracefully. You blasted fool, I'm had now."

It took a second to process, but Kale finally caught the meaning of this conversation. "No, we can't leave him behind. We'll carry him."

From the edge of the room, Atus stared in fixed curiosity. In broken speech he attempted to make himself understood in the common tongue. "No, we won't. I not help. He slow me down."

Kale stood and walked confidently towards Atus, "When we get out, you can do whatever you want, you old cod. Run ahead of us. I don't care. But, we aren't going to leave Jenkins behind."

Stonegrave chimed in from the background. "No, Kale, he's right. If we take him, we will have no chance. We will have to make all haste away from this place. In the morning they will be chasing us. He would just die. He has to stay. It's his only chance."

"They're right, Kale. Leave me here. I ain't wantin' to die here, but I will die for sure if I go. Bugger it all, and curse the lot of you. Better if I stay. Sadly enough, better if I stay."

Riggs walked to the grate. "If we don't get to work, we will miss the time frame anyway."

The grate had a singular cut all along its edges. It had

already been loosened from the framing. Smiling, Atus walked to the grate and picked it up, showing that the bottom grate had been removed as well. He said something to Riggs in his native tongue.

Riggs turned to Kale with a smile. "He says you're weak and work too slow. Well, a better translation is, he called you a sluggish weakling."

A tingling sensation of anger and resentment flooded Kale's mind. Putting his feelings in check, Kale took several minutes before speaking, "Well, anyway, let's get to work. Have we talked with the prisoner below to make sure he is on board?"

Atus spoke again in his native tongue. Riggs turned to interpret with a worried stare, "He says that we don't need to worry. He's taken care of it. Dead men tell no tales. Or, at least something close to that."

Smiling, Atus leaped down into the bottom cell unassisted by rope or person. It took the rest of the group, minus poor Jenkins, several minutes to climb down. The grate at the bottom had been partially started. Off to one side, the bodies of two unfortunate pit workers lay in a heap. Their eyes were closed as they leaned against the wall. Such an unnecessary waste of life. Surely they would have gladly joined the escape.

Atus knelt down and began to work. His flame burned much stronger than Kale had realized. Focusing it through one finger, he wielded a thin, very powerful beam rather than flame. It cut through the bars with utmost rapidness. Kale began to burn through the other site. His flame looked very weak extending from the palm of his hand. Its brightness dimming in comparison to the sharper, brighter light from Atus' flame. Still, the triple grating on each end took nearly a week. Both Atus and

Kale were tired, but the deadline was drawing near. The final night was approaching. Two more days and the digging crew would be close to the wall. None of the group were fortunate enough to be a part of this crew, but word from a few passing by confirmed they were close. This aligned perfectly with the plans stolen weeks earlier.

On the last night, the wait for the guards to leave their post was almost unbearable. Each passing moment a hundred possible reasons for failure flooded Kale's mind. What if the guards walked the tunnel and noticed the loosened grate? What if someone they talked to squealed? What if they were betrayed by Atus?

Riggs busied himself, collecting his possessions and wrapping them in a bag. Kale walked over to him and offered him the last of the food brought by Makko the day before. "We might want to save this for the road. I don't think we will have much time to hunt. I have a concern that has been wandering around my mind the last few days. Why did Atus kill those men? Even at worst case, they would have split from us early."

"It doesn't take much to figure that one out, Kale. We all have to run the same direction. We will head toward the Stone Kingdom borders and then trail along the wall until we reach the Uriki forest. The more of us that travel that way, the more of us likely to get caught. I've been thinking of it myself. We are going to have to be careful of Atus, and I daresay Stonegrave, as well. He has shown more than one time he is concerned for himself only; a sad addition to the Stonegraves, for sure. We'll need to keep an eye on them. Letting them out of our sights will be very risky."

"I agree. I don't know if I've ever been so nervous. Makko

hasn't shown up tonight, either. I wonder if he knows something's amiss."

The hour finally came. The sound of the guards moving to their night time post a few floors below echoed up the hallways. Climbing down, they found Stonegrave comforting the sobbing Jenkins. Jenkins dried up his tears and looked them straight on. "My apologies, it's just a hard night for me. Not being able to escape this place would make any man loose his composure. Kale, may I have a moment with you?"

"Sure thing, Jenkins," Kale agreed.

Kale walked over as Stonegrave took off his shoes and handed them to Jenkins with a smile. Then he retreated.

"Might I ask a favor of you? You have been very kind to me; you've treated me like any nobleman, despite my placement in life. But, I wanted to ask one more kindness. Your sash, can I have it? The guards know not to beat the man wearing the sash. It will protect me for awhile, " Jenkins explained.

"Of course, Jenkins. Might I also suggest you climb to the top cell. It has a bit more air, and you can see the sky. Plus, being at the top of this place has its advantages in the waste disposal area. The guards don't pay attention to our looks. We are the same height with the same hair color. I doubt they will notice the switch. Most cycle out every few weeks," Kale suggested.

"A very good idea. Do you think you can weld the bars back into place? If they come to investigate, they will assume I am there alone. If the bars are not loosened, they may assume the escape started with this floor and not yours." Jenkins waited anxiously for Kale's response.

"Surely, I think we can. To be certain I will weld at least a few of the bars to keep it in place," Kale stated.

It took a few minutes to help the frail fellow up to the top floor. Placing the grate in place, Kale lightly welded the two bars together. Jenkins sat staring through the bars with as much sincere thanks as the sorrow he felt to the morrow of his bones.

Finally ready, Kale lowered himself down to the bottom floor to meet the others who already waited for him. Atus had been busily removing the last section of grating. With a shuffled clank, the weight of the grate shifted, and then Atus handed it up through the hole. The group entered the dark tunnel, only vaguely lit by the two hands of Atus and Kale.

Riggs shifted to the right. "This way, We need to move quickly."

The group made its way through the tunnels, turning more out of instinct and memory than sight. Coming to the tunnel that led to the exit drain, they slowed their pace. Riggs stopped at the entrance to the tunnel and began to take mathematical steps along the tunnel. Riggs progressed slowly, exposing the plans to the light every few seconds to check his distance and calculations. The wall came into view. Stopping, Riggs lifted his head. "Oh, no, they aren't on time. They're half of a day behind. There is an extra four feet," distraughtly he said.

The tunnelers had left their picks and shovels lying about. Stonegrave leaned down and picked one up. "There is no help in just sitting. We need to dig through."

"It won't matter, Stonegrave. I've watched teams dig down here. We have eight feet to go, and the outer edge is stone. They will surely be through tomorrow and have the grate put in place. And it's not something we can burn through in one night," Kale began.

Atus spoke from the back of the group in a reluctant tone.

Riggs, in his normal fashion, played the interpreter. "That might work. He says that they use small bags of powder to break through large sections of rock in the quarry. The bags are kept in the blacksmith's storeroom."

Riggs turned to address Atus. "Do you think you can get them, Atus?" Atus replied with a nod.

"Okay, Atus. You go. Take Kale with you. Stonegrave and I will start our way through this dirt to make a place for the bags," Riggs commanded.

Riggs turned to Kale, giving him a glance of concern as if to say, "Watch yourself."

Moving up the tunnel without the presence of a guard and with the freedom to gaze freely gave the place a strange feeling. Atus lead the way, motioning with his hands as he peered around corners. As they made their way closer to the entrance, both turned off their flames to keep the light from drawing attention. The guards were placed on the outside of the walls, but most were sleeping or playing dice. The few watching their post were concerned with the land outside the city as the slave pit became an uneventful place after dark. The two made their way through the shadows, darting behind carts and mounds of dirt.

Across from the cart they were hiding behind stood the blacksmith's shop. Smoke from the coals in the furnace still smoldered as they died down from the day's labor, and off to one side stood a small storage room. Atus pointed to the room. Kale nodded his understanding. They both darted from the cart, crouching down to minimize the chance of being seen. Approaching the blacksmith's shop, they entered into the open work area. Passing by the cooling trough, Kale paused, remembering the first day of his arrival. The memory of being suffocated under the water by that brute of a taskmaster haunted him. A firm tap from behind got his attention, and Atus walked over to the door that was locked from the outside by a padlock. With little effort, Atus burned through the loop and pulled off the lock. Opening the door, he disappeared into the room. Kale waited a few seconds. Then Atus came out holding two large bags the size of a pig. In his other hand he held a handful of the water skins used during the day to quench the thirst of the workers. Atus threw the skins towards Kale and pointed to the water trough.

It felt odd working so closely with the man Kale had come to fear and dread each week. His actions were brisk and thought out but always in a superior and strangely friendly attitude. As Kale filled the water skins, Atus quietly rummaged through the shelves and small boxes lying about. Kale began to think intently about Atus. Could he have misjudged this man? Surely he was a brute, but what else could survive this place. Was he not just the outcome of a harsh environment? Even Kale had changed over the years. Death held little importance in his mind. How crude he had become! How much he had grown from that first day he had been brought to this wretched pit! Smiling, he corked the water skins and grabbed a bag from Atus.

The sound of guards walking along the road caught their attention. Ducking behind the building, they listened as the guards strolled by talking. Most of the guards Kale could not recognize. This wasn't uncommon with the high turnover of guards in the quarry. But one, one distinct voice, he understood very clearly. It was Celic accompanying the guards as they made their rounds, talking about his clever upset of the late taskmaster. As he walked, he boasted about how he had bested that ignorant old fool at last.

They passed by the building and made their way up the path. Kale barely noticed that he had been holding his breath in suspense. Atus, too, let out a relieved sigh when their voices trailed around the corner towards the gate. Kale followed the troop with his eyes. Out of the corner of his vision, he saw a flicker of shadow pass by a wall. Turning, he saw a rag waving in the light breeze of the night, and his heart sank back to its normal position.

* * *

Sneaking quickly, they made their way back to the tunnel. Atus was moving a bit slower than Kale, trailing behind a few feet. They entered the tunnel and started to make their way down the dark corridor. After the first turn, Kale felt a chill run up his spine. Something wasn't right. He could just feel it. The air felt muggy, and his mouth tasted metallic; every inch of his body felt agitated. Suddenly a strong arm wrapped around his throat from behind, and a sharp pain sunk into his back. Kale could hear Atus' laugh as the makeshift shank pierced his flesh. Atus' breath was warm against the side of his face as he spoke in a foreign tongue. Then he pushed Kale to the ground and stood above him smiling.

Overcoming the pain emanating from his back, anger filled Kale. Out of sheer instinct, he kicked up his feet, knocking Atus' leg to one side. Atus started to form a flame in his hand, but last nigh's work of removing the last of the grates had drained him. Kale took this chance to make his move. Kale kicked Atus in the chest, forcing him to stumble back several steps, and then Kale arose to his feet. His blood was leaving his body fast; every second lost could be his end. Kale rushed Atus in blind fury, hurling punches at the man's head. They came quickly, but soon

128

Kale found his energy almost spent. Atus was able to side-step a punch; as Kale passed by him, Atus kicked the shank further into his back, sending it in several inches deeper.

The pain was paralyzing, and Kale only had time to turn his body around to prevent Atus from continuing the onslaught on his most vulnerable position. Kale could feel the energy in his body bubbling up in rage. As Atus rushed him, Kale summoned what energy he had left and filled his palm with a ball of flame. When Atus was within arm's reach, Kale planted it in his chest, forcing the brute back a few feet and knocking the breath out of him.

This was what Kale had hoped for. While Atus was struggling for breath, Kale jumped as high as he could and wrapped his legs around Atus' neck. With all of the might and strength he could muster, he twisted and sent Atus' body sideways. With a pop, Kale could feel Atus' neck snap and his body flew into the dirt, the convulsions of death its only movement.

Fortunately, the fight made little noise and was short for Kale could barely stand after the exertion of energy. Reaching back, Kale attempted to grab the shank from his back. It was perfectly positioned out of reach, a deathblow. Kale slung the water bags over his shoulder and dragged the bags behind him. Each step caused more blood to seep down his back. The pain quickly became unbearable, and his vision wavered as he trudged on through the darkness. When he got close enough to Riggs and Stonegrave, he couldn't hold a straight course and wavered back and forth, staggering like a drunk.

Seeing Kale alone, Riggs ran to him. "Are we discovered? Where is Atus?"

"He betrayed us. He's dead now." Then Kale collapsed into

Riggs' arms, unable to stand any longer.

"Help me with him, Stonegrave. Grab the bags," Riggs demanded.

Stonegrave had found a lantern and lit it during their absence. Now Riggs drug Kale's body into the light.

Turning Kale onto his side to examine the wound, Riggs let out a gasp, "Oh, my, Stonegrave, hand me that water skin. This is deep. I'm afraid it's punctured his lung."

Stonegrave began placing a bag of powder in the hole. "Then he's lost. We don't have time to deal with him. I'm sorry. He will have to stay," Stonegrave declared.

"No, give me that water, you cod," Riggs retorted.

Taking the water skin from Stonegrave, he poured a little on the wound to clean it. Then, with a gentle movement, he removed the shank. Blood began to pour out, and Kale's moans increased.

Lowering his head in concentration, Riggs placed his hand above the wound; slowly, a blue light filled the area. The water stopped its downward motion with gravity and worked its way into the air to from a small sphere. Riggs held it suspended in the palm of his hand and then pressed it into the wound, concentrating intently. A warm feeling spread through Kale's back, and slowly the pain started to recede. His strength was still spent, but it no longer seemed his life was fading. The glow stopped quickly, leaving a small, painful throbbing behind. Riggs breathed a sigh. "I'm sorry, Kale. That's all I have in me; I'm spent. Can you walk?"

Kale gazed at Riggs with amazement and concern. "You're a Gehage, a Water Gehage?"

"Yes, Kale, but now's not the time. Can you walk?" asked

Riggs.

Kale knew he was lying, but optimism was more acceptable at this moment, "Yeah, I think I can."

Weakly standing, Kale made his way behind the wall while Stonegrave unraveled the fuse around the rim of the bag.

Stonegrave brought back one of the bags and set it on the ground. "We only needed one."

From down the tunnel they could hear the voices of the guards. Celic's voice could be heard above all, "I've found a body. Go and alert the other guards. Something's going on, and I'm going to go check this out."

The footsteps of the heavy man running echoed throughout the corridor.

Stonegrave lit the fuse and ducked back. There were a few seconds of suspense. Then, a loud roar as the explosion went off. The air was filled with a cloud of dust. A gush of fresh air rushed in. creating a new air current. Slowly, emerging from the cloud of dust, appeared a hole no more than four feet tall. Rocks and small shrubs could be seen as the dust settled outside. Above, an alarm was sounding, and the shouting guards could be heard rushing out of their resting spots. Ever closer drew the sound of Celic's steps. Stonegrave wasted little time rushing out. Riggs took a few steps before he turned to see Kale stumbling to the ground. "Go, Riggs, I can't move! Just go!"

"I can't leave you, Kale. I'll carry you." Leaning down, he began to pick him up. Kale grabbed his hand and pushed it away, "We both know that won't do any good. You'll be lucky to make it out now anyway with the guards alerted. Go, before it's too late."

As they were speaking, the shadowy form of Celic rounded

the corner. "Halt there!"

Riggs gave one last glance, "I'm sorry, Kale. I'm so sorry."

Ducking, Riggs ran through the door. Celic was just paces away now and headed straight for the hole, ignoring the wounded Kale. Kale grabbed the remaining bag of powder as he got close, and, with a swing, he threw it into the entrance. Celic paid little attention to it for the first few seconds before his logic caught up with his zeal of pursuit. It wasn't in time to shield himself fully. As he turned, Celic tried to dive out of the way of a small fireball. The last of Kale's energy passed by him and struck the bag. Again the sound of a huge blast filled the corridors. Rocks and dust filled the room.

A second after the blast, the rumblings of the entrance and ceiling came crashing down burying Kale under several rocks and a few inches of dust. Fortunately, two rocks landed in a way that left an airway to breathe from. From his position under the debris, Kale could see the whole of the tunnel, still slightly lit by the half-covered lantern. After a short pause, Celic emerged, coughing from the rubble. Dusting himself off, he stumbled to the center of the corridor. Remembering the cause of his injuries, he scanned the room, looking for Kale.

In the dim light Kale saw his gaze stop in his direction. Feeling the cold on one of his feet, he knew it was exposed. Celic drew his sword and hobbled slowly through the darkness toward Kale. With a satisfied smile, he started to lift the blade into the air.

Emerging from the shadows behind him came two powerful arms. They wrapped around his neck. In an instant they twisted rapidly. With a loud crack, Celic rolled to the floor. As his body went limp, Kale could see the taskmaster standing behind him. "I said I'd get ye back you pompess weasel. I can see it now. Dim der stuck up boys at yer funeral. 'Poor Celic, got his neck done snapped by dat dere Riggs feller during da escape. Poor Celic'." Laughing, in low, silent reverence, he turned, not noticing Kale. Walking further into the tunnel, the taskmaster disappeared into the darkness.

When he was out of site, Kale unburied himself. Feeling along the walls, Kale started to make his escape. Sounds of guards coming into the tunnels echoed throughout each passage. Kale had to hide; he had to go deeper into the tunnels. Working his way along the walls, using them for support, he went further under the city; moving farther and farther away from the freedom that lay outside the walls. A pebble being kicked caught Kale's attention. A slight light was waving back and forth in the darkness, disappearing behind a large body illuminating the outline of the taskmaster as he moved further into the tunnels.

Kale followed quietly behind the taskmaster as he made his way. He stopped suddenly and doused his light. Kale's heart sank with the thought that the taskmaster had heard him trailing behind in the shadows. Would he sneak up behind him in the same manner as he had Celic? The taskmaster moved so quietly for such a large man. He could easily move around Kale and wrap those powerful hands around his neck. A few seconds passed, and the hair on Kale's neck began to rise in fear. A few feet ahead, a light appeared from above. A latch was being opened, and Kale could see a ladder leading to a hatchway as the taskmaster made his way through it. With a few grunts, Kale pulled himself up and shut the latch; quickly afterwards, the sound of a second door opening could be heard, followed by the low click of the door closing gently.

SIX

****

A NEW PRISON

From down the hall Kale could hear the guards making their way through the tunnels. It was now or never. Moving to the ladder, he forced himself up it. Gently, he pushed against the latch. It went up easily. Kale climbed into a small armory of swords, armor, and shields neatly arranged for easy distribution.

An idea came to mind. Kale locked the floor latch to prevent anyone else from coming up through that entrance and then put on a set of armor.

"Oh, no, no boots!" he thought.

At that moment the door swung open, and three guards came in. Kale's heart sank. He was caught.

The lead guard looked at Kale. "Hey, go with Gitta up to the guard tower and tell them to come and help us. We've got some runaway slaves we need to track down."

Kale stared for a moment in surprise and then said, "Yes, sir."

"And next time, bath when you're done working in the quarry. Your face is filthy," the lead guard continued.

"My apologies, sir. Right away!" Kale responded.

Kale walked out the door, proceeded by a man he assumed to be Gitta.

Walking down the hall, Kale realized he was in the keep. His bare feet patted on the floor as he walked behind the guard. Several groups passed on their way to the armory or towards the exit. A large group was forming into ranks outside receiving orders. There was no way to sneak by them. Up and up they went; each stair taking away any hope of escaping this situation.

Finally, they reached the top and turned down a hallway. Gitta addressed two guards standing by the door. "We're supposed to inform you that you're needed downstairs. We've had a prison break, and you will be in the search party."

The two guards left the door and started their way down the stairs. A few seconds later, Gitta turned to Kale "It doesn't take more than one person to guard this old man. I'm going to go assist. You stay here and guard him."

Kale felt a small twinge of hope return. Surely if this man had stayed, he would have noticed Kale's lack of shoes, and all would be over. "Yes, sir."

Gitta turned and went back down the stairs in haste. As soon as he was out of the way, Kale started to look for a window but found none. They must be inside. Kale unbolted the door and walked in slowly. The room stood four stories high. Three of them were filled with winding bookcases; Kale was standing in a massive library. The fourth was barren of books, windows, or ladders leading to a coned ceiling with two unbarred windows. On the bottom floor tall twelve-foot barred windows interlaced the bookshelves surrounding him. Long red curtains were hung, and fine furniture and candle light filled the room.

From one side of the room Kale heard, "Can I help you?"

Looking over, Kale saw an ancient looking man no more than five feet tall with long gray hair streaked with white. His eyebrows wisped out from his face, and his thin long beard hung down below his chest. His hands were withered and spidered with wrinkles. In one hand he clutched a walking stick, and in the other hand he held a book.

But, what Kale noticed most were his eyes. They were young, vibrant, intelligent gray eyes hidden behind his broad short nose.

Coughing gently, Kale put on the most authoritative voice he could muster. "I was just checking on you, making sure all the exits were sealed."

The old man walked slowly over to Kale, leaning heavily on his walking stick. "Oh, I see." Then with a quick pump he brought the end of his stick down on Kale's foot.

Kale's composure tightened, and he fell to the floor holding his foot.

The old man turned and sat down in a chair and opened his book. "Tell me quickly, and tell me truly. Who are you? The guards will be back shortly, and I assure you there is no way out of this place but through the front door."

"My name is Kale; I was a prisoner in the quarry these last eleven years and have now escaped. I need a place to hide until things settle down. Can you help me?" Kale implored the old man.

"That depends; tell me how you got in the pit and how you escaped," the old man responded.

Kale went over his story starting at the death of his mother to the death of Celic and his luck, thus far, in the keep.

The old man listened intently, nodding at key moments while he read his book. After Kale had finished, the old man sat for a few minutes until he had reached a good point in his book. Then, lifting his cane, he pointed it towards a portioned room on the side of the circular area.

"There is a change of clothes in there. I think they're your size. Hide your armor under the bed, and, for goodness sakes, wash yourself in the basin. I'll handle locking the door," he finally said.

Kale rushed to the room and pulled back the curtains enclosing the door. Instantly he was taken aback by the site of a caged bear cub and a young man in a bed laying next to the cage. His face was cleanly shaven, and his hair was cut very nobly. Kale thought to himself, "This must be Riggs' friend." A small oak closet was set next to a wall. Kale opened it and saw several garments. Choosing the plainest of these, he pulled out a red tunic, a white shirt, and a pair of casual breeches. Several pairs of boots lined the bottom of the closet. Kale grabbed a pair of common house shoes and then proceeded to wash himself in the basin. The entire time the bear pawed through the cage to play with him.

Kale stuffed his armor under the bed and filled a mug of water to quench his thirst from all the commotion. Kale came out into the room with his water just in time to hear two guards arguing outside. "I left a guard here. I swear, sir. I know I did. He must have taken off to help in the search. These recruits are useless."

The lock slid open. "He'd better still be in here, or it's your head."

A young officer walked in with Gitta behind him. When they saw the old man, they both sighed in relief.

Looking up from his book, the old man spoke in a frail fake tone, "Dear, me ,what's all this commotion about? Here I am trying to study, and you all are busting in on me."

The old man looked over at Kale, "And you, you've been here two weeks and you're still as slow as a sloth. Am I going to die of thirst before you get me my water?"

Catching the hint, Kale bowed slightly and handed the old man his water. "Of course, master, I will work in haste next time."

"That you'd better. That you'd better," warned the old man.

The officer looked at Kale questioningly. Then he turned to Gitta, "I wasn't aware he had an assistant. When did this happen?"

Gitta lowered his eyes in servitude. "I do not know, sir. I have only been here two days, reassigned with the last regiment."

The officer took a step forward to seize Kale. "We'll need to confirm this breach of protocol with the slave master. A slave isn't supposed to own any slaves."

The old man stood with a weak, pathetic air "Now, just wait a minute, you, I had to bug Celic for two months to get someone to help me. You know I'm not a young sprite, not by a long shot. But, go ahead, bring him to Celic and ask him, and while your at it, tell Hakot his son died because you were too negligent to let an old man have an assistant to help him with the tedious task of keeping his only son alive."

The officer's face went white at the sound of Hakot's name. "I don't think that's necessary. Your work here is very important, and I would never deprive you of the assistance you need in serving Hakot."

Turning, the officer swiftly retreated, locking the door behind him. In the distance, Kale could hear him unloading his frustration on Gitta. Screaming profanities and swearing, he threatened if he ever found that guard who abandoned his post

138

he would be drawn and quartered.

"Thank you, sir. Thank you very much. Now, I just have to find a way out of this place," Kale explained.

The old man put his book down on a shelf. "I am afraid that the only way out of this place is through the bottom floor. And when they give up on finding you, this place will be full of troops again. You should get used to this place. I assure you, it's a bit more comfortable than your old prison cell."

"Comfortable or not, it is still a prison. May I ask what has prompted you to be held here in such comfortable shackles," Kale continued.

"In due time, but for now let's get you settled in. The room you were in holds Hakot's son, Kain. It's a very remarkable situation, but I am near a cure. Or at least something to work around his problem. This room, of course, used to be the grand library of the Fire Kingdom. It was a retreat for the earliest Fire kings. Over the years it was abandoned until recently. Now this city is being built around it. There is no way out of this place except the door in front of you and the windows up above. Those being nigh unreachable."

"And your name, sir?" asked Kale.

"Oh, I am known by many names and many titles. You may call me Zube," the old man replied.

"Again, thank you, Zube. I will not forget your kindness," promised Kale.

"Oh, posh, stow your sentimental blabber. We are both prisoners. And I would have done it anyway just to take a jab at those imbecile guards who hover over me day and night. Though I have to admit, your story intrigues me. Let's sit and have some tea. I am curious to hear a more detailed account of your experiences so far." Zube said as he headed towards a seat.

Tea, could it be true. Kale's stomach turned in a joyous rumbling of desire. "You have tea, real tea?"

"Of course, I have tea; I would do nothing without it. I have a fresh pot for every meal. Now, sit boy, sit. You youth are so lofty in your thoughts. No tea, for goodness sakes," grumbled Zube.

Picking up the fragile cup proved almost more than Kale could muster. His rough hands had grown accustomed to brutal hard labor and tedious work. The cup felt so breakable in his hand that he was forced to place his palm under it and sip it like a canteen. Even then, when returning it to the tray, it made a clanking noise from his harsh movement. "Oh, that was exceedingly good. Thank you."

"Well, let's start at the beginning again; this time with detail. It's a very interesting story," said Zube.

Kale began to recite his story yet again. This time Kale emphasized his feelings and included the experience of killing the guards the day his parents were murdered and the effects it had had on him. He also went over Riggs' story just to be thorough.

"That is very interesting, Kale. Now, you tell me that you were in the quarry for eleven years. And how old were you when you were taken?" he asked.

"Nineteen, or roughly so. We don't really keep track of birthdates, but I would have been between eighteen and nineteen, based on the harvests."

Zube stroked his wispy eyebrow gently in deep thought. "I dare say, really. So your father was a Fire Gehage. How interesting. So, have you always been naturally young looking?"

"I looked fairer than most my age, I suppose," Kale said.

Zube stood and turned to a desk. Reaching a drawer he pulled out a mirror. Taking it, he turned it towards Kale. "Then tell me, Kale. Why is it that you haven't aged a day since you were taken? I would state my many years of experience and my reputation as a physician that you look no more than seventeen."

Kale took the mirror in his hand and began to run his fingers along his face. The prison cells allowed little opportunity to reflect on personal appearance, and in no time had Kale found the opportunity to gaze upon his reflection. His hair had grown out, and the whiskers on his face were cut to a suitable length with the help of Riggs' makeshift knife. But, his face, skin, eyes, and body structure still resembled that young man who had been left behind in his consciousness all those years ago.

Looking toward Zube, he handed back the mirror. "I don't know. It is very intriguing, indeed."

Zube replaced the mirror and headed toward another portioned room just next to Kain's. "I am tired, and I am going to bed. But, we will resume this in the morning. Your age is neither here nor there, but, still, your story gives me such enlightenment. Either you are lying to me, or I have made a most interesting discovery. Good night, Kale there are some pillows on the reading sofa near the window."

Tea and now pillows, this day was getting better by the minute. Kale stopped in front of the sofa thinking of which way he would enjoy sleeping in it the most. He positioned himself finally with his feet up above the armrest and his head sunk deep in between two soft pillows. Shortly after, his back started to ache, and he switched to lying on his side curled up like a ball. But his ribs now ached, and he turned and put his head on the armrest and his feet dangling, only to have them fall asleep. To make it worse, the ever-moving ache decided to rest in his hips. The couch and cushions were very soft, and his mind told him it was the most comfortable thing in the world to sleep on. But his body argued. A position of comfort was not to be found. Hours passed, but eventually Kale resigned to his body's impulses and resorted to lying on the floor with a pillow under his head. "Now this, this is true comfort," Kale murmured to himself as he sank into peaceful ecstasy.

* * *

Kale awoke to a sharp pain in his side. The first thought that passed through his mind was that he had slept on it wrong and now was reaping the consequences. But the pain quickly went away. Then it appeared again, then again, and yet again. His ears finally caught up with his sense of pain and his eyes shortly after. Zube stood above him, hitting him lightly with the end of his cane. "Get up already! You lazy youth these days. The sun has been up for a full twenty minutes. Get up."

"I'm up. I'm up." Kale stood and placed the pillow back on the couch which had been mauled from his constant squirming the night before. Sitting on a small coffee table laid a freshly made bread roll and a pot of tea.

"Join me for breakfast, Kale. I do not get much company up here, aside from the bear that is," said Zube.

"Surely, Zube, I would be glad to. Bread, oh how my mouth has coveted it!" exclaimed Kale.

"Eat up. I'll need you strong for the operation today. I believe I have struck upon a remarkable find in the young Kain." Sensing Kale was utterly lost and only nodding out of politeness and the hope for the last piece of bread, Zube got up and motioned Kale to follow.

The only movement in Kain's room had been that of the young bear pacing back and forth in his cage. Zube walked up to Kain using his shoulder to gently roll him on to one side, exposing his back. Zube pointed at the top of the neck, right above the shoulders.

"You see this, here. Can you see any scarring, anything that would indicate a puncture of the skin?" Zube asked as they looked at Kain.

"No, I can't. It looks as unabashed as the day he was born. Why?" asked Kale.

Zube grabbed Kale's hand and put it on Kain's shoulder, "Hold him. We might as well find out. It won't take but a second."

Rolling up his sleeves, he retrieved a tray with some surgical supplies and a basin of water. As he swabbed the area, he began to talk. "I was told that this young man fell and hit the back of his head upon a rock. But the fall should not have been so great as to affect the boy like this. It has stumped me until now. I have tried running his blood through this bear to purify it, but it doesn't appear that works. However, if my theory is right, today I will try another method. This bear may prove worthy of more than just becoming steaks for us."

Cutting the skin slowly, Zube moved it aside and then began to, ever so delicately, separate the muscle.

"Can I ask you something, Zube?" Kale asked.

"Surely, asking is free. It is the answers that cost people," Zube answered sarcastically.

"Why do you work so hard to save someone from the nation that imprisons you? I wanted nothing more than this person to live for the sake of Riggs' release, but now that is of no value, I have little desire to see this man live. He will only wreak havoc on the poor people under his control," predicted Kale.

Zube looked up from his patient with utmost distain. "Keep your bias words to yourself. I have heard them more times that any would hope. In every country there are those who strive for power and those that choose to serve the people. Most are honest people trying to get by. They deal with the brunt of their leader's greed and battle lust. Just because a country has a bad ruler who directs his armies to conduct themselves poorly does not give you the right to assume all people of that nation are evil. Now hold him still," Zube demanded.

Kale tightened up at this unforeseen rebuke. As Zube continued his work, he ranted on half under his breath, "What's wrong with people these days. Everyone is so caught up in the fantasy of one evil entity, one person, or one group of evil people. They are colorblind, only seeing in black and white," he grumbled.

Returning his gaze to the now fearfully silent Kale, Zube continued, "And I assume you think that the King is the soul source of all this misery; that his will alone causes the masses to fault and strike out in murderous rampage." The look on Kale's face betrayed his ignorance and his narrowed mindset. "Just as I thought, another imbecile. Well, I tell you this much. I may not be able to save the world, but I will deliver you from your stupidity. I will rid this world of one narrow minded ingrate if it kills you."

Then his white eyebrows lifted slightly, and he returned his attention to Kain. "Ah, just as I thought. Here it is."

Pointing down at the open flesh, his finger guided him to

a small rock lodged between two vertebras. Muscles had grown around and in them. "Do you see that, young one? Agonite, small and imperfect, but agonite it is. How appropriate the name, in this case."

Renewing his composure, Kale jumped at the possibility of shifting the old man's scrutiny to something more remote than his personal stupidity. "So, now is it just a matter of extracting the rock, and all is well?"

"Oh, how I wish that were the case. If it were limestone, or granite, or shale, or any other rock in existence, it would be that simple." Replacing the skin, he put a few stitches in it to hold it in place but did not sew it up completely. "Look at this, referring to Kale as any unlearned ingrate. I call it a stone; most of the world calls it a stone, so alike in properties and appearance. Have you heard of agonite before?" Zube asked.

"No, I have to admit I haven't, but I have never been one on studying the rocks in my surroundings," explained Kale.

"On this I will not fault your ignorance. Many know about agonite, but few know what agonite really is though it has been used in the making of almost every king's weapon since the first leader took up his stance to form the clans of this world." Pointing to a dusty bookshelf with a cob webbed ladder running up its side, he said with a grin, "Take the book that is on the second shelf from the top, third book from the right. About yeh big and has a red outline of a dragon on the spine."

Kale walked up to the ladder and broke it free of its many layers of webs. Moving it to the right side, he began his assent up the creaky ladder. Step by step he made his way up to the top. Now, thirty feet in the air, he reached out and grabbed the book shaking it lightly to get the dust off of it. On his descent, one of the steps of the ladder snapped, and he went down a few feet before catching his foot on a more solid landing.

Walking over, he placed the book on the reading table. The old man spun the book around and opened it with ease as if he had read it a hundred times. In two quick motions he flipped to the page and put his finger carelessly down on a passage of text. "Can you read Kale or should I describe what Monk Heartly discovered about our geological discussion?"

Kale began to read aloud; proud that he could show some superiority in intellect above most illiterate commoners. His experience as a messenger gave him ample practice at reading and writing.

The passage read:

"Here, on this eleventh day of the forty first year of this age, I have discovered a most amazing thing while bringing some meat to our neighboring dragon. Along the dragon's normal walk, its feces had dried among some grass. To my fortune, the dragon allowed me to examine it. A most interesting dissection, I assure you. To my greatest astonishment, I found that there were parasites living among the waste. I can only assume these parasites live inside the dragon's stomach assisting in the digestion process. I will collect more samples and see what I can make of this phenomenon."

Kale began to read the next paragraph but was cut off, "Very interesting, isn't it? Now let's skip ahead in this summarized diary a few years." With another flick of his wrist and placement of his fingers, he pointed to another text.

146

The passage read:

"We have worked these many nights on our new experiment. We have found that the parasite does indeed inhabit all of the feces of the dragons. It acts as a natural digestive, breaking down solid mass into its basic energies and passing it to whatever it touches. We have found that the petrified feces quite resembles coal but are the heaviest substances in relevant size to weight ratio we have ever experienced. The smith who assisted us in our collecting has discovered it is very sensible to smelt it, and it makes a fine metal. Nigh unbreakable but has the amazing aspect of draining energy from you if you touch it for too long. In any case, he has been assigned to work on some blades for the local villages and plans to make a sword as a gift to their chiefs."

Leaning back, Kale's smile turned to a smirk. "Feces, you mean to tell me that's dragon dung?"

Zube gave a satisfied smile, "Yes, dung my boy, dung. All the kings of this world strive with all their heart to be honored with a blade. A blade of dung that they can wield in battle. How ludicrous, don't you think? What uneducated morons they are."

Sitting on the sofa, Kale relaxed "So, what makes the agonite difficult to remove?"

Zube looked over, "At least now you're asking questions to fill your ignorance rather than making faulty assumptions. There may be hope for you, yet."

Zube walked over to a barrel and uncapped the lid. Removing two pieces of black rock, he set them on the table. "Here are some samples. It isn't the rarest stone in the world, but it isn't exactly easy to find. That quantity I have over there cost the senator a mountain of treasure, I am sure. Anyway, you see, even preserved in its petrified state, the 'stone', shall we call it, lives. The parasites multiple, slowly to be sure, but still they grow, and they begin to absorb the elements surrounding it.

That is why one dung pile eons ago now amounts to an entire vein of agonite. That poor lad has had that stone in his neck for almost twelve years.

It has absorbed parts of his flesh which are of little consequence, but, more importantly, it has fused to his spinal column. It distorts energy from passing to his brain. I'm afraid he is imprisoned in his own consciousness."

"Is there nothing you can do, Zube? You seemed to have had some hope of saving him still," Kale said.

"A mere experiment from the past may help us. I will send this barrel down to the forge tonight. Within a few days, we should have what I need to attempt this. His energy must flow unhindered and pure throughout his body. To do so, we need to filter off of the parasites and channel it back clean to his body."

A slight knock on the door signaled the entrance of the guard, "What is it, Zube? I am about to get off of my shift."

"I know, but I need you to take this barrel down to the smiths with these instructions. And take this note also to the Senator Haken. He will be most interested to get this news so waste no time," Zube instructed.

"I'll send a messenger, anything else?" asked the guard.

"No, that will be all. Thank you," Zube answered.

The door closed with an echoing clank. The bar slid into

place, locking them in their prison. From outside, the patter of rain came streaming down the windows. "It sounds so different in here. In the cell with Riggs, it was nothing but a loud crashing that echoed throughout the air hole. Here, it is almost peaceful," Kale commented.

Zube retrieved a loaf of bread from his stores and started a pot of tea. "I dare say, for a prison, it isn't unlivable. I have long gotten over my need for travel. Locked away with these books has been a useful experience. At least it reduces the risk of any harm coming to those around me."

Zube's voice trailed off at this last sentence. Almost as if he were hoping Kale hadn't picked up on it.

The tea had been made and the bread, along with some fresh fruit that had been cut for dinner. It felt as if he were lounging around the Inn on a calm, slow day.

Zube turned and began to recite Kale's history of his experiences that had led him to this point in his life. "So, it seems you are not very attached to your own life?"

Kale sat up with an anxious air, setting his tea down gently. Still, it was difficult to manage the fragile object "Why would you say that? I love my life as much as the next man."

"Why, in your own account, you have twice forfeited your life to save a friend. Either you are heroic by nature, or you hold your life in little esteem. I have found neigh a true hero in all my years abroad so I must deduct by reason you wish to die."

"On my word, what a load of horse dung! What would you have me do, let Reagan and Latus die for nothing? Either it was all of us or just me. And, as for Riggs, I was wounded and wouldn't have made the journey anyway. What other option was there than to cover their retreat? I had given myself over for dead anyway."

Smiling, Zube took a sip of his tea. "So, the hero is the route you chose. Sacrificing yourself for others. A noble trait for one so young, but a few things come to mind. They interest me most highly. You say you were wounded as if it were a thing of a month ago. Has it not been but a day? Yet, you get around like you were not even scratched."

Kale lifted his shirt to show a scar now well healed and fading into his dark complexion. "It must be the work of Riggs. I told you how he surprised me there at the end. The scoundrel was a Water Gehage the whole time and never said a word."

"That, indeed, is what unlocked the mystery of this Kain fellow. I have racked my brain to find why a mere bump would cause such intense issues in his being. But, now I see the picture for what it really is. This young man fell onto a rock protruding from the ground. It lodged in his neck. In an attempt to save him, this Riggs healed his wound not realizing there was a piece hidden between the vertebras. I dare say, that may even be what Riggs referred to as Hakot's 'doubtless proof' that Riggs was not his son.

"It would, indeed. I hadn't thought of that. Well, anyway, I hope that he made it away from this place," Kale said.

Zube brushed some crumbs from his beard. "Escape from this place. He will have to run far, indeed, to outstretch Hakot's arm. Hakot is no ordinary politician. He has connections in all the kingdoms. He is considered quite highly in the Water and the Stone kingdoms. And, with Alora being his only conscious child and a daughter, at that, he will pursue them to the afterlife if need be to retrieve her. And, to boot, he is second in line to inherit the thrown. Only his brother, General Qame, stands in

150

his way, and, I dare say, they are as thick as thieves. Both masquerade as patriots, but each are equally villainous in their greed for power."

Kale's body jerked with surprise. "General Qame is Hakot's brother. He is uncle to my retched enemy, Fike. And, you say that we shouldn't stab the heart of that man in the other room. Every person in his family has done nothing but seed pain and suffering."

"Calm yourself, Kale. Can anyone pass the faults of a father, or anyone for that matter, on to the son? Is that boy not entitled to make his own choices? Should we condemn him because of where and to whom he was born? Surely your mind must stretch farther than that. Even if he turns out to be a snake like them, will it not all balance in the end?" Zube demanded.

"I don't agree with your logic, though I see where you are going. These people are trained from birth in the pursuit of lush greed. War mongers with power lusts from the time they can walk. They should be eliminated, every one of them," Kale bitterly replied.

Zube's face turned red with anger. "Now, hold your tongue. There will be no talk of genocide while I am around. Now, I have been around long enough to speak to you out of experience. The Fire Kingdom is on the rampage now, but it will not last. The whims of a madman are fleeting. It may feel like an age during his reign of power, but he is victim to death like the next and then things start to come into place. Was it not two hundred years ago that the Stone Kingdom had tried the same thing? Wars for over sixty years, conquering much of the land the Fire Kingdom is fighting for now.

In the grand scheme of things, is it not just as rightly the

Fire Kingdom's as it is the Stone Kingdom. No, things will go back and forth but even out in the end. No one country has any real hold on the other's lands. They are each suited to best fit their Gehage and, on home turf, they will always eventually overcome their attackers even if it requires an uprising after the leader of the opposition has died and been replaced by a less zealous successor. I tell you, death is the ultimate soldier, the equalizer of nations. Death is the fate that keeps things swaying, never in the same direction but always in equal motion."

"Zube, I do not pretend to conquer your experience though I am not as young as I may seem. It will take a lot more than your spirited talks to change my opinion of the Gehage of the Fire Kingdom. In all honesty, in a way, I hate myself for being one of them," Kale admitted.

Kale surveyed the books sitting around the room. Most hadn't been touched in many years. Thick blankets of dust sat on the higher shelves and cob webs littered the tops of everything above the meager-sized man's reach.

"I have a question for you if I may, Zube?" he asked.

"Certainly, certainly, without questions we would not gain knowledge. Ask away. Oh, pass me that tin there...yes that one. Would you like some grass? I have an older pipe in the drawer at my desk," Zube said.

"No, just a simple question; how long have you been here?" Kale asked.

Zube stroked a match and puffed on his pipe for a few long draughts. Seeing it sufficiently lit, he leaned back and folded one arm under the other and puffed rings in the air. "Going on sixty nine years, eight months, and four days, roughly; off and on throughout the years."

152

"Dear me, you've been here almost seventy years. But, you mentioned off and on. Have you ever escaped?" wondered Kale.

"Escape, why would I want to do that? I am guarded by a small army. I have all the books I could wish to read, I've traveled the world more times than any man could dream. Why would I want to leave? This is my retirement, my giving up, and my final abode," Zube explained.

"So, you have no desire to leave?" said Kale in disbelief.

Zube added some more grass to his pipe and puffed a bit more. His countenance went from an entertaining house guest to one of almost depressive remembrance. The whiteness in his eyes shaded over, and the wrinkles on his face crinkled, exposing their maximum depth. Looking away from Kale, he replied in a distant solemn voice, "Let's just leave it that it is better for everyone if I stay where I am."

"Now you've sparked my curiosity. For a man who is up on all knowledge, you seem to be hiding a great berth of it. What could you have done that was so heinous as to warrant this life of solitude?" wondered Kale.

Standing, Zube tossed his pipe into a small dish lying on his desk. Then, turning briskly, he began to walk toward his room. "I am tired. I'll see you in the morning."

* * *

Such abrupt change in mood was new to Kale. Riggs had always maintained a monotone emotion: strict seriousness, military etiquette, and no sense of humor, though most of that had been due to their lifestyle. But, in Kale's opinions, Riggs had always been open. That was until he revealed his birth lineage. Kale had also thought Riggs to be truthful. On the other hand,

153

this ancient being harbored some great mystery. He appeared frail and immensely intelligent.

While Kale sat contemplating about the old man, a glint caught the corner of his eye. Looking over, he saw that Zube had left his cane. The reflection from the polished handle had caught his eye. Kale rewound his memory to just moments before to replay Zube's exit. He had stood and walked briskly with no help of his cane. no waddle, not even a limp. He didn't need it. It had been a ruse!

The next morning, Zube awoke with his cane propped up against his nightstand. Taking it with little thought, he proceeded from his room in his limping, elderly fashion. Kale had already made breakfast and sat perusing a book about the tale of King Heaken and the Wolfkin King; a favorite story for campfires but much more intriguing to read the unmodified version.

"Kale, could you bring me that basin of water?" called Zube.

Looking up from his book, Kale took a bite of his toast and then returned his attention to his book. "I think you're perfectly capable of getting it yourself, old man." At this, his eyes rose above the edge of the pages to give Zube a knowing glance.

Smiling largely, Zube hooked the edge of his cane on his forearm and walked confidently to the bowl. "Two days, very impressive. In seventy years no guard has caught on. You must understand that for a man of my age I need to seem...old, as you put it."

Kale closed the book with a clap. "You seem very spry for someone so aged."

"Oh, really, well look who's talking, young one. And I can say young even if you are thirty. You look overly young for your age. Tell me. Was your mother very short, a gnome perhaps?" questioned Zube.

"Oh, don't jest about my mother, you old cod. She was of normal height, and she was real enough. No fairy tale," Kale admonished Zube.

Tossing his cane to the couch, Zube pivoted ever so gracefully. "What, you don't believe in gnomes. And I'm not talking about the kind small children speak of. They aren't prancing do-gooders, spreading flowers and protecting trees. But, gnomes do exist. I can assure you of that."

"Prove it; prove you're not just toying with me, another ruse at my expense," Kale challenged him.

Zube paused for a second. "Third floor bookshelf, four-teenth shelf, fifth from the left."

"Why don't you climb up there and get it yourself?" Kale said.

"Kale, I am the physician. You are the assistant. Now, do your duty and assist!" Zube commanded him.

Climbing the spiraling staircase, Kale made his way to the book. Then he retrieved it, returned, and plopped it on the desk in a childish manner.

"Oh, stuff your whining, boy. My ruse was going on long before you got here. I wasn't going to let up for a stranger," Zube calmly informed Kale.

"Let's see what this storybook has to say about your gnomes," Kale said as he began examing the book.

Zube, in his regular fashion, opened the book up in one flick and walked away. The page he had opened to had some cryptic writing but displayed a head and shoulders drawing of a gnome plus a smaller, full-body picture. It was, indeed, not like the

155

children's stories he had read about. The gnome was very short. It stood about four feet tall by the dimension diagram at the side of the page. But, it was clad in warrior armor. The gnome was plated from head to foot and armed to the teeth. Two thin blades hung on either side of the gnome, and a broadsword style blade was slung across its back. The gnome's hands where adorned with spiked gloves, and its feet had long spikes off of the tip of each boot. Arrayed along his belt were several small daggers, and even his helm was topped with an axe blade, reaching to the sky. The gnome was a very formidable being, indeed.

The head and shoulder shot was of a gnome in a common shirt and bare head. Every feature was outlined in detail. Hair grew in thick bushes down its facial sides. Its chin had a thick patch of hair. But, what took him back most was the broad nose and rounded ears, the shape of the eyebrows, and the proportions of the head. It reminded him of Zube. Could it be?

Looking up from the book, Zube sat on the couch, peering at him as if awaiting the knowledge to sink in. When Kale met his gaze, it became obvious he had made the connection.

"You're a..." stuttered Kale.

"A gnome, well, half-gnome, anyway. It's no real secret. I've lived for so many years I am well-known among many of the nations. It didn't take them long to figure out what I am," Zube revealed.

"So, it is true that gnomes don't age. Do they live forever?" Kale asked.

"Oh, the forever part is a tale, for sure. No, we can die like anyone else. But, yes, we live for a very long time. Some die of old age at four or five thousand years. Others have been alive for eight thousand years and are still very much alive. I, myself, am young for my kind, a meager twenty four hundred and twelve years," Zube said.

"Twenty four hundred years? That's impossible," exclaimed Kale.

"Why? Prove to me its impossible as I am living proof that it is true," challenged Zube.

What an amazing discovery! This ancient being was not just metaphorically ancient. He, by any standard, was, indeed, ancient. This cast an all new respect and reverence in Kale's mind. What he could learn. The possibilities were endless!

"So, in all those years, I would imagine you have been around several Gehage, then?" guessed Kale.

"Many, very many. I had the privilege of raising a prince in the Earth Kingdom. His great grandson is now ruler, I believe," said Zube.

"Could you help improve my abilities? Maybe if I could strengthen them, we could escape. Or, at least I could escape if you wanted to stay," Kale corrected.

"And what would you do with this new-found freedom?" questioned Zube.

"Well, I would, um. Well, I would find Reagan," explained Kale.

"And then?" continued Zube.

"We would live out our lives. See where the road would take us, so to speak," he said.

"Would you now? You would find him. I am sure if he is living, that is. But, you would go on living just as blindly as you do now. Take my advice. Stop, think of your options, and then decide. There is a vast quantity of knowledge in this room. You will find it not only in these books but from the thousands of years of knowledge in this old cod, as you might call me. Why not take advantage of the Fire Kingdom's hospitality and advance yourself here?" Zube said persuadingly.

"That is what I am asking; can you show me how to use my abilities to a greater extent?" wondered Kale.

"What a fool thing to ask for. Power, that's all people want these days. Power, bah, knowledge my boy, knowledge is what you need. Power will come in due time. But, power can be reduced, taken away. Knowledge, that is an ever-growing commodity. It is something you can only build on but never spend. Knowledge is where true power resides," explained Zube.

"I see your point, but, please, I mean no disrespect. I haven't seen this world many times over. The lust for freedom still burns within me. I have no intention on this being my last abode. But, for now, until opportunity presents itself, I will be patient and a humble student. These last few days have been a very good rest, but I am beginning to get bored of changing sheets and emptying pans. There is too much leisure. Something to do would be welcomed," said Kale.

"Then, let's begin. What do you know of the five elemental races?" asked Zube.

Kale checked himself from correcting Zube for a moment but then couldn't help himself, "Four, sorry, you said five. Go on."

"Am I the teacher or the student? I said five, and I meant five. Your ignorance answers for you. We'll start way at the beginning for this. You already know of King Heaken and his bond with the dragon, Eriki. Good, and you know of his four sons. Those, you say, are the four elemental races. But, few know that there was a fifth child, a daughter. You see, she traveled with her father when he went among his sons to train them. He didn't realize for many years that she had been watching very closely and in secret had trained herself. It wasn't until he passed on his life-force to her, granting her immortality.

His sons, he knew, could not be allowed to live forever with such power at their fingertips, but he longed for some shred of family to stay with him as he lived out his long years. Years that were granted to him by the dragon's life-force. His daughter now shared in it, and her life was extended many thousands of years. During these years, she practiced feverishly in secret until she had mastered all of the four elements.

But, her father eventually found out, and he cursed her. He could not allow the world to be loitered with humans of such power, but he also did not want to deprive her of an heir. So, he limited her child-bearing abilities. She could only bare one child, and that child could bare only one, and so on. Her lineage would be a feeble thread. If only one of her heirs died before siring an offspring, the Wind Gehage bloodline would end. Gnomes are, indeed, thought of as myth, but the Wind Gehage is an even rarer story. Passed down among royalty, it too is a bedtime story. But, they are real," Zube told Kale.

"Wind Gehage, why do they call it that?" asked Kale.

Knowingly, Zube replied, "Her husband was killed, and in her distress, her emotions flared within her, a mighty storm of power. You see, she commanded raw energy, and she could focus this energy into any one of the five life-force veins running through her body. But, when stricken with grief, her pain had been too much. Her emotions became clouded and confused. The energy welled up and spilled out of her. The raw energy caused static discharge that affected the wind near the Gehage."

159

Kale sat quietly, reflecting. Could it be that he was a Wind Gehage? Could it be that his father was not just a master of one element, but all? How else could he explain the wind on that day his parents died or his lack of aging? "Do you think I may be one of these Gehage?"

"It appears to be so although I am doubtful. I don't see how it could be," Zube said.

"What do you mean?" asked Kale.

"Because the last Gehage died over forty years ago. It was by the teeth of the Wolfkin, and the greed of the Fire Kingdom that ended the lineage of the Wind Gehage," explained Zube.

Zube stood at the window reflecting. His mind began reeling over those many years, silently contemplating. Out the window he could see the statue of King Heaken, and next to it stood a band of riders, twelve in all. With a start, he turned to Kale. "You need to hide!"

* * *

Rushing to the window Kale looked down into the street. There, amidst the soldiers, rode Fike. His black hood was pulled up over a masked face. But it was his knives, those hideous weapons he lashed around his body, that drew Kale's attention. "Fike!"

"Yes, Fike, but more importantly General Qame, his father. He would only come here if it was to see me. And if he comes up here, Fike is sure to follow. You must hide," Zube told him.

Kale searched for an adequate place to hide. The desk was open at the bottom. The rooms were filled with smaller furniture, and shelves lined the walls. The only place he could think of was to be covered by a blanket behind the bear cage in Kain's room.

160

Several minutes passed, but then there was a sliding of the bolt outside. The door swung open. From a small hole in the blanket, Kale could see Qame and Fike entering the room. Following them was Hakot.

Fike's size had changed little, but his garb was altered. He now wore a black shirt covered by a leather vest. Stretching across from one shoulder to his hip was a lined procession of blades. On his side, he carried his sword. But, his face was completely covered by a black metallic mask engraved with red stone carvings of flames. His eyes were all he could see as the rest of his head was shrouded in a thick, black cloth hood.

His father, Qame, looked almost as surprising as his son. He had a long thin jagged burn from the top of his head down his right eye across his nose and down his cheek. His white beard was thick and full except for where the singe made its path proceeding down his neck. One hand was covered with a glove, but, as he moved, his shirt lifted slightly so Kale could see that the streak of scar ran down his wrist and into his glove. He wore a magnificent chest plate and greaves, and his sword was very similar to Fike's.

Hakot walked toward Zube. "So, I hear you have a proposed solution to my son's misfortune."

"Yes, I do, Hakot. It will require cutting into his spine. I found a large piece of agonite there. If this works, he will have to forever filter his essence through some animal. A mountain bear would be my choice. They are resilient and live for years. I have one caged now. I was going to use him for a different experiment, but the bear will do nicely for this. Do I have your consent?"

"If it even has a remote chance of saving him, then do it.

But if he dies, I will hold you responsible," Hakot promised.

Zube waved his hand in a non-caring fashion and then turned his attention to Qame. "So, General, what brings you to my humble abode? This must be your son. I see he has decided to take up the family tradition of getting burned."

Fike stepped forward and drew his sword, "Who do you think you are, slave? If you wish to anger me, I'll put you out of your misery right here!"

In mid-step his father held out his hand to prevent his son from stepping any closer to Zube. "Hold it right there, captain. I gave no order. You will learn to take your lead from your superiors."

"My apologies, father; it is clear he wishes to anger us. Why do you allow him to live?" he asked.

"It is not us we should worry about getting angry. Do you remember the day you gave me this scar, Zube?" A respectful smile broke out on his face. "No, I would not allow you to get angered again. At peace you are as harmless as a lamb. We remember what happened the last time you lost your temper. Don't we, Zube?"

Zube's head dropped slightly in silent remorse. "What do you want, Qame? I've already told you I have no intention of assisting in your tactics to take over the Stone Kingdom. I no longer meddle in political affairs."

"No, this is not political but a family matter. Would you mind explaining, Hakot?" he asked.

Hakot folded his arms as he peered inside the room that contained his son. Without turning around, Hakot began, "My daughter has gone missing. My scouts tell me she boarded a boat heading to the Water Country's waters. They also tell me she was headed to a remote island bordering the shipping lanes. I can have all the known islands searched, but I know there are several islands not on our maps. But you, you have traversed those waters many times. You also hold several copies of our up-to-date maps. I am not adapted to talk to slaves as equals, but I know your history so I ply past all ceremonies. She is my only true living child. I need to find her. Can you point out any other islands that may not be listed?"

Zube folded his arms in his normal thinking pose. His head bowed with wisps of hair floating on either side. His big nose crinkled, and then, with his hand cupping his chin, he replied, "So, what is in it for me?"

Hakot's face rose with a smile as Kale's heart sank deep beneath his feet. "That scoundrel, he knows exactly where they will be! How foolish I have been to tell him everything!"

"Why, I will grant you your freedom so long as she is found, of course," he answered Zube.

"I can make no promises of her getting found, but I'll point out the islands your people negligently left out." Grabbing a map from a shelf, he dipped his pen into a bottle of tar ink and began to feverishly scratch and doodle. The minutes passed by with Kale's heart pounding feverishly with both fear for Riggs and utter hatred for all four men leaning over the map.

Stopping quickly, he allowed the men to survey the map. Hakot gazed in amazement. "I didn't realize there were that many islands so far out to sea! Why has an island of this size not been found before?"

"Mostly the currents do not naturally progress that way. The wind inevitably dies out thirty miles before you get near the island. Bring lots of oarsman. The sea current pushes away from the island. It will be a hard approach," warned Zube.

"And you think she would go there?" her father asked.

"Well, there or any one of the sixty four smaller island circling it," replied Zube.

"Dear me, this could take longer than I thought. Well, I'll make several copies of the map and send it over to my ships' captains," he said.

"You'll do no such thing!" commanded Zube.

Hakot, Qame, and Fike's heads all snapped up in the same feverous pitch. "What! Do you presume to tell me what I can or cannot take in my own city!" exclaimed Hakot.

"Look at the corner of the map. Do you see there? That is the sign of the king's secret library. This map doesn't leave this room. You both know what will happen if it does. The person responsible will be hung for treason. You see the latitude and longitude of the island. Note it, and let it be. I will not redraw the map," said Zube.

Fike bounded forward with his sword drawn. "You will do as you're told slave!"

Two steps into his charge, Qame's mighty arm came swinging through the air, striking him on the chest and sending him against the door with a smash that echoed the cracking of the thick bolts. "I warned you about stepping out of place. And you, you old haggard memory, I grow tired of your mockery and tricks. You press my patience, and one day we will finish what we started so long ago."

Zube tossed his cane to one side and rolled up his loosely hanging sleeves. This was the first time Kale had seen his arms. They were baggy with skin, but under them, he could see taut muscles emerging from where the skin was pressed flat. What intrigued Kale the most was the sight of small black bands that circled his arms. Each connected to the other with a loose wire leading up until it was hidden by his robe. "Let's finish it now, Qame, I grow tired of this contention."

Qame hesitated a moment, and then his face flushed with anger. "Now is not the time to settle old debts. I must organize the search of my niece." With this, he grabbed Fike and pushed him out the door following hastily. Hakot took another look at the map and then turned silently and left.

Emerging from his hiding place, Kale strolled over to Zube, "Before I choke the life out of you for betraying Riggs, I am compelled to ask what these men could possibly have to fear from you. Anyone else would have lost his head to the axe for that."

"Those who know the truth about gnomes know to fear us. There are few who can rival us in battle. A young Gehage against an old gnome is still a one-sided fight. Before you anger yourself, I'd suggest you take a look at the map," explained Zube.

Walking over to the table, Kale surveyed the outstretched map. In it were many islands outlined in gray. Kale realized these must be hidden islands for the king's eyes only and far out to sea were the drawings that Zube had recently added. In particular was one large island surrounded by many smaller ones. But, this didn't make sense. These islands were north of the Fire Kingdom borders, not south as Alora had told Riggs.

"You did not reveal the island to them," Kale determined.

"No, Alchemete is here." Zube stretched his finger to a blank spot on the map to the farthest southern shipping lane. "It will take many years to scout all of those islands. And they won't be anywhere near her or Riggs."

"You are a sly devil, Zube. Is everything a ruse with you?" asked Kale.

All Zube did was smile and walk away. "The blacksmith should be here tomorrow. We'll begin as soon as he arrives. So, how did it feel to see your most hated enemy?"

"I felt that my skin was crawling with fire ants. If only I had had a sharp knife, I could have gutted him. Though I have to admit, I enjoyed watching him get chastised by his father," Kale remembered.

"It is that very treatment that turned him into the monster he is today. A person's upbringing determines more about who they will be than what they are made of. Gehage, human, gnome, Wolfkin, or beast, all are affected by circumstance. But hatred does get easier," Zube explained. "Some say the hate never goes away and it doesn't. But, if you see them often enough, it doesn't burn as diligently in you."

"And Qame, he is your enemy?" asked Kale.

"Beyond anyone who walks this earth, I would enjoy nothing more than to tear him apart. But I gave up on revenge a long time ago. Hatred, I still hold onto, but I cannot bring myself to kill again." Zube stood at the far window looking out into the quarry yard. Kale wished to press him further but was cut off by the waving of Zube's aged hand motioning him forward.

Peering out the window, Kale saw a group of slaves lined up many floors below them. Pacing from side to side walked Fike. The taskmaster waved his hand, and a familiar figure walked through the crowd.

It was Jenkins. Kale could tell by his severe limp and the red sash tied around his waist. Some preliminary discussions took place that Kale could not make heads or tails of, and then,

166

as quick as a rattlesnake, Fike pulled a dagger from his belt. It burned bright red. With a flash, he plunged it into Jenkins' chest.

Kale screamed, "No!" and grabbed the bars, shaking them furiously. Jenkins' body slumped over and then fell to the ground, a mass of blood collecting around him. The burning in his hands started to smolder the metal he gripped, and the world began to go hazy. A breeze stung his face with its harsh coldness, and blackness started to overtake him. Before utter darkness sucked him in, he felt a cold compression on his back, and it began to tingle. It felt like a torrent of water was pouring out of his body. Slowly, his vision started to come back. He released the bars. The area around where he stood contained many books that had flown off of the shelves, and, turning around, he saw Zube standing, holding a large cylinder black disk.

Zube stepped forward, "I have no doubt now that you are a Wind Gehage for you share their common flaw. When you loose control of your emotions, your life essence goes wild and pours out of you. And what a strong essence you have, Kale!"

"What did you do to me? How did you stop me?" he asked.

Zube held up the disk. "This is tempered agonite. Although it doesn't grow after being tempered, the ability to transfer energy is increased. I used this to capture the energy running rampant in you. Like water descending down a mounting if given a proper outlet, the energy will always take it. I must tell you, Kale, it is of the utmost importance that you learn to control this. If you don't, you run the risk of killing the innocent as well as your enemies."

A creaking from the door opening broke their conversation

167

and in walked a burly man covered in black dust and dirt. In his hands he had a long black chain. "I have your order. Where do you want it?"

"A day early, good man, put it on the table. Thank you," Zube said.

The chain appeared oddly shaped; each link had a steel cylinder forged between the two halves of the link preventing it from touching the other. At both ends were oddly shaped clamps with five claw-like extensions and a long needle sticking out of the center.

Zube picked up the chain and motioned for Kale to follow. They entered the small room where Kain rested in his endless slumber. The mountain bear paced in his cage. "Hold this for a second, Kale; I need to subdue the bear before we begin." Handing the chain to Kale, Zube retrieved a pouch of herbs from a drawer and sprinkled its contents over a piece of meat. Tossing it into the cage, the bear devoured it with ferocity. Slowly, the movements in the cage lessened, and the bear laid with his eyes half open in a dreary daydream.

Cutting the stitches, Zube revealed the agonite implanted in Kain's body. Slowly, he took the needle at one end and pushed it into Kain's flesh around the stone. When that had been completed, Zube clamped the claws into his skin and locked them to keep the needle in place. Next he opened the cage of the bear and ducked in to cut an opening in the bear's neck. The mountain bear sat with disconcert as Zube performed the operation attaching the same clamp to its neck.

"There, now in a few weeks we should see some progress. I hope," Zube said.

Kale examined the attachment in wonderment. "What is

this thing? Exactly how will this help Kain?"

"Ah, good, a question, I love questions. Here let me show you." Pointing to one of the links he began, "This chain is made out of tempered agonite. It took me years to perfect the process. I've tested it on another occasion. The blacksmith is a brute, but he is effective at his craft. You see, each link is separated by a plate of steel. This prevents the energies from crossing. Now the energy from Kain is redirected into the mountain bear. The mountain bear is young and full of life. In its youth, it is very strong and its energy is potent; far more potent than a tame bear needs. We use the bear's energy to cleanse Kain's energy. In addition, it gives any extra energy to Kain. This should restore the energy flow to Kain's brain, providing him with clean pure energy."

"Surely there must be side effects. Amazing, I admit. But what risk do you run?" asked Kale.

"Normally, the side effect is death. If the energies are incompatible, they will be destroyed instead of cleansed when they pass through the bear. But, I've tested this already, and the bear will be a good fit," he continued. "As well, the bear will gain a heightened intelligence and a mental link with Kain. I'm still searching for how that happens, but it is immensely interesting. You'd be surprised how complex animal thoughts are."

"I'll have to take your word on it, and I look forward to seeing Kain improve. If only to see what he will make of himself," admitted Kale.

By the time they were done cleaning up after the surgery, Zube looked very drained. His face seemed pale, and his eyes were just slightly dimmed. Rubbing his forearms gently, he drudged off toward his bed. "I'm retiring for tonight. Finish up here, Kale." Exhausted, Zube fell into a deep, but disturbing, sleep. His mind raced back to the past.

SEVEN

****

REMNENTS OF THE PAST

The day was sunny and bright. Small birds chirped on their perch just above the arched walkways of the monastery. Running among the trimmed green grass, a dozen children played a game with a ball of deer hide; it was such a peaceful day, so bright and full of life.

A young boy came running by chasing a ball that sped along the terrace, stopping just short of the robed man.

The boy in his plain cloth pants and patched shirt retrieved the ball from the man holding it in place with his cane. "I'm sorry. It got away from us."

"My dear boy, surely you and your friends can play in the courtyard. We need you to do your part and stay out of the way today," the robed man explained.

"Yes, sir, I'll make sure everyone of us stays within the courtyard," the boy promised.

The old man continued down the walkway and through the great doors. As they swung open, the peace of the monastery was overwhelmed with the commotion from outside. In the streets, groups of men rushed about carrying bundles of swords and arrows.

A young soldier in Fire Kingdom armor approached. "Commander, Sir, they are forming battlement positions. I foresee them attacking before nightfall. What are your orders?"

"Zeke, my friend, first I would find a suitable covering for your armor. You are likely to get confused with our enemy in that garb. The blacksmith should be able to at least sear off the symbols. Secondly, pull the catapults back a hundred more feet. They can easily cover the field with their debris. I don't want some lucky shot from those makeshift contraptions out there taking them out. We are secure behind the walls. Keep everyone close," the man commanded.

From south of town the sounds of a trumpet erupted, signifying the approach of a messenger. The two men rushed toward the outer gate and mounted the wall, passing armed soldiers preparing for battle. The walls were constructed of eight foot thick square boulders molded into a forty foot impenetrable barrier. Edged around it stood six archer towers roughly thirty feet in diameter. Stretching out beyond the gate sat a low corn field and beyond that the recesses of the forest.

From the edge slowly marched the Fire Kingdom army. An entire division formed into ranks, carrying their red banner high above each section. The division was easily two thousand strong, armed with the cruelest of weapons. Several small groups moved within range with their catapults and began to stake their ropes to the ground.

Zube surveyed the soldiers. Many were trained soldiers, but some were just townsmen drafted for the defense of their home. "Take heart, my brothers; they cannot take this fort so easily. Their weapons will barely chip away at it. Hold your ground for your families lives are your reward. Beyond us is the great city of Japada, and in it are many innocent who should not have to face this army. We will stop them here. On the walls of Drakholme, they will be defeated."

Even Zube's confidence sank when, from the edge of the wood on either side of the fields, lines of Wolfkin entered. Both

172

breeds were lining up along the Fire Kingdom's flanks. On one side, the Black Paw tribe adorned in its dark fur advanced on all fours until it was in position. Then the mighty savages made battle lines that rivaled the trained solders positioned next to them. Their saliva dripped from their gruesome mouths as they growled and howled, preparing for battle.

Opposite them, on the other flank, stood the Grey Paw tribe; this tribe took on a resemblance closer to man than canine and wore armor as well as brandished shields. They marched with their own flag above their ranks. They did not growl or snarl but stood stern as stone. It was hard to determine which looked more fearsome, the Black Paw with their ferociousness or the Grey Paw with their marked discipline and obvious battle experience.

This put a new spin on the outcome of this battle. The walls made little difference to the Wolfkin. They could leap more than halfway up and dig their claws deep into the stone, as if pouncing on a defenseless creature, to make their way over the wall.

He walked slowly back toward the monastery with the young officer, Zeke, beside him. "Zeke, I must ask you a favor," the officer began. "I know of your history, and you would be a most welcome addition to our defense. But, in case things go wrong, I need you to get the children and their watchers out of the fort. You know the passage way leading north. Take it until you get past the great river and then head towards the Eriki forest. You know I am entrusting my treasure with you. Keep them safe."

Zeke extended his hand, with only a nod acknowledging his responsibility, and then he turned and headed toward the blacksmith to darken his armor.

Two guards approached with a Fire Kingdom messenger between them. He was a younger officer, not more than twenty five. "Commander, the messenger has been searched. He is unarmed."

The two went through the customary bows before continuing with the message. "I am Lieutenant Qame, and I bear a message from General Falkhurst. He demands that you raise your flag of surrender and throw down your arms. He knows this is primarily an orphanage outpost and does not wish to kill a bunch of children to get to Japada. He will wait until morning for your response."

Folding his hands behind his back, Zube observed a troop of small ones walking along in single file towards the wall. "There is no need to wait for a response. Our wall will hold, but, even if your army batters through or you send your pups over the wall, we will fight until the last breath. We are the guards of Japada, and your general will find this group of 'children' quite a match for his men."

With a glare of anger, Qame turned and headed back with his message. As he left, a small hooded person approached. From any distance he would have been mistaken as a child, but, removing his hood, it was easy to see he had seen many winters. His hair had already turned gray, but his beard was well trimmed and his mustache cut short beneath his wide bumpy nose. "Commander, the younglings have been put in the tunnels with Zeke. They will make their way out when the battle starts. My men will line the walls to repel the Wolfkin as they breach the top."

"Thank you, Grewen. I'm glad Japada could spare a few of the King's Guard. Your group is much needed today," replied

Zube.

With a bow, the gnome left, and summoning his soldiers, he directed them to the wall. After seeing that everything was in place, the commander made his way back to the wall to lead his men in the defense of the city. Seconds drug on for what seemed hours as the messenger made his way into the enemy lines. All was still across the field; the cold from the early winter had set in and each soldier rubbed his hands together to keep them nimble. The gnome warriors seemed like small children standing near the human men, but they had long-earned the respect of everyone. No ten men could match the weakest of their race. Their presence encouraged the men to seek victory.

The tense silence was broken by the creaking beams of the catapults being loosed, echoing in the silence. Each blow struck with force across the mighty wall, but few were injured. A single catapult was moved closer to test for range. As the makeshift catapult was being pegged down, the artillery officer ordered the firing of the Drakholme artillery. Simultaneously, twelve boulders flew into the air. Most flew far to either side of the catapult. Three were off their mark only by a few feet. One solitary mass crashed into the forward catapult. A cheer broke out from the men along the wall. The makeshift catapults didn't have the range to get close enough to defend against the massive basilisks. Echoing down the ranks the words, "Prepare for ladders," was passed.

A line of latateers came to the front of the line. Then, with a swinging of their red flag, the troops were given the notice to charge. The roars, clanks, and screams of the men were deafening as they headed into a barrage of arrows from the towers. The ladders were placed quickly; some breaking halfway from the weight of the men clamoring up them in haste. The men were slow in their progress up the ladders, but the Wolfkin, the true threat, ran with majestic speed. With one pounce, they were halfway up the ladders, many times landing on a comrade and sending him sprawling to the ground. A second later, the beasts had cleared the distance and were perched on the walkway, clawing and biting.

The men could barely hold off the ladders while they attempted to drive back the fierce activity of the Wolfkin soldiers. Each swipe of their mighty paws laid waste two or more men. It wasn't until the gnomes got into the fray that any progress was made to check the Wolfkin's advance.

The Wolfkin were agile and strong, but they could not match the prowess and speed of the gnomes. With leaps and spins, they ducked and jumped over the Wolfkin's blows. Then, with a well-placed attack, the gnomes ran their blades into the beasts' hearts, the only real spot to cause serious damage to these abominations of mankind.

Finally, the ladders were cast off, and what was left of the first wave of troops subsided. Zube limped forward, grabbing a staff to brace himself. During the attack, he had received a wicked slash across his thigh before dispatching a rather large Black Paw.

"How do your men look, Grewen?" asked Zube.

The gnome cleaned his blade and sheathed it. "Four dead and twelve wounded, sir. Not too bad, but I see they reserved most of the Wolfkin on this attempt."

"Yes, that was their test. Most of those men were new or too old. I'm afraid the real onslaught is yet to begin. We must find a way to keep those ladders from making their way to our walls.

Those Wolfkin barely need more than the length of a man to clear the distance to our wall," observed Commander Zube.

Several minutes passed as the Fire Kingdom reorganized their lines for the main assault. After a half hour, things began to get uneasy. Then another trumpet announced the arrival of the enemy's messenger once again.

Riding through the gates, Qame was met by Zube. Qame tossed a bloody sack on the ground. "That is all that is left of your guard and the caretakers of your children. The little ones are safe for now, but it is very difficult to keep the Wolfkin from tearing them apart. A delicacy for them, I hear. Surrender and the children will be spared."

Grewen leaned down, and, from the sack, he produced the leg of Zeke; recognizable by the recent blackening tint to his armor.

Zube flushed with anger. "I have a message to bring back to your General." His fists tightened, and his breath came in short spasms. A flash of light blinded the area, and Qame sank to the ground, holding his face and arm; a long black searing gash trailed the length of his body. "Tell him to bring his horde; it will save me the time of hunting down every last one of you."

Zube slowly walked back to the wall. Shock kept his mind from accepting the reality of the situation. They were dead. A few inquiries from Grewen did little to restore Zube to his surroundings. The roar of the full advance echoed in the distance. The sound of new ladders slamming against the wall only seemed like a distraction in the unreality of Zube's mind. His hands began to burn. His face tingled with heat. Then things blurred, and the screams were all he could hear.

* * *

Zube awoke sweating, and above him Kale sat. He had been awakened by Zube's screams. His face was worried, and in his hand, he held a wet cloth. "Are you all right, Zube? You've had a high fever for a few days now. I gave you up for a goner." Zube lay in his bed in only his canvas breeches. His body was lean and muscular hidden beneath a canvas of drooping skin.

Around his arms and leading up to his shoulders were bans of agonite leading down to a cylinder disk placed just at his back. "So, I see you found my little secret."

"I had had my speculations before. You know a little too much about bending for someone with no experience in it himself. What is the meaning of this contraption?" Kale inquired.

"They are my shackles. They prevent me from bending." Sitting up, Zube slid on his robe and stood. His weakness vanished quickly, and he strode to his patient's room as if nothing had happened. "How has Kain been doing?"

"Nothing, I've changed his sheets and bathed him daily; he looks less yellow than usual. That's about it." Zube approached and began to examine the man. Kain's features hadn't changed much at all, but, turning to the bear, he could see its continence had totally altered. Instead of pawing at its visitors as normal, it sat watching the two in the room. The chain leading to its neck jingled as the bear turned his head from side to side, following the movement of the two as they glided around the room. "His intelligence is already increasing. This is very interesting."

As Zube spoke, a subtle grunt escaped Kain, and then he began to sweat profusely. "This is good Kale. He has taken to a fever, and his body is reviving."

Kale had begun to understand that this man was rarely mistaken. Even though a fever to him would be considered a step in

178

the wrong direction, Kale decided to concede to his new master's understanding of the matters. The fit passed later that night, and as they sat hunched over their afternoon tea, they heard a weak voice from Kain's room. "Hello..where am I?..I'm so thirsty."

Both rushed in and were delighted to see Kain lying with his eyes open. Zube stepped forward and took his pulse. "I see our treatment worked. How are you feeling, Kain?"

"Very thirsty. My head is pounding, and I am so weak I cannot so much as move my arms," he replied.

"Ah! That is atrophy. You have been unconscious for twelve years, and it will take a considerable amount of time, years even, I might add, before you will be able to even walk the way you used to. But, within a few months, you should be able to feed yourself. In time, you will even use the facilities without assistance. For now, rest and we will start the function of getting your belly used to solid food again," Zube instructed.

"Riggs, he was with me. Is he ok? Was he hurt?" Kain anxiously asked.

Kale took this as his opportunity to introduce himself. "He is fine. His horse was not spooked, but he did his best to save you. He is somewhere in the Water Kingdom right now." This was all he felt best to disclose, and he could see a shadow cross Kain's face. Even in this poor man's dilapidated state, he seemed to pale as he grasped some hidden meaning in Kale's words. Something was amiss to the young man, but neither Zube nor Kale then knew the meaning.

It was many weeks before Kain could digest food, and, as his appetite grew, so did his pompous attitude. It wasn't that he was cruel but that he had grown up as a prince and was used to the constant servants at his beck and call. Even for an invalid, he required

179

more to be done than was necessary. Kale had been convinced for more than a month that the man could bring his own mug of tea to his lips if only he would try. It wasn't until Zube interceded that Kain was told he must attempt everything himself from that point forward, aside from walking to wherever he needed to go.

For a man who had slept for twelve years, Kale could hardly have anticipated how much the man still slept. On the other hand, his bear, always at his side, seemed to never sleep. Rarely did it even lay its head down to rest. Always, it was watching its surroundings, absorbing as much detail as possible.

Aside from his superiority complex, Kain seemed shifty. He always smiled and seemed to be in good humor, but Kale had long learned to judge someone by their subtle traits. Kain's eyes were always serious and, in many instances, malicious. He never acted wrongly, but something about the way he eyed Kale and the way he sat stiffly in his chair when Zube came near him indicated he was hiding something. Kale felt a distrust growing daily toward the crippled prince.

Kain's long naps gave Zube and Kale much needed time for study. Kale learned more of the geography of the countries than he could have thought possible. He learned of each nation's history and of their great battles. By the time his stay with Zube had reached almost a year, he had read most of the books on bending and many of the rarer peoples.

Gnomes were his first study. It was odd to him that they would be so rare, but he found that was due to the rarity of producing female offspring. A male's life was insignificant compared to that of their fairer gender. Female gnomes were smarter, stronger, more agile, kinder, fiercer, and far better warriors than their male counterparts.

Unfortunately for the gnome race, the females were also prone to die in childbirth. It was almost unheard of for a gnome female to be able to live through more than one birth every ten years. Nine out of those ten children were born male. If not for their near immortality, their race would have long been extinct.

Next, Kale's study led him to the Wolfkin; this race primarily lived in the Eriki forest bordering Japada, the ancient city of the gnomes, and the Earth Kingdom. Formed from a blood bond with wolves, their race wanders the thick forests and out skirting territories, destroying and devouring anything they come into contact with. The Wolfkin are separated into two clans. The Black Paw clan, a ruthless tribe of dark furred Wolfkin with legendary ferocity, and the second clan, the Grey Paw, a more human-like Wolfkin with gray fur and an extremely cunning mind. In their perspective practices, both can be as formidable as a gnome in battle.

***

One night while Kale sat up late reading, a small white mouse crept up on the table. Its eyes were nearly sky blue, and its walk determined. Kale had seen many rats since the beginning of his imprisonment but never a mouse. Slowly, he reached for a glass setting on the stand to his side and positioned himself to pounce on the rodent so he might keep it as a pet. From above, somewhere on the third level of the book cases, Kale heard a light shuffling. Then, a few small bits of dust and cob webs floated down out of the darkness into the candlelight.

Often Kale had experienced the same thing when a large rat would scurry through the terraces. Returning his attention to his newfound prize, he slowly stood from his chair and approached the mouse. After only a step, he realized he wasn't the only thing stalking this prey. From the foot of Kain's bed, he could see the bear who had been named Olan standing with his head lowered and his back legs poised to chase the little creature. "Don't you even think about it, Olan. You can have all the rats you want, but the mouse is mine, at least until Zube takes him away from me."

But the bear had no intention of giving up so easily. He released the steel springs in his legs and pounced at the same moment Kale sprang with his glass. The mouse made a dash for the safety of the bookshelf. At the sound of a screeching roar reaching from above, each of the three were stunned to immobilization. From the darkness, as quick as a falling stone, a light brownish mass rushed into the fray. Kale's heart nearly stopped with fear. The beast was not after the mouse or Kale but smashed into the grown bear, knocking the massive beast onto its side. Then, in a flash, it was up on its feet, standing in front of Kale, hissing and snapping at Olan.

The beast didn't seem to regard Kale at all but stood with its back to him. Its full attention was on the bear. Kale had a few seconds to survey the animal before the bear regained its footing. Kale had never seen anything like it. It stood as big as a large dog, nearly four feet high and five feet long. It walked like a feline, moving gracefully but with a slight hobble that Kale attributed to smashing into the bear. Its tail feathers were ruffled, and on its back were two enormous light brown wings folded neatly into two shield-like ovals. Its face remained hidden from Kale, but, from behind, its head appeared to be that of a large, brown eagle. A bird, for sure, but what bird had four appendages?

During this brief pause, the bear had regained its footing and was in the middle of its pre-battle tactics, bearing its fangs and ruffling up its fur. It was unlikely that anything as large as this bear needed to impress upon his foes the shear mass of destructive power in him, but years of nature had enamored him with the impulse. Never had he seen the forest, yet he looked wilder than any beast of the wood.

The epic battle that would have followed the collision of these two titans, one the most ferocious of the land and the other, seemingly the king of the sky, would have to be postponed by the smallest of all beasts. From under the bookshelf, the all but forgotten mouse came out, standing on its back legs. It began to squeak in the queerest way; although the large birdlike creature never altered its attention, that of Olan changed instantly. The mountain bear may be the greatest of the known beasts, but it is also the most curious and most easily distracted.

Instantly, Olan went from savage warrior to cunning hunter. It again went to spring on the mouse, but, as before, was checked. A sudden jerk of its chain assailed him to the fact that the mouse was out of his reach, and its post had been securely fastened next to the bed.

Seeing the bear was restricted to a parameter that did not extend to Kale, the birdlike creature turned. Kale had forgotten the danger to himself and backed slowly to the table. Only seconds passed, but he was sure his doom was near. This creature would devour him in a manner of seconds. But, his fear fleeted as fast as it came, replaced by overcoming joy and wonder.

The bird faced him and had an expression of intelligent happiness. The bird had a scar running down its face and across his shoulder that led down to a deformed front leg. The two back legs looked very birdlike, but the front leg had only one fully-formed limb that appeared cat-like; very similar to that of the sand cats. It took Kale little time to deduce that it was Makko. A much larger, altered Makko, but it was Makko all the same.

Leaning over, he caressed the head of his long-lost friend, "Makko, my friend, you have grown. I have missed you. The question is what have you grown into?"

Zube's voice was startling as he spoke from the background. "I think I can answer that."

Kale turned, and there was Zube standing in his night robe, propped on his shoulder sat the mouse. "You know what he is?"

"Of course, I do. I'm surprised you don't. You read that book last month from cover to cover and had many questions. Second floor, fourth bookcase from the right, second shelf, third book from the right. Title, 'A Griffin, Myth or Fiction.'"

"A Griffin, I never thought they were real," breathed Kale.

"You also never thought Gnomes, Wolfkin, or the diseased, outcasts of the Stone Kingdom's underworld were real, but they are," assured Zube.

"I never knew there were diseased outcast in the Stone Kingdom, how could I believe they weren't real?" Kale asked.

"Oh, that is neither here nor there. The point is that your presumptions on reality have been steadily wrong. Try opening up your mind. Presume it's possible until otherwise proven to the contrary," admonished Zube.

At this, Zube walked up to Makko and began to examine him. "A very intelligent animal, I've never heard of one be-friending a human...most irregular."

"Well, he didn't at first. In fact, he bit me several times. This is the bird I saved long ago and who brought me food in prison," explained Kale.

Zube sat at his chair smoking his pipe as the mouse curled up and began to rest on his shoulder. "I dare say, what a fine creature! I see his loss of sight in his eye and his mangled limb have not impeded his ability to survive. That is most remarkable."

Kale took his seat, and Makko laid his head in his lap like a faithful companion, allowing his feathers to be stroked. Kale's hand ran along his feathers until they became soft fur at his back and patted his side as if the animal had always been that size, and it was the natural thing to do. "How did he come to be in this area? I've never heard of a griffin, not a real one, anyway. Anything this odd or this large would have been noticed," said Kale.

"Not necessarily, what your book didn't say was that the griffin, like most animals, are born with a defense. Like some bugs and birds, it is cloaked in appearance. Bugs can be colored like bark or shaped like a stick. The griffin is disguised as a hawk, at any distance mistaken for the bird. This is why not many live long. They lay their eggs before their front legs develop to the point they must be removed from the sack in the chest," Zube explained to Kale.

"I do remember him having an abnormally large chest. It seems to have regulated, now," noticed Kale.

"Yes, yes, that is due to the fact he was hiding his front legs in them; another part of his disguise. But many are killed very young, extremely young for an animal built to live for a very long time. You see, hawks, in general, are killed as a nuisance, but a griffin when it is young is very ferocious and eats continually. Actually, Makko hawks are quite tame and don't normally go after livestock. But the Griffin who is always mistaken as a Makko hawk has given it a bad name. It will eat anything and is very cunning and intelligent. I seem to have heard of a most aggravating Makko hawk in the area years ago. My spy told me that whole pens of chickens were reduced one by one every night, and more recently, goats and pigs have been disappearing. Folks believe it is a rogue sand cat, but I think we've found our thief."

"How do you know about the farmers in the area? You've been in here the whole time," questioned Kale.

"My spy, I told you. Guess I should say my little spy." Zube gave a satisfying grin and then lifted the mouse off of his shoulder and placed him in his palm, "Meet Alkaz, my first experiment."

Kale had wondered why the mouse had taken to Zube, but now it made sense. Zube had said that he had experimented with an animal before trying it out on Kain to test out his theory. Kale, however, had never thought the animal still existed.

After a short pause, Zube continued, "I had to test on something that was unlikely to do me harm so I chose the smallest mammal I could get my hands on. Now that the test is over, Alkaz roams the castle and sometimes the outskirting farmlands, giving me knowledge of current events, so to speak. You would be surprised how little planning really goes on in those formal cabinet meetings of the war room. Anyway, back to the more interesting topic, Makko."

Kale could hardly suppress his feeling of happiness. He could finally put his hands on something that felt like the life he had before, before when he was free. "Zube, you mentioned that Griffins have a long life. How long do they live?"

"Many have been known to live thousands of years, but most don't make it to adulthood. They are very fragile in their youth," Zube explained.

"Will he live as long as me?" wondered Kale.

"I'd say a griffin is one of the few beings on this earth who might. But, Kale, you will have to accept something, and it's better you accept it sooner rather than later. No one will live as long as you. Even the gnomes eventually die of old age. You are destined to loose everyone you know and love at some point. Immortality is its own curse as well as reward," Zube began.

"Immortality? I've felt physical pains like the next, and I have the scars to prove it. I am not immortal," argued Kale.

Zube leaned forward and folded his fingers together. "But you are, Kale. I didn't say you were invulnerable or a god. I said you were immortal. You cannot die from old age, sickness, or even starvation. Although to starve would make you wish you were dead. The energy that runs through you preserves your life. But, the blade can still kill you like any other; it is harder to strike a killing blow than most, grant you, but still, it is a way to die."

"Why do you say it's harder?" asked Kale.

"Your body will naturally heal itself. The more times you get hurt, the faster and more adequate your body gets at healing itself. Pain is as much a part of your training as exercise. Exercise hardens your physique and enhances the amount of energy flowing through your body, but physical pain increases the rapidity in which your energy is replenished, and therefore, the faster you heal."

"This is all so odd, but it doesn't matter much. I'm locked up in perfect safety," Kale said.

187

"Kale, do you really think this city, as I guess it should be called now, will outlive you? Maybe a few hundred years at best. Things change. That you can always be sure of. Things are changing even as we speak. The Stone Country was expected to put up a resistant defense, but it was not expected that the Stone Country would go on the offensive. There are talks that they may attack this very city. It is only hearsay from the townsfolk, but it does enhance the argument that, at some point in time, you will cease to be a prisoner here," suggested Zube.

Makko lifted his head at the sound of scurrying from somewhere on the terraces. With a flexed leap, he took to the air, leaving eight deep groves in the floor from his talons. A rodent squeaked, and then the moonlight was blacked out of the tower's opening in the ceiling for a brief moment as Makko made his way into the night.

Zube sat smiling while his little mouse played on his hand. "Left as quickly as he came, I see."

"What can you expect from an animal of the wild? He is a friend, not a pet."

EIGHT

****

THE UPRISING

After a few months, Kain was removed to the Fire Kingdom capital, Uphar, to be attended to by several personal physicians and a host of servants. It came as a great relief to Kale. Between Kain's annoying attitude and Olan's constant troublesome meddling, Kale had begun to long for his freedom. After Kain left, things fell back into its normal routine, with the exception that Makko regularly came to visit, sometimes staying as long as three days. Makko was a curious animal, constantly examining Zube or Kale as they worked or trained. Despite all of his curiosity, he seemed very distracted. Rarely did a day go by that he did not poke his head out into the wind. Many times Kale could hear him whine as if he were sobbing for a lost one.

Alkaz's spying kept a constant stream of news from the outside world. The Fire king died in battle a few years after Kain went to the capital. Having no son, Hakot became the new king, making Kain a prince. The wars between the Fire Kingdom and the Stone Kingdom became more intense. Steadily, the amount of troops around the town began to deplete as orders for new soldiers were needed elsewhere. The troops were preparing for a massive assault on the great wall. Many of the townspeople followed the armies to keep their businesses alive, and the remaining few only scraped by on the purchases of the skeleton crew of guards protecting the city.

One day, almost seven years after Kain had left, Kale awoke to a strange site. Awaking from his sleep, he could hear shuffling. Zube stood hunched over his desk busily working with two backpacks hurriedly packing his tobacco pipe set and a few books.

"What's going on, Zube?" inquired Kale.

"We have to leave. We have to go, now!" Zube urgently answered.

"Go, what is it Zube? I've never seen you so flustered. What's going on?" Kale wanted to know.

"Oh, dear, oh dear me, what have I done! Kale, you must understand that I didn't know. I didn't know what kind of monster he would be," insisted Zube.

"You're not making any sense, Zube. Again, what is going on? What is the matter?" Kale insisted on knowing.

"That villainous rat, that boy, he's coming for you, Kale. Alkaz has been spying in the war room, and I'm glad his curiosity led him to do so. Alkaz heard Fike talking with a guard. He's been ordered by Kain to take you to the palace along with all the surgical equipment from his operation. That fiend, I should have let him die like you suggested the day you saw him," Zube agitatedly continued.

Kale stood for a moment staring blankly in the air, trying to connect the pieces of the story that would lead Zube, the impediment of pessimistic thought, to such wild emotions. Catching his lingering expression, Zube exhaled in a frustrated blast. "Don't you see, boy. He plans to replace his bear with you. I don't know how he knew about your long life. That's the only reason he could possibly want to use you. But, in any case, we have to get out. I won't allow him to become immortal. An immortal king will never do. Never do, I tell you, Kale. It is destined to cause ongoing misery. We have to get you out of his reach."

190

Wandering to the window, Kale allowed his hands to rest on the cold steel of the bars. Outside it, a mass of over two thousand slaves, many as innocent as himself, worked at a never ending task.

"How do you plan on escaping? Surely you wouldn't have packed unless you knew a way out," Kale wanted to know.

"Of course, I have a plan. What do you take me for? Your flame has long been strong enough to burn through bars. We could go out the same way your friend Riggs did. We'll cut through the bars and be on our way. We've only got to make it down to the armory that you came in through. Simple, but it should work," Zube informed him.

"Zube, surely you must realize that they would have that entrance guarded now. Granted, the guards are cruel beasts, but not fools. We would be lucky to get two people through that grating before they covered it with crossfire from the towers they built on that side of the city. I have little doubt they built them specifically to cover that one, now very noticeable weak spot," Kale countered.

"Lucky if we could get two people through, you say." Zube contemplated for a moment, streaming his wrinkled fingers through his beard. "I've been watching you the last few days. I see you standing at that window counting the guards along the walls and looking down on those people with eyes full of pity. You're planning on taking them with us. Aren't you?"

"No, not with us, I have little idea where to go myself, but I can't just leave them here. Not when there is a chance to free them," he vehemently stated.

"I understand your feelings, Kale. The guards are as thin as they will ever be with the war raging at the great wall, but, even

191

so, your chances of failing are great, and your chances of being one of the ones to fall in the fighting is even greater. Are you really willing to risk that?" Zube asked.

"I can't just leave them, Zube. I can't," Kale insisted.

"Very well, then, I think I have an idea. Listen closely," Zube began.

* * *

At mid morning, the clanking of footsteps indicated the new guard replacing the old in front of the cell, marking the beginning of the day.

Kale stood silently with his bag packed, and Zube, dressed in his old guard outfit, stood behind him. Zube held a chain attached to a set of shackles that restricted Kale's hands and feet.

Zube gave two loud bangs on the door. "Hey, you, what do you think you're doing? You're not suppose to lock me in here with him. I've been ordered to take him to General Fike immediately. Now, open the door already," shouted Zube.

There was a short pause before the bolt slid open. The door creaked as it swayed. A young private stood rigidly in the hallway. "My apologies." The private took a pause to inspect the symbol on the soldier's shoulder pad. "Sergeant, sir. I wasn't informed you were already here. I was told that you wouldn't be here until next week."

"Well, obviously you were misinformed, and tell that knuckle brain to watch what he is doing next time, or I'll inform General Fike of his incompetence," Zube spoke authoritatively.

"Yes, sir!" answered the nervous guard.

Zube led Kale down the corridors and out the front of the keep. The city had changed dramatically over the course of the years. Many of the shops had taken on a weathered look, and

192

some of the shops Kale remembered as just opening when he was brought into town were now closed and decaying. Other areas that had been barren were now filled with new shops or housing. But, the one thing unchanged by time was Heaken's statue.

The guard led him down the street and through the commons to the back of the city. Standing guard to the quarry was a tall, dark man in a sand turban.

"What do we have here, soldier?" he asked.

"Just another for the quarry. Now, out of my way," the guard replied.

"That's okay. We'll take it from here. The quarry guards are now employed by the city and not the army," the man answered.

"This here is a special case. General Fike, himself, has ordered him to be brought here and given some specific duties," the guard replied.

"General Fike, I'm glad I'm not this poor fellow. Go ahead. Just make sure you get him marked before you put him in with the others," he said in relief.

"Very well, I'll stop by the smithy to have him branded on the way through," Zube said as they left the man.

The ramp leading down the quarry felt just as lonely and even more terrifying, even though Kale knew this time it had been voluntary, and that his stay would be short. Whether it be short by the reward of freedom or death, the stay would not be prolonged.

"I knew that old set of armor would come in handy one day. That was a crafty plan of yours, Zube. It looks like they are carving away at the outer wall for the new northern gate. That's got to be where we plant the bags," Kale decided.

"Yes, yes, of course it is. Now, stop your talking before someone notices." At this, Zube gave Kale a well-placed slap on the back of the head that would fool any onlookers; probably because it was done in earnest.

"Now, lower your head already and use your eyes instead of that mouth. We need to find the speaking trumpet. It's the only way they will hear you over all this racket," Zube ordered him.

At the bottom of the ramp stood the same blacksmith station with the exception that its storeroom had been enlarged and its door had been secured by a large lock.

Located on the side of the storehouse stood a large barrel of water, and next to it, on a spike in the beam, hung the coveted item; the speaking trumpet. The blacksmith stood ready at the bottom with the number nine hot and ready.

"Ah, a late comer, I see. Well, bring him here. He's nine thousand." the blacksmith began.

Kale gripped the handle of the iron, and before even the next syllable could be uttered, he drew the red, hot pole across the defenseless mans' throat, rendering him mute. With Kale's next action, he brought his fist against the blacksmith's head, sending him to the ground in a heap.

"Quick, Kale, grab the trumpet, and let us hope they haven't had time to be beaten into submission," Zube said.

Kale grabbed the trumpet and mounted the barrel on the side of the shop. With a nimble leap, he made his way to the top of the roof.

With a swallow to wet his throat, he began in as authoritative and commanding voice as he could muster. "My brothers, today is your day of freedom. The army has gone to the great wall, and we outnumber our captors ten to one. It is now or never. Rise up and take back your freedom. Fight and be free again!"

A short pause in the commotion of the general workings was the only initial response to this plea. During this speech, the guards on the surrounding walls fitted their arrows. Then, with repeated thuds, the arrows from the watch towers began to rain down on the small building's roof. The fear of failure mounted in Kale's mind as he dodged off the roof behind the barrel. The arrows danced for a second wave as he crouched behind the barrel, awaiting the piercing blow of one of the many arrows. Then, from the mud pit, Kale heard a familiar voice. "Tor'lam not be slave. Tor'lam be free. Tor'lam hungry!"

Kale gave a quick glance and saw Tor'lam, the giant that he had once feared facing in the Arena, sinking his teeth into the neck of the guard nearest him. The guard towers changed their aim and sent a volley toward him, but he had been ready for it and lifted the body to shield himself. Tor'lam inspired them by taking the first leap. Now there could be no resisting the reality that the captors could be overcome. The sounds of the quarry were soon overtaken by the battle cry of two thousand slaves. Two thousand men chiseled from a constant state of work. Two thousand abused men suffering the cruelties for crimes they had not committed, or for a country they did not swear allegiance to. If all the Wolfkin were to swarm that quarry, they could not have elevated themselves to the ferocity that these slaves threw themselves at their attackers.

Zube, in the meantime, had opened the cellar door and threw bags of the black powder into a pile. "Okay, Kale, I'll get some help getting these to the wall. We'll need every last one of them to break through. You have to hold the main force of the guards at the ramp. It's the only way down. If they get in, they will overpower us with their weapons. Keep them funneled, and we have a chance to hold them off."

Kale grabbed the iron from the furnace and then turned to head back to the top of the ramp. Raising the blazing rod above him, he gave his command. "To the ramp, hold them back until we blow the wall." The swarm of men began to come off of the excitement of the initial assault, and this bit of direction had been perfectly placed. Tor'lam was the first to climb the ramp with Kale, followed by a multitude of men wielding hammers, picks, shovels, and an occasional sword from a fallen guard.

The first to cross his path was a young guard with a new uniform and clean armor. "Halt there, or you die, slave." Pulling out his sword he lunged at Kale. Kale had never handled a weapon in battle before, and the rude iron rod was a most unfortunate first. The man had been well trained, but Kale noticed that his movements, that everyone's movements seemed slow. He parried the blade out of his hand and then struck him down with the searing blunt edge of the rod. Leaning over, he replaced his rod with the guard's weapon and made his way to the top where a mass of soldiers were pouring in to settle the uprising.

The two groups met with a ferocious clash. Kale made up for his lack of skill with his extraordinary speed and dexterity. The slaves fell by scores, but the soldiers were also starting to slowly dwindle. Tor'lam had been the only one besides Kale from the front of the mass to hold his ground. Choosing to batter down his opponents with his massive fists or in some cases grabbing a fallen victim and swinging him with both hands like a doll, he drove back their attackers. It was his girth, his monstrosity, that kept the soldiers from charging with their full force. The minutes ticked by with increasing slowness. Kale could feel his energy draining, and just when he felt that he could not hold out much longer, another familiar figure met his gaze. Pushing up from the back of the crowd appeared a masked man; Fike was advancing to the front line, stringing curses to both the prisoners for their boldness and the soldiers for their incompetence.

As he came to the front of the line, Kale conjured up all the reserves he could find and lunged toward him. Unlike the other soldiers, Fike fought not only with skill but a finesse. He was not just slightly better than Kale, but it became obvious with the first few parries that he was well out of Kale's ability with his blade. Then, as if taken aback, Fike noticed who he was fighting, "YOU! I already killed you!"

Kale's anger burned with the memory of Jenkins and his fate dished out by this animal. "No, you beast, that was only another innocent you have slaughtered, and today you will be repaid." Both men now burned with anger, and the battle raged on in a more personal war.

Fike immediately opened up his palm and launched a fiery blast directly at Kale. Digging down Kale pulled from his reserves, so feverishly supplied from his rage and hatred of this man and swatted at the ball, sending it flying into the crowd of guards behind him. Fike's bewilderment quickly faded and was replaced by a deep-seated hatred of this Fire Gehage that defied him. "So, Gehage, I see we will settle this like the Ukrin dogs that surround us. So be it!" At this, Fike lunged forward with his sword in hand.

The first few blows on each side were parried, but Kale's

197

speed failed him and he took a serious stab to his left shoulder. Kale continued on, but again and again Fike lunged in, piercing his flesh. His shoulder, then his leg, then his forearm, and lastly a lung to the body that sent Kale to the ground caused his blade to go skittering down the ramp to be picked up by a slave reinforcement. Fike stepped closer and raised the blade high above his head to steady it. "Now, you little sand flee, I will finish what I started so many years ago. Now, the son of that traitorous whelp will die."

Looking up, Kale could see the insanity that burned in the eyes behind the mask. But behind the mask, behind Fike altogether emerged a dark mass quickly blotting out the view of the blue sky. Fike's hand began its quick downward thrust but was checked. To Kale's relief, a second later Fike had been driven to the ground. Above him stood Makko with his front paw clinched around Fike's arm, and his massive wings pounding Fike's body. Makko's roar-like shrieks could barely penetrate the mass of sound swirling about. Then, with a heavy beat of his wings, Makko took to the sky carrying away a nearby guard and leaving Fike unarmed and bruised.

Kale struggled to his feet at the same worn out pace as Fike. Both paused long enough to draw in one long breath. Then they came charging together like bulls. Kale was worn, but now the fight turned in his favor. For many years, all he had trained at had been hand to hand combat, and he was well beyond any normal Gehage. His speed and dexterity, coupled with Riggs training and the many lessons Zube had taught him, made him a most formidable opponent.

Fike swung, fueled with rage and hate, but Kale was the one implored with finesse now. Ducking under the swing, Kale brought his fist squarely into Fike's chin knocking his mask off. Exposed after many years was the white distorted figure. Each burn, each wrinkle, exactly as Kale remembered it. The battle continued on. Each time Fike would come forward only to be assaulted by a volley of blows. Each blow felt like an ecstasy of release. Finally, Fike went down and did not get up but only groaned. Kale searched for a weapon to finish him off. While searching, he saw Zube coming up the ramp. "Kale, there you are. We need your help. We've got the bags moved to the weak side of the quarry, but the guards have the towers full now. We need to take out the archers so we can get the bags against the wall."

"Okay, I'll do what I can." Looking back, Kale discovered Fike's body had either been moved, or he had slunk away. At one side of the ramp a ladder led to the top of the wall. Kale scaled it with utmost pain as each of his new wounds ached. Blood ran down his side and dripped down his leg. "This wound will drain me to death. I have to stop it." As he walked along the trenches to where the guards were hauled up, Kale placed his palm on the wound under his shirt and sent a quick burst of flame, searing his wound closed. "That hurt a lot more than I thought it would."

The archer walkway served as a great guard against the other towers' arrows but gave Kale little cover when he came within range of the tower blocking the weak spot in the wall. Twenty archers positioned themselves on the one tower platform. The sun beat down on them as they sent hails of arrows upon the slaves below. One archer spotted Kale coming down the walkway and sent an arrow his way. Kale's senses and movements were still sharp and keen from the recent engagements.

With a sidestep, the arrow sailed harmlessly by, and he kept his pace. The archer alerted his comrades to the approaching danger, and they all took aim and let loose a volley. With but a second to react, his instinct kicked in right as the arrows came near. The energy pulsed down his arm to the base of his palm as if by reflex, and with outstretched hand, the air filled with a red mist of flame. The arrows hit it, dissolving into ash as the arrow heads skipped harmlessly to the ground.

Air began to rush around Kale as if some unleashed being had overtaken him. Every inch of his body burned, and, as if directed by some ancient guidance, he flung his hand forward. Seconds later the archer station erupted in flame, sending the front line of archers over the edge, plummeting a hundred feet to the ground below. The remaining archers grabbed their blades and rushed down the narrow platform toward this new attacker in a last attempt at survival.

Kale had entered that state in battle where his logic no longer prevailed, but he was guided by sheer instinct. His pace was a brisk stride, and each archer made his charge only to be met with their inevitable fate. Each, in succession, made a lunge at Kale and were thrown aside over the wall or had his weapon taken from him only to have it returned through his heart. Reaching the tower, Kale was able to compose himself and take a bearing of the battle.

Below he could see the slaves loosing ground on the ramp as the last of the bags made their way to the wall. Zube stood by the shop a good distance away only awaiting Kale to get clear of the danger. Every second was precious as the wave of slaves steadily backed down the ramp. There would be no time to make a descent. The guards would be in the courtyard and with limited space could subdue the slaves. The wall must be breeched so that these people could make a run for freedom before the guards overtook them. Kale took a few steps back, drew a breath, and, with a run, lunged himself off the edge of the tower. Turning as he fell, he mustered what was left of his energy and sent the ball of energy towards the stack of powder. The next few seconds blurred as the explosion erupted. First a bright light, followed by a wave of scorching heat that checked his descent, sending him flying back into the air. As the light faded, the last thing he felt were sharp talons sinking into his flesh and the roar of Makko echoing in the darkness.

* * *

Kale awoke to the sounds of laughter. Opening his eyes, he could see a dark room and at the end of it the opening of the tent. Outside a fire was blazing and many men could be heard laughing and carrying on. A heavy object lay across his waist. With a grunt and a fatigued effort, Kale maneuvered himself into a seated position. Lying, half asleep, by his side was Makko with his large feathered head placed on Kale's waist. The light from the doorway was blotted out for a moment as a figure entered. Kale's eyes were adjusting now, and he could see Zube seating himself.

"Oh, good, you're awake. That was some stunt you pulled. Very few people missed it, and it has circulated to all the men who have. I can't tell if it was another of your attempts at heroism, or if you really do want to die," Zube stated.

"I only remember the blast. What happened afterwards? How long have I been out?" Kale began.

"Oh, you've been out of it for about a week now. And, I might say, it's been a week you would have wanted to miss.

201

These men, though many innocent beforehand, are now all thieves. They ransacked the surrounding towns in the Fire Kingdom for supplies before moving out into the Deadlands. Can't say I blame them. It was just restitution for many years of work, I guess, but I still feel for those poor cattle farmers and the various shops. Oh, well, can't be helped, I guess."

"But, Zube, surely the city sent out a patrol to recapture the slaves," Kale said.

"Recapture! Now, Kale, you are funny. They were already depleted to a minimal number before the uprising. We lost nearly a thousand men on our side, but they suffered just as many. Maybe they even lost a few more, seeing as that blast of yours threw stones into some of the other towers, knocking them down. What a sight! But, no, they would not dare send out even a soul at this point. That would leave their city defenseless, and now that they have a big gaping whole in their outer wall, I would say they are weak enough as it is. No, we are on our own, and now that we are well out of the Fire Kingdom country, all we have to worry about now is provisions and some idea on what to do with all these men," Zube told Kale.

"They should all go back to their families. They should disperse," Kale said.

"A few left to return to their families, but the majority either don't have family living or, in most cases, their families live inside the Fire Kingdom. They dare not return; not now, at least," Zube began explaining.

"Well, what are we to do with them," wondered Kale.

"They followed you out, Kale. I guess that's up to your planning now. Being the hero can have its downsides. By the way, they talk about your battle at the ramp, and I can't get through a day without hearing a reenactment of that leap of yours off the tower. Well, in any case, we're moving at a steady pace towards the Japada Pass. It borders the Leaf Kingdom forests. I'm hoping we can find a more permanent solution before we get there," Zube said.

"The Japada Pass...you're taking me to Japada?" asked Kale.

"What better place, Kale? It is the only place that neither brute force or politics can get you. No matter what, we must keep you out of Kain's reach. If you were forced to be attached to that infernal contraption of mine, he would be endowed with your life-force and therefore become immortal. That cannot happen. No ruler can be immortal. Without death, there would be no balance," Zube insisted.

"I understand that, Zube. I really do. But, by what you tell me of the gnomes, they won't let just anybody in. We'll be hard pressed to get me in, not to mention all these men." Kale paused for a second to try and calculate the size of the force he could hear. "Exactly how many men do we have following us?"

"Twelve hundred and thirty three was the unofficial count. And, let's be clear. They're following you, not us. I want no part of that. You freed them. It's your problem. My only concern is keeping you out of Kain's hands," Zube said.

Kale struggled to his feet. With an exasperated breath while holding his sides he said, "Very well." Then he walked out of the tent. Directly in front of him burned a large fire with several men around it talking and still enjoying their newly restored freedom. Scanning the foreground, Kale could see a hundred or so smaller fires with shadows bouncing to and fro as the men walked in front of the light. The expanse of space was breathtaking. The stars were out in full grandeur, and the openness of the Deadlands with its calm breeze and flat landscape made the immensity of the world grow to an overwhelming size. So overwhelming that Kale's heart began to beat very rapidly, and his breath came in short fits. The strength in Kale's knees began to ebb, and within a few seconds they buckled. Grabbing his heaving chest, he labored through the dirt to return to the safety of the tent. As he entered, the darkness surrounded him, and the confines of the small space comforted his body. His heart rate regulated, and his breathing evened out to a steady pace.

"I don't know what happened, but I can't go back out there. I don't know how to explain it. It frightens me. I know it sounds absurd, but the space is just too big," Kale anxiously explained to Zube.

Zube had watched the event from inside the tent and had already made preparations for the remedy. "My boy, you've been coupled up in a tunnel or a tower these many years. Just as it took you time to adjust to the confines of your prison, it will take time to readjust to the expanse of the free world. I know something that will help." Taking a cape and black cloth from his bag, he wrapped the cloth around Kale's face leaving only a slit in the front for Kale's eyes to gaze out and placed the hooded cloak on his shoulders.

"Now, pull on the hood. This will act both as a blinder and will give you a sense of confinement even when you are outside. It doesn't get rid of all the panic, but it does help a great deal. Trust me. This isn't the first time I've seen this," Zube promised Kale.

* * *

"Well, Kale, try it again. Your men will want to see you out and about," encouraged Zube.

Kale reluctantly approached the tent opening and stepped back out into the dimly lit camp. "Freedom, I don't know if I'm ecstatic or terrified. Maybe I'm both."

From the darkness, just outside of the campfire, a large shadow appeared and stepped into the light. Tor'lam the giant slowly approached. His arm hung in a sling, but he walked with reserve, keeping his distance from the men. "Little one, you walk about," he commented.

"Hello, Tor'lam, it is good to see you survived. You fought like fifty men. How is your arm?" asked Kale.

"Tor'lam arm hurt only little. Tor'lam come to see little warrior. Why does little warrior wear mask?" he said.

"It's nothing, Tor'lam, just a bit of an adjustment. Why aren't you celebrating with the other men? Surely you have earned your freedom," suggested Kale.

"Tor'lam fight like many men, as you say, but Tor'lam is still Tor'lam. Tor'lam make men afraid," he replied.

"You do not scare me, Tor'lam. I would be honored to share a campfire with you. Tell me where you come from," Kale asked.

Tor'lam came near the fire and sat down. The flicker off of his tanned skin and bald head made him appear very somber. His eyes softened as he reached back into his memory. "Some say Tor'lam slow in head, but Tor'lam not slow in head. Tor'lam slow in mouth when he talks little men tongue. Tor'lam fast in head."

"I know that, Tor'lam. I've seen you fight. Your actions are quick and decisive. No one who thinks slowly could be as effective in battle," agreed Kale.

Tor'lam smiled a large grin. "Tor'lam people live high in mountains in Stone men's country. Tor'lam people and Stone men fight for land. Tor'lam great warrior among his people. One day Tor'lam kill a Stone man whose father was a great man. He was chief...no that is not word....he was prince. Yes, prince. Tor'lam went away from people so Stone men not hurt them for Tor'lam battle. Tor'lam went to Fire people land, but Tor'lam big and people try to hurt Tor'lam because Tor'lam not same as little men. Tor'lam great warrior. Tor'lam kill a few men. Then many men come. Tor'lam kill many men and a large number come. Tor'lam kill a large number and a whole clan come and Tor'lam not able to kill them. Tor'lam taken to city to be slave fighter. But now Tor'lam is free, Tor'lam is free because little warrior fought many men like Tor'lam. Tor'lam and little warrior are same."

"My name is Kale. I would be honored if you would use my name," suggested Kale.

"'Kale' not fierce, 'kale' green thing that Tor'lam eat that comes from ocean. No, Tor'lam not make fun of little warrior. Little warrior fiercest warrior of whole people. Little warrior is leader of people. Tor'lam know what little warrior is. Tor'lam call little warrior Chief," he promised.

"Chief, I'm not a chief. I'm only a man fighting for freedom. This isn't my army. I'm just a man," protested Kale.

"Chief does not want to be chief. Only bad chiefs want to be chief." At this Tor'lam stood and walked back into the darkness.

* * *

The next morning Kale awoke to the sound of a large group arguing outside of his tent. His limbs still ached, and the stiff, dry dessert air had heated the tent into an oven. The feeling was unpleasant in its physical aspects, but the familiarity of sweat running down his face and his clothes clinging to his body brought back distinct memories of his home. The home he had left nearly twenty years ago. Makko sat lazily by the entrance ignoring the commotion outside as he basked in a slanted beam of light that penetrated into the darkness of the tent.

Making his way to his feet, Kale put on his mask and hood before making his way outside to check out what was going on. As he leaned down to duck under the flap of the tent, the multitude of arguing voices quickly came to a standstill. Zube stood complacently next to the tent examining the social behavior of this unorganized flock of humanity.

One of the men stepped forward out of the crowd. "Kale, sir, we are terribly low on food, and our water supply will be depleted today. The men do not know how to ration themselves. We took enough to make it to the Earth Kingdom, but we are less than a sixth of the way there and these gorging animals have depleted it." The man had obviously been in the army, possibly even a foot soldier for the Fire Kingdom. Kale saw an immediate need to organize the men. Fifty men all taking command of this group would bring about utter chaos. Kale had never commanded men before nor did he have a desire to do so now, but Zube had already ingrained a sense of responsibility over these men into his being. He could not turn away from them now.

The men stood silently awaiting Kale's decision. Kale had rarely in his life felt embarrassed, but standing there in the sun with hundreds of eyes settled on him brought the blood flowing into his cheeks. As a leader, Kale knew they could not see such petty emotions, and the mask around his face worked to guard both the world from him and his weakness from the world. "Who here has served in an army?"

Several hands went up, along with the specked, "I have," that sounded in from the back.

"Come forward then," he commanded. Roughly thirty men stepped forward, and, not to Kale's surprise, the spokesman for the group placed himself at the front. "How many of you men here were scouts?" A rough handful of six signified they had been. It was time for Kale to set an order to this madness. His choices here would decide if this group of men were to survive the week. Spending a week fully rationed after speeding away with their freedom was an easy task compared to keeping the men rationed and organized for a long period of time. Over a thousand starved and thirsty men that would brawl over a slice of bread if given the chance. This situation would stress even the most experienced leaders. Kale lifted his finger to the spokesman. "You, sir, what is your name?"

The man stepped forward almost out of instinct. "Caos, sir, I fought with you at the ramp though I doubt you would remember me." Kale had to change the flow of the conversation. Favortism or personal attachment to these men could cause more trouble than it was worth. "Very well, I'm putting you in charge of the scouting parties. Each scout will recruit five men and canvas the area. There is a plant called yukata. It has small purple flowers with a yellow core. Have any of you scouts encountered this?" Many acknowledged they were familiar with it. "If it is around, you will find it in patches of several hundred. Collect all you can and bring it back. That will provide some liquid and food sources. Also scouts, while you are out, you are to keep your eyes open for buffalo tracks. They feed off of the sand grass where it grows more thickly. That will be a primary food source if we are fortunate. Can you handle that, Caos?"

Caos gave a small suppressed grin. "Yes, sir."

Kale turned to the remaining men who had served. "Now, each of you make a line. You will command forty men each. After your roster is filled out, you will give me a list of every man who serves under you and their skills. Choose four men whom you feel stand out and put them over nine others. Those will be your squads. Caos will lead seven platoons along with the scouting party." At this Kale randomly selected seven of the newly appointed platoon leaders and signified their places. "Tor'lam, come forward, please."

From the side of the his tent, Tor'lam spoke. The sound was so close Kale almost jumped with surprise. "I am here already, little chief."

"So you are. Tor'lam will be over eight platoons." The men all started to murmur at the thought of subjecting themselves to this giant monster. Kale had to immediately take charge or his command would never last to do these men any good. "Silence! Tor'lam may speak slowly, but he had the courage and the intelligence to hold the ramp for the duration of the battle. Many of you know how feared he was in the arena. He has killed many men and led many men into battle. You will submit to his authority while you are here, or he will rip you in two."

The crowd of men became deathly silent. Kale quickly selected the eight men to serve under Tor'lam. Standing casually in the front of the line an older man leaned on a long stick. Clearly he had seen many battles. His face and arms were strewn with scars, and several of his fingers were missing. His long black beard and shaggy hair was streaked with grey, and he stood leaning on a makeshift spear. Kale was drawn to him. While all the other men were balking and chatting, he stood still, taking in the scene and absorbing information. Kale approached him. "You, sir, what is your name?"

"My name, well my name is of little importance. You can call me whatever you like. I've been just a number for some time now."

Now this was a man Kale was deeply interested in. Here was another man who stayed reserved to protect his past. "What would you be called then?"

"You may call me Druwen. I would have stepped forward, but I have never served in the Nations armies, nor do I plan to," he replied.

Kale stared into Druwen's eyes to gauge if there was any malice to this attempt. The man only stared back with his honest blue eyes. "This has become an army, not by my choosing, but it is what it has become. I, apparently, have been called to lead. Do you wish to stay with us?"

"We all have to belong to something. If not here, I would be a part of another group. I just have no intention in serving in a Nation's army. This is many men, but it is hardly a nation. We are but men keeping our necks from stretching. I'd rather be here, living free."

"Would you object to leading some of these men?" Kale asked him.

"I will do what I am called to do," Druwen assured him.

Kale stood back. Now this was truly a man of value. "You, sir, will lead the remaining eight platoons." With a slight step back, Kale drew himself up so that he might project his voice. "Now hear this! If we are going to be an army unto ourselves, we must have order. You are all free men. You may leave when you wish, but if you stay, you will keep order. You will respect those in command, or you will die. We do not have the political world to deal with. Either leave or stay and fight with us. Every man will work. Every man will pull his weight, and every man will stick to a ration allotted. We are free, and together we will stand against those who try to crush us. As one man we can be chained. As one man we can be subjected to cruelty. But, as an army, we can bite back!"

The men had now worked themselves up into a cheer. Kale stepped back into his tent. Why had he ended such a well or-ganized endeavor with a speech of grandeur? The men were in high spirits, and Kale could hear the men lining up to get as-signed to their platoon leaders. Zube came in grinning from ear to ear and chuckling like a child. "Oh, no, you don't want to lead! This isn't your army. 'As an army we can bite back'. Oh, Kale, you fool yourself. Every man of power is pulled into lead-ership. It is almost inevitable. Do what you must now, but make sure you don't get too attached with being at the top of the food chain. The speeches are all well and fine, but managing over a thousand men will not be as enjoyable. Just remember, I'm here to get you to Japada. As far as I'm concerned, these men are nothing more than a protection detail. But you have fun playing general."

Zube's words meant little at the time, but over the course of the next few weeks, Kale came to realize exactly what he had gotten himself into. Rarely had his eyes closed for more than an hour before someone came to interrupt him. Men got into brawls or didn't obey the leaders over them. Many of the lead-ers proved to be incompetent and had to be removed or rebuked.

211

Stores for the men fluctuated with what could be found during the travel. Even with the water and food rationed, many days the men went without, and Kale was bombarded with constant complaints and questions. Kale had finally grouped many of the more general items that came to his attention. Any issue with the supplies would be handled by Caos, and anything disciplinary would be handled by Druwen, except in rare circumstances. But, even after this delegation, Kale could barely sleep with the amount of demand on his time.

* * *

Kale sat around his camp fire eating a piece of buffalo that the scouting party had hunted down. Zube sat next to him examining some of his books. "Zube, I don't know if I can take this much longer. I'm not cut out for administration. I haven't walked more than thirty paces out of camp for over two months." Zube's only response was to look up and give a "you brought this on yourself" smile. "I know, I know, you warned me from the beginning, but really. What was I to do? I couldn't just leave these men behind, not when there was a chance."

"That's just it, Kale. You could have left them behind, but you chose not to. Now, I'm not saying one way or the other if it was right, but I tell you now, I believe all of these men should die before you are captured by Kain," Zube calmly stated.

Kale's face began to flush with anger. "Surely someone as enamored with the preservation of life would not condemn these men to death for me. It is better that I die to save even one of them than a thousand to die to save me."

Zube placed his books on the ground and rolled up his sleeves so that he could light his pipe. "Now, Kale, you know I hold life in high esteem, but you must understand. If these thousand or so die to save you, it is but a small loss compared to the hundreds of thousands that will die if Kain captures you."

"Am I really that dangerous? What could I possibly offer that would give cause for so many deaths," lamented Kale.

Zube stopped the lighting of his pipe, and his eyebrows furled as they did when he was speaking as seriously as he could. "It has nothing to do with your gifts. Wind Gehage or not, it makes no difference. You don't age, Kale. Don't you get it? When Kain becomes king, he can use his armies to conquer the lands. If he is only mortal, then so be it. A few years of turmoil and things will right themselves when he dies. But, if he is immortal, then what hope do the people of this world have? He will use his infinite life to slowly conquer the nations. He will live as a tyrant, an immortal tyrant over the people. We cannot let that happen."

Kale stood up and brushed the dust off of his pant legs. "I have to get a breather; I can't stay coupled up like this any longer."

Zube resumed reading his book. "Well, then take a breather. You're in command. You don't have to ask my permission. I'm sure your men can handle themselves for a bit. Just make sure you take your sword and a few men."

"I'll go out with one of the scouting parties. They're suppose to canvas ahead of us, and that should give me at least a half a day's peace from making decisions," he decided.

Scouting the Deadlands was nothing more than spreading out every hundred yards and walking briskly. Each patch of green or dip must be examined for a possible food or water source. It was a monotonous task, but to Kale, it was a sweet relief from the constant mental demands of the previous weeks.

Far in the distance, the slightly raised grey blotch indicated the location of a small town. Its clay wall could just be made out by the thin straight line that defined its edge. The necessity to speak over a hundred yards proved to be a challenge so the scouts resorted to cactus whistles. Kale sounded his whistle to indicate he had seen the town. A half mile later, the scouts whistled back to signify they saw the town as well.

As they got closer to the town, the scouts shortened their distance from Kale until they were huddled together behind a dune a few hundred yards from the wall.

Crouching down, Kale eyed the edges of the town looking for the guards. So far, no one had made their rounds. This pricked a warning in everyone's mind. Here in the sands, no town could relax their watch. This was very odd. Kale leaned forward and listened intently for signs of life. Not a sound. It was eerily silent. A light breeze picked up coming from the direction of the town, and faintly it brought to Kale's ears the sounds of a screaming woman and woven into the background the crying of a child. Something was, indeed, wrong. There could be no time to wait.

Jumping to his feet, Kale took off running at a swift pace, waving for the other scouts to follow. As he approached nearer the town, the signs of a recent siege littered the town. Guards laid lifeless in the ditches, and the tops of the walls were covered with blood. The main gate's doors had been ripped off their hinges. As Kale entered the town, the barren streets took him by surprise. His heart was racing with the expectation of action, but there was nothing awaiting him. No enemy to face. His hands clutched the handle on the sword that he had at sometime drawn by instinct in his sprint toward the town. "Keep your eyes and ears open men. Someone is here. I heard a woman and child screaming." Now that his heart had settled back down, he calmed himself and listened intently for any sound that would direct him. Then, as loud and clear as if they were next to him, he heard the sound of the woman screaming from somewhere to the right.

The group of scouts followed him as he moved down the streets. Again the scream rang out, but this time it was cut short. Kale came around the corner of the building just in time to see the limp body of a woman fall to the ground, a bloody mass. Above her stood a dark haired Wolfkin. It was black as the night, with fangs streaming with the woman's blood. His neck was wide and his head was broad. On both arms were bands of leather. His chest and legs were armored with black plate mail.

Upon seeing Kale and the other scouts, the beast reared its head and let off a deafening howl. Then it turned its bloodshot eyes toward Kale. "I thought we killed all the guards. Oh, well, more food for my clan." A trickling of rubble from the houses behind them brought their attention to two other Wolfkin leaping down from the rooftops. They were clad only in fur. Upon landing, they took the first few steps on all fours before standing up and waiting for orders. The armored Wolfkin began to snarl and took a step forward. "The hooded one is mine; you two take care of the rest."

The dark Wolfkin lunged forward. With just a second to spare, Kale dodged his claws. Immediately Kale could see that this was not going to be a regular battle. So far, all he had faced in combat were dwarfed in speed and strength. This Wolfkin was not his inferior, and from the first lunge, it was obvious that his speed was beyond any Kale had ever seen. As the Wolfkin

215

passed, Kale shifted his weight and brought his sword down across his back. The blade glanced off the armor, and within a moment the Wolfkin had spun around to engage his enemy. "So, you are no common guard." The Wolfkin sniffed in Kale's direction. His nose crinkled and his eyes squinted. "Yes, you are no common man, but neither are you a common Gehage. This could be interesting."

Swiftly the black paws of the Wolfkin darted out towards Kale. Each blow sought a vital vein. With labored dexterity, Kale leaped and twisted to avoid the blows and often taking an opportunity to make an attack. Then, a mistimed blow left Kale open, and the claws of the Wolfkin slashed down on his shoulder cutting through his pads and sinking deep into his flesh. Pulling back, Kale grabbed his shoulder and recovered his balance just in time to dodge a killing strike to his throat. A quick glance towards his fellow scouts displayed a pitiful sight. All but two of the scouts lay on the ground either dead or heavily wounded. The others were doing all they could to keep the claws and fangs of their foes at bay.

Kale's heart began to race from the pain and the sight of his fallen comrades. Now each blow from the Wolfkin seemed to come just a little slower until the blows were manageable. It was Kale's turn to draw blood. The Wolfkin's teeth came to a popping snap just inches from Kale's forearm. Taking advantage of this opportunity, Kale brought his blade down in a quick motion upon the Wolfkin's head. Deep into the flesh it sank until it hit the skull and was deflected. The blow was not delivered in vain. The Wolfkin stood dazed from the blow and laying on the ground in front of him was a large hunk of flesh along with his right ear.

This pause gave Kale a moment to check on his party. The sight was even more despairing than before. The two other Wolfkin were tossing the bodies of the last two to the ground and had begun their charge on Kale. The black Wolfkin resumed his assault with a heightened hatred while the other two wolfkin joined the fray. Now the blows came slowly but were many. Kale dodged and parried, moving about the street to gain an advantage by putting distance between his attackers. Slowly, Kale's energy began to lessen. Each blow by the Wolfkin came closer and closer to hitting its mark.

From down the street, the sound of hooves could be heard on the rough earth street . In second long glimpses as he dodged the blows, Kale perceived a rider clad in a large red cloak that hung down over one side. Relief was on its way. Moments later one of the Wolfkin groaned in pain as a spearhead pierced its chest. The cloaked figure urged his horse forward and leapt at full speed onto the ground, hitting squarely on his feet in a dead run and engaging the remaining Wolfkin. Kale turned his attention to the armored Wolfkin. Now that the battle had been evened up, the blows were easier to dodge as both were close to exhaustion.

From the background, the wail of the other Wolfkin pierced the battleground, and, stepping to his side, the cloaked warrior took his stand. The black Wolfkin looked at his opponents. Realizing that now his chances of success were very small, he backed away. "This isn't over, Gehage. I know your scent, and I will have my vengeance. We will finish this." With a leap, he mounted the nearest roof and began his massive flights from rooftop to rooftop until he cleared the wall and disappeared out of view.

217

The caped stranger turned to Kale. "Looks like I came just in time, friend."

Kale sheathed his blade and stretched out his hand. "That you did, and I am very thankful for it." The caped man sheathed his blade somewhere under the cape that covered his left side and shook Kale's hand. This man was older. His curly black hair was specked with gray, and his cheeks were lined with the onset of an early wisdom. His eyes were very familiar to Kale. They gave him a warm feeling of peace. The man took his cape and flung it over his shoulder as he turned to look at the fallen scouts. "Your men are very hurt. We should attend to them." It was at this moment that Kale saw the amputated limb. How could it be? Looking up into the man's face, Kale addressed him directly. "Latus?"

The man's brow crinkled as he gazed back at Kale. "Apparently you know me, friend, but I have yet to place you. Would you be kind enough to remove your mask?"

Kale had long gotten used to his mask and upon removing it the fear of the open space pounded down upon him. Only the joy of finding his friend of years past could he master the urge to put the hood back on. As his face was revealed, Latus's eyes widened. "Who is your father boy? What kind of joke is this?"

"This is no trick, Latus, and I am no boy. I am the very Kale who left you at the great gate so many years ago in the back of my friend, Reagan's, cart. I know it may seem odd, but I do not age. I am so glad to see you again, old friend," Kale assured him.

A moment's hesitation commenced as Latus examined this youth in front of him. "It is you," he said. Then Latus broke out in a burst of laughter as he embraced Kale. A groan from the fallen men brought the two to their senses, and they quickly ran to attend to the men's wounds. As they were bandaging the men who were not yet dead, a faint cry from a nearby barrel caught Kale's attention. As Kale walked over to the barrel, it moved ever so slightly. Upon lifting the lid, Kale saw a young child no more than twelve but very petite crouching down. Turning to Latus, he pointed to the body of the women "Latus, my friend, would you be so kind as to cover that body? I have found a child hiding."

As Latus gently covered the body with his large red cloak, Kale lifted the child out of the barrel. She was very weak and had a gash across her arm from one of the Wolfkin. "Dear child, you are safe now." The child did not speak but buried her face in his arms and sobbed. After burying his dead soldiers and taking a stranded cart, Kale loaded up the wounded and made his way back to camp with Latus at his side.

NINE

****

ENEMY ALLIANCE

Walking next to Latus after all these years helped Kale to forget the pain of his shoulder. "Latus, you must tell me how Reagan is. What happened to you two after I was captured?"

"Oh, that horrid day so long ago. Yes, I remember it well. After you were taken Reagan fromed a group of volunteers to go and retrieve you. They left and came back shortly after. Reagan was in tears. He said he had found your charred body lying in the dirt next to a freshly deserted camp. I've never known a man who grieved the loss of a friend so much. I believe it was your death, or should I say your presumed death, that drove him to be the way he is."

"I'm sure that would be hard to endure." Then, looking Latus in the eyes, he asked, "What do you mean 'the way he is'?"

Latus lifted his hand slightly, "Oh, it's not a bad thing. Don't get the wrong impression. I won't go into too much detail as I want to leave his story to his own telling, but he was changed that day. Your sacrifice for us set him on a course that has won him great honor and....well, great infamy. Since that day he has been obsessed with protecting the Stone Kingdom people from the Fire Kingdom. It has cost him much, and he has been through some very treacherous perils but has stood his ground. The people know him as their defender and now hold out hope he can hold back the armies of the Fire."

"He always talked about joining the Stone Kingdom armies. I'm not surprised to see him leading men against the Fire Kingdom. You talk as if he is actively doing this. Is he fighting at the great wall? I was led to believe the Fire Kingdom mounted an attack there. I could only assume they were successful."

Latus gave a look of dismay "Oh, the battle still rages on. Though Reagan has been abandoned by the Stone army, he and his men still hold their ground at the gate. Why the King has pulled his troops away from what seems to most the obvious place of weakness is beyond me. Though I assume he is protecting what is most valuable to himself, his gold mines.

Reagan, on the other hand, values the people and has set himself against the king by standing his ground. He has lost many men. That is why I am here now. I just came from the Leaf Kingdom petitioning for help, but their councils work too slowly to be of any help. The battle will be decided on before they can decide whether or not to meet to decide what to do. I am left to my only hope. I have been told there is a renegade army wandering the Deadlands. I must find these renegades and hope beyond hope that they can be hired to come to Reagan's aid."

Behind the mask Kale smiled deeply. Deciding to let his position in this army be a surprise, he kept walking silently. Many minutes later they mounted a small hill and could see the army encamped close to a small stream. Latus's face brightened with surprise. "Oh, Kale, you sly thing, why didn't you tell me you belonged to such an army? You must introduce me to the leader so that I may make my petitions."

"All in due time, Latus. I assure you, you will have your sentiments heard." Kale replied.

The wagon pulled up into camp, and the men quickly started bandaging the wounded. "This way, Latus, the leader's tent is just a bit further." As they approached the tent, two guards parted and allowed Kale and Latus to enter. When the flap was closed behind them, Kale sat down on a pile of furs exhausted from the day's work.

Latus took his seat as well. "I guess your leader is not at his tent. Should we wait for him? I hope he hurries. Every hour is precious."

Zube entered, carrying a book and his lit pipe. "Oh, Kale, you've returned, and I see you ran into some trouble. Can you ever be left alone?"

Latus stood and bowed, "Dear sir, may I introduce myself. My name is Latus. I knew Kale many years ago, and, forgive me for being forward, but I must beg your assistance. Please, sir, will you hear my request?"

Zube's bushy whisping eyebrows furled, and then he laughed openly. "Me? Surely you are being jested with; I am not the leader of this ravel, no not me. If it is the leader of these men you seek, you only have about three feet to travel. He rests, smirking under that mask, in this very tent."

Latus turned and smiled an embarrassed grin, "You? You are the leader of these men?"

"My apologies, Latus, I did not mean to jest with you. I just couldn't help myself. Yes, these men follow me though I do not hold anything over them. They are free to come and go as they please. As for your request, I see it fit to leave it to the men to decide."

Zube blew out a puff of smoke as he questioned, "And what request is this?"

Again Latus put on a pleading air. "Reagan, both Kale's friend and mine, is fighting with his men to protect the great wall. He has been able to hold off the attacks for now, but he

222

cannot hold out much longer without men. The Stone Kingdom has abandoned the people and ran to protect their mines. We need men, sir, men willing to fight the Fire Kingdom. I have a fair sum of money from my father-in-law's estate. It's only a diamond mine, but I'm sure that I can provide payment to your men and ensure they are fed and clothed during their stay."

Zube put down his books on a small table and pulled a stool out of the corner to sit on. "As Kale said, we'll need to put that to the men though I see it solving a few issues we've been wondering about lately." Then, turning his gaze to Kale, Zube said, "Did you tell him? You know you must."

Kale cleared his throat before speaking. "I cannot go with you, Latus. I must continue my journey to Japada. It is imperative that the Fire Kingdom not get their hands on me."

The color from Latus's face went pale. "You...you will not accompany us. But, Kale, you do not know what this will do to Reagan. You, of all people, cannot shrink from battle. It would devastate him."

Kale's hands wavered in the air as he tried to vocalize his reasons, but after a few seconds, his hands went back to his sides and his head leaned a bit forward in frustration. Zube chimed in from the background to give him assistance. "Latus, you must understand. Kale does not wish to run from battle. To be honest, I can't seem to keep him out of it. But he holds a power too great for the Fire Kingdom to control. The new prince has found a way to steal the power of other beings to survive."

"I still do not understand what makes Kale so powerfully dangerous," Latus said.

"Don't you understand, my friend? I do not age, and I heal rapidly. If the Fire king were to get a hold of me, he would gain

223

these abilities. Would you want that kind of a leader for the Fire Kingdom? Would that not cause more harm than me coming to Reagan and giving him a short joy? No, it saddens me that I cannot come to his aid, and I hope that one day we will see each other again. But I must continue my journey for his sake as well as ours."

With disappointment, Latus waved his hands. "I see your point, but it will not make it any easier to break it to Reagan. He may understand more than I do. Please promise me you will find a way to see him again. I know it would bring him great joy. He has had so little these few years."

"I do not plan to hide forever. I must strengthen myself so that one day I can stand against the Fire Kingdom. At this time I don't stand a chance against the Fire Kingdom Gehage and even less against their king. Give Reagan my best. I promise one day I will visit him," Kale solemnly said.

The tent flap opened allowing a burst of light and fresh air to rush in, overtaking Zube's pipe smoke. Caos stepped in, "Kale, sir, the girl you brought back is very sick. She's running a high fever, and the other soldiers who were injured have died."

Zube put down his pipe, "Bring her to me."

A few minutes later Caos came back leading two guards who were carrying the girl on a stretcher. Caos pointed to the table, "Lay her down here."

The girl was streaming with sweat. Her clothing stuck to her body, and every breath was labored and slow.

Kale stood and examined her while Zube rummaged through a trunk. "What's wrong with her, Zube? She didn't look that badly wounded."

"She is suffering from the poison in the Dark Paw's claws.

Those foul beasts are riddled with parasites and disease. Their claws carry such horrible poison that it will kill most who are cut deeply with it," Zube explained.

Kale's heart sank with despair. "Zube, you must know how to save her. I can't bear to watch one so little die. Is their anything I can do?"

"Yes, Kale, there is. You can go outside and let me do what I can. I have the herbs here, but it may be too late."

With a nod, Kale left the tent to wait with the others. Each minute added more and more stress as Kale paced like an expectant father, every cry or groan enticing him to run back into the tent to save her. With each attempt, Latus outstretched his hand to prevent him from entering. "She will be okay, Kale. Either she will be healed, or she will find rest with her parents. Either way, she will be okay."

Zube requested bucket after bucket of water to be brought in. Each time a guard brought another in, he would carry out one full of blackish red liquid.

"If only I would have come sooner. I could have gotten there and saved her parents, too," Kale said.

"You can't blame yourself for every awful thing that happens. Sometimes that is just the way it is. You can only confront the things in front of you. The things behind you matter little," replied Latus.

After what seemed like an eternity, Zube appeared. His sleeves were rolled up and surprisingly his gauntlets were not on his arms. His face poured with sweat, and he looked as if the life had been drained out of him. "Water, I need some water."

Then he lowered himself down on a log to rest. "She may live, but she'll need to be tended to by a Leaf shaman. They have the medicine to treat her now. The poison destroyed much of her internal organs. I've repaired them the best I can, but her system will need to heal."

Latus lowered his head in thought. "Kale, you received some very nasty slashes from that brute. You should have Zube take a look at it before it sets in like it did with her."

Zube gave a half smirk. "Latus, my boy, you don't understand yet. Kale is immune to poison. His body treats it like anything else, a consumable resource. Everything that passes through him is broken down into its basic form, Energy."

Latus sent a questioning eye to Kale. "Yes, I can see why it would be wise to keep you out of this new Fire king's grasp. Ancient life, vast healing ability, and impervious to just about anything; truly that would not be the best thing for this king to possess."

"Latus, I know we haven't seen each other in many years, but I am the same person as before. I bleed just like the next. I can die. I am not immortal. I'm just a bit harder to kill than most. But, still I agree, I need to keep my distance until I am strong enough to face his armies. I just hope Reagan understands."

While Zube prepared the girl for the trip to the Leaf Kingdom, Kale called together his officers to discuss the proposal in front of them. Sitting in a circle in his tent, they began discussing what must be done.

***

Kale stood, "Good, so it is decided. The army will assist Reagan at the wall. I am sorry that I cannot come with you, but I'm sure you can see why. I will go to Japada to prepare for an assault on the Fire Kingdom. It will take time but I must do what I can to keep the Fire Kingdom at bay."

Druwen walked over to a chest that he had brought in with him. "Kale, we were going to wait to give this to you when we reached Japada, but I guess now is just as good a time. One of the men is an armorer and we salvaged enough materials to make it." He then reached in and pulled out a shield and a leather chest plate. The shield was brandished with the crest of Makko with his limp leg and scarred face etched within a triangle which decorated the background and on each point were strange words of a language unknown to Kale.

"This is a very fine shield, Druwen. Thank you. Thank you all. What do these words say?" he asked.

Druwen replied, "Strength, Courage, and Wisdom. Zube helped us with the wording. He says it is of the gnome language."

"You had a hand in this too, Zube. Well, you do keep secrets." smirked Kale.

Druwen next presented the leather chest. "We have been saving the hides of the buffalo in the area to make these. We felt you should have the first one. The armorer is very gifted."

Kale took the leather. It was blacked with dye and in white stitches the same symbol as the shield was imprinted on the upper right chest region. On the left shoulder were the markings of a general, and on the right where the nation's symbol would normally be were wording in the common tongue. It read 'The Kalian Army'.

"You all honor me beyond my merit. I only did what was within my power, nothing extraordinary." Kale was beyond honored.

Caos, Kale's lead scout, now stood. "Oh, sir, you did much more than that. Your courage saved us all from an awful death at that prison. Your strength kept us together in this barren land, and your wisdom has kept us all alive. That is why we chose those words for the crest. No one could do what you have done. No one could have stood their ground at the front of that line and held back such an army. No one would have tried to sacrifice his life to save us by jumping off of that tower. We all saw how drained you were keeping us together. You were the first one up and the last to sleep. You ate last and the least, and you worked twice as hard. You showed us how to find food and how to work as an army and not a group of bandits. No, Kale, you of all people deserve our respect."

Now Tor'lam stood. "I speak now, little chief. You save Tor'lam and give him home. Men fear me, but now men follow me. Tor'lam serve little chief until Tor'lam close eyes for deep sleep."

Each officer spoke his peace. Fortunately for Kale, his mask covered his face hiding his emotions. If the men were to see how deeply this affected him, it might dampen this image of the strong leader they had built him up to be. After they were done, Kale put on his new armor. "I will miss you all very much. I will not forget any of you and will hasten to ready myself to face the Fire Kingdom. Every man here has proven himself worth the weight of any ten Fire Kingdom soldiers. I thank you, again, for your kindness."

As the men were leaving, Kale requested Caos to stay behind. "Caos, my friend, I need a favor of you. I must travel with Reagan and the girl but I need someone to run ahead and get the shaman from Katela, the Leaf Kingdom capital."

Smiling, Caos replied, "Of course, sir, I would be glad to be of service." After a pause he began again, "Sir, I have a request.

I am not shy in battle so I beg you not to get that impression, but I wanted to make a request. I would like to accompany you on your journey."

"I do not know when I will be able to make it back to the army, but you're welcome to come. I assure you it will not be a safe passage. We must pass through the Black Paw Territory and then through the Gray Paw's Territory before we reach the Japada gate.

"Sir, I do not fear death. I feel that my destiny is closer to your path than the armies. I hope you understand. I will serve you well," promised Caos.

"I have had enough of being treated as a king, Caos. Until I rejoin the army, I am just Kale," he insisted.

"Yes, sir, I understand," Caos said.

"No need to call me sir, Caos. Kale will work fine."

"Of course, sir, I understand," he replied.

"What I mean is...ah, well, never mind. You need to hurry. Do you know the way?" Kale asked.

"Yes, sir, I already anticipated the need and have reviewed the maps for the quickest route. I have two copies. One for the scout going. I guess in this case it is me, and one for you, sir," he replied.

"You are a very efficient scout, Caos. I will be glad to have you," Kale assured him.

"By my calculations, we should converge somewhere around the edge of the Delimar," Caos said.

"The Delimar?" asked Kale.

Zube stepped closer to the two. "Caos, you should hurry. I will get things taken care of here. We have no time for history lessons. Let's pack up and go."

"Yes, sir." At this, Caos quickly left the tent and the sound of him tossing on his pack and taking off at a run was clearly heard over the din of the army breaking camp outside.

"We must go, Kale, or the girl will not survive. The men have already packed the cart. You will need to pull it though. I am drained," Zube said.

Night was falling, and Kale pulled the cart in a furious pace. Makko would fly above circling them and occasionally fly down next to Kale for a moment and run beside him. For the first night Zube slept. He always seemed drained of life, but rarely had Kale seen him sleep so much. Plowing through the roughly formed roads and paths was amazingly easy. Each hour Kale waited for his energy to deplete, but his zeal to save this poor little creature seemed to keep him fueled with an endless resource.

After the third day, Kale came to the edge of the thick woods. This was the edge of the Leaf Kingdom's main borders. It wouldn't be much further before he reached the capital. The roads indicated it was only thirty miles. Stopping only to eat a bite of food and to feed the girl they pushed on. Zube still slept nearly the entire time, and the journey would have been lonely except for Makko and his visits from the sky. Knowing that his friend was circling above ready to swoop down and help him was comforting. The next day they came to the edge of a vast grassy field. Deep in the distance, the outline of another set of trees was visible very tall and geometrically placed. Kale assured himself that must be the Delimar.

The next few miles went by at a frightening speed. With the goal in sight Kale pushed on at a hectic pace. The girl was growing weaker, and he knew every minute counted. To his surprise, he did not feel weaker for all of the constant pushing. On the contrary, he felt very much stronger and contained more energy than he ever had before. Pulling this load for so many miles at such a pace had strengthened him. As he approached the Delimar, he saw a small camp set up on the edge of the road. Even from a distance he could see Caos running towards him. As he approached, he gave a slight bow. "Sir, you made amazing timing. We only just got here from the capital. Let me assist you with this cart. You must be exhausted."

"I am fine, Caos. Just run ahead and make sure they are ready for the girl. There is no time to lose. She is very sick. I'm not sure, but I think there might even be something wrong with Zube. He has never slept this much," Kale explained.

"Yes, Sir, I will see you at the camp," Caos said.

* * *

As Kale entered the camp an old man in green and brown robes briskly walked to the cart. "Oh, dear me, Zube. It is true. Caos bring the girl and Zube into my tent. Halos get this young man some food and water. Hurry now. There is not much time."

"Sir, will they be okay? What is wrong with Zube?" Kale questioned worriedly.

"Young man, I don't know yet. I'll tell you what I find, but we can't waste any time. Hurry now. Hurry," he insisted.

Again Kale sat outside of a tent awaiting news of how those around him would pull through. Sitting, deep in thought, he contemplated the surrounding area. The edge of this Delimar was strange. All of the trees on one side were tall pines. On the other side each tree was an oak. The ones in front seemed newly planted, but, as it progressed back, the trees got larger and larger

231

as did their age. Each was placed a specific space apart giving the lanes of trees a narrowing appearance as it moved off in the distance.

A feminine voice of elegant grace penetrated his thoughts, "Hello, you must be this Kale Caos speaks of so highly."

Kale turned to see who was addressing him. Standing before him was a young lady. Unlike the two women who stood behind her, she did not wear elegant gowns but instead a full set of leather armor. She was nothing like the tales he had heard of the female Leaf Kingdom warriors who were so rare. She did not dress in scanty clothing to draw attention to herself. Nor did she remove vital pieces of armor to expose her flesh to entice the men she served with. Everything was in its place, and everything fit to best enable her to fight in battle. Her eyes were not one of meek submission nor was her stance. She truly was a thing of beauty.

"It is Kale, isn't it? I assume there are not too many masked generals of this Kalian army," she inquired.

Recognizing that he had been addressed and yet unable to speak, Kale began, "Yes, my name is Kale. My apologies, I have had a long journey. My mind wonders. Whom do I have the honor of addressing?"

"I am Rea. My father is tending to the girl you brought. I am very interested to meet this Zube. Father has spoken of him for as long as I can remember," Rea told Kale.

"Your father knows Zube?" Kale asked.

"Yes, Zube raised my father from a very young age. He taught my father the healing arts. I hear Zube is a great man," Rea answered.

"He is wise and an idealist to be sure. I am worried about

him," confessed Kale.

The old man stepped out of the tent and walked over to the small group. "Welcome, Kale. I am Platos. I see you have met my daughter, Rea. The girl is responding well to the treatment, but we will not know for a few days how she will pull through. As for Zube, well, maybe you can help me persuade him to help himself. There is nothing I can do for him."

"Just tell me what to do, and I will," promised Kale.

"Come with me. Rea, you must wait here. I know how anxious you are to meet him, but you must control your curiosity for now," her father told her.

Kale entered the tent. The girl seemed to be sleeping, and Zube lay on the cot sweating and shivering. "What is wrong with him, Platos?"

"He absorbed the poison from the girl to try and save her life. His body is fighting it, but it is so weakened that he may not be able to overcome it," explained Platos.

"You said that he could help himself. What must he do?" Kale asked.

Zube's weak voice echoed out, "Platos, you and I both know that I cannot do what you ask. It is too dangerous."

"Zube, it would only be for a moment. Just take off those infernal shackles and that disc. You will be better in a few minutes, and then, if you wish, you can put them back on," Platos told Zube.

Zube rolled over, putting his back to the group, "I will wear these shackles to my death. I will never let that happen again."

Kale stood, staring in confusion for a moment. "What is he talking about, Platos?"

"If he didn't tell you, it isn't my place to. Nor will anyone

233

else speak of it. We must begin the journey back to the capital. To get to Japada, you will need to go out the northern road. If he hasn't beaten the poison by then, he will be dead," Platos explained.

The camp packed up, and Kale was able to ride one of the extra horses. It was a new experience. Kale had only ever ridden a mule, and that was to bring it to a trader it had escaped from. While they rode, Rea often would ride next to him.

"Rea, I have a question for you. What is the Delimar?" Kale asked.

"You don't know. The Delimar is where we bury our dead. Each of the eight families has a section of the forest. At birth we are given a necklace like this one. Reaching inside her armor she pulled out a gold chain with a small glass container on the end; inside it rested a seed. "When we die, we are planted in the ground, and the bulb is broken. The tree grows above us and consumes our essence so that we live on in the great trees," she explained.

"That is an interesting tradition," Kale commented.

"What do you do in your country, Kale?" Rea asked.

"I have no country, Rea. I am from the Deadlands. My people consist of misfits of various people trying to survive outside the nation's control. Most of the land is sandy desert so when we die, we burn the bodies and cover the bones with whatever rocks we can find. This keeps the animals from eating our dead," Kale explained.

Rea made a disapproving motion of her nose and mouth. "That is an...interesting tradition, as well."

Kale would have told her any number of interesting traditions to see her crinkle her nose just once more. As the day moved on, he began to make reasons to ride next to her, and she seemed to do the same. They sat down to dinner next to a secluded fire. Her assistants were always watching over her, and her father kept a close eye on them both. They sat on a fallen birch tree where one of it's saplings had taken root next to its felled parent. Rea was tending to it and removing the surrounding weeds.

Rea sat for a moment. "You seem different from the young men. So much more aged in mind," she said finally.

"I am much older than I look. I still feel like a youth in body, but I am much older than you may expect," he told her.

"Why do you hide your face, Kale? I still haven't seen what you look like," Rea said.

"Oh, it is not my face I hide but the world I hide from myself. Open spaces frighten me," he explained.

"Frighten you! Oh, I find that hard to believe. Caos has told us all tales of your heroic feats in battle. He speaks as if you were invincible," Rea exclaimed.

"Caos has an overreaching zeal. I do what I must to protect those around me. That's all any man can do, I guess," he modestly answered.

Rea moved closer to Kale. "May I see? I want to see what you look like."

Kale hesitated for a second. The trees were spaced out so that the sky could be clearly seen. This place felt overwhelming. But, how could he deny her such a request? Maybe it would make her nose wrinkle up again. Slowly he removed the hood and unwrapped his face, closing his eyes by instinct to shield himself from the immenseness of the world around him. Then, through the darkness, her thin fingers, chilled with the night air, touched his face. His eyes opened, and he could see her staring in amazement at him. "You look just like him. It is amazing. Your body is very young, but I can tell in your eyes that you have seen much."

Then she leaned in and kissed him. Never in all of Kale's life had something felt so good. The world around him went into a haze. If the phantom world he had entered into when he lost control of his anger was the extent of anguish then this was the other side of the coin. This was ultimate bliss. As they parted, Kale looked toward the camp and was startled to see Rea's father, the guards, Rea's assistants, and even Caos standing next to them as if they had rushed over and were halted by something. Kale turned his head. Before them no longer stood a small sapling but an aged tree well into its adulthood sprouting with flowers.

Kale wrapped his head up again while everyone stood staring at the tree. He broke the silence, "Wow! Rea, how did you do that?"

"I...I didn't," she stammered.

The sound of flapping wings ended the inquiry into the mystery of the blossoming tree. Through the light of the fire, the majestic landing of Makko struck awe into the would-be group of heroes. Makko landed next to Kale. With an unusual sense of urgency, Makko tucked his wings in and began to pace next to the tree line, snapping his jaw at some unknown element.

"Something is wrong; Makko never acts like this unless he is protecting me. Keep a look...". From the edge of the darkness a black figure sprang into the air towards Kale. Makko checked it with a leap of his own, ramming his body into the figure and sending it to the ground only to have it spring up quickly to its feet. Now that it had been knocked into the light, it was clear it was a Black Paw. With a deadly lunge, it made another attempt at Kale. By this time, Kale had armed himself with his blade, but this Black Paw was uncommonly quick. Between the twilight merging with his shadowy form, each attack from the beast was cloaked by the natural shadows of night.

Only seconds into the fight, Kale found himself thrown to the ground by a heavy blow. Makko took his position over Kale spreading his wings to protect him, but to Kale's surprise, Makko was not the only one standing in the gap between this assassin and his prey. Caos and Rea both drew their swords and took a stance.

Caos made a preemptive charge on the beast, only to receive a nasty slash on his shoulder pad while Rea chose to wait until the beast made its attack. Each of the guards rushed in to attempt to ward off the creature. All but one lay at the Wolfkin's feet, sprawled in the death squirm as their lives drained from them.

Now that the odds were more in the favor of the beast, it charged forward to thwart this last line of defense. Kale had regained his feet, but each breath was labored as the wound in his chest seemed to suck the life from his body. This Black Paw carried that deadly poison in its claws. The beast advanced and began to spring and dart from side to side as it closed in. Such dexterity could only be rivaled by a rabbit racing to its home.

Finally the beast clashed with Rea. Kale couldn't steady himself enough to go to her aid, but, through the haze of his injured state, he could see she didn't need his help. Each claw was parried or blocked with skillful success. Finally, with a half turn, Rea pulled a second blade from her back. Before the creature knew otherwise, Rea spun and took its head from off its shoulders.

Kale attempted to take a step forward, but, in doing so, he lost his footing. The haze around him began to close in. Just when he thought he would slip into darkness, he felt a warmth encircle his body, and all of the cold chill and darkness turned into energy and light. The poison now began to be absorbed by his body and converted into pure energy. Rea's face leaned over his prostrated body. "Kale, are you okay?" she whispered.

"Yeah, I guess I am. It just took me a minute. Are you okay?" he asked.

"Yes, I will be fine. Father, help him, please," she said.

Kale sat up and wiped the blood from his chest. The wound had already stopped bleeding. "No, I will be fine. It appears my body is getting more used to healing itself."

Reaching down, Platos helped Kale to his feet. "The more you are wounded, the more accustomed your body will become to healing itself. It seems you have led a painful life so far. We need to pack up camp and go deeper into the Delimar. It seems we are being tracked by the Black Paw. That is one of their scouts, not one of their assassins. He must have known Makko had discovered him. There is no time. We must move now."

Each day the group traveled into the Delimar brought Kale closer to Rea. Zube was showing signs of progress, but it was still unsure if he would pull through. Platos attended to him regularly, but it seemed he was not without his own health issues. Kale saw him hiding a bloody rag that he coughed into from Rea on many occasions. Kale prided himself on the study he did of the sicknesses and healing remedies. Zube always seemed especially passionate about these sessions. But, this sickness was something Kale knew couldn't be healed with roots or medicine. It couldn't be healed with water healing or a change of climate. Platos was dying of old age, and his body was failing. How long would it be? Did Rea know?

After many days they reached the walls surrounding Katela. The Leaf Kingdom capital reached far into the sky as the large building climbed the mountain. Each road ran in a perfect arch allowing for easy travel and outlined the city in perfect semetry. Kale had always imagined the tree lovers dwelling in the tops of trees like rogue warriors, but this was no fairytale. Most houses were larger than the rich estate homes in Durian. They were carved from the finest oaks and decorated with marvelous wood workings and carvings. It was a beautiful sight to see at a distance. Platos had gone to talk with the counsel. Apparently, the guard had indicated an issue with allowing the group to enter into the city. Shortly afterwards Platos returned. His brow was furled and reddened with anger.

"Kale, my friend, I am sorry, but the council will not allow Zube into the city. We will give you all the provisions you need and allow you to travel along the outer road to the north to continue your journey to Japada." His hands dropped to his side in frustration, "I am sorry."

Rea stepped forward in her usual haste. "Father, how can they do this? Zube is a great man. Why, father?"

"My child, there are parts of history that even our people chose not to repeat. If Zube hasn't made it known, I will not betray that secrecy," he insisted.

"Then, I will go with them, Father. The Black Paw are only days behind. I am sure. We cannot leave them alone like this," she declared.

Platos' hands were raised in protest, but his words could only agree with the council. "I'm sorry, Rea. The council has their motives. But, Rea, you must bend to reason. Even if you outrun the Black Paw to the Gates of Japada, you have to do it by traversing through the Gray Paw Territory. It is too dangerous, my child. I cannot allow you to go."

"I won't leave them alone, father. We both know I have experience fighting the Wolfkin. Your guards are no match for them. I must escort them, at least until Zube is feeling better," she said.

* * *

It took two days to get the group to the northern part of the city. At night the sound of large wolves could be heard in the distance. Their howls filled the air in response to a very close wolf's summons. It would not be long until the Wolfkin closed the gap.

The entrance into the Japada forest gave Kale both a sense of hesitation and comfort. The woodland area grew so thickly that visibility was limited to a few dozen yards at best. But, this wood also gave the added comfort of seclusion. The tree canopy blocked out the majority of the sky, making it both dark and enclosed. After the first hundred yards into the woodland path, Kale removed his hood. The relief of being able to expose his face without the overcoming fear of the wide space enabled him to admire Rea more freely.

Zube was also benefiting from the new environment. The poison had begun to lose its effect on his body. This came as a great relief to the small troop who had been pulling his cart along. The guards and even Rea's father had little desire to track into this Wolfkin lair. Although for the few days' travel to the

Japada Pass entrance, Rea continually argued with her father about her decision to accompany Kale. He, in the end, had to give up on convincing her to stay.

But not everyone was particularly happy with the woodland area. Makko walked next to Kale for the first half of each day but found the confinement to the ground too much to bear. After licking Kale's hand with affection, he took to the trees until he had clawed his way through the canopy, glancing back at Kale just before taking to the sky. It was apparent that he was going on another one of his flights to heaven knew where.

Caos proved to be a capable guide as he cleared the path in front of the group. He was always diligent to check the parameter during every break, and when it finally came time to make camp, he insisted on taking the first watch. Sitting around the fire, Kale began to prepare the meal while Zube settled back into his old habit of smoking his pipe. He wasn't yet fully restored, but he was recuperating now. He had spoken very little the last few days. It seemed something was on his mind, and he was struggling with some inner turmoil. "Kale, how much have I told you about the Japada wars?"

"Not much, I'm afraid. Mostly we have focused on the Gnomish history and the political leanings of the four nations. Why?" asked Kale.

"Many years ago this forest not only belonged to the Wolfkin, but it was also inhabited by humans, gnomes, and even the Leiken. But, the Fire Kingdom was at war with the Earth Kingdom over a small strip of land. Japada had taken the Stone Kingdom's side in the matter, and the Fire Kingdom saw that as a declaration of war. They began a siege on the Japada city. The Fire king understood that he could not make it to Japada without the Wolfkin's assistance. Besides the fact that the gnomish war-riors guarded even the outposts, the woods were so thick with Wolfkin that they would not make it to the gate with enough men to take the city. So, the Fire king made a pact with the Wolfkin leaders. If each would join him in his battle, they could split the land after Japada fell. The Wolfkin clans had already been in a territory war with each other for years and both chiefs felt this could save their people any further bloodshed by providing enough land for both clans to survive."

"That is very interesting. I didn't know that, Zube. But I've seen the maps of this region. The pass is very large. How was it that the Wolfkin did not have room enough for two clans?" Kale asked.

"Oh, Kale, do not misunderstand the meaning. Clan may seem small to you, but it is how the Wolfkin address their group-ings. Each clan is made up of several packs. At one time, both clans had over thirty thousand Wolfkin warriors. Now, I am sad to say that the Black Paw retain the majority of their troops while the Gray Paw are reduced to only a few dozen packs."

Before continuing, Zube took a puff of his pipe. Caos rushed from the brush followed by Rea. Before speaking they both kicked dirt on the fire to put it out. In the darkness that fol-lowed Kale heard the sound of Rea drawing her swords. "They are very close. We have to hide. We cannot outrun them. Maybe they will pass by."

Standing, the group prepared themselves for the inevitable. Rea's voice carried little hope in stating that they may pass by. They all knew that it would only be a matter of time. The silence of the forest was only broken by the labored breathing of a few of the guards. The darkness was complete, and in the air the group could feel danger moving closer. Each second brought a stronger metallic taste to Kale's mouth. His senses began to get sharper as his nerves prepared for battle. Each second seemed like an eternity as the ears of the party strained to hear their pursuers. Nothing, the only sounds in this forest were their heaving chests.

In the darkness two green eyes began to glow. Then four, eight, sixteen, more, and more eyes appeared encircling the group until there was a veritable ring of green trapping them. Seconds passed without a sound; just a multitude of watchful eyes.

Zube's voice pierced the silence, "Kale, I think a little light would be in order."

Not knowing where his companions stood, Kale lifted his hand high above his head. In an instant he had formed a fireball that rested in his palm. The pack of Black Paws began to snarl when the light reached them. Their eyes were weakend by the sudden change in light.

Zube drew his cane as if it were a blade. "Stay close together. They will first try and thin us out. Don't leave the circle."

At that very instant one of the Wolfkin charged into the group. It met a quick fate at Rea's hand. With a smooth slice, its jaw separated from its body, and the Wolfkin fell to the ground moaning. One of the guards finished it off with a quick lunge. Seconds later a second charged. Only this time one of the guards became overconfident and went out to meet it. The second his body left the range of the party's weapons, two larger, more agile Wolfkin snapped his arm and leg in their jaws and drug him into the pack. His screams could be heard for many minutes.

Zube again made his appeal. "They are baiting us. Stay

together. Don't leave the circle." In the light of the flame, a familiar shape emerged to the front. Kale noticed the slashed ear and that familiar armor. He had fought this Wolfkin before. Standing silently, the Wolfkin kept his eyes on Kale; waiting for the moment to strike. Nearly an hour passed. Each member was growing weary of the relentless attacks of the Wolfkin. There was never more than two, but always they were testing and teasing, awaiting for a mistake that would allow them to separate a member from the group.

Already all but one of the guards had fallen to these schemes. Rea was almost taken twice, but her agility spared her. Kale could not understand why the Wolfkin kept their distance. Why did they not swarm them? What were they afraid of? His arm was getting tired of holding the flame. He had rarely held a flame of this strength for so long yet he could feel as if even the air around him was granting him energy. It was as if the situation itself called for a deeper well of strength.

Then the unexpected occurred. As the lone guard dodged out of the way, he bumped into Caos, sending him out beyond their reach. Instantly the Wolfkin clamped down on his arm and began to drag him away. Caos was able to cut the first Wolfkin off of him, but it would only be a matter of a second or two before the rest surrounded him. Out of reflex, Kale lunged the fireball in his hand toward the group approaching Caos. To his horror, he realized his folly for as soon as the light left the group, something clamped onto his arm and began to drag him away. The burning carcass of the Wolfkin gave enough light to see that his old foe had seized his opportunity to take Kale from the group.

His mind was clear as the pain shot through his body from the Wolfkin's iron jaws. His doom was fast approaching. In a few seconds he would be dragged into the horde of Wolfkin to be torn to pieces like the fate of the other men that day. The blood running from his flesh began to quickly cloud his vision. Then, a bright light filled the area, and the howling of the Wolfkin brought Kale back to the reality around him. The Wolfkin were scattering now. A ring of flame now encircled the group. The mauled Black Paw who had clamped onto his shoulder had retreated with the others. Kale's mind whirled, trying to decipher what had saved them. Had he created this wreath of flame? Something inside suggested not, but whom else had such ability?

Zube's strong grip pulled Kale to his feet. "Let's go boy. They won't pull back for long. We have to run. We have to get to the Gray Paw lands, or none of us will live to see daylight again." Kale was comforted by Caos who although injured was handling the pain pretty well. "Sir, are you all right?"

"Yeah, Caos. I'll be fine. Just give me a second to gain my bearings," Kale assured him.

Zube smacked Kale on the chest with his cane. "Hush, you fools."

Ria stepped ahead, guiding the now dwindled group through the black foliage. They were off the path now. Each step was taken with baited breath. The Black Paws now paid little attention to stealth. Their prey could easily hear their pursuit. The sounds of crunching branches and rustling leaves penetrated the darkness on all sides as the Wolfkin searched for their escaped prey. Rea's father trailed closely to Zube, peering into the darkness. A loud snap of twigs up ahead forced the small group into a tightly woven thicket. Once a din of some large game, it offered adequate cover.

245

Now that the fighting had reached a moment's respite, Kale's heart began to beat more steadily. His nerves remained on high alert as he took inventory of their group. Caos nursed his injuries while Zube gently applied the herbal remedy to counteract the poison working its way into his system. Rea stood guard with her father, and despite the old man's frailty, his stance denoted that he would hold his own when the time came. It seemed none of the guards had made it through the fray. This would, indeed, be an interesting night.

Close by another crunch of branches alerted Kale to the oncoming danger. A familiar voice echoed in the darkness. "I smell you boy. I will find you. And when I do, I will dine upon your flesh savoring each limb while you writhe in agony." The sound of two other Wolfkin's sneering laughter indicated the Black Paw was not alone. The slight breeze through the branches behind Kale's back subsided into a calm still. His mind raced to the conclusion the Wolfkin had found him and was blocking the airway. With a quick jolt, he lunged into the darkness of branches with his blade. A piercing howl rang out as the group stumbled out of the thicket and prepared to take what may be their last stance in this life. Learning from his previous mistake, Kale sent a flame into the thicket providing a light for the group to fight by and freeing up his hand.

Blind with fury, the armored Black Paw leapt with ferocious speed towards Kale, snapping his jaws. Kale dodged nimbly but with labored efforts to evade the death that awaited him should he hesitate. The sounds of the battle echoed around him as the others engaged the Wolfkin in battle. With each passing second, the blood in his veins pulsed more rapidly. The world slowed around him, and his foe's movements became easier to anticipate. With a quick step, Kale moved out of the way of this armored Black Paw and sent his blade deep into the back of his skull.

Now that his immediate threat was eliminated, he turned to check on Rea and the others. He was not surprised that during the battle more Wolfkin had moved in and surrounded them. But these Wolfkin were different. They were all armored and carried large blades attached to metal gloves. Their fur was light and reflected the firelight in an ominous way. Several had blades held to the necks of Rea and her father. A large group had surrounded Zube but were oddly keeping their distance with blades held high. These were not Black Paws but Gray Paws. It flashed into Kale's mind that with all of the fighting, the Gray Paw would surely be alerted to his group's intrusion into their lair. Kale began a futile onslaught to save his friends.

Zube stepped forward, and the Gray Paw around him flinched in fear. "Kale, steady yourself. They are not our friends, but, for now, neither are they our foes. Well, at least they are not your foes."

A large Gray Paw took a step toward Kale, his face hardened by years of war and famine. Although his armor and weaponry differed very little from the others, Kale could sense in his stride and the way the others looked at him that he was a seasoned leader.

His voice echoed out with labored words, each obviously foreign and difficult to remember as he addressed this young warrior. "Few have we seen of your kind who fight like the viper strikes. You move like the wind, young pup. But, you travel with dangerous company. You trespass on our land. Have your people not reduced our land far enough?"

Kale lowered his blade and relaxed his muscles. Looking down at the armored Black Paw who lay lifeless at his feet, he said, "We are on our way to Japada; we do not come to harm your people or to take your land. Let my friends go."

"My chieftains must decide the fate of your party, pup; they will not take kindly to the Bashert's presence."

Kale silently repeated the word 'Bashert' to himself. He had heard this word before but could not connect its meaning. The Gray Paw anticipated Kale's confusion and lifted his blade hand in Zube's direction. He firmly repeated, "Bashert."

"You must come with us, young pup. There are many Black Paws on our borders tonight, and we cannot allow you to come through our territory without the permission of the chieftain council," the warrior stated.

The march toward the Gray Paw camp was made in silence. Some of the Gray Paws carried torches to light the way, but it became clear this was done only for the benefit of the humans they now escorted. Kale took this time to rack his brain for the meaning of the word 'Bashert'. It must be a Wolfkin term. Zube had spent many months working on this language. Although it was rare, it was one of the most useful dialects. Many of the giants of the mountains spoke it fluently as a second language, and all the Wolfkin tribes used it. But this word eluded him. The meaning teetered on the edge of his tongue.

TEN

****

THE GRAY PAW

After many hours the group was led towards a large encampment of thatched buildings. It was surrounded by a wall of poles sharpened at the tops to provide a barrier to attack. This sophistication, even in such a rudimentary form surprised Kale. He had envisioned the Gray Paw living in holes in the earth and eating their meat raw. But, instead, he noticed many fires lit and an occasional small game being prepared over the fire. The majority of the Wolfkin wore rough clothing although, in large, they felt no shame in going without it. A large wooden structure was erected in the center of camp. Unlike the surrounding buildings, it was a long square building with a roof of planks and two large doors. As they entered into the room, Kale was further amazed by the tables and chairs that lined both sides. A large fire rested in the middle of the room. Further in sat a chair. One, Kale imagined, that was for their High Chieftain. On either side sat four smaller seats. These were obviously for the lower chieftains of the clans.

"Little pup, you and your band may stay here." The Wolfkin then turned his attention to Zube. "Bashert, you must promise me you will not try to harm my people. Unless you do so, we cannot allow you to stay. We will escort you out of the valley, but your friends will remain."

Kale noticed Zube's face was pale, and his eyes were filled with a mixture of sorrow and rage. "I assure you I will not harm your people unless provoked. But, Kannov, I give you my word

249

if you harm Kale," at this he lifted his hand toward him, "I assure you, you will be the first to die."

Kannov gave Kale a searching glance. "Bashert, you need not threaten me, but know this. I will abide by whatever the council decides. Our females and cubs are being escorted out of camp as we speak, and the call has been made for my chiefs to come into court. We understand what we face here, but know that we have no fear of death. If things turn hostile, we are sure that your blood will be spilled with ours this day."

With this, Kannov walked over to Kale, getting close enough to inspect him. "Hmm, for a human, you are oddly gifted." Carefully Kannov took two long sniffs of Kale. "You look like a cub, but you are no youngling. I smell many years in you. You're no mere human, but neither are you a...." Kannov halted mid-sentence and peered long at Kale. His brow tightened, and the skin on his nose curled involuntarily into a snarl. The snarl was not one of malice but one of knowing disbelief. Stepping back as if from a dangerous jolt, he stepped quickly toward the door. "There is food on the table. Eat your fill. I have my guards posted around the building. Do not try and leave."

The large doors creaked shut, and the sound of the large wooden beam was heard sliding into place, sealing the group into the wooden prison. Kale rushed over to Zube. "What is going on here? Why are they acting so strangely toward you.... toward me?"

Zube only response was to step over to a stool and collapse from exhaustion. "We must wait and see what the council has to say. It is likely that our battle is not over. Eat and rest while you can."

Many hours passed as the group sat in silence eating what

250

small rations lay on the table. Kale brooded on the day's events. His body had been stressed, but he seemed in better shape than the rest of the party. They lay limp, exhausted from the day's pursuit; all but Zube that was. He sat staring at his palms with his sleeves rolled up. Occasionally he traced the edges of the metal bands; this man contained so many mysteries. Kale suddenly came to the realization that it had not been him who had made the ring of fire that had saved the group from the Black Paw. It had been Zube. He was a Gehage, and by the looks of it, a very powerful one. It was obvious the Wolfkin feared him. That was why they kept their distance. That was why he was imprisoned. That was why the Fire general had feared him, and why everywhere he went he was known even though no one was willing to speak of him. What atrocity could he have committed? Another realization hit Kale, and he walked steadily over to Zube.

"Zube..." Kale began.

Lifting his sorrowful eyes, Zube met Kale's. Gaining a bit of composure Zube replied, "Yes, Kale."

"Now I remember the meaning of Bashert. It is Wolfkin for widow maker," Kale told him.

Zube's eyes begin to tear up. "Yes, Kale, that is correct. The word originates from the gnomes. In gnomish it means "Destined One". It is my birth name. But the Wolfkin have adopted it. They associate the name with death."

"But why? Why do they refer to you as the widow maker?" Kale wondered.

A new voice, harsher, gruffer voice chimed in from the background, "You mean you didn't tell him, Bashert?"

Turning, Kale saw a Black Paw dressed in the Gray Paw

garb and weaponry. His words were spoken fluently, unlike Kannov's. His eyes and stance resembled the Gray Paw, as well. The Black Paw had burns from head to toe on one side of his body, and his step was gated with a limp. One arm hung lashed to his belt. It appeared he had not used it in many years. Still, his body denoted an authority, a power not to be trifled with. His age far exceeded any Kale had seen among the tribe, at least in the males. "You travel into our domain, OUR domain, with this boy yet you do not share its history. You do not let him know what danger you bring him to. Oh, Bashert, you are a heartless one. Oh, wait, now you go by Zube, right. Is this another gnom-ish word we must now associate with deceit?"

Zube stood from his table. His face was flushed with anger. Kale had seen Zube upset once before with the Fire general but never to this degree. His muscles rippled under his skin. The room filled with a tense presence; the hair on both Kale's body and the rest of those in the room begin to rise.

Zube's face flushed bright red. "You!" With a step forward, Zube's hand moved to the band on his right arm to rip it off. From behind the charred Wolfkin several guards flooded the room and aimed their crossbows at each of the party members. The charred Wolfkin sneered, "I wouldn't do that. The second those bands come off, we will kill your friends."

Zube slowly lowered his hands. "Pravus, you half breed traitor. I tell you this now, I will not rest until your corpse rots in this earth."

"Now, now....what happened to the self proclaimed peace-maker, the righteous outcast? Where is that nobility we saw so many years ago?" Pravus took a leisurely step toward Kale, barely noticing the anger raging in Zube's eyes. With his good hand he reached up and tilted Kale's head from side to side. "Very interesting. So that is why you have taken to him. I see."

"So, cub, I assume that this old man here has taught you well," growled Pravus.

Despite the feeling that he wouldn't last five minutes against this half-mangled old Wolfkin, Kale straightened his head and defiantly looked Pravus in the eyes. "He has taught me well, Wolfkin, in all forms. He is a great man, a great teacher, and an even greater friend. If death awaits us today, I assure you, you will lose more men than we will."

"Oh, I don't doubt that, cub, I don't doubt that at all. But, you see, our women and children are out of harms way. It is only the warriors that remain, and we don't fear death."

With a glance at Zube, Pravus emphasized his remark. "Do we...." Smirking, he returned his glare to Kale. As each second passed, Kale could see the Wolfkin devouring him in his mind, imagining how wonderful it would be to destroy Kale. His eyes ran along his body looking for the tender flesh he would like to rip from Kale's body. Kale had never experience such hatred. Not even in Fike, the enemy that had assailed him for so many years because of the scarring Kale's father had given him. Fike, the killer of his mother and father, his imprisonment and the killer of so many innocent lives. Even this man contained less hate in his heart than this crippled Wolfkin. Unlike Fike, this Wolfkin's hatred was channeled, controlled with the patience that only the aged possess.

"It sounds as if your pupil has been neglected in his studies. Surely you have told him about the battle at Drakholme?" After a pause, his vicious grin spread to a broad sneer of joy. "Oh, I see! That would be a no then. We still have many hours before

253

all the chiefs are gathered in camp; there's plenty of time for an educational trip down memory lane. You, guards, if I am not back in three hours, assume the worst and kill the prisoners."

Rea put her hand on Platus' shoulder. "It is all right father, isn't it?"

"Don't worry, child. Kannov gave no such order. We will be fine. It is Zube I worry about. Oh, how I hope he can control himself," Platus worried.

Zube and Kale were led out of the gates heading deeper into the Japada pass. An hour passed in silence, and the moonlight shined brightly ahead. Kale was astonished to see a clearing in this dense forest. As they approached it, he covered his head to protect himself from the expanse of the clearing. As his eyes adjusted to the full moon's brightness, he was bewildered by the sight he beheld.

Before him was a massive charred plain. The charring appeared many years old, and Kale noticed that not one blade of grass grew in its desolation. The ground was blackened. Even the earth itself had been burned to a coal black substance that misted into the air with each step. Further into the clearing appeared tall black objects. They were difficult to make out at this distance. With each step, the closer Kale got to the objects they became more clear. Eventually Kale was able to see large stone columns, dilapidated and blackened. Large sections of what could now be distinguished as stone walls littered the surroundings.

With close inspection, Kale filled in the massive holes in the structures with his imagination. This had once been a massive outpost, possibly a small city. But what could have happened to it? What could have destroyed it in this way? A few hundred yards from the buildings Kale started to notice rows and rows of flat stones propped up in rows. It was a graveyard, a massive graveyard of thousands and thousands of tombstones, closely packed with faded writing. Finally they got to what used to be one of the walls. Each row of graves seemed to focus around one point on the wall, one section of uncharred structure. This column of stone wall contained an inscription in a foreign tongue.

Pravus turned on his heel and faced them both. "And here we are. It's time for a history lesson, cub."

* * *

"Many years ago the Fire Kingdom contracted both Wolfkin tribes in a war to infiltrate the lands of Japada. With our lands shrinking and our numbers growing, we eagerly agreed so long as after the Japada nation was defeated, we were given the land. The Gray Paw collected all of our warriors. We were an honorable breed; no Wolfkin male over the age of twelve was exempt, and every last one of us came to the battle. The Dark Paws were less zealous and brought only their experienced fighters, leaving many of their sons to attend to hunting and protecting their borders. We came here, to Drakholme; the first real obstacle in taking Japada by force. But we met resistance. The great Bashert had gathered his gnomish army here to make their stand. But, in their confidence, they neglected to send the women and children away. It was a mistake that I, and I am sure, the gnomes regret to this day.

The battle raged on, and soon Bashert ordered the children to be taken out through what they assumed to be a secret passage. But, it was not so secret. You see, I was the diplomat who negotiated trade agreements between Japada and both tribes. Being a half-breed of Black Paw and Gray Paw, I was accepted

255

by all. While at Drakholme many months prior to this, I scouted the keep for entrances in preparation for the assault. I found this tunnel and posted myself and a few Gray Paw guards outside it.

When they tried to escape, we killed the woman and lone guard assigned to protect them. Oh, what folly that was! They sent only one woman and one Fire Kingdom betrayer to protect their younglings. We took the children to use for negotiations and if need be kill to provide the leverage to enter Japada. But, this tactic proved to be ill-conceived.

Are you listening cub? This is where it gets interesting. We stormed the keep again after our demands were rejected by this noble leader. We stormed it with every Wolfkin and every Fire Kingdom soldier present. We would have taken the keep, too, except we did not realize what abominable force we had unleashed. Apparently, we had killed someone close to Zube because this self proclaimed man of peace lost all control and unleashed the most powerful display of Gehage ability this world has ever seen.

It only lasted seconds. I was just entering the area with the children when a massive explosion of heat and fire engulfed everything. Thrown to the ground, I rolled around and put myself out. Because they were cowardice enough to stay at the back of the battle, some of the Fire Kingdom commanders survived and me....one Wolfkin out of thousands. There was also one gnome who was fortunate enough to be standing next to Bashert who survived.

Men, women, and even the children Zube was so upset about losing were burned to death. His rage was so complete that nothing could slake his anger. After losing consciousness,

I woke up a few weeks later to learn that the advance had been called off. The Fire Kingdom had lost too many men, and without the help of the Wolfkin, who now after seeing the power of one Japada Gehage, had decided it not worth the risk, they could not advance.

But the Gray Paw realized their loses much later than that day. Our warriors went in hopes of dying a glorious death. But, what we did not realize was that now all of our warriors, all of our men and boys had perished. There was nothing to protect us from the Black Paws advancing forces to take our land for their own. Now, many years later, we are so reduced that we are backed into the edge of these woods. At our front stands the Black Paw. Our back is to Japada, and to our side is the Leaf Kingdom; each year our lands are reducing . And why, why is this? Because of one man, Bashert, the widow maker. Shall I read the passage to him? We can't move on without that, now can we, Bashert?"

Kale had lost focus on his surroundings. His mind was conjuring up the images, the screams, of so much destruction. Looking back at Zube, the old man's face was downcast. Tears rolled freely down his cheeks. Without looking up, he began to recite. "Here stood Bashert, the embodiment of anger. Destroyer of Wolfkin, man, gnome, and child, alike. Here stood death in its unbiased fury. Here stood the Widow Maker."

"Ah, so you remember. That's good. You see, cub, after the battle Bashert was banished from Japada. His own kind was afraid of the fury he had unleashed upon those he had killed. The Wolfkin shrank from his very presence. The Fire Kingdom imprisoned him in a tower that had once served as Bashert's own personal study back in the days of peace, and around him,

257

they built a prison. Unwilling to encounter his wrath, they left him in his seclusion."

***

The trip back to the camp was slow; Zube's head remained down as they walked, tears still running down his cheeks. "Kale, I'm sorry I didn't tell you. It's not something I choose to remember."

Kale placed his hand on Zube's shoulder. "I can't imagine what it must be like to carry such a burden. I know understand a bit why you are the way you are. And those bands...those bands. It makes sense now." Entering the camp, they were once more escorted to the large building. Inside the atmosphere had changed dramatically. The place was filled with Wolfkin. Rea, Caos, and Platus sat in front of the row of chairs as if facing an inquisition; two seats remained. Kannov took his place at the high chieftain's seat. This, at least, answered one of Kale's many questions. He was only glad that Pravus did not hold that place of authority over their lives.

Pravus walked to his seat just to the right of Kannov. All of the other chieftains were younger than Pravus by many years, but they all looked aged and full of wisdom. Some of the eight chieftains looked at the group with ravenous hate; a few only looked at them with questioning glances. Kale was worried as none of them seemed happy to see the group of intruders.

Kannov looked at Pravus. "I gave no such order to take them to Drakholme. What do you have to say for yourself?"

Pravus looked back at Kannov with respectful authority. "My Lord, what better test than to bring him to the place of his downfall?"

Kannov dismissed this excuse with a wave of his hand and

returned his attention to the group. "I will not hide the grievous situation you have placed us in, Bashert. But, what has been done is done. Now we must decide the best course of action. If it is decided you and your party are more of a threat to us than we are willing to risk, we will execute you. And, in doing so, if a battle commences, so be it. But, your timing may have been destined. I have talked with my chieftains. And though some of them wish for me to order your execution. Others, including myself, may see another option. Do you wish to hear our demands?"

Zube lifted his head. "You can speak of whatever you wish. But know this; I will preserve my life only to protect my party. Your demands are meaningless, as we both know that should you provoke me, no one in this camp would survive."

Kannov sniffed in frustration as the chieftains around him filled the room with their snarls of contempt. "There is no need to threaten us, Bashert. We know what we are tampering with. But, know that we do not fear a battle with you or your student. Also, know that we first ask for you to put aside your anger and your hatred for us as we are trying to do against you. Please remember that we killed only two of your people maliciously. You destroyed our nation. You killed even my very own father at Drakholme. You killed all of our fathers. And, in Pravus' case, you killed all three of his sons. If we are willing to put that aside for the sake of preservation, you must do the same. It was war. That was the way of it."

Zube looked down again. "What are you proposing."

"Our land has been taken from us over these many years. We have no land to expand on, and our children starve while our numbers dwindle. We barely have enough warriors to keep the

259

Black Paw at bay, and now we have heard that the Fire Kingdom has raised an army to take Japada. What makes things worse is that the Black Paw have agreed to help them. This campaign will be led by their new general, General Fike, and I fear my people's time is coming to an end."

At this, Kale's attention sharpened. Could he not escape this man?

"We are strong and mighty warriors though limited in numbers. We need someone to go to the gnomes of Japada and plead our case. We want to make an alliance with them. If they allow us to live in their lands, then we will fight by their sides in the upcoming battles."

Zube smiled dimly, "We both know that I cannot make this request. I am only here to escort Kale to the gates of Japada. I will not enter."

"According to what Pravus tells me, Kale is the one we should expect to make these negotiations. If anyone can persuade them, it will be him," Kannov predicted.

This unexpected gesture sent Kale's mind spinning. What could these Wolfkin think he could do to convince the gnomish people to do anything at all? How was he to create a political alliance against a long engrained and hated rivalry?

"Me? But I have never even stepped foot in Japada. I'm not sure they will even let open their gates to me. Why would you expect them to take my advice?" asked Kale.

With a chuckle, Pravus ran his tongue over his teeth. "Oh, so he hasn't told you yet....very interesting. Let me just enlighten..." But before he could finish his sentence, Kannov gave him a glance that made the old Wolfkin snap his jaw shut and sit rigidly in his seat. Kale realized that although Pravus was surely no warrior to trifle with, not even he dared to cross Kannov. "That explanation will be up to Zube to confer. For now, we will only say we have complete trust in your ability to negotiate with the gnomes."

Kannov waved his hand in a motion that the rest of the council members took to be a sign to be silent and leave the hall. Slowly they all rose and left. Kannov stood and walked toward Kale. "I will not deceive you. It is unlikely that the gnomes will agree to our request. But, it is a chance we must take. The normal path to the gates will take too long to get through. The only way to reach them in time is over the mountain range to the north. With winter setting in, it is unlikely that we will reach it before even that pass is overrun with snow. But, unless we do, unless we can secure an alliance, my people will be snuffed out in the spring when the Fire Kingdom launches its attack.

Every mile of their advance will push us farther toward the gate. And, as we approach the gate, we will have to fight the Fire Kingdom and Wolfkin on our right and the gnomish warriors on our left. We won't stand a chance. If you agree to go with us over the pass to negotiate peace, we will send our clans through the Japada pass to meet us a month after we are to be there. Hopefully that will give us time to convince them. Come with me, cub. I want to show you something."

Kannov walked to a large window covered by an outside hatch. With a knock, the panel was removed, and Kale could see several camps outside. One large tent sat directly in front of the window.

"This is my favorite spot in my entire land. And, do you know why?" he asked Kale.

Instantly Kale responded, "No, I do not."

261

"That is my hut." As if on queue, a small cub tumbled out of the hut followed by a young female Wolfkin. Kannov gave a loving growl, "And that would be my wife and my son; my only son."

Kale sat watching the cub toddling around. Its clumsiness reminded him of every other young child learning to walk. With each step, it overcompensated the sway until eventually it attempted to sit down on an imaginary chair, only to find the ground was further than it thought. And with the surprise of landing on hard dirt, the little Wolfkin began to whimper. Its mother scooped it up and rubbed her nose gently with his.

"Kannov, I thought the women and children were sent away?" Kale said.

"Yes, most were, but I know that it wouldn't matter. We are all that stand between my people and the points of the Fire Kingdom blades or the fangs of the Black Paw who want nothing more than to take our lands. "You may see us as vicious monsters, but we are not, at least not all of us. If you were gauged because of the actions of your fathers, or grandfathers for that matter, solely because you were of the same family, would you not feel unjustly accused?" Kannov asked.

"I can see your point, Kannov, but it will be hard to convince the gnomes to trust you within their gates," Kale pointed out.

"I do not deny that, Kale. It will be no easy task. It will be extremely difficult to get through the pass before winter sets in. We may just have time. But, before I can put all my nation's power behind this plan, I must know if you will help us. Even though they may not want to admit it, the gnomish people will need us, as well. The Black Paws are great in number, and the

Fire Kingdom has been mobilizing for some time for this attack. They have been recruiting from every corner of their empire; from every sand ridden town to the mountains of neighboring nations. Defeating the Japada nation has been something attempted by almost every king of the Fire Kingdom. And, unless the gnomes get assistance, they will lose this time."

Kale sat thinking, staring at the small Wolfkin cub making his way through basketfuls of grass. "I will do what I can. I know that you are only concerned for your family. But, there are a few conditions," Kale stated.

"And what would that be, cub?" asked Kannov.

"My friends, including Zube, are to be set free. And Rea, her father, and anyone else who wants to go back to the Leaf Kingdom are to be given an escort; that condition is non-negotiable. Are we agreed?" Kale asked.

"Although it will be difficult to find guards willing to escort Zube, as you call him, I will see to it. None of them will be hurt, and they will be given safe passage back to within one mile of the Leaf Kingdom's borders. We dare not approach any closer. And what are your other conditions?" Kannov said.

"Just one, I want some information," Kale told him.

Kannov inhaled, believing Kale wanted to know more about Bashert. But, before he could speak, Kale lifted his hand, "I will leave Zube to tell me what he wants when he decides it is time. This is on a more formal level."

"What is it that you wish to know?" Kannov asked.

"If I am going to convince the gnomes to join forces with you, I will need to know the size and condition of your forces. I must know the numbers of your tribes that will need safety behind the gates and all the knowledge you have on the Fire

Kingdom army, the Black Paw forces, and, most particularly, General Fike," explained Kale.

Kannov gave a quizzical look into Kale's eyes. It was not malicious or devious but more of surprise and wonder. "You remind me of a man in a story my father used to tell me about so long ago. He, too, was young, but he also was naturally drawn to lead. Although he took his power through battle, it is much the same with you. He was a good leader, and many followed him because of the man that he was. I can see in your eyes that same man. I can smell battle seeping from your very breath. You are a warrior, and because of your lineage, I am sure you will prove a mighty man in battle. You ask the very question any leader should ask first. Not to gain personal knowledge, but to attain the information you need to complete the task at hand. It is a shame you were not born a Wolfkin."

Kale's mind again began to spin. He had only asked a basic question that he thought was crucial to the task at hand. Why did so many admire him for taking the only steps he felt were in front of him? Was there any other choice than to help two nations survive the onslaught of the Fire Kingdom and the fury of the Black Paw? "You give me too much credit, Kannov. I am only a man trying to survive in this world, and if I can keep a few of those around me alive just a little longer, I would be happy. I haven't known a day of peace for many years now, and sadly I have shed more blood than I care to remember. Even though I look back and know that it was the only logical course of action, I can't help but to despise myself for it." Kale turned to look at Kannov. "Can you give me the information I need?"

"Yes, Kale, I will have my war table brought out, and we will go over what we know so far as well as our strategy for the winter," Kannov promised him.

* * *

Kale sat next to Zube around a large table. Its edges were gilded with gold and in the center carved into the wood was Telekkar. The map's details were impressive. It expanded further than any map Kale had seen. And, after being in the library with Zube, that was notable. The Wolfkin chiefs took their place as Kannov stood and, with a large stick carved for this purpose, began to explain the position of the armies.

Kannov first pointed to Durian on the map. "Durian has been under development for many years and now has developed into the military capital for the Fire Kingdom. With the river at its side, the mountains at its back, and its geographic position between the water and Stone Kingdom, it makes the perfect base of operations.

The Fire Kingdom has been recruiting heavily for the last year and a half. This has provided them with a significant army. The Fire Kingdom has already openly waged war against the Stone Kingdom. Although our scouts report that they were unable to take the great gate, they were able, with little resistance it seems, to take the south eastern most quadrant of the Stone Kingdom's lands. The Stone Kingdom now fights to keep what lands it has left, but the land they lost was the most significant to the Fire Kingdom's plans. It gives them a place to refit and re-supply near the Japada forests. They must have this to wage a war on Japada. In our current state, the Gray Paw are only numbered enough to keep the Black Paw at bay."

Kannov allowed a brief moment for the information to sink in. "The Fire Kingdom has gathered its army at the edge of the Japada forest and is completing negotiations with the Black Paw.

They will not be able to sustain themselves for long in the forest. There is little enough for the Wolfkin to eat, and transporting the needed siege equipment will be difficult. They cannot start the journey to Japada until spring. It is likely it will be mid-summer before they can make the assault. We estimate it to take roughly two months to complete the assembly of the siege equipment.

They know that they cannot starve out the gnomes. They have lived behind their walls for hundreds of years. They must breech the wall and sweep through the land. No one knows the size of the gnomish forces, but we can estimate them to be under twenty thousand. The Wolfkin alone will number thirty five thousand. The Fire Kingdom troops, even after we deduct the amount that will die in the journey to the wall will be another forty thousand. If the gnomes accept our offer, we will add another eight thousand to their forces. That includes every male over the age of twelve. The Black Paw will inevitably leave their young at home. This is fortunate for us. As you can see, we will be outnumbered almost three to one."

Glancing over at Zube, Kale could see his eyes fixed in worried thought, wisps of hair dangling slightly in front of his face. Kannov noticed this as well and turned to the old man. "You see, Zube, it could be the end of both of our people. This wave of death will consume your loved ones as well as mine."

Zube pushed back his hair, "I must go to the Leaf Kingdom. They have had a long standing alliance with Japada; they would not dare refuse to send troops."

Kannov spoke, choosing his words carefully. "Zube, much has changed in these years you were away. The Leaf Kingdom fears Japada as much as we do. They lost many at the battle of

Drakholme. But, I agree, a petition must be requested, however, you know their democratic system better than anyone. It will take many months to convince them to help and longer to get them to act on their decision."

Zube folded his hands as his old self began to return. He stood and grabbed his cane. Life again showed in his eyes. "Kannov, I must leave Kale in your care; you must get him to Japada. I will go to the Leaf Kingdom and do what I can to convince them to come to Japada's aid, and if that fails I will seak aid elsewhere. Yes, you are correct. The Leaf Kingdom can take an age to make a decision. It has been the downfall of their political system, but it is our best hope."

Kannov motioned for the table to be taken away. Several guards lifted the massive table and removed it from the room. Although it was a simple task to these Wolfkin, Kale did not fail to notice the strength these Wolfkins possessed.

"Pravus and myself will take Kale to Japada. We dare not take more Wolfkin. They may be seen as a threat. Pravus has crossed the pass to Japada many times. He will know the way. I must be there to negotiate any terms. Sending a messenger back and forth will just waste time. While we cross the mountain, my people will take the longer path and make their way through the pass," Kannov decided.

"Caos, Rea, and her father will come with me. It will be safer for them," stated Zube.

From the background Caos stepped forward. "By your pardon, my Lord, but where Kale goes, I go." It was clear from his stance that he had no intention of being persuaded otherwise. Zube could only admire this scout. He had just heard that they would be outnumbered three to one in the upcoming battle yet he did not waiver. Instead of taking a safe route to the Leaf Kingdom, he would not abandon his commander. "Okay, Caos, that is your decision. You will accompany Kale. Kannov, may I have a few moments alone with Kale?"

The room was cleared, and Zube sat on one of the chairs. His slow movement and exhalation let Kale know that this was not another ruse but truly the fatigue of someone aged and tired of war. "Kale, this may be the last lesson I am able to teach you so listen carefully. I know my people. They can keep a grudge for hundreds of years. You will be engaging in a battle not of blades but of wit. You will be battling a bias, an idea."

"It is important that you realize it is easier to fight a man than an idea. An idea is much more difficult to defeat. A man dies with his last breath, but an idea lives on in the hearts and minds of people. It can spread and multiply like a disease, infecting the weak in mind just as a disease infects the weak in body. The only way to overcome this idea, this bias, this hatred, is to plant another idea in the minds of the people. They must feel more strongly about allowing the Wolfkin to join them than about the history of war with them. I, for one, do not know how that can be achieved. I still harbor my hatred for them, but I am willing to put aside my distain for most of them for the benefit of my people. I, though, am only half gnome and therefore only half as stubborn."

Kale grinned at Zube's attempt to lighten the mood. "Tell me, Zube. Why does the Fire Kingdom desire to take over Japada so badly? They are not interested in occupying it. If they were, they would not have agreed to let the Wolfkin live there so many years ago."

"They do not want the land Kale. They want what is in

it, what grows on it. Japada has the largest deposit of agonite in existence. It has the tallest trees of the greatest quality for ship building and some of the deepest diamond and gold mines known to this day. The land is the best in Telekkar. That is why the king of old chose it as his homeland. With the agonite, they can equip their armies. With the gold and diamonds, they can buy allegiance or mercenaries. And, with lumber, they can build ships to wage war on the Water Kingdom. This take over expands beyond their power of today. You see, they need Japada to fund the war to take over the rest of Telekkar. If Japada falls, so does the rest of Telekkar."

Kale sat back. The weight of this new responsibility weighed heavily upon him. "So, what you are saying is that if I fail in negotiating peace with Japada and the Wolfkin, or if even after that impossibility I fail to protect Japada during the invasion, then the blood of the rest of Telekkar is on my hands?" As Kale spoke, he could feel the blood draining from his face. His mind worked desperately to contain itself and not lose itself in panic.

Zube leaned forward and placed his hand on Kale's knee. Instantly Kale felt calm "My boy, you cannot blame yourself for whatever takes place. What happens will happen. We can only do our best to prevent it. You are accountable only for your own actions. Now I must tell you something else. I know when you get to Japada they will tell you anyway, and it is best that you hear it from me."

"At Drakholme those many years ago I had my child with me, no older than nineteen. During the attack I ordered all of the children, including my own, to be taken to safety. When I got the report that they were killed and that the Fire Kingdom soldier was killed, his leg bitten off and presented to me as proof of

269

their demise, I lost all control of myself. The thought of my only child laying in the dirt, covered in blood, caused my anger to rise to such a level that I could not contain the rage that welled up inside. You saw the destruction it caused, but I found out through you that my child had not died."

Kale began to take in all that Zube was saying. All the odd situations, the silent whispers when people met him. The story of the soldier and the young lady entrusted with the care of the children. Then it hit Kale. The soldier with his leg ripped off.... His mind began to whirl. It must be as he was thinking even though his mind had trouble taking it all in. His father's leg had been missing. He had been a Fire Kingdom soldier. The drinking...it must be. Looking up at Zube, his eyes opened wide with amazement. "You, you are..."

"Yes, Kale, I am your grandfather," Zube finished his sentence.

"But, my father..." stammered Kale.

Zube's eyes burned, "No, you misunderstand. Not your father, my boy, my child was your mother."

"My mother?" Kale asked.

"Yes, Kale, she was a Wind Gehage. Though like me, she chose to be a person of peace until we were openly attacked. She cared for the orphans of the cities. She must have thought I had died. I'm not sure how they survived, but like you, she would have been extremely difficult to kill. Your father was a great man, one of the greatest swordsmen we had ever trained, but he was not a Wind Gehage. He was a powerful Fire Gehage. But, that is all. Oh, how I miss my Ellien...." he grieved.

For a few moments Kale sat stunned, and then he began to get angry. "Why didn't you tell me? I thought I was alone...why didn't you tell me?....why didn't they tell me?!"

"They must have chosen to hide, my boy. And I did not want to make your life more complicated than it already was. But, you have the same weakness I do. You have trouble controlling your anger in times of despair. You must learn to control your anger. You must keep it in check. You saw Drakholme. Do not make the same mistake I did. You cannot let your personal feelings get the best of you. It is a hard lesson, but I do not want to see you kill those you love. You would never forgive yourself," Zube assured Kale.

"I understand, Zube, and, in a way, I think I always knew. At least a part of me did. You seemed to know much about me. You seemed to know just the right questions to ask. It was as if you already knew the answers but were just confirming something to yourself," said Kale.

"You are much like the first king, my grandfather. He was a warrior at heart, but, unlike him, you have your mother's love for those around you. An odd combination, but so far it has served you well," Zube said proudly.

"Served me well! I would not change any of the decisions I have made, but they have hardly served me well. Years in prison, countless scars, lost loved ones, lost friends and exile. Not from any nation but from those around me. The only one I can be open with is you. Everyone else treats me either like some pompous royal that they must keep a distance from, or, in most cases, a venomous snake that they fear will strike them if they get too close," Kale said.

"Such is the curse of leadership, Kale. It doesn't get easier. There is another point I must make before we prepare to part. Kannov seems well intended, but do not be fooled. His chiefs

271

are not as loyal as they appear. I can assure you of one thing. Pravus will harm you if he can. He is likely playing both sides. He knows the odds and has proven he sways easily. His hatred for the gnomes, as well as me personally, will play a big part in his decisions. Keep a watchful eye on him during the journey. If you die so does any hope for the Gray Paws and, more importantly to me, the gnomes."

Zube then reached into a large pocket and lifted out his small mouse. "Here, take Alkaz with you. At least then I'll have some idea of your state during my travels." Zube ran his finger over the mouse's head. "He likes the crust of bread."

Kale gave a nod of understanding. "I'll keep that in mind. We should get ready. Every minute could make the difference between success or failure."

Rea approached Kale as her father packed their bags. "I won't see you for some time. If you survive this year, you should come to my home in the fall."

Kale grabbed her hand and held it. She was the only soft thing he had felt in so many years. "Why the fall?"

"Because in the fall the contest of courtship begins, and if you are there, I will announce I am ready to wed. Then it will be up to you to win my hand. I am sure you will defeat any of the other suitors and get first choice of a bride," she stated.

"You have some strange customs, but it will give me something to look forward to. But, the chances of me living that long do not look very promising. Are you sure you want to wait that long?" Even as Kale said the words, he wanted to take them back. They must have been very callous. Why did he try and push her away? He knew she cared for him though he could not tell why, and he felt strongly for her. But, he knew that if she

272

waited, she would be disappointed. He held no delusions that he would survive the year, and he didn't want to see her hurt.

"Kale, you are a fool. But, I think that is part of why I am drawn to you. Even now you are sacrificing your feelings for me to spare me some girlish pain. I am not soft like some others you may have known. I do not fear death, and I know that you face a great challenge. But I will wait for you because inside I know you will succeed. You have to. It's in your nature," she assured him.

"Rea, how can you have so much confidence in me? You barely know me," Kale asked her.

"Anyone who can inspire thousands of men to follow them can overcome any obstacle. The fact that you even have just one man," at this she raised her hand to Caos, "who would follow you into the jaws of death itself proves to me the kind of man you are. Be safe, and I will look for you in the fall." She leaned in and gave him a kiss. Then, without so much as another word, she turned on her heel and walked to the party preparing to leave. Kale stood, wondering at what had just happened.

Kannov spoke from just to his right. "You seem to have attracted a mate though I do not know if I would want to share a tent with that one if she were to get angered. Are you ready to go?"

"Yes, let's get going," replied Kale.

ELEVEN

****

THE JAPADA PASS

Parting with Zube was more difficult than Kale had realized. The time spent with him had greater significance in his mind. He no longer was alone. He had a grandfather. His remembrances were broken by Caos tossing a blanket over his shoulders. "Here, sir, we don't want you dying of a cold. Need to keep your strength up to fight off these Black Paws."

"Thank you, Caos. You know you don't have to call me sir. We are no longer with the army," Kale said.

"Of course, sir," Caos replied.

"Caos, really you don't have to." But Kale didn't finish his sentence. He could see from the look on Caos' face that it would be of no use; yet another person who trusted him so deeply. What was there about him that gave these people so much faith in his ability? He was nothing special. Yes, maybe he was a Wind Gehage, but he could be bested by any of the elite Wolfkin. He was no match to a large number. He was still only one man.

Pravos lead the way. His eyes continually darted to see where Kale stood. Zube was right to warn him. Pravos' every move, every word, even the way he smelled the air when Kale passed him, made Kale's skin crawl. His eyes were filled with a malicious appetite.

Kannov seemed to trust him and Kale found that he even respected the old Wolfkin. Each day they marched toward the mountains, and Caos proved to be an excellent companion. He looked after Kale like a nurse maid, ensuring he ate, had dry boots, and was kept warm. He scouted the trail ahead and foraged for food along with a multitude of other small tasks. He had always shown a loyalty to Kale, but after hearing of the significance of this treaty and Kale's crucial part in it, he treated Kale as a fragile glass jar. One he took personal responsibility to care for.

Kale sat next to Caos by the fire feeding Alkaz and allowing the mouse to get a few minutes of exercise by running up and down the length of his arm. Looking at Caos, he was surprised to see that the man was staring into the fire; his eyes betrayed a worried look. "Is everything all right, Caos? You seem disturbed tonight."

"Oh, sir, it is nothing. I'm just thinking..." His voice trailed off, and then he looked at Kale. "What if we fail?"

"Then we will die, and it will not make much difference," Kale stated.

"Sir, I wish I could be like you. You do not fear death; none of this seems to worry you at all," Caos said.

Kale could only guess that his hood must hide his face from betraying much emotion. "I fear death as much as the next person. But when we are dead, what we could or could not have prevented will matter very little. And as for you, I've seen you in battle, Caos. You fight bravely. Your comming on this journey proves your bravery. The fact remains that you came with me alone with two Wolfkin to a city of gnomes who may kill us on site to fight an army three times the size of the army we hope to have, and that is only if we succeed. You are both a good warrior and a good friend."

"Friend, sir? I hadn't thought you considered me a friend. You're always so distant; no disrespect intended, sir. I just mean you have so much more serious matters to attend to than a lowly scout. I'm sure you're used to leading men. I hear you were a great general before." This last statement was filled with a hope of getting an answer.

"A general! What nonsense," Kale began to laugh, his stomach aching from the spasms of his sore muscles. Caos, at first, stared in wonder. Never had he seen his commander laugh. Then, slowly he began to chuckle, too. He had no idea what he was laughing at. He just knew that the moment called for it. Laughter being contagious, he eventually found himself holding his stomach as well. The moment passed, and Kale sat thinking, guessing that the men probably came up with all kinds of stories about their commander. Without a real story to circulate, they would be forced to come up with their own.

"Caos, do you know what I did before being imprisoned?" Kale asked.

"I've heard talk, sir, but no," Caos confessed.

"A sand runner," Kale looked at Caos to see if the man believed him.

"A....a messenger sir?" stammered Caos.

"Yes, Caos, I was a messenger. I ran messages to the sand locked towns of the Deadlands," Kale told him.

Kannov appeared out of the darkness and sat down. "Well, pup, that explains why you are so fast on your feet."

Now the lot of them broke out in laughter. Kale began to laugh even harder when he heard Kannov giggling like a hyena.

It amazed Kale how the stress of the task in front of them had made each man, whether a regular man like Caos, a Gehage as himself, or even a king of the Wolfkin tribes more susceptible to release their stress by laughing. It made him miss Reagan deeply. He rarely thought of his friend but at times like this. Small moments like this made him think of those memories now many years in the past. He remembered their times of wrestling outside town or even the night they spent at the local inn so many years ago. How careless their life had been back then."

Caos' words echoed in Kale's mind. "What if we fail?" What would happen if the Fire Kingdom overtook the lands of Japada? They would have a near endless supply of valuable commodities to fund a long war effort. Many thousands of lives would be lost in just the first few months. How many thousands, how many millions of lives would be lost during the years of war that would follow? Kale worked hard to push this from his mind. He must not allow himself to think about what he could not prevent.

What was within his control now involved this Wolfkin sitting across from him more than his friend sitting next to him. If he failed to persuade the gnomish people to agree to a pact with the Gray Paws, his whole race would be wiped out. Already his people were making their way through the Japada Pass towards the great gates of the Japada Nation. This Wolfkin was risking everything on Kale's ability at diplomacy. His people would most likely be stuck in between the Fire Kingdom and the great gates.

Their only option was to flee further north up the wall to the abandoned port city, its name long forgotten. But, what would that serve? They could not swim, and they had no ships for transport. Even if they could swim, even if they could manage to find ships, where would his people go? They would find no safety among men. No, it was a hard fact to swallow, but if Kale could not negotiate the treaty, they would be cut down by the

Fire Kingdom army or worse yet by the gnomish people who, like Kale, probably only saw them as murderous beasts. Those around him held out such hope...yet Kale felt there was none. The thought made him sick to his stomach.

Kale returned the mouse to his pocket and stood to shake off the ghostly feeling of hopelessness that was surrounding him. Tossing another log on the fire, he sat back down, closer to Kannov. "Kannov, may I ask you a question if it's not too forward?"

"Of course, Kale, anything you wish to know, I am willing to share," Kannov answered.

"What is the story with Pravus? He seems more like a Black Paw than one of your people. He also doesn't seem to agree with your plan yet you seem to trust him to accompany us." Kale was hoping this wouldn't reveal too much of his apprehensions, and that it would not offend Kannov.

Kannov didn't seem to notice but went right into an explanation. "Pravus has grown more....aggressive toward the gnomish people as the years go by. He lost his sons in the battle of Drakholme, and when he came back, he was the only surviving adult male. He had no choice but to take leadership of the clans until I and the other chieftains were old enough. It was a very heavy weight to carry.

He has tried several times to have more children, but either age or his battle wounds have prevented it. I pity him. His line dies with him, and as his end of years gets closer, he gets angrier about his loss. He taught us all the warrior's path, and he helped us keep what land we could from the Black Paw. This cost him much as he is half Black Paw. Secretly, I feel he still holds some sentiment for them. But he has stood by the Gray Paw. He was the only father figure any of us ever had. But, no, he doesn't agree with my plan. He would prefer we make an allegiance with the Black Paw and blend into their clan. But, my people could never live as they do. We are a separate race despite the similarities. Speaking of Pravus, he should have been back by now."

The hours passed and Pravus was nowhere to be found. Nothing was said, and each was left to his own thoughts. It was obvious something was not as it should be. Kale sensed that even Kannov felt something was wrong. After many hours, the Wolfkin king rose and grabbed his pack. "We must keep moving. We do not have time to look for him. He may have left us to find our own way, unable to proceed with a plan he disapproved of. I'll deal with his insolence later."

Caos asked, almost hoping, "Could he have been killed by something in the woods?"

Kannov gave a low grunt. "There is nothing in these woods that could best that Wolfkin. I would barely be a match for him. And, even if something engaged him in battle, we would have heard his howl. I cannot even smell his scent on the wind. I've been trying for some time. He is many miles away. We must make our own way. Let's get a move on. We reach the mountain pass in a few hours. After that, there will be nothing to burn for warmth. We won't want to stay put long. If we are lucky, we will find a cave to take shelter in at night."

The climb the next day was very steep. Each mile brought rougher terrain and colder weather. After clearing the tree line, the icy winds came in heavy bursts down the mountain. Caos seemed to handle the cold better than Kale. Each hour drained Kale of more energy than he thought he possessed. Occasionally

Caos would stop to check on Kale. At the end of the second day, Kale noticed the cold weather coupled with the rough terrain was playing havoc on his body. Caos noticed it as well and came to him. "Here, take my cloak, sir. I'm not very cold."

"No, Caos, you keep that cloak. You need to keep warm. I'll be fine. We will be topping the mountain today or tomorrow. Then it is all downhill from there. We will be heading back into the warmth of the forest," Kale told him.

"As you wish, sir." Kale took a closer look at this man of woods. Although his attitude presented a strong front, Kale picked up on many subtle details. His lips were paling, and his movements were slowing. He contained extraordinary fortitude, but he was just as cold as Kale.

Kannov continued on in silence. Occasionally he would look back and sniff the air. He was worried about something, but he didn't choose to speak. That night they found a small cave to bed down in. There was little to burn so they had to make do with no fire. Caos sat close to a large boulder. At first Kale thought he was sleeping, but upon a closer look, he noticed his eyes were opened slightly, and he lay shivering.

Kannov sat next to Kale. Kale chose to ask a question that had been on his mind the last few days. "You don't think Platus just left us, do you?"

"No, I don't, young one. Something troubles me greatly with his disappearance." He then looked back at Caos and with an obvious effort changed the topic. "Your friend will not survive long if we cannot get him warm. We still have several more miles before we begin our descent, and the winter snows will begin falling soon. I can smell them in the air."

"I know. I just don't know what to do for him. I could use

my fire bending and warm him for a short time, but that won't last long. I can't sustain a flame for more than a short time without draining myself. I can barely keep myself standing," said Kale.

"When the snows set in and we begin to get cold, my people will heat up flat rocks and place them on our skin. The back is a good place to start. It has gotten us through many cold winter nights. Maybe it would help your friend; maybe it would help you, as well. They last for many hours," suggested Kannov.

"That is a very good suggestion. Thank you." Kale got up and gathered a few stones. Placing them in his palm, he heated them gently so that they were just cool enough not to burn the skin. He handed them to Caos. "Here, place these under your shirt. They may help."

Caos grabbed the stones and placed one on his stomach. "Oh, sir! That feels so good. What an ingenious idea." He hurriedly placed the others under his arms and between his legs. "I feared I would freeze to death. Honestly, I did."

"Don't thank me, Caos. It was Kannov's idea. I merely provided the flame. I'll renew these every hour or so. You may even be able to carry some with you as we walk,," Kale told Caos.

"I won't even notice the extra weight, sir if it means I'll be warm again." With this, he shut his eyes and rubbed his hands together enjoying the warmth of the stones on his body. "You know, sir, they aren't such a bad lot, the Wolfkin, that is. Not all of them, anyway. I don't much care for this Pravus character. But Kannov, well, sir, he reminds me a lot of you."

"I like him, too, Caos. They are nothing like what I imagined," Kale agreed.

That night a heavy snow set in. Caos woke him up periodically to request his stones be reheated. Kale noticed on the last request that his friend was shivering uncontrollably, his body blanketed in snow. "Why are you covered in snow, Caos?"

"I had to step out for a second, sir. It was dumb, I know. Can I get these stones heated extra hot?" he asked.

"Sure, Caos, and for all love, man, stay inside tonight. Use the back of the cave if you need to relieve yourself," Kale instructed him.

"Yes, sir," he answered.

Kale heated both his and Caos' stones and rolled over to get another hour or so of sleep.

When they prepared to leave the next morning the ground was covered with a foot and a half of snow, and it continued to come down in large flakes. The march that day left them tired, but they managed to top the crest of the mountain and begin their descent. Caos' walk was labored and slow; each step deliberate and restrained. He kept a steady stride, but it had slowed to a casual walk rather than the hurried pace they had been taking. The extra load this man had taken to look after Kale was catching up with him.

During a momentary reprieve of snow the clouds parted allowing the group to look at the landscape below. For the first time Kale could see the lands of Japada. They were contained on one enormous peninsula; there were thousands of miles of the richest land in all of Telekkar.

Roughly in the center of the entrance to the peninsula stood the largest wall Kale had ever seen and, by his history lessons, the largest wall ever built. Even from this distance he could tell it stood many hundred yards tall. It stretched for many miles until it eventually met a mountain on each side. Each mountain stretched far above the cloud line at such a strong angle that Kale was sure no army could climb it. The mountains then ran to the sea where they created a wall for many miles out before they sank below the surface.

Before the northern mountain, the abandoned port city could be made out. It was a mesh of lines and white, crowding a massive bay. The end of the bay was closed off except for a few miles stretch of open water. It was perfectly defensible yet massive enough to hold the whole of the Water Kingdom's fleet.

Beyond the wall, Kale could see small circles cut out in the landscape. They had to be gnomish towns. Toward what Kale assumed to be the entrance stood a massive city. Some of its large buildings were visible even from this great distance. Kale was amazed at its beauty, but the massive expanse caused his heart to start to beating quickly, and his body began to seize up with fear. His legs felt heavy and sweat droplets rolled down his cheeks. What a weakness to have! Of all the ridiculous fears, how could he overcome it? His mind seemed to process that there was no danger, but yet the feelings of anxiety and fear washed over him like a flood. The picture of massive beauty passed quickly and with it the baseless paralyzing fear as the clouds came back to begin their onslaught of snow and drizzle.

* * *

The march down the mountain was slow. Celic lead the way, scouting ahead while Kannov lingered behind the party. Every few hundred yards Kannov paused to raise his nose to the wind and spend a few minutes in thought. The concern in his voice and his obvious anxiety began to grow with each passing hour. Finally he came to Kale.

"Young pup, we must increase our pace. I fear we are being

followed by a pack of Dark Paw," he explained.

"You think Pravus is leading them to us. Don't you?" asked Kale.

Kannov lowered his head. "I'm sure of it. I can smell him very distinctly. He has at least seven others, most likely Dark Paw hunters. We won't stand much of a chance. I may be a match for Pravus, but can you and your friend take on six or more Dark Paw elites?"

"No, I'm sure we could not. I had a time with just one. How much time do we have?" Kale questioned Kannov.

"Maybe two hours." Kannov paused before making his next statement. "I know you may not want to hear this, but we could probably make better time if we left Caos behind. I know we have slowed our pace to match his. It is imperative that we make it to the wall."

Kale's anger began to flare at this cruelty but was driven away by the look in Kannov's eyes. He had lost hope. He was grasping at any chance to make this mission succeed, and he now was choosing between one foreigner and his entire race.

"Kannov, let me make this perfectly clear. I will not abandon Caos. If you wish to run ahead, then feel free. Even if we die, at least I will die knowing that I did not leave behind a friend to die while I fled for safety. No, if they catch us, then we will take out as many of them as we can before we are killed," Kale declared.

"Pup, I am not afraid for my life. It matters little. I find it an honor to die in battle...but my people. I have to try everything I can to keep them safe," Kannov explained.

"I understand. I really do. Let's get moving." Moments later they caught up with Caos who sat resting on a rock.

"Caos, we need to talk. It appears that we are being followed by six or so Black Paw and Pravus. We need to increase our pace and try to get to the wall before they reach us," Kale told him.

Caos looked up, his face grave with concern. "I know, sir. I heard you talking. I doubled back last night while you were sleeping and caught sight of them at first light. And there are eight, not six. I spotted them from a distance, but, sir, I can tell you they looked more vicious than the ones we took on in the forests. They looked armored, that is. Like the one you cut down."

"More of those, we really must get a move on," decided Kale.

"Sir, Kannov is right. You will be able to move faster if you leave me behind. I can move steadily, but I can't seem to shake this chill. It keeps me from moving swiftly," Caos said.

"Caos, we aren't going to leave you behind. We can outrun them..." He was cut off by Caos raising his hand in protest. "That's not all, sir. Look." Lifting his pant leg, he removed his boot. His foot was soaked with blood. The bottom of his foot was blistered and split.

"I don't know how the two of you can make such a journey without much impact, but I cannot push on at this pace for another day. I am no Wolfkin and definitely no Gehage. I'm just a man, just one man at that. Leave me. I'll hide the best I can, but you two should be able to outrun them. After all, you were a sand runner, sir." He said this last statement with a slight smile. His pride at being the only one in the Kalian army who knew anything of the commanders past was obvious.

Awaiting his decision, Kannov and Caos looked at Kale for

many minutes. Kale's head was lowered, causing his hood to hide his face completely. "Drop your pack."

"What sir?" Caos asked in confusion.

"You heard me. Toss your pack on the ground," Kale told him.

Caos obeyed and looked at Kannov to see if he knew what Kale was doing. Kale then dropped his pack and grabbed Caos' arm, pulling him to his feet. "I am not leaving you behind. You will let me carry you."

"No, sir, leave me," begged Caos.

"That's an order, Caos! Kannov, if you want to go ahead, I understand." Kale bent down and placed Caos on his shoulder. Then he began the fastest pace he could manage down the hill. Every few minutes Caos would grunt an argument between the jerking up and down as Kale navigated the steep mountainside. When he became overly argumentative, Kale would purposely bounce him on his shoulder to knock the breath out of him.

To Kale's surprise, Kannov did not run ahead. To the contrary, he kept a hundred yards to the rear. The descent for the next few hours was hard, and Kale thought many times that he could not carry Caos any further. But each time he reached what he thought was his limit, he found another reserve, small and just enough to push on another mile or so. The bottom of the mountain still lay many miles away. Kale was sure that they could not make it in time. It was still half a day's hard walk. Even at this pace they would not reach it for five or more hours.

Kannov came up to his side. "They aren't far behind now. I can see them in the distance."

Kale stopped and sat Caos gently down on a boulder. His breathing slowed with the much needed rest. Kale looked ahead;

the path was beginning to even out into an easier slope. "Kannov, take Caos as far as you can. I will do my best to hold them off."

Caos stood quickly and drew his sword. "Don't touch me, Kannov, or I will cut you down." Then he looked at Kale. "Sir, with all respect. You can order me all you want, but I'm not leaving you here to fight alone. If we die, we will die together. If you don't like that, I don't much care so you might as well let it be."

Kale couldn't help but be impressed with this man. He could barely stand and would be no match for the weakest Dark Paw elite. But, who was he to tell this man what to do with his own life.

"Very well, Caos, I can't begrudge you for feeling that way. My friend, it was a pleasure serving with you," he told Caos.

The eight Wolfkin were swooping down the mountainside in a frantic pace. Their prey was close at hand. Leading a few yards ahead, Pravus was running not on his hind legs like the Gray Paw, but on all fours like his Dark Paw brethren.

Kannov lifted his nose to the wind again. "Pup, something else is coming."

Kale looked down the mountain but saw nothing, just sparse trees at this altitude, rocks, and patches of mossy grass. "I don't see anything, Kannov."

The Black Paw was within two hundred yards of Kale's group. Kale could see their bodies heaving up and down as they made their flight toward them. Each drew their blades in preparation for the onslaught. Pravus advanced fifty yards ahead of the other Darkpaw. With a growl, Kale saw Kannov lunge forward and begin his charge toward Pravus. Kale took off at a sprint to try and help Kannov dispatch Pravus before the other group reached them.

Over the sound of his feet pounding against the floor and the beat of his heart, he could hear another sound. First a steady swoosh and then a sound that brought hope into his heart. Over the sound of their screaming battle charge, he heard the roaring scream of his winged friend, Makko, flying by swiftly toward the Wolfkin. In his talons he carried a small person armored from head to toe and carrying a massive sword on his back and two smaller swords on either hip. Kale took his eyes off Makko just in time to see Kannov crash into Pravus, barking and biting like a pair of ravenous wolves fighting over a mate. The armored body was dropped behind Kannov, blocking the advance of the remaining Black Paw. It was a gnome warrior.

Like all battles, what followed next happened quickly yet seemed to flow in slow motion. The gnomish warrior drew the swords from his sides. With one swipe forward and another backwards the gnome dropped two of the Wolfkin dead in their tracks in a process that seemed like a dance while the other six Wolfkin lunged at him.

The small warrior jumped from one's back and, with acrobatic grace, spun over the others, lopping off the head of the tallest on his descent. Kale was mesmerized by this small man. His movements were so graceful and yet so familiar. He had seen this style of swordsmanship before. But where? Makko swooped down and tackled one of the Wolfkin. It clamped down on Makko's gimp front leg, causing Makko to yelp in pain. But then the bird let out a ferocious roar as he snapped his razor sharp beak over the wolf's throat, ripping it wide open. He then took to the air, leaving the wolf to convulse in its death spasms.

By the time Kale reached Kannov, Pravus was pinned on the ground. Both were covered in slashes and bite marks, but Pravus had surrendered. Kale continued his charge toward the gnomish warrior and the remaining four Wolfkin. One of the Wolfkin lunged toward the gnome to bite his arm. The gnome lifted his arm just enough to evade the bite and brought the spike on his elbow down on the Wolfkin's head. Its body went limp, and it slumped to the ground.

A fifth snapped at the gnome, only to meet a similar fate as the gnome warrior lifted his knee up, impaling the Wolfkin on his knee spike. The last three lunged in sequence. The first was sliced down the middle while the second rushed past, missing its target completely. The third managed to clamp down on the gnome's helmet. Just as quick as it did, the gnome used a spike on his glove to cut the strap and slipped out. With one spin, he rammed his elbow into the helmet, causing the blade on top to sink deep into the Wolfkin's jaw.

The remaining Wolfkin in the last assault continued its advanced toward Kale, the object of his mission. Kale gripped his sword, glad to be able to take out at least one of these Dark Paws. As the Wolfkin got within twenty feet, Kale let out a battle cry. But, before the wind had left his lungs completely, the sound of a soaring object cut through the den of noise. A sword blade was stuck in the Wolfkin's chest. The gnome had thrown his blade into the advancing Wolfkin.

The gnome ran to Kale and drew his blade from the body. He reminded Kale a lot of Zube. He was shorter, and his hair was a darker shade white. But, it too was long and scrubby. After pulling the blade from the Wolfkin's body, he mumbled something to himself. "Just two left...". Kale was surprised to smell a heavy scent of alcohol coming from the gnome. This reminded him of his father from so many years ago. The smell brought Kale's father into mind and, in doing so, answered a question he had been asking himself. He now knew where he had seen this fighting style before. He had seen his father use it on the day of his death. Kale now could place a familiar property in this gnome. As he stood, he swayed from side to side, ever so slightly. The gnome was drunk.

The gnome began to advance on the two Wolfkin. Kale reached out to stop him. "No, the Gray Paw is a friend."

Before he realized what had happened, he found himself lying on his back with the gnome above him holding a blade close to his throat. Kale lay motionless. The gnome seemed to be looking past him, unaware of what he was doing, acting solely on instinct. His pupils adjusted as he focused on Kale. "Don't sneak up on me like that....." With this he gave a low burp. The smell made Kale wrinkle his nose in disgust. In slurred speeach the gnome mumbled, "What do you mean...no. They're Wolfkin, aren't they?"

"He's my friend, an ally," replied Kale.

"I've heard that before.....oh, blast it. At least there is one more of them I can kill." The gnome stood and began to walk over to Pravus with his blade drawn. This time it was Kannov who interjected. "Do not kill him."

The gnome's face reddened. "Blast it all! What do you mean DON'T kill him. Zube didn't send me here to shake hands with the bloody things. What is he, an ally too?" The gnome staggered back over to the closest Wolfkin body. As he spit on it, he reached behind his back and grabbed a bottle that was hidden away on his belt. The cork made a pop as he opened it and took a long swig. "Bah, only eight. Barely worth enduring the ride." The gnome looked toward Kale but didn't seem to be talking to him when he said, "And, Zube, the next time I see you we are going to discuss this flying business. If gnomes were meant to fly, we would have been born with bloody wings!" He then turned on his heel and used the body as a stool.

Kale kneeled in front of him to get down close enough to look him in the eyes. He could see the gnome was well past drunk. "Don't you think you've had enough to drink?"

"Enough? Enough....now look here boy, I'll tell you when I've had enough. Now bugger off," the gnome replied.

"I'm sorry. I didn't mean to offend you. My name is Kale. Who are you?" he asked.

"I know your name, boy, and I know what you are going to attempt to do." The gnome waved nonchalantly in the air. "Pure waste of bloody time." He then cupped his hands and yelled toward Kale. "Do you hear me, Zube? Pure waste of bloody time! Anyhow, my name is Grewen."

Kale thought for a moment. The name sounded familiar, but he couldn't place it. "You said Zube sent you. When did you meet him? Last we knew, he was on his way to the Leaf Kingdom to negotiate for their assistance in the upcoming battle."

Grewen took another swig and put the bottle back into his hiding place. "Battle....more like a massacre. Yes, Zube sent me. As soon as you all knew you were being followed, he sent me after you. Luckily he had that griffin with him, or I would have never made it in time; magnificent creature...except for the flying part, that is. Though how a descendent of Zube could be bested by a handful of Wolfkin is just down right disgraceful. You should be ashamed of yourself."

Kale's anger now began to flare. "Ashamed! Who do you think you are? I may be no gnome warrior, but I handle myself pretty well."

"Oh, stuff your pride, boy. I see you at least inherited Zube's lack of self control," he commented.

Kale realized that he was beginning to pick a fight with a person he clearly could not win against. In any case, he still had questions that needed answering. "Grewen, how did Zube know we were in trouble? I only sensed it recently."

"He gave you Alkaz, didn't he? What, do you think he wanted you to take that critter just for the fun of it?" Grewen asked.

Lifting Alkaz from his pocket, he stared into its small red eyes. "The little spy, I should have known you were keeping an eye on me. How easily I forget your craftiness. At least now I know this old gnome isn't as crazy as I thought."

With more effort than Kale thought would be needed, Grewen stood to his feet staggering slightly as his body hit full motion. "Well, what are we going to do with that Dark Paw if we can't kill him?"

Kale turned to Kannov, "Well?"

Kannov looked down into Pravus' face, resigned to his fate but still full of hatred. "For all the years you were faithful to our people, I am going to let you live. You are banished from the Gray Paw tribe. Your name will forever be looked on with disgrace. Go to your Dark Paw brothers and tell them we will fight to the last Gray Paw. We will not make the same mistake we did so many years ago and set ourselves against our gnomish neighbors."

Pravus looked back towards his king, and his lip began to

snarl. "You are a fool, Kannov. You should kill me now. Your people will join the Dark Paw, or they will be destroyed. Think, pup, take allegiance with your brother Dark Paws. Do not side against them."

"Our people were to blame, just as much as the gnomes for what happened at Drakholme. If we would have let those children go free, Zube's wrath would not have been triggered. It was our desire to preserve our race that brought it to its knees. No, I will not make the same mistake as my father. We will stand against the Fire Kingdom and the Black Paws, as well, if that is what it takes to regain our honor."

"Fool, I will see you on the battlefield." Pravus stood and began to make distance from the group. Kannov narrowed his eyes and slowly his lip began to snarl. "If I see you on the battlefield my old friend, I will kill you."

Grewen had stood silently, his face betraying his disapproval. "You're going to let him go? What has this world come to, letting a Dark Paw go free? Might as well stick yourself in the back and save them the bloody trouble. And Pravus, to boot, the wickedest, backstabbing betrayer of the bunch."

Kannov walked slowly over to Grewen. "I know you do not understand, but all I have left is my honor. My people's only hope is to obtain a treaty, an alliance from the gnomes. I know that is almost impossible. In all likelihood, my people will die at your great gate, but we will die with a clear conscience. We will no longer be plagued by our mistake."

Grewen rubbed his chin, his hair had clearly been unkempt for many months. "An honorable Wolfkin; who would have thought. Very well, we will make our way to the gate. I will walk ahead. If they do not spot a gnome first, they will likely kill both of you. One arrow for you boy, one for your friend, and the rest would make this Wolfkin look like a cactus."

"Very well, we will keep our distance," he said.

Grewen made his way ahead, his walk slumbered and off balance. Occasionally he would reach behind his back and pull out his bottle, taking a swig as he walked.

Kale took this time to greet Makko. His gimped arm bled from the bite he had received earlier. Kale bandaged it and caressed his head. "My friend, how did you know to bring him here? You're always swooping in to save me. Aren't you?"

The next few miles were taken in slow stride so that Caos could keep up. Grewen paid little attention to them but walked on slowly, taking breaks now and then to drink from his bottle.

Kannov no longer stayed in the rear but walked next to Kale and stared at Grewen. His look was not filled with hate or distrust, but rather with amazement.

"Kannov, I know I have heard of Grewen, but I cannot place him. Admittedly he is the greatest swordsman I have ever seen. But why would Zube send a drunk?" Kale asked in confusion.

"Pup, he is the greatest swordsman to ever live. And, if you had seen what he has seen, you would need drink to drown out the memories, as well," Kannov stated.

"What he saw?" Kale asked.

"He is the gnome survivor of Drakholme, the only survivor next to Zube. Story is told that he was standing next to Zube when Zube lost control. He stood on that platform and watched everyone around him. Women, children, and warrior alike burned alive; their screams filling the air. Unlike Zube, he remembers it all. How could anyone see something so horrible and come out unscathed. No, Zube sent the only person the gnomish people would listen to. He sent the great Grewen, captain of the King's Guard. What walks before us is the greatest warrior to ever walk this earth. Albeit A shadow of what he once was, but you would be wise to watch closely."

"He was Zube's captain at the battle. That is why I remember his name. Zube said it in his sleep shortly after I met him. He must still dream about it," said Kale.

Caos was now staring at this gnome who was looked on with such respect, "Wouldn't you, sir?"

Kale walked on, thinking back on his life. "I guess I would. My father was at the battle, as well. I think I understand now why he drank so much. He must have witnessed it, too."

Kannov placed his hand on Kale's shoulder, a simple gesture but his hand betrayed the massive strength it contained. "Your father was well known by our people, also. He was the only human to ever be trained by the gnomes in the way of the sword. The King's Guard are very selective of who they teach their battle tactics and swordsmanship to. If it wasn't for Zube's recommendation, they would have never allowed it. But for Zube's daughter, the King's Guard would do anything. She loved him, and Zube felt it best that his daughter's future husband should have the means to protect her."

"I never saw him use his sword until the day he was killed. It was so long ago," Kale remembered.

They were making their way through a thin wood at the bottom of the mountain; the trees eventually thinned until they stood at the edge of a large field. The grass was grown four or so feet high, and it stretched for a few miles before it met the great wall. Kale could see to the north the edge of a massive gate. Grewen stood for a moment and then squinted before shaking his head. "Come out of the grass. I can see you. It is Grewen and Kale, grandson of Zube."

The grass began to move and six armored gnomes stepped out into view. They knelt and bowed their heads "Sir, we were ordered to investigate the intruders."

"And now you are ordered to take us to the Gate safely. The Wolfkin and the humans are with me and under my protection. This is a political parley."

"Yes, sir, we will lead the way sir," they said.

Grewen motioned with his hand for them to follow. As they walked through the grass, many more gnomes came out of the grass and followed them. Looking over of the tops of the grass, Kale could see around fifty more gnomes making their way through the grass to take up their places around them.

"I never even saw them," Kale admitted.

Kannov looked very uneasy. "And I never smelled them. They must be the King's Guard."

A few miles further and they came out of the grassy plain and onto a road, old and unkempt but clearly one of quality in years' past. The road led westward and between two great mountains. Kannov pointed to it, "That is the Japada pass. My people will be making their way through it. I suspect they will reach us in a few weeks. It is windy but easily navigated and shouldn't close up with snow for another few weeks.

Grewen turned to face them when they reached the road. "Kannov, north is the abandoned town of Tritos. The town may offer some shelter for your people or at least the supplies to build them. A river runs into it from the west. There will be fish as well as wild vegetables. The grasslands are full of rabbits and other rodents. Your people can eat as much of them as you can. They are a nuisance to us. When your people arrive, you will have them settle there while we attempt to negotiate. If any of your people, child or adult alike, comes within one hundred yards of the wall, they will be killed. No exceptions. Are we understood?"

"Understood. May we use your trees to begin fortifications on the town? In the event we cannot come to a treaty, my people will have to make their stand there," Kannov explained.

"My people care little for the land outside the wall. Any tree outside of the one hundred yard perimeter is yours if you desire. Kale, stay with Kannov until I can discuss this with the Magistrate. He will want to talk with you," Grewen said.

***

Tritos contained many dilapidated buildings; the wood are barely worth reusing. But it did contain a few stone structures that with minimal repair would offer shelter for a majority of the women and children.

Grewen was not exaggerating about the rabbits and smaller mammals. They plagued the area by the thousands. Within a day, they had secured enough food for themselves for the next few weeks, caging many in an old chicken coop.

"This place offers an abundance of food. How could so many survive here? How does the landscape sustain them?" Kale wondered.

Kannov was able to answer this as they sat by the night fire eating some of the product of their day's hunting. "They don't. Many of them die of starvation. The gnomes drive them out of the gates by the hundreds every day. Unable to eat meat themselves, the plant eating animals are nothing but a nuisance. They keep many meat eaters solely to kill off the multitude of small game."

"They won't eat meat? I find it hard to believe that they oppose killing animals. I've seen their ferocity in battle," Kale said in disbelief.

"I didn't say they wouldn't eat meat, young pup. I said they were unable. They are plant eaters themselves. Their stomaches cannot digest meat. It makes them ill. It is much the same with us Wolfkin. We can only digest certain vegetables, and even that can make us feel ill. But when it comes to starving or eating a carrot, we choose to suffer the digestive struggle."

Grewen sent one gnome with a letter to the magistrate and then ordered the remaining to surround the town. Grewen himself only sat on a sawed off dock post staring out into the bay, occasionally taking a drink from his container. Kale stood next to Grewen, looking out at the harbor. Neither spoke, instead choosing to enjoy the beauty of the water. Kale saw Grewen tip up his bottle and shake it to get the last drops out. He took a long look at it and then tossed it into the water. "Bugger it all."

***

Over the next week, Caos feet began to heal. He proved both a great hunter as well as carpenter, all the while taking special care of Kale.

After the initial food supply had been gathered and a basic roof was put on one of the stone structures, Kale began to wonder how long it would take for a gnome diplomat to come out and meet them. It had already been close to three weeks, and it appeared the gnomes had chosen to ignore his presence.

TWELVE

****

FALL OF THE PRINCE

While Kale and Caos were working on the first wall to the entrance to the town, Kale spotted a small group coming out of the smaller gate located on one of the massive doors of the larger gate. Caos gave a whistle after Kale pointed it out to him. "A gate within a gate, amazing isn't it, sir."

"Yes, it is amazing," agreed Kale.

An hour later the gnome group made their way into the town comprised of a few contingent of warriors. Four of the soldiers carried a cart on their shoulders. On top of the cart sat the oldest being Kale had ever seen.

A gnome who, when straightened out, would stand around four feet tall. However, due to his hunched shoulders and awkward back, he appeared to be closer to three feet in height. His hair ran in wisps down his shoulders and hung close to his lower back. It was braided and well-kept. His eyes shone a bright grey, a shocking contrast to his white skin blotched with age spots. On his hip, he carried a small dagger, and in his hand an aged cane.

When he stepped down from the cart, he made his way over to Kale. His steps were slow but steady, and his eyes were fixed on a point behind Kale. It only took Kale moments to realize his destination wasn't to reach him but beyond him. Turning he saw Grewen standing on the edge of the camp. He must have seen them coming as well and came from his place on the dock. Grewen knelt and bowed his head in respect. "Magistrate, sir, this is Kale, grandson of Zube."

The Magistrate paid no attention to what the gnome was saying but kept steadily walking over to him. Once he reached Grewen, he began to speak. His voice was clear and authoritative, yet somehow soothing. "It has been many years, Grewen."

Grewen kept his head bowed. "Yes, sir, many years."

"Stand Grewen," the Magistrate ordered.

Grewen stood but kept his eyes averted, a look of shame on his face. He stood in silence, seemingly awaiting some horrible event. The magistrate drew the dagger from his belt and then slowly reached for the back of his head, pulling his braid of hair to the front. With one clean swipe, he sliced it off at the knob. The old gnome dropped both blade and braid and fell into Grewen embracing him. "My son has come home."

Grewen's face wrinkled as he began to sob. Not the sob of a drunk or of someone mourning, but a sob of relief. "Father, I'm sorry. It was my fault. I should have attended to them myself. They would have been safe then. It's my fault."

The Magistrate placed his hand on his son's cheek and looked up into his face. "No, no son. It was no more your fault than it was Zube's. What has happened has happened. I have sent many scouts to look for you. Where have you been hiding all these years?"

"I was with the giants of the northern Stone Kingdom; Zube found me and told me of the battle to come. He sent me to protect Kale."

Both Kale and Kannov looked at each other with a worried glance when they heard that Zube was in the Stone Kingdom and not the Leaf Kingdom. Kale also noticed that there now stood over a hundred gnomes encircling the meeting place.

They had come in during the last few minutes from their posts around the town.

The Magistrate touched the handle of the sword hanging on Grewen's back. "I see you still carry your burden. I assume this means that Zube did not wish to have this returned to him?"

"No, sir, he said that he would not return to Japada. That he leaves all of his rights to Kale," Grewen explained.

The Magistrate turned to stare at Kale. "Yes, Zube's protégée." The Magistrate's look was neither warm nor loving. He was carefully inspecting him. Kale felt as if he was on a weighing platform and being scrutinized, inch by inch. "He seems to be as I have heard."

"Kale, I am Magistrate Balic. As you have guessed, Grewen is my son. I cannot force you to stay outside of Japada. Neither can I allow the Wolfkin to enter. The people do not believe that they are truly on our side. They fear, as do I, that when the battle begins the Wolfkin will not fight against their Dark Paw brothers but, instead, turn on us. With the Gray Paw already behind the walls, the taking of our lands would be almost too easy," he explained.

Kannov took a step forward and began to speak "That is not..." His words were cut off by Grewen's blade placed under his throat. "This discussion does not involve you, Wolfkin. Be silent."

"Magistrate, you say that you cannot force me to stay outside the wall. Does that mean that the people and even yourself do not want me there?" asked Kale.

"Kale, the people fear that you will lose control of yourself and cause us more damage than we can sustain. You are the descendant of Zube, and although we miss him greatly, we would

301

hope he would keep his distance, as well. We fear both yours and Zube's capabilities," stated the Magistrate.

"I see. So, you would judge me for my grandfather's weakness. You would judge the Gray Paws for the sins of their fathers. Is it right that we should not be allowed to earn or loose our own honor?" questioned Kale.

"You speak as a youth, Kale. This is much more difficult than you believe. If you go to the Gray Paws now, they may still have time to turn back and get out of the way of the advancing army. If after the battle they prove to truly be our allies, then we will be able to further our discussions. We have full confidence that we can hold off their advances on our wall," the Magistrate said.

"After the battle! Do you not realize that the Gray Paws will not exist after the battle? Even if we ran to them now, we could not possibly risk backtracking with women and children into the arms of an advancing army. And even if we managed to get out of the pass before we collided with the army, where would we go? The Leaf Kingdom would give them no asylum. And as for holding them off, this is not an ill-thought out plan. They have been working their way to the border of Japada for years, building up their forces and resources for this attack."

Balic turned to Grewen, " 'We', he acts like he is half Wolfkin, too. I am sorry, but I cannot allow it. We will not even entertain the idea until we are sure of the Gray Paws intentions."

A gnome broke into the crowd in a stiff run. His chest heaved as he attempted to catch his breath. "Grewen, sir, there are ships along the Japada Pass where the trail meets the sea. They bare the red flag. Thousands of Fire Kingdom soldiers are unloading."

This time Kannov could not stay silent, "Are their Wolfkin ahead of them? It would be a large number."

The scout looked at Grewen. After he had received a nod of approval, he spoke. "Yes, there are many Wolfkin making their way down the pass ahead of the Fire Kingdom. They are making a quick approach."

"How many miles out are they?" asked Kannov.

"The Wolfkin should reach us by morning and, at this rate, the Fire Kingdom a few hours later," the scout predicted.

Kannov sighed with relief, "At least they made it through."

From the north side of the group another gnome scout came running. "Sir, there are ships in the harbor, and they carry warriors. We are being sieged from both fronts."

Kale ran to the docks. Eight large ships each packed with men on their decks breeched the harbor's entrance. They flew the Fire Kingdom flag and were in the process of making anchor. "We will not be able to run to the sea, Kannov. Your people will be trapped between two armies."

The lead ship ran down the Fire Kingdom flag, and in its place it ran up another flag. This one was all too familiar to Kale. "No, we are saved. They were sailing under false colors. That is the Kalian army's symbol. Let them dock."

As the first ship docked, Kale could already see some familiar faces among the crowd. Tor'lam stood several feet taller among the rest. The first to come off of the ship was Druwen, the man Kale had left in command of his men. "Sir, I see you have made your journey to Japada. As you can see, we have grown a bit since last we met."

"I do, indeed, Druwen. How did you come to be here at such an opportune time?" asked Kale.

"After the battle at the Stone Kingdom Wall, we had heard that the Fire Kingdom was marching on to Japada. We knew you were here so we petitioned to the Stone King for assistance. It so happened that some ships from the Water Kingdom were at the northern dock petitioning for his assistance, as well. He negotiated their assistance, not that it took much, sir, after their captain heard who we served," Druwen said.

"What do you mean?" Kale questioned him.

"Maybe it would be best if I introduced you to the captain of this fleet," he replied instead.

A man in a well-tailored outfit came walking toward Kale. His face was strained in a stern face. As he got closer, Kale recognized him. He took off at a quick pace. As he approached the man, he could not contain his smile any longer. They both embraced each other. "Riggs, my old friend. But how...."

"That story is for another time. I see you made it out of that prison, after all. I truly didn't believe your men when they told me who you were. Their story of how my friend, who could not so much as take on a stone cutter when we met, had led an uprising that resulted in their freedom. I guess my lessons were not in vain," Riggs teased.

Makko came swooping down and landed next to Kale. Men, gnome, giant, and Gehage alike stopped to admire this creature. Riggs kneeled down to get a better look. "Ah, Makko, I owe you many a dinner. It is nice to finally get a look at you outside of the bars."

"Riggs, there is a large army that has landed to the west. We must prepare to defend ourselves in the plain," said Kale.

"I know of the army, Kale. We sailed in with them," he replied.

"You sailed in with them?" Kale asked in confusion.

"Yes, it was the idea of a young man from the Stone Kingdom. You should meet him, as well. He will be commanding the Stone warriors," Riggs said.

"Very well, where is he? I would be happy to greet anyone who brings assistance for this battle," Kale answered.

Riggs pointed toward a large crowd of men forming on one side of the dock." He is just over there."

Kale's heart began to beat even faster now. Standing with is back to Kale, was a large man, broad shouldered and massive in size addressing the crowd. "It can't be..." Kale took off at a brisk walk. "Reagan!" His walk slowed as the man turned around. His face was young. He looked so much like Reagan, but it was not his friend. His face was unscarred. As Kale got closer, he could tell the man stood a few inches shorter than his old friend had been in his youth.

"I'm sorry. I thought you were someone else," Kale said.

"My name is Cicero Darkwater. Are you Kale?" the man asked.

"Yes, I am. Darkwater? So, you are related to Reagan?" Kale said.

Cicero's eyes glissened with tears. "Yes, sir, my father spoke of you often. He would have given anything to have been here with you. It is an honor to meet the man he spoke of every night in my bedtime stories. It is a shame he never got to meet you again, sir."

Kale's heart sank at the thought of Rigg's death. "I look forward to talking with you more about your father after this battle.

305

Are your men ready? Even with the Wolfkin, we will be greatly outnumbered," Kale reminded him.

"Wolfkin, sir. They are fighting on our side?" Cicero asked in disbelief.

"Yes, some of them." Then, turning to Caos who had constantly kept to his rear, Kale said, "Caos, gather together the various leaders and bring them to the monastery's main building. We will discuss our battle plan there. We don't have much time."

"Yes, sir," he replied.

Minutes later Kale sat at a large table, a wide variety of warriors surrounded him. There was Riggs who sat in his normal formal attitude, much strengthened with his new role as captain of the fleet in the harbor; Kannov, the Wolfkin chieftain and commander of the largest contingent of men; Druwen, an exile and a man who had seen many battles, Kale's captain and current leader of the Kalian army; and Tor'lam, a mighty warrior of the Mountain giants.

Kale had noticed that his men no longer held Tor'lam in contempt but had gained a high respect for their slow speaking captain. Grewen sat in his full armor, an advisor from Japada. Caos had earned his right to sit among them and gave his opinion of the matter. His knowledge as a scout counted for much. Then there was Cicero, son of his long friend and captain of the Stone Kingdom troops, a story there, for sure, but one that would be told another day. Even Makko made his way to sit next to Kale's side.

"The Fire Kingdom will be meeting us blade to blade at dawn, mid-day at best tomorrow. We have a few thousand Gray Paw on their way, most only women and children, but there are many warriors among them. They will make up the majority of our army and will be much needed. Druwen, how many men do you command in the Kalian army?" Kale asked.

"Sir, you command roughly four thousand. We have seen many volunteers, including a large number of giants who serve under Tor'lam," he replied.

"Cicero, what of the Stone Troops?" Kale continued.

"Two thousand roughly, sir, and around one hundred Stone Gehage," he reported.

Kale folded his hands. "With the Gray Paw's eight thousand, we still only number fourteen thousand."

Grewen spoke up, "Don't forget about my men, Kale."

"I thought Japada was not going to assist us?" he replied.

"The armies of Japada will not. They will stay behind the wall, and they will still kill anything that comes within a hundred yards of it. But I was ordered by Zube to protect you. His guard units will fight alongside you to offer protection. We number four hundred. That's four hundred of the finest, hand-picked gnome warriors in all of Japada. They are as good as any four thousand Fire Kingdom troops or any two thousand Dark Paw elites," Grewen proudly stated.

"And they are very welcome. Still, we will be outnumbered nearly four to one. Well...let's do the best we can. Cicero, how quickly can your Stone Gehage build a wall?" Kale wanted to know.

"If it isn't terribly large, it can be done in a night, sir. They will be pretty drained for the battle, though," he said.

"The wall will count for more than their strength in this matter. The opening to the pass is roughly a mile and a half wide. If we build a half circle around it with a small opening

307

at the end, we may be able to funnel at least some of the troops and deal with them in a smaller quantity, at least lessening the advantage of their numbers. It worked well at Durian. No reason it shouldn't at least help here," Kale strategized with the others.

Kannov spoke up, "That will work for the regular men but not the Dark Paw. Scaling any wall that is not at least a hundred feet high will be of little difference to them."

"It may, at least, slow them down. We will have to count on your Wolfkin to help us. I know that you do not normally use your women and children in battle, but we may need to equip them with bows and have them shoot arrows over the wall. After all, if they do not fight, their chances of survival are very small," Kale reminded Kannov.

"We will do our part," he answered.

Kale looked around at this ragged group of warriors drawn from all over Telekkar. "Well, let's get to work."

Kale had never seen a Stone Gehage at work. With each heave, they produced a large column of stone thirty six feet high, four feet thick, and four feet wide. Every few hours they had to break and recuperate their strength. Kale hoped his decision to weaken them for the sake of a protected front would be of a greater value.

* * *

"Kannov, can you smell your people yet?" asked Kale.

"No, young pup. The wind has shifted with the weather. It blows away from us now. I cannot smell anything from the west," he replied.

"At least the Stone Gehage finished the wall during the night," Kale said.

"Yes, the wall will help against the Fire soldiers. I will feel better when my people reach us. I will feel better when I know our young ones are safe," Kannov said.

"I will feel better when they get here, as well," agreed Kale.

From the top of the wall, Kale could see several miles down the pass up to where it shifted to the left. Close to mid-morning, Kale spotted a large group of Dark Paw making their way around the corner of the pass. His heart sank with fear. He turned and shouted over the wall, "The Wolfkin are Dark Paw! Prepare for battle!"

Moments later Grewen was standing next to him on the wall. Looking out at the advancing Black Paw army, he reached to his back but then realized he had tossed his flask into the sea. "Bugger it all! I picked a fine day to stop drinking." He then turned and yelled to this men. "Guardsmen, on the wall!"

With grace, each of the four hundred gnomes leaped from ladder to handhold until they all reached the wall and stood side by side equally spaced along the wall. Each held a shield in one hand and a blade in the other. Grewen looked out at them. "Hold the line, my brothers. Let's show these mangy dogs what a real warrior looks like." In unison, the gnome warriors lifted their swords and gave a loud 'whorah'.

Kale looked down at the men below. "Cicero, your men along with the Kalian's will hold the mouth of the funnel. We're sending them all to you."

"You can count on us, sir," he assured Kale.

"I don't understand why they wouldn't wait for the Fire Kingdom. Why not wait?" Kale wondered.

Grewen scratched his beard and then noticed everyone was

309

looking at him. "Oh, well I imagine that they cut off the eight thousand troops for the Gray Paw and figured they had a good chance of catching us out here alone. It would be clear that Japada wouldn't sign a treaty soon, and if they knew of the help coming our way, they would want to reach us before we received reinforcement. Again, their own zeal has wounded them. And I'm glad of it."

"Me too, Grewen, me too. The situation is still bleak but at least not as hopeless," Kale said. Caos made his way up a ladder and over to Kale. Drawing his sword he prepared himself for battle.

"Caos, it may be better if you fight with the other men at the mouth of the funnel. It is going to get pretty nasty up here," Kale told him.

"Oh, sir, you don't think I'd spend all this time keeping you alive to let a bunch of mangy good for nothing dogs kill you." Caos then turned to Kannov, "Present company excluded, of course. And anyway, we do hold the high ground."

The Dark Paw were advancing at a rapid pace, but to Kale's disappointment, they were well organized. The front line carried large shields to protect from archery, and the well formed lines behind did not please him much. "I had rather hoped for a disorganized group."

Caos tested his footing on the makeshift wall. "We'll hold them off, sir. Those Stone soldiers did a good job on this wall. Wish we had had a few of them working with us in Durham. It would have made life a bit easier."

Kale couldn't help but smile. "Yes, it sure would have."

The approaching Wolfkin army started their advance. From either side of the pass large boulders began to roll down on top of them. Looking up, Tor'lam and his giants worked to push down the rocks off the ledges above. It was only mildly effective, but every Wolfkin killed was one less they would have to worry about at the wall. "Very good idea, Caos."

"I thought you would like that one, sir," he said.

Grewen reached behind his back and pulled off the large blade. "Guess you might as well use this during the battle. But, mind you, it belongs to Zube, and until that bugger dies, it is his."

Kale unwrapped the blade from its cloth covering. As he drew it out, he felt magnificent power seeping into his pores. The blade was easily recognizable. He had seen a statue of it in Durham. It was the high blade, the king's blade.

"Thank you, Grewen. I will return it after the battle," Kale assured him.

The Wolfkin hurried their advance now, seeing that the longer they lingered, the more likely it was they would be crushed under the boulders crashing down the mountainsides.

"At least that got them disorganized. Ready yourself, men," Kale instructed.

A din of arrows from the Dark Paw flew toward the top of the wall. Each man used his shield to fend them off. Luckily, none on the wall were injured. A few of the men to the rear of the group fell, but the wall provided sufficient protection for the majority of the men. They would only have to endure the arrows until the front lines collided. Then it would be too risky to fire into their own men. The Wolfkin army smashed against the wall. As each Dark Paw got within range, it jumped through the air aiming for the top of the wall. The gnomes began their onslaught, cutting down each Wolfkin as it made its attempt to scale the wall. Kale looked to the rear, "Archers, Fire!" The back line of the Kalian army unleashed a volley of arrows over the wall. Kale could see sporadic Wolfkin falling, but the sea of fur and fang rushed over the dead. Looking down, the Stone Kingdom warriors and Kalian army were keeping the Wolfkin at bay, but only barely. Each minute they were faced with a new foe. His strength new and unused. Their strength was dwindling quickly. From his left, Kale could hear Grewen yelling, "They are pushing back our line." And then the gnome leapt from the wall into the sea of Wolfkin flooding the narrow passage way through the wall.

Kannov looked down into the sea, and his teeth set to a fierce snarl. "Pravus! Today you die!" Kale could see the old Dark Paw pushing his way through the crowd to reach the front. Kannov joined Grewen in the battle below, awaiting Pravus' arrival to the front line.

After dispatching another Wolfkin who had made a leap for the top of the wall, Kale peered out over the mass of bodies. Kale could not make out the back line of Wolfkin. How long would they have to fight? Kale had made the mistake of letting up his guard, and as his mind came back to the task at hand, he found himself a second too late for a vicious slash from an advancing Wolfkin. The blade opened his flesh from his shoulder down to his ribs. The Wolfkin hit him with the back of his hand, sending him flying into the mass of Wolfkin below.

The bodies of the Wolfkin broke his fall, and he found himself fighting to stand up, being kicked and mauled over by those advancing. Then a hand reached down and pulled him up. It was Caos. He was hacking and slashing at Wolfkin as they advanced toward him. Kale regained his footing and began to fight off the advancing horde.

"Make your way for the opening; move!" Kale shouted.

Both men began to step backwards, guiding their way toward the opening while cutting down any Wolfkin that came near. The blades were coming from all directions, and Kale found it hard to keep up with defending himself. He was unaware of a Dark Paw who, unlike the rest, was not trying to get to the wall but was working his way to Kale now out in the middle of the fray.

Caos noticed Pravus just in time to step in the way of the oncoming thrust. His groan caused Kale to turn quickly enough to parry the second attack. The third was not to come as from behind him, Kannov wrapped his hands around the old Wolfkin's head and sank his teeth deep into his neck. Pravus fell to the ground. Grewen leapt over them both and took on a position protecting them as Kale bent down and hauled Caos onto his shoulder and began to make his way through the opening.

As he made his way past the defenders, he sat Caos down on an opening just inside the wall "Caos, are you okay?" he anxiously asked.

"I'll be fine, sir." At this, he coughed up a margin of blood and spit it out. "You had better get back in there, sir. It was an honor serving with you." Caos closed his eyes and his breath became slow and labored.

Kale's heart began to beat quickly. He felt the flood of emotion building in his chest. His anger pulsed. He heard many things as he turned to head back into battle. "Sir, they are pushing through.", "Sir are you okay?", "Sir, where are you going?". The images around him began to flash. He saw Wolfkin coming at him. They came so slowly, and he cut them down with

such speed and such ruthless fury. He heard himself screaming. He was rage-filled, the high blade cutting down everything
that came near him. His fury was building, reaching higher and
higher. The pressure inside Kale climbed to a point that he felt it
pushing out from the seams of his being. He heard Grewen yelling in a pleading voice, "For all love, close the wall! Everyone
run for your life!"

His mind watched for the background as his body began to
pulsate with uncontrollable fury. Something inside him clicked.
He realized that he was about to commit the same act Zube had
so many years ago. He knew he must channel this anger. With all
of his will, Kale attempted to direct the release of this energy to
the front of his body. If only he could keep it in a general direction there may be hope. Then everything went white for a brief
second, and the sounds of screaming Wolfkin filled his ears.

Slowly, Kale could see the things around him. He was on his
knees staring into the dirt. It was black and smoking. Looking
up, the Black Paws were rolling on the ground in death spasms.
Thirty thousand burned corpses stretched all the way until the
pass veered to the left. His heart sank at the thought of what
must lay behind him. Slowly, he turned his head. To his eternal
relief, the wall was still there. The tunnel had been closed in
time and climbing up on the walls were the gnomes taking their
places once more. Kale could barely stand. His heart still raced
from recent events. His chest was bleeding through his armor.

His hand felt the ground begin to tremble. From the distance
ahead, he heard the uniform stomp of advancing troops. From
around the bend a massive force, both Fire Kingdom troops and
Water Kingdom troops marched in line. Kale could recognize
Fike mounted an a horse to the right. To his side rode another

foe of old, Kain's bear, Olan. The bear was unchained from its master and clearly there to convey to Kain what the outcome of the battle would be.

Forcing his body to obey him, Kale stood. His mind wandered in and out with fatigue. Gripping his blade, he steadied himself to meet his end. Large balls of flames flew over his head from the Fire Kingdom Gehage. They crashed against the wall, sending pieces of it flying. Makko swooped down and took his place next to Kale, his feathers ruffled in defiance. A horn from the Fire Kingdom announced the call to charge.

Fike took off at a fast gallop on his steed, outpacing the army quickly. Olan was close on his heels. He reached Kale far in advance of the others. His blade came swooping, clashing into Kale's at the same moment that Makko crashed into Olan, both biting and clawing at each other's throats.

*21 YEARS EARLIER

Standing in tense emotion, Reagan watched Kale make his way across the sandy plain. Horsemen were quickly closing in from the rear. Clinching the cart handle, his knuckles began to whiten. Latus lay on his back, his breath coming in heated waves; the journey was almost too much for him. His recently amputated arm left him weak and now disoriented.

Kale had made it to the safety of the Earth Kingdom's archers. Surely the horses would not follow him further. "Come on, Kale. Use those legs of yours. You're almost safe," Reagan yelled.

Then, from the masked man on the lead horse, a crossbow arrow zipped ahead, closing the distance. It pierced Kale's leg, causing him to tumble to the ground. The horse stopped, and the rider twisted the rope around his saddle as he began to drag Kale back out of the safety of the guards.

"No! Kale! Let me go! I've got to save him!" But before he could charge out, the guards had seized him, each doing their best to hold his massive body.

A guard planted himself in front of Reagan, "If you go out there, they'll hang you, too. We can't interfere with them when they are in the Deadlands. I'm sorry, but your friend is gone. I saw what he did for you. You must be very fortunate to have had a friend like that."

Reagan hung his head. What had he let his friend do? "Kale...."

Made in the USA
Charleston, SC
22 October 2011